FINDERS KEEPERS

B BASKERVILLE

HYEM BOOKS

ISBN: 978-1-7392445-0-7 (Paperback)

Front cover image: DrNickStafford. Pixabay.

Cover design: B Baskerville

www.betsybaskerville.com

- CHAPTER 1 -

SNOW CRUNCHED BENEATH THE thick tread of the touring bikes' tyres. Delicate flakes fell gently in the night as Rhett and Laurel approached Alston. At over one thousand feet above sea level, the village shared the title of England's highest market town.

"It's so pretty," said Laurel, looking around.

She brought her bike to a stop as she caught her breath. Christmas lights twinkled in living room windows; holly wreaths covered every door.

"It's almost magical," Rhett said as he pulled up beside her. "I feel like we've ridden into a Dickens novel."

Above them, a Victorian streetlamp glowed orange. In the distance, the sound of revellers singing Christmas carols carried up the hill. *God Rest Thee Merry Gentlemen* if Rhett wasn't mistaken. He checked the second-hand Garmin watch he'd bought from eBay: midnight was fast approaching.

1

A pint before closing was tempting, but their BnB and a warm bed awaited. The owner said she'd stay up for the pair after they were delayed by a puncture, and Rhett didn't want to take advantage of her generosity. Still, he paused to soak up the atmosphere.

Laurel flexed her fingers, easing them from the handlebars. Mud spattered her leggings and a layer of sweat covered her red face. But to Rhett, she'd never looked more beautiful. He reached out and cupped her chin. "You were brilliant today."

"It felt like my legs were on fire back there. I can't believe we made it," she said breathlessly.

"I can. You're fitter than you give yourself credit for."

Laurel looked away in a cute, shy manner before her face flooded with excitement. "Look, Rhett. Mistletoe."

Tied with crimson ribbon, a bunch of mistletoe hung from the Victorian streetlamp, its pearlescent berries tinged yellow from the light.

Rhett jumped from his bike and wrapped his arms around his fiancée. They kissed passionately for over a minute. When Rhett reluctantly pulled away, he looked at the Garmin once more.

"It's midnight. Merry Christmas, Laurel."

"Merry Christmas, Rhett."

RHETT EMERGED FROM THE shower and dried himself with a fluffy white towel. He may have been tired and aching but his soul swelled with pride. While plenty of people cycled the coast-to-coast route from Whitehaven in the west to Tynemouth in the east, the vast majority tackled the challenge in spring or summertime. Hardly anyone did it in the dead of winter. Fewer still went straight from one challenge to the next. Rhett pictured a map of the north of England in his head. A blue line wiggled from one side of the country to the next, then snaked up the east coast towards Edinburgh.

Laurel, naked, her strawberry-blonde hair still damp from the shower, popped the cork from a bottle of sparkling wine and poured two glasses. A fire burned on one side of the room, its golden light flickering over her toned body. Rhett watched open-mouthed and mesmerised for a moment. They were – as their friends liked to say – completely loved up.

"It's true what they say about northerners," Laurel said, handing him a glass of bubbly.

"That you can't understand a word they say?"

"No, silly." Laurel laughed before taking a sip. "That they're friendly. It would have been enough for Martha to stay up for us. She didn't have to go to all this trouble."

Martha, the hunch-backed lady who ran the BnB had not only lit the fire in their room, she'd kept some food warm and placed hot water bottles in their bed. Laurel was over the moon with the complimentary bottle of wine she'd given them to celebrate Christmas.

"She gave me the creeps," Rhett said.

"Don't be ridiculous."

3

"She looks like a witch. Like the one from Hansel and Gretel."

"You're one to talk." Laurel ran her fingers through Rhett's long locks. He usually kept his hair tied back in a bun, but he'd just washed it. Reaching his shoulders, his hair was almost as long as hers. "Grow this any longer and you'll start to look like a young Gandalf."

Rhett wiggled his eyebrows at her. "A young, sexy Gandalf?"

Laurel placed her glass on the bedside table and removed Rhett's towel from his waist. "Very," she replied.

Rhett and Laurel fell into bed and into each other's arms. He laced his fingers between hers and felt her wooden engagement ring press into the sides of his fingers. They weren't rich; they couldn't afford diamonds or gold. One day maybe, but not yet. Fresh out of university with a mountain of debt, neither of them had much in their current accounts, but they were wealthy in other ways. They were young, fit, and stupidly in love. They had a shared passion for adventure and achievement. Doing the *coast-to-coast* and *coast and castles* back to back in winter had its dangers. Still, they were excited and prepared for almost any eventuality. Rhett bought an exercise bike from a gym that was closing down and they used it two hours a day, three days a week throughout autumn. Laurel had taken a first aid course and Rhett was experienced in survival skills.

Laurel wrapped her legs around him and gripped his behind. Cuts and grazes covered her shins and Rhett's hands were blistered and raw, but none of their aches and pains would stop them from making love until dawn.

Rhett was prepared for a hard winter, but whatever the elements threw at him, he was confident they'd get through it together. Yes, Rhett had prepared for many eventualities, but like the best-laid schemes of mice and men, so too would Rhett's plans go awry. They had a train booked from Edinburgh to Hampshire on the second of January. Neither of them would be on it.

- CHAPTER 2 -

Two weeks later.

DETECTIVE CHIEF INSPECTOR ERICA Cooper held her hand over her swollen belly as she entered CID at Northumbria Police's headquarters in Wallsend. Her body had changed dramatically over the past two years. She'd dropped several kilos thanks to cancer, chemo and an inability to cook; now, she was well into her third trimester. She had scars and tattoos, and her long, pre-chemo hair was now kept short in a manageable buzzcut that her teenage daughter called *totally badass*.

The room was abuzz with all the usual noises that come with office environments: phone calls, photocopiers, printers and constant banter. DI Neil Fuller was in talks with Durham Police, trying to link their missing child cases and pool resources. DS Paula Keaton rushed by, her face stony after a troubling domestic violence case. Martin, Whyte and Boyd huddled around cups of milky tea, discussing their actions for that day. But as always, Cooper searched the room for a pair of eyes she'd never see again. While things had improved since the death of their colleague in September, things would never be normal. There was no normal without Tennessee. Though she knew better, Cooper looked for him again; he wasn't there. She exhaled – her heart as heavy as her belly – and sought out Elliot Whyte for an update.

"What's the latest?"

Whyte straightened his posture as she approached and tucked strands of his dark hair behind his ear. "Tea?"

"Please."

Cooper took the cup in both hands and savoured its warmth. She was sure the bean counters had turned the heating down in the building to save money.

"We're struggling to find leads in the drive-by. The locals are scared to talk, and it's not like the victim's going to wake up any time soon. If he wakes up at all."

Nodding, Cooper asked, "Do we have anything to go on?"

"Gent at number forty-three says he saw a dark blue Vauxhall, but the woman at forty-nine says it was a black VW."

"Has the weapon turned up yet?"

Whyte shook his head. "Casings are in the lab. No prints, sadly. Still no sign of the gun."

"Great," Cooper said with sarcasm. "Keep at it. You had a contact in the Roker Boys, didn't you?"

Whyte made a pessimistic grunting noise. "He's been off my radar for a while, boss. I'll stick some feelers out, but he's either on the straight and narrow, or he's in a ditch somewhere."

She was about to tell Whyte to update her later in the day when the doors to CID opened and Superintendent Howard Nixon pushed his puffy face into the room. "Cooper. My office."

She shared a look with Whyte. Cooper hadn't wanted him to join her team back in April when they worked together on the murder of a crime boss. The atmosphere had been tense between the pair, though, to be fair, it was Cooper who was the frosty one – Whyte had been professional. He'd deserved it, Cooper told herself. But having forgiven him, they now worked well together.

Whyte's mouth curled at the corner as Nixon disappeared from view. "Good luck," he said.

———

INSIDE NIXON'S OFFICE COOPER pulled out a chair and sat down without being invited. One of the perks of being heavily pregnant was that people didn't expect you to stay standing a second longer than was necessary.

"There's very little progress in Friday night's drive-by shooting. We're looking into a dark vehicle.

Might be blue, might be black. The brand begins with V. Possibly a VW or a Vauxhall." Even as she said it, Cooper felt like an idiot. "Whyte's taking the lead in speaking to witnesses. As for the Summer Holt case, Fuller's losing momentum."

"Yes, yes. Never mind that," Nixon said, cutting her off. "I've just had Hampshire Constabulary on the blower. Their CC's from up here originally. A Geordie ex-pat. He's a right piece of work, and unfortunately for me, I owe him a favour."

Cooper opened her notepad; she had a feeling she'd need it.

"Rhett Campbell, twenty-four, and his fiancee, Laurel Deacon, twenty-two, have been cycling around the northeast."

"In this weather?" Cooper asked, unable to think of much worse.

"Indeed. An adventurous pair by all accounts. They were due back on the second of January; it's now the tenth. The last correspondence from the pair was a Whatsapp message from Rhett to his mother on Christmas morning."

"Why are we only hearing about it now?"

"The girl's father's been away on business, and as for the lad, his parents didn't think to worry. Apparently, he's not the best at staying in touch when he's on holiday. It's quite normal for him to plan on visiting friends for a day or two and end up staying a week."

"Last known location?"

"The Discovery Museum," Nixon said, tossing a file at Cooper. She caught it before its contents fell to the floor. "It's all in there."

"CCTV?" she asked, thumbing through the file.

"At the museum, yes. Anywhere else, not really. They were meant to catch the eight a.m. train from Edinburgh Waverley to Southhampton on the second. CCTV shows they never boarded the train."

"So we don't even know which side of the border they're on?"

"No." Nixon rubbed his neck and held Cooper with a steely stare.

Cooper closed the file, placed it on her lap and folded her arms over it, readying herself to challenge her superior. "Sir, another missing persons case will take a lot of manpower. We only have one DI, and his hands are full with the Summer Holt case." She gestured to her bump. "I'll be on maternity soon. If DS Dan—"

Cooper's voice caught in her throat at the thought of Tennessee. She tried not to think of it, but the image of his dead body flooded back to her.

Nixon's face softened. "If DS Daniel was here, he'd have been promoted to DI and could lead the team in your absence?"

Cooper nodded, holding back tears for fear of looking like the sort of hormonal wreck Nixon despised. To her astonishment, Nixon offered her a tissue.

"I know you're all suffering. DS Daniel was a good man and a great detective. This case is a real-head scratcher, the sort of case DS Daniel would have loved. Focus on that and solve it in his honour. Look, I'm not blind to the fact he's irreplaceable, but I get it, Cooper. You're understaffed."

"I need a DI."

"And I'll get you one."

There was a brief moment when a spark of hope warmed Cooper's chest and eased the tension in her shoulders.

Then Nixon added, "Once you solve the case."

Clumsily, she got to her feet and seethed. She smelled the lie on Nixon like cheap aftershave. A new DI would be a carrot dangling forever just out of reach. There'd always be another case, another murder to solve, another rapist to throw behind bars. She was stuck. If she found Rhett and Laurel with her limited team, he'd say she didn't need more help. If she failed, then he needn't fulfil his promise.

"Between a fucking rock and a hard place," she whispered.

"What was that, Cooper?"

Cooper turned at the doorway and painted a perky smile on her face. She held up the file. "Just saying it's an effing rock-hard case."

- Chapter 3 -

When Cooper returned after her trip to Nixon's office, she found CID much quieter than she'd left it. Busy with their workloads, the detectives of the northeast had dispersed, visiting crime scenes, taking witness statements and liaising with other agencies. Cooper knew summoning them back to HQ would take time. She sent a message requesting everyone's presence at one o'clock that afternoon, threatening any latecomers with twenty push-ups.

Collecting her coat and the flimsy file concerning the missing cyclists, Cooper headed to the canteen to purchase a salad bowl and a carton of coconut water. She pulled on a woollen hat and gloves, then went to see Jack 'Tennessee' Daniel.

Following Tennessee's death, the team requested a memorial to their fallen friend, a place for quiet reflection and thoughts of the things Tennessee held dear: family, loyalty, and friendship. They'd settled on a bench engraved with his name and had it installed at the side of the wagonways – a cycle path that ran close to HQ. It was near enough for colleagues to visit on their breaks, but away from the main road, surrounded by trees and wildlife, it felt like a world away from the incident room.

The fresh air and five-minute brisk walk helped Cooper clear her head and did her and her baby a world of good. As she approached the bench, she was glad she'd made an effort to leave the office, even if it was colder than a penguin's arse that day.

Sitting on Tennessee's bench, she opened her lunch and took a mouthful, regretting having not asked for a hot drink.

"I don't know if you can hear me," she started when she'd finished her food, "but we think about you all the time."

Cooper took a deep breath, leaned back and closed her eyes. Her mind wandered as she listened to the distant rumble of traffic and robins chattering to one another on bare branches.

Shivering, Cooper wrapped her coat tighter around herself. She had a decision to make. She could sit here perturbed between her grief for Tennessee and her annoyance at Nixon, or she could do the right thing and push on.

She opened the file.

THE THREAT OF PUSH-UPS worked wonders. When Cooper entered CID the troops were assembled like the worst Avengers impersonators one could imagine. The only one vaguely resembling a superhero was DS Paula Keaton, and that was because she was built like a tank. Unlike Cooper's flimsy frame, Keaton had neither dainty feet nor a thigh gap. If she looked like she could bench press a horse, it was because she probably could.

"Last one here, boss," commented a PC with a wispy moustache. "Down and give us twenty," he joked.

At least Cooper hoped he was joking. She gave him the benefit of the doubt as she cast her eyes down at her stomach. "If I get on the floor, I won't get back up. Right, boys and girls, take your seats and make yourselves comfortable."

There was a collective groan as they realised this was no five-minute catch-up; something big had come up.

Two photographs were pinned to the whiteboard. "Rhett Campbell, twenty-four, and Laurel Deacon, twenty-two," said Cooper. Both Rhett and Laurel appeared young and healthy, their eyes a striking shade of blue, their teeth unnaturally white. Rhett sported wavy brown hair that reached his collarbones. He looked like a Hollywood A-lister with clear, tanned skin and a dimpled chin. Laurel's distinctive strawberry-blonde hair was braided in an elaborate style, reminding Cooper of a Viking warrior woman.

"Both from Totton, Hampshire," Cooper continued. "Keen cyclists, they were cycling the coast-to-coast and the coasts and castles routes back to back."

Keaton whistled. "Impressive."

"Indeed, especially at this time of year. Hampshire MISPERS have already interviewed Rhett and Laurel's families. The pair weren't looking to break any speed records. Instead, they were taking their time, stopping a few days here and there to explore the area. If the weather got too bad, they'd hunker down in a BnB or a pub and wait for the storm to pass. When the weather allowed it, they saved money by camping."

Several pairs of eyebrows raised as the group imagined camping in the northeast in January.

DC Saffron Boyd visibly shuddered. "Each to their own," she scoffed.

"Rhett and Laurel budgeted just enough for their current travel itinerary, which, aside from cycling, involved low-cost activities such as visiting churches and museums. They were due to travel back south by train and had tickets booked from Edinburgh on the second of January. CCTV shows they never boarded the train."

Cooper paused to rub her lower back. Three constables tripped over themselves to offer her a chair. She thanked the young woman who got to her first and sighed as she sat. Without a seat, the constable moved to the back of the room and leaned against the wall.

"Anything specific we can go on?" Keaton asked. "Brightly coloured bikes, for instance?"

"Yes," Cooper said. "While Rhett rides a Boardman ADV in black, Laurel's bike is a more unusual bright orange Cannondale. Their tent's also easily identifiable, green with yellow trim, and they wear matching wooden engagement rings."

A uniformed policeman made a note on a jotter and then suggested, "Maybe they decided to extend their stay. Enjoy Newcastle's nightlife?"

"It's possible," Cooper said, "and it's not totally out of character for them to stay somewhere longer than planned or indeed change their plans. However, we know they were low on funds and were on a budget for this adventure. Also, while they hadn't been updating their parents regularly, they were updating social media. Laurel's last tweets were on the twenty-sixth and twenty-seventh of December. On Boxing day, she wrote, *We arrived late, soaked and frozen to the core, but we were greeted by towels warming by the fire and a bottle of fizz on ice. It's true what they say about northerners. Everyone is so friendly! If I could understand the accent, this would be the perfect place. Almost.*"

"Almost?" Keaton echoed, apparently personally insulted that the northeast wasn't everyone's idea of paradise. "What did she mean by that?"

"No idea." Cooper checked her notes. "And on the twenty-seventh, Laurel posted a photo of the Turbinia with *hashtag discovery museum.*"

"What's the Turbinia?" asked Whyte."

"A steamship," said Cooper.

She hadn't been to the museum in years, but she'd seen the image Laurel posted and vaguely remembered going on a school trip in the nineties not long after the Turbinia exhibition opened.

"You can see it for yourself," she told Whyte. "You and I are heading over there now. Boyd, I want

Rhett and Laurel's images everywhere. Liaise with the pressroom and prepare a statement for the six o'clock news. Get stories in all the local papers."

DC Saffron Boyd nodded and got to her feet.

Cooper turned to another DC, Oliver Martin. "Martin, I want every officer in Northumbria Police and Police Scotland on the lookout for Rhett and Laurel, as well as their bikes and tent."

"I'll put a pack together with images of the bikes," he replied.

"Paula, can you start the basics?"

Keaton nodded and closed her notepad. "I'll get warrants for their bank accounts, see if they've withdrawn any money or used their cards, speak to their mobile phone providers and set up a hotline for when the story hits the news. Want me to check the hospitals? I know they liked camping, but the weather's been atrocious. They could have been injured."

"Please do. And thank you, Paula." Cooper awkwardly got to her feet before addressing the room. "The twenty-seventh of December was fourteen days ago. Two whole weeks. We know they made it to Newcastle; let's find out what happened next."

- CHAPTER 4 -

ONE HUNDRED AND FIVE feet of green and white painted steel greeted Cooper and Whyte as they entered Newcastle's Discovery Museum. The steamship Turbinia dominated the ground-floor exhibition space. At forty-four tonnes, it was impossible to miss. The detectives were drawn to the vessel like magnets. Cooper had to stop herself from running her fingers over the polished hull.

"Made right here on Tyneside." A man with thin grey hair and friendly eyes smiled at Cooper. His build was similar to Cooper's in both height and stomach size, and he wore a blue polo shirt displaying the museum's logo. "She was the fastest ship in the world in her day."

Cooper took a few moments to appreciate the boat, marvelling at the sleek lines and curved propellors.

"DCI Cooper, I presume? Your colleague phoned and said we could expect you."

She showed him her ID. "Yes. This is Elliot Whyte. We wanted to speak with you about some visitors you had between Christmas and New Year. Have Hampshire Missing Persons spoken to you already?"

"They have indeed. Sent over some photographs to see if I recognised the couple."

"And?"

"I did. Charming pair." He introduced himself as Rowan Stevenson. "The young lady, Laurel, was it? She was an inquisitive young thing."

Whyte looked up. "How so?" he asked.

"So many questions. I'm not complaining, of course." Rowan interlaced his fingers and rested them on his belly. "Most people come to the museum as a couple or as a family. It's an outing and they want to spend time together. Usually, the only interaction we have with them is in the gift shop. If people ask us questions, it's usually to find out where the loos are."

"But not Laurel?" Whyte asked.

"No. I thought they were marvellous guests." Rowan bit his lip and spoke to himself. "Thought the story of the Turbinia at the navy review was hilarious."

"I'm not familiar," said Cooper. Something about Rowan made her want to hear more. He seemed like the sort of man who had a story for all occasions.

"It was Queen Victoria's jubilee and the might of the British navy was on display. Over one hundred and sixty battleships and destroyers were sailing at Spithead when the Turbinia turned up unannounced and steamed past them all. Literally steamed." He paused to chuckle. "She was two to three times faster than any of the warships. Parsons – the engineer who designed her – made the navy look like fools. It was a huge publicity stunt, and he landed a large naval contract out of it."

Whyte looked amused. "That was a ballsy move, showing up the military like that."

"That's what Laurel said. 'Course, it was the enigma machine they were really interested in. Follow me."

Rowan wandered away at a surprisingly quick pace for a man who must have been in his late sixties. Cooper struggled to keep up. As they walked, her suspicions were confirmed. Rowan had another story for them, this time about Tommy Brown, a man from North Shields who seized documents from a German u-boat. Documents that allowed the code-breakers at Bletchley Park to solve the enigma code.

"They were both into computing," said Rowan. "Hence their interest in code-breaking. Now my memory isn't great these days..."

Cooper doubted that very much; the man seemed to have a knack for retaining information.

"... but, I'm fairly sure the young gentleman said he was into programming and artificial intelligence, and the young lady studied cyber... Erm, cyber something."

"Cyber security?" suggested Whyte.

Rowan pointed a finger at Whyte. "That's the one. Now would you two like to see our—"

Cooper cut the man off. As much as she'd enjoy a private tour, they didn't have all day to spend in the museum. She needed facts.

"What time did Rhett and Laurel leave?"

"It was about half two. I remember because they said they wanted to get to Tynemouth before nightfall. I thought they were cutting it fine, seeing as it gets dark about four."

That was more like it; Cooper knew where the pair had headed next.

"I don't suppose they said where they were staying?"

"They didn't know. Didn't have anything booked. I thought they were a little naive. I mean, what are the chances of getting somewhere in Tynemouth at the last minute between Christmas and New Year?"

Cooper estimated their chances were slim to none.

"They weren't fussed, though. Said they'd put their tent up if needed. Youth, eh? My bones ache just imagining it."

"You and me both," said Cooper as she made notes. "Anything else you can tell us?"

Rowan used the hem of his blue polo shirt to rub a fingerprint off the glass case that housed the enigma machine. "Hmm. Not really. Rhett bought a souvenir pen from the gift shop if that's any use to you."

It wasn't, but Cooper thanked the man anyway. They were laying the first foundations in tracing the pair after their last known communication.

As they left, Cooper took a moment to browse the gift shop, buying a notepad and pen for her daughter. Tina would be jealous that she went to a museum while she was stuck in school.

"Oh, check it out," said Whyte, his eyes like saucers as he stared at a Red Arrows flight simulator. "Fancy it? All work and no play and all that."

Cooper pulled an are-you-serious face. "In case you hadn't noticed, I'm a little bit pregnant. But don't let me stop you."

Whyte peered at her for a moment, perhaps wondering if it was a test. Deciding to chance it, he practically skipped over to the ride.

His excitement was short-lived. When Whyte exited the machine, one of the detectives looked like they had morning sickness; it wasn't Cooper.

- CHAPTER 5 -

"EARLIER TODAY, THE HOME secretary approved the extradition of Francisco Peña to the United States."

Cooper watched the national news that evening in the comfort of her Tynemouth home. Her mother, Julie, cooked dinner while Tina tidied the dining room. Julie had recently moved to an apartment in North Shields with views over the mouth of the river. Her new place was a twenty-minute walk away, but she made the journey to Latimer Street every Friday evening for a family dinner.

"Peña, from Santo Domingo in the Dominican Republic, is serving a life sentence at Belmarsh Prison for the attempted murder of his former landlord. He is wanted in the US for the 2017 murders of Sophia Grey and Emma Huxley and will likely face the death penalty. Peña has fourteen days to appeal the decision."

Cooper zoned out, the smell of beef casserole reminding her that she hadn't eaten much that day. She was waiting for the anchor to hand over to the local studios for the regional stories. Hopefully, Rhett and Laurel's disappearance would be the main feature. She needed exposure for the case, and the sooner that happened, the better. The longer they waited, the more challenging it would be to find the pair.

When the report finally came, it was short and to the point. The reporter, a slim woman in her late thirties, had the perfect voice for regional television; smooth, local and motherly.

"Police are investigating the disappearance of Rhett Campbell and Laurel Deacon, who were last seen here at Newcastle's Discovery Museum on the twenty-seventh of December. Rhett and Laurel, from Totton in Hampshire, were cycling through the region and told a staff member from the museum that their next stop would be Tynemouth."

Close-up images of Rhett and Laurel's faces appeared on screen, followed by pictures of their bicycles and a description of the green and yellow tent they travelled with.

"Anyone with information on their whereabouts is asked to..."

Cooper sat up and turned the television off just as Julie called through to the living room to say dinner was ready.

"Where's that handsome man of yours?" Julie asked, spooning casserole onto three plates. "It's family Friday."

"Running late," Cooper said. "He'll not be long."

Justin Atkinson, a scene of crime officer, was at a house in Houghton-le-Spring where the death of a child was being treated as suspicious. Cooper knew he found cases involving children difficult, especially now that he would be a father again. He'd drive home slowly, detaching himself mentally from work, so he could focus on family when he walked through the front door. It was a skill Cooper was practising but finding tricky; she wasn't one for switching off after work. As she took a mouthful of delicious beef and vegetables, she hardly registered Julie and Tina's conversation about schoolwork. Cooper made a mental note to be fully present at the next family dinner, but for now, her thoughts turned to the missing cyclists.

THE LOBBY AT HQ was bustling with people when Keaton arrived on Monday morning. She waited at the entrance and greeted Cooper with a Starbucks and a smile.

"You're an angel," Cooper told her.

Feeling like Cooper's own personal bodyguard, Keaton nudged officers and civilians out of the way as she guided the pregnant DCI safely towards the stairs.

"Don't get too excited. It's de-caf."

Cooper tilted her head up and scowled at Keaton.

"Now, now. Grouchy doesn't suit you." Keaton was likely the only one at Northumbria Police who could call Cooper grouchy and not get reprimanded. "Besides, I have some good news."

"A lead?"

Keaton smiled and savoured the moment. She'd had little to be happy about over the past few months, but Rhett and Laurel's disappearance had given her renewed enthusiasm.

"Some twitchers saw the story on Look North. They recognised the bikes. One of them's come in to give a statement. Care to join me?"

Keaton offered Cooper an elbow to help her up the stairs. Cooper rolled her eyes and took a swig of the de-caf coffee. "I might be fat, but I'm not completely useless. I can still manage the stairs."

"Fat?" Keaton snorted. "You weigh about as much as my left leg. You make marathon runners look obese."

"Would you feel better if I let you carry my coffee?" Cooper handed her the Starbucks and followed the DS up the stairs to CID.

"Mr Gilmore?" Cooper approached the man. He was talking to Oliver Martin by the first-floor vending machine, the latter debating between a Snickers and a Mars Bar.

"Call me Billy."

When Keaton told her their lead was a twitcher, she pictured an anorak-wearing man with grey hair, a moth-eaten hat and a pair of binoculars around his neck. Billy Gilmore was no such thing. He was a muscular man in his thirties with full-sleeve tattoos and a head of thick red hair braided into a long plait. Martin introduced Cooper and Keaton before entering C6 into the keypad. The coils of the vending machine rotated and a Snickers bar fell into the drawer.

"So, what can you tell us?" Keaton asked, showing Billy to a table and offering him a seat.

Billy pulled a small spiral-bound notepad from the pocket of his jeans and flicked through the pages. "It was the twenty-ninth of December."

That was two days after Rhett and Laurel were seen at the museum.

"I was at Hauxley Nature Reserve with two of me mates – Archie and Liam."

Keaton typed the location into a tablet and a map appeared on the screen.

"Here?" Keaton asked.

"Aye, that's the one."

Cooper stole a glance at the tablet. The nature reserve was on the coast, north of Druridge Bay, south of Amble.

"A cattle egret had been spotted so we headed up with our cameras." Billy unlocked his phone and showed Cooper a stunning black and white image of a bird with a long neck and beak coming into land on the water, its white wings spread like great fans.

"Beautiful," said Cooper.

"I took that snap at about eleven a.m., and I think I'd been at Hauxley aboot an hour at that point, so it was aboot ten when we saw the bikes. They were just lying on the grass with two backpacks. There

27

was nee one aboot, so we assumed the riders had gone for a walk or gone into the reserve."

"Can you describe the bikes?" Cooper had images of the bikes in her file but she held them back for now in case she influenced Billy's memory.

"Aye. One black, one orange. The orange one was smaller, and it had Cannondale written on the down tube in thick black letters. Archie made a joke aboot the orange one matching me hair." His mouth curled into a mischievous grin. "Ah gave him a clip roond the head for that."

Cooper nodded. He'd described Laurel's bike to a tee. "And the backpacks?"

Billy stared into space for a few moments. "Soz. I divint remember exactly. They were pretty hefty, looked heavy like."

"But you didn't spot Rhett or Laurel?" asked Cooper. "Rhett was five-eleven with wavy brown hair and—"

"Nah. The only other people I saw were Archie and Liam. The bikes were still there when we left."

"What time was that?"

"'Boot one, half one mebies."

Keaton got to her feet. "I'll send Martin up there."

"Divint bother. I was back up that way on New Year's Day, blowing the cobwebs away. They weren't there then."

Deflated, Cooper thanked Billy for his time. At least they knew Rhett and Laurel had continued up the coast as planned. Billy stood and shifted his weight from one leg to the other. "Sommat bad happened to them, didn't it?"

"We don't know," Cooper said, "but we're trying to find out. If you remember anything else, get in touch."

Billy pushed his phone and notepad back into his pocket. "I will." He turned to Keaton. "You have me number?"

She was about to answer when Martin loudly called for Cooper's attention. They all turned their heads as the young DC with short dark hair and a youthful complexion pointed to a computer screen.

With a mouth full of Snickers, he said, "I found them, boss. I found the bikes."

-Chapter 6-

"WELL, THIS IS DEPRESSING." Oliver Martin looked up and down a neglected street in Ashington.

Some argued that Ashington was a town, while others considered it a village. Either way, it was once a major centre of coal mining. So connected was Ashington to the industry that the distinct Pitmatic accent, developed from mineworkers' jargon, could still be heard today. The last mine closed in 2005, leaving behind empty streets and empty hearts. New estates were cropping up on the edges, fancy new builds with extensive gardens, and there was investment in business parks and leisure facilities. But for some in the dense terrace colliery houses, while life had moved on, they'd been left behind.

"Not much to do around here," Keaton said. "Unless you're into betting or sunbeds."

Martin wouldn't admit it in front of his mates, but he was glad to have Keaton with him. She was a no-nonsense woman with a build that terrified insecure men. The street gave him a bad feeling. The houses at either end of the terrace were boarded up, the walls covered in crude graffiti.

"It's this one. Number ten," he said, pointing to a garden with long grass sprouting up around an old fridge and washing machine.

Martin had taken a punt and looked for Rhett and Laurel's bikes on eBay and Facebook Marketplace. It had paid off. He contacted the seller, a man named Adam Squires, and posed as a prospective buyer.

Squires opened the front door. "Alreet?"

He was a skinny bloke with a pointed, stubble-covered chin. Despite the chilly weather, he wore a vest. His face widened into a massive grin which Martin presumed was at the thought of making an ill-gotten four hundred quid. The smile vanished when Martin and Keaton flashed their ID.

"Don't bother running," Keaton warned him. "Not unless you want all your neighbours to see you tackled to the ground by a woman."

His eyes flashed nervously around the adjoining houses. A net curtain twitched, and Squires lost any bravado he may have had.

"Fine, you got me. The bikes aren't mine. I found them, okay? I'll give them back. It's not a big deal."

"Oh, but it is." Keaton stared at the man until he moved aside and invited them into his home.

Martin tried not to wrinkle his nose at the smell; it was somewhere between wet dog and old bin liners. The two touring bikes propped against a dining table were the only clean things in the place.

31

Squires had the heating turned up high, and a collection of beer cans and ashtrays covered the floor.

"Where did you nick the bikes from?" Keaton asked.

Squires edged around the room uncomfortably. "I didn't nick them. I found them."

"Listen, son," Keaton said, being purposefully condescending. "Your mam'll be home soon, and she won't be happy when she finds out her little pride and joy has been trying to sell stolen goods."

"How'd you kna I live with me mam?" Squires frowned and folded his thin arms.

"Because we do some research before rolling up to a suspect's home."

"Suspect?"

"Yes, suspect. The house is in your mother's name, and as you both put every minuscule detail of your lives on Facebook, it wasn't hard to work out your schedule. Your mum works part-time at Argos on Station Road, so I reckon you've got a quarter of an hour before she comes home and wonders why the police are here. These bikes are evidence in a missing persons case. You can either tell me where the bikes came from – the truth, this time – or I'll have to assume you had something to do with the disappearance of a lovely young couple from Hampshire."

Rubbing a bead of sweat from his forehead, Squires looked to Martin as if he would help him.

"The truth, Mr Squires. Or you'll need to accompany us to the station." Martin looked at a carriage clock on the mantlepiece. "We have all day. You have ten minutes."

"Bollocks." Squires slouched and sat on the windowsill. "I took them from the back of a van. That's the truth. I don't know anything aboot any missing people."

Finally, they were getting somewhere. Martin scrawled notes while Keaton continued to grill him.

"Where?"

"It was parked near the train station at Pegswood, by the community park."

"When?"

"Erm." Squires hesitated. "Aboot a week ago. The sixth, I think. It was Monday morning."

"Describe the van."

"It was black, open at the back for carrying shit."

Keaton tried to picture it. "You mean a pickup?"

"Yeah. A pickup. Proper old, like. V-reg. Black and dirty. Loads of mud in the tyres."

"Did you see the driver?" Martin asked.

He shook his head. "Think I'd take the bikes with the driver aroond? I'm not that daft."

Martin thought about contradicting him but instead remained quiet. Keaton was less kind.

"We'll see about that," she said. "Did you take anything else from the back of the pickup?"

"No. Just the bikes."

"What else was in the pickup?"

Squires thought for a moment then shook his head as he tried to remember. "Just some old tools and that. A spade. Rope. It was under some dark green plastic sheet."

"A tarpaulin?"

"Aye," he said.

"Any backpacks?"

"Not that I saw."

Both Martin and Keaton stared at Squires. He didn't cave this time. Either he'd toughened up or Rhett and Laurel's backpacks weren't there.

"Final question," said Keaton. "You seen these two?" She showed him photos of Rhett and Laurel.

Squires' eyes flicked to the clock and then back to the photos. "No. Honest. What happens now?"

Keaton put on some nitrile gloves and picked up both bikes. "I'm going to take these bikes to the forensic lab and DC Marin here is going to arrest you under section twelve-five of the theft act – the taking of pedal cycles."

Squires' face dropped. "You said you wouldn't arrest me if I telt the truth."

Apparently Squires was that daft after all.

Keaton shook her head. "That was concerning the missing persons case. You've just confessed to theft."

Squires' groaned like he'd just lost a game of pool. "Can I call me mam first?"

WITH SHAKING HANDS, PORTIA Holt unlocked her front door. The key jammed in the lock, and it took much jiggling and cursing to finally turn. She placed her shopping bags on the kitchen counter, vowing never again to put herself through the ordeal of shopping at the local Waitrose again. She used to enjoy shopping, browsing the aisles as she planned meals for Michael and Summer, but Portia could no longer stand the stares. A gaggle of young, yummy mummies clutched their chests and adopted pained expressions, rocking their prams and fretting over their babies. They'd never let *their* children out of sight; they were good mummies, unlike the rotten woman in the fruit and veg aisle. Then there was the man by the fish counter who couldn't meet her eye and the loved-up couple giggling as she struggled with her trolly. Worst of all was the woman from the estate agents snapping sly photos of Portia to plaster on Twitter or sell to a tabloid. Her pain was their dopamine hit. From now on, she'd have her shopping delivered.

The kitchen-diner in the Holt's Ponteland home was clean and stylish, filled with modern gadgets and gizmos, but it was also quiet. Children came with noise; the silence of a missing child was deafening. Portia boiled the kettle and selected a podcast to listen to. She didn't care which one, as long as it provided some background noise. She opened her laptop, signed into Facebook and scrolled through her feed. There were the usual proclamations of sympathy from well-wishers, but there were also the trolls. Since the moment the news had broken, every half-wit on the internet had weighed in: *The poor woman. What kind of a mother loses her child? The planet was overpopulated anyway. It was a natural selection thing. How does she look so good? Maybe it's a publicity stunt? How can you trust a woman who looks like that? She's clearly had botox. Don't you know that she's probably in it for the money? How can she live with herself?*

When the kettle boiled, Portia made a cup of tea and switched tabs to GoFundMe. A complete stranger set up a fund for her, Michael and poor Timothy Harding's parents. It had raised a silly amount of money – over thirty grand already. Not that Portia needed the money, she had her own and would spend every last penny to have her daughter back. Regardless, it was consoling to know some of the population still cared. The others thought she was to blame; some even suggested she'd killed Summer. The thought made her queasy.

Her laptop pinged as another donation came through. Her husband wanted her to forget about Tim and concentrate on Summer. The other boy was unfortunate, but he was not their priority. Michael was partly right, Portia thought. She didn't have the mental health to cope with the disappearance of her own child, let alone someone else's. Still, knowing another woman was going through what she was – that she wasn't completely alone in the world – brought her a strange sense of comfort, so much so that Portia had contacted Tim's mum. Nadine Harding was younger than her and remarkably pretty. She was strong and resolute in the hope her little boy would be found alive. When they'd met for coffee to discuss what to spend the fund on, Nadine did her best to make small talk, to hold Portia's hand and pretend her heart wasn't breaking. Portia admired her. Nadine was a doctor but hadn't worked a day since Tim's disappearance, and though she was now eating into her savings, she was adamant she wouldn't use the money herself. They thought about keeping it as college funds for their children or donating it to charity should the worst happen. In the end, they decided to spend a large chunk of the money raised on something useful, something to show the world they hadn't given up.

- CHAPTER 7 -

ELLIOTT WHYTE PINNED AN enormous map of the north of England to a bare wall in CID. He took stickers and placed one over Alston before writing the words *Christmas Day* on it. He added a sticker over the centre of Newcastle and labelled it *twenty-seventh*, and another one at Hauxley Nature Reserve, marking it as *twenty-ninth*.

Cooper thanked him as she took a seat facing her colleagues. "Theories?"

"I don't know why they'd leave their bikes and backpacks out on the grass by the reserve?" Saffron Boyd asked. She flushed slightly as everyone turned to face the shy DC. "The bikes were their mode of transport. Their entire adventure depended on them."

"We know they wanted to do some hiking as well as cycling," said Whyte. "They might have gone for a wander around the reserve to give their backsides a rest. I hate bicycle seats."

"I still think it's unlikely they'd leave the bikes and all their belongings just to go for a walk," Boyd said. "They'd lock them to something, surely?"

Cooper agreed with both of them. When she, Keaton and Tennessee took part in a charity triathlon last spring, Cooper had reluctantly tackled the swimming leg. She thought she'd drawn the short straw but looking back, she would've been just as unhappy having to run or cycle. She'd never been a fan of the seats they put on bikes and wondered when they would invent something as fast as a bike but as comfortable as a beanbag. Still, like Boyd, she didn't think Rhett and Laurel would leave their things unattended unless... Cooper's thoughts turned once again to Tennessee and something he'd told her about him and his wife, Hayley.

"They were young and in love," she said. "Maybe they left their things for a few moments to go and..." She searched for the right word.

"Get jiggy with it?" said Keaton.

"Do some horizontal dancing?" said Martin.

"Play hide the sausage?" said Whyte.

Cooper pinched her nose. "Yes, yes and yes," she said, looking at each of them in turn. "I mean, people do stupid things for sex. Would you leave your bike and backpack out in the open if alfresco nookie was on the cards?"

Martin, Whyte and Keaton all nodded.

"Okay. So, the reserve is quiet. No one else is around." Cooper stood and pointed to the map. "There's tree coverage here and here, or they could have gone on to the beach, hidden between the dunes?"

"And when they came back, someone had nicked off with their things?" said Martin.

Boyd's dark blonde brows lowered and she bit her lip. "It still doesn't make sense. Even if their bikes and bags were gone, it doesn't explain why no one's seen or heard from them."

"Boyd's right," Keaton said. "I mean, granted, they were in the sticks, but it's not like they were in the middle of Siberia. They could have walked to the main road, hitchhiked, or waited for a bus. There's a caravan site there," she pointed to the map. "They could have asked someone to phone us and report that their stuff had been stolen."

Whyte raked his fingers through his dark locks. "The file said Rhett was experienced in survival skills. Even if they took a wrong turn, got lost, and spent the night outdoors without their camping stuff, he'd have known how to make a shelter."

Unless he was hurt. Cooper listened to what the team had to say and considered the possible outcomes. "How cold was it that night?" she asked.

"Effing freezing," said Whyte. "But if you want a more precise answer..." His voice trailed away as he typed into a tablet and consulted a weather app. "It was two degrees and raining."

Cooper grimaced. It wasn't looking good. "You checked the hospitals, didn't you?"

Keaton confirmed she had. "I'm still waiting on information from their mobile providers. It's due tomorrow. As for their banks, I should hear from them by the end of the week."

"What do you think?" Whyte asked Cooper.

Cooper placed a hand over her belly for a moment while her baby practised kickboxing her bladder. "I suspect foul play and think you all do as well. I want a major search arranged for first thing tomorrow morning. Everything east of the A1068 from Druridge to Amble. As many boots on the ground as we can get."

"We're looking for bodies, aren't we?" Boyd asked, her large eyes filled with sadness.

"I'm afraid so."

THE FOLLOWING MORNING, COOPER awoke to the smell of croissants and freshly brewed coffee. She pulled on her dressing gown and followed her nose, finding Atkinson in the kitchen. The radio was tuned to Classic FM and played relaxing orchestral music. It wasn't Cooper's usual choice – she was an Absolute Radio Rock kind of gal – but it suited her slower pace now she was weighed down. Besides, Atkinson liked it; now that they lived together, compromises had to be made.

"You're up early," she said.

Atkinson was smartly dressed in a grey shirt and dark patterned tie. He wore new glasses that suited his angular features and his recent haircut was short and tidy. He looked every inch the professional he was.

Atkinson pulled out a chair and poured her some coffee.

"That better not be—"

"De-caf? No, it's the real deal. I know better than to deny you your morning coffee."

He pulled a croissant from the oven and made *ooh ooh* noises.

"Hot," he said, dropping the crescent-shaped roll onto a plate, cutting it open and slathering it in butter. He placed the plate in front of Cooper then knelt down and rested his head against her abdomen.

"What are you doing?"

"Listening."

"What for?"

"A heartbeat. I should be able to hear it through your skin now." Atkinson's eyes widened. He looked up at Cooper, his face full of wonder. "I can. I can hear her heart beating."

"Her?"

"Just a hunch."

Cooper and Atkinson had decided not to find out the sex of the baby until it arrived. Atkinson had twin boys from a previous relationship; perhaps his use of *her* was him wishing for a change. Cooper wasn't one for old wives' tales, but if the one about sweet or salty cravings was to be believed, then Atkinson would get his wish. She'd been dreaming of sticky chocolate cake all of yesterday evening.

"Oh, it's amazing. A teeny tiny heart, with teeny tiny valves and ventricles, going boom-boom, boom-boom. No ultrasound, no stethoscope, just a powerful little heart."

Cooper wiped croissant crumbs from Atkinson's head as she ate. "There's still so much to do."

"We have plenty of time," he smiled. "Now Julie's moved all her things to Harbour View, we can transform the spare room into the nursery. How about we pick a colour scheme tonight?"

"Deal," said Cooper. She had a long day ahead of her with the search teams heading up the coast, but as she sat in the kitchen enjoying the coffee, croissant and Classic FM, she felt very much at peace.

Five seconds later, the peace was broken by Tina's screams that she couldn't find her netball kit.

- CHAPTER 8 -

TAMZIN CAMPBELL CLUTCHED HER handbag to her chest as she and her eldest son, Ashley, took their seats on a LoganAir flight from Southampton to Newcastle. Her hands shook as she tried to secure her seatbelt.

Ashley took the metal clasp from her fingers and clicked it into place. He held her hand, squeezed it gently and gave her a reassuring look. He was a sweet boy; he knew she was a nervous flyer at the best of times. During their last family getaway – a package holiday to Benidorm two years ago – Tamzin had clutched the armrests so tightly her arms went into cramp. Not that this was a holiday. She'd always wanted to go to Newcastle, but not like this. Her friends had arranged a girls' weekend a few years ago, but Tamzin couldn't go because Darren found out Lisa had booked tickets for Dreamboys and he'd hit the roof. All her friends had a great time drinking on the quayside, posing for photos with the Tyne Bridge in the background. She'd stayed home with a grumpy bastard.

Now Darren was dead, and she could have gone to Newcastle any time she bloody well pleased. But she hadn't. She'd become a recluse. Tamzin was only going now because she couldn't stand the idea of her little boy being missing.

He'd always be her little boy. It didn't matter how tall he grew or how independent he became, Rhett was always her little boy.

Ashley ordered two coffees and two brandies. He'd practically read her mind. It was early, but the drink would help her nerves. Hearing that no alcohol would be served during the flight almost brought tears to Tamzin's eyes.

"I tried," Ashley said with a shrug.

He was so unlike Rhett. Ashley was built like his father. Blonde, gaunt and pale with artistic fingers and menacing eyes. Rhett was built like Darren's friend, Peter. He was tall and athletic, with thick brown hair and electrifying blue eyes. *The less said about that, the better,* she thought, letting go of Ashley's hand and taking some headphones from her bag. She'd downloaded a relaxing hypnosis track to help her through the flight. Of course, it wouldn't do a damn thing. Rhett had vanished, and there was no hypnotising her way out of her maternal pain.

THREE HUNDRED AND FIFTY miles north, search teams had already been hard at work for several hours. Some focused on Amble in the north of the search area, speaking to residents, showing them photos of Rhett and Laurel and trying to spark any memories from the twenty-ninth of December. Others started in the south by Druridge Bay Country Park. They spread out over farmland, sand dunes and golden beach, searching quiet lanes and hedgerows. A third team focused their search on Hauxley Nature Reserve and the nearby caravan park.

Cooper shoved her feet into a hefty pair of green Wellington boots and stepped out of her vehicle onto a muddy trail. As much as she wanted to, she wouldn't be helping with any fingertip searches, not in her condition.

"Any news from the Campbells?" she asked Keaton as she pulled a woollen hat over her head and wrestled the hood of her coat over it. She felt sorry for the search teams. They were braving drizzle, slippery landscapes and a bitterly cold sea breeze.

"Flight left on time," Keaton told her. "Martin's driving Denise over to meet them at the airport."

Cooper knew family liaison officer Denise Oswald from a previous case when a man had been murdered on Holy Island. She was a kind woman and an excellent choice to work with the Campbells. She would take care of the family and keep them informed of any updates. Her role also involved listening to the family and gaining their trust. If there was anything unusual about the

Campbell family and their relationship with their son, Denise was their best bet for discovering it.

"They want to meet you," Keaton told her.

"That's understandable." Cooper struggled to zip her coat over her belly. "Bring them up here once they've taken their luggage to the hotel and had time for some food and a shower. I want them to see all this. It's important they know Northumbria Police are taking Rhett and his fiancée's disappearance seriously. I want his mother to see how many people are out looking."

Keaton relayed the information to Martin then followed Cooper into the nearby caravan park. Cooper had called and arranged to meet the owner in the park's clubhouse.

Standing under a wooden shelter, a friendly-looking man finished a cigarette. "You're late," he said. "Oh, sorry. That sounded rude. I mean, were the directions I gave you okay?"

"They were fine." Cooper smiled at the man's awkwardness. "It's Mr Watkins, right?"

"Right. But, call me Olly."

The man's hair was almost black, forming tight curls that matched his eyebrows. Four moles on his cheek formed a perfectly straight line. He stubbed his cigarette out in a metal grate over a bin and opened the door for the two detectives.

The room was large, with a bar at one end and round tables scattered throughout. Olly gestured to a table by the bar. "Can I get you anything?"

Cooper declined, but Keaton asked for tonic water. Olly made himself a tea from a machine that dispensed boiling water at the push of a button.

47

"So, how can I help you?"

"You may have seen on the news recently that two tourists from the south have gone missing in the northeast," said Cooper.

Olly's face showed a flash of recognition. "The cyclists? Yes, I saw on Look North."

"Have you seen them before? Perhaps they stayed here?"

Olly pulled his thin lips into his mouth and leaned back in his chair. "Sorry, no. We're an owners-only site, not a holiday park. We don't have any caravans to rent out."

"We think Rhett and Laurel's bikes were stolen from the nearby reserve," Keaton said. "They may have come here looking for accommodation. Could you check with your staff?"

"Certainly."

"And we'd like to speak to any of your guests who were here at the same time," Cooper said. "Someone may have seen the couple, and we really need as much information as we can get."

Cooper pulled an A5 notebook from her bag and opened it to a blank page. "Obviously, you'll need to check your records, but if you could list any staff, cleaners and so forth that we could speak to, it would be a great start."

Olly took the notepad. "What dates are we looking at?"

"Their bikes were seen at the reserve on the twenty-ninth of December."

Olly looked Cooper in the eyes. "In that case, I'm afraid it'll be a very short list." He pushed the notepad back across the table, its page still blank.

"We close in December. We shut everything down on the thirtieth of November and opened up again on the second of January."

Cooper's internal monologue flooded with swear words.

"Damn it," she whispered out loud. "You mean no one was here? No guests? No owners? No staff?"

He shrugged, filled his lungs with air and adopted an apologetic expression.

Keaton finished her tonic water, propping her elbows on the table. "If someone owned a caravan here, they'd have their own keys, right?"

"To their caravan, yes, but not to any of the facilities."

"Could someone still come here during December and just not tell you?"

Olly paused and sucked on his thin lips. "I guess." He drummed his fingers while he thought. "But we lock the gates. You'd have to park in the village or on the main road, jump the fence and lug all your stuff in that way. I've never heard of anyone doing that, though." He suddenly sat up straighter. "I have a camera trap. Set it up to take pictures of the badgers. They're dead cute. I just love them. I could load it up to my computer, see if anyone set it off on the twenty-ninth?"

Cooper and Keaton shared a look. It wasn't much, but it was worth a shot. "Please do, Olly. If you could also check for a few days on either side, I'd be very grateful. Here's my card. I'll be in the area all day. Let me know what you find."

CHAPTER 9

COOPER'S WELLIES SUNK INTO wet sand. Though she wore thick socks, the coldness of the water permeated the rubber material and numbed her toes. Seagulls squawked above, occasionally diving for a fish or fighting over another's catch. The breeze carried a smell of salt and seaweed.

The water at Druridge Bay was calm, like a mill pond; it must have been slack tide. Cooper turned to look at the trail of footprints she'd left behind her. They ran parallel to the edge of the water. Her eyes followed the prints until she spotted four figures walking toward her. Two men and two women. It was Martin she recognised first.

Tamzin Campbell looked slightly lost. She was somewhat shorter than Cooper, in her mid-fifties, and walked with a bit of a limp. Her frizzy brown hair poked out from under a bobble hat. The man accompanying her, Ashley, Rhett's brother, seemed on edge as he held out a hand to Cooper. She could hardly blame him.

"You're pregnant," said Tamzin almost instantly.

"I am. Thirty-one weeks."

"So you understand," said Tamzin, "what it's like to love something as much as a parent loves a child?"

"I do."

"Maternal instinct is a powerful thing." Tamzin breathed in the sea air. "I just know my little boy is okay. He might be hurt or lost, but he's going to be fine. He's out there. I know it."

"Oh, Mother." Ashley looked torn. His love for his mother and the instinct to protect her conflicted with the need to be realistic, to not allow her to hold too tightly to false hope. He rubbed a gloved hand over his face as he gathered himself.

Cooper took a moment to explain what actions Northumbria Police had taken so far. She gestured to the sand dunes where dozens of men and women completed a painstaking search, looking for any signs that Rhett or Laurel had been there.

Her phone rang. "Excuse me." Cooper walked away, leaving the Campbells in Denise and Martin's care. "Hello?"

It was Keaton. "Boss, the phone company just got back to me. The bad news is there've been no outgoing messages or calls from either of them and they can't find a location for the phones since the twenty-ninth. Good news is they've sent their records through. I'll head back to HQ and start going through texts and calls, see if anything unusual jumps out. Unless you need me up here?"

"Get yourself away," Cooper told her before returning to Rhett's family. "Is Laurel's father joining us?"

Tamzin shook her head. "Not today. He couldn't get time off work."

"He works for himself," snorted Ashley.

"Very busy man. Runs about five different businesses," Tamzin explained. "He can't just drop everything at the drop of a hat."

"Drop of a hat? His daughter's missing. Probably murdered!"

Ashley looked to regret the words as soon as they left his mouth.

"It's not like you rushed to help either." Tamzin's tone was harsh. She wiped a tear away.

Cooper looked at Ashley and waited for him to say something else.

When he finally spoke, he said, "My brother and I haven't seen eye to eye for a while. We had a falling out. About a girl."

"Laurel?" Cooper asked.

"No."

The group walked south along the shore as Ashley continued speaking.

"A girl Rhett used to out with in sixth form — India Hays. They'd been broken up for a long time when I started seeing her. Rhett was with Laurel by then so there were no hard feelings or anything like that."

"Then what was the problem?"

Ashley picked up a piece of driftwood and turned it in his gloved hand a few times before casting it away. "He would bad mouth her. Call her names. Said she was loose and that she was probably cheating on me. He said she was only interested in money, always wanting presents. He said she viewed men as credit cards and thought it was a boyfriend's job to spoil his girlfriend."

"And did she?"

"Not at first. I was besotted with her. Thought she was a gift from God. Problem was, she thought she was God's gift as well. Worked it out eventually, but by then I'd already cut ties with Rhett. He tried to warn me, but I didn't listen. The damage was done."

Denise Oswald, the FLO, patted Ashley on the arm and asked if he wanted to go into Amble for a cup of tea. He did. Martin went with them, leaving Cooper with Tamzin, who was looking out to sea.

"Brothers, eh?" she said, forcing a smile.

"I'm an only child," said Cooper. "I can't relate. I'm sorry you're going through this. We're going to do everything we can to find your son."

"Do you think he's dead?"

The bluntness of the question caught Cooper off guard.

"You can be honest with me, DCI Cooper."

Cooper wondered if she could be truthful. She thought it was near impossible that Rhett and Laurel would turn up unharmed. Still, she couldn't bring herself to say that to Tamzin. "Right now, we don't have enough information," she said diplomatically. "We have no evidence that they've been hurt, and equally we have no evidence that they're fine. I wish I could tell you more."

"You're trying, though?"

"We're doing everything we can," Cooper echoed.

Tamzin looked at her shoes and toed the sand before pulling a photo of Rhett and Ashley as young boys from her purse.

"Tell me about him," said Cooper.

And she did. Tamzin started her story with Rhett as an infant, sickly and premature. He was often off school with asthma attacks and constant coughs and colds. Slap cheek, chicken pox, scarlet fever. You name it, Rhett had it.

"Then one day, he just seemed to grow out of it. He discovered sports, which helped his asthma, and he grew big and strong. He was an athletic teen, doing every sport his school offered. He was on the rugby team, the squash team, captain of the football team."

"And then what?" asked Cooper. "What's he like now?"

As she asked the question, the wind picked up and blew sand across the rocks where police searched for clues. They turned their heads, shielding their eyes until the wind settled again.

"He's still the same person. Loves riding his bike, a bit of hiking, canoeing, that sort of thing. Then there's his computer. He's always playing games - oh, what's that one he's into?" she asked herself. "World of—, Call of—, Age of—. I don't know. He even made a few games of his own. Clever boy."

"He did programming at university?" Cooper asked, remembering her conversation with Rowan at the Discovery Museum.

"Yes. That's where he met Laurel. They hit it off straight away. He didn't go straight from school like she did. He worked for a couple of years to save up for some of the tuition. Worked weeknights at our local Wetherspoons and weekends at a computer repair shop."

"Sounds like a good idea," said Cooper. "Tuition's ridiculously expensive now." She thought of Tina and wondered how much debt she'd be starting her adult life with once she had three or four years of uni, rent, textbooks and food under her belt.

"Free in my day," said Tamzin. "Not that I went to uni."

"Me neither," Cooper told her. She liked Tamzin; she seemed friendly and open, even in the face of her worst fears.

"I'm not sure what else to tell you about Rhett. He was well-liked and didn't court trouble. He wasn't one to start fights. In fact, I'm sure I remember someone saying he was better at breaking up fights in the pub than the bouncers were. He was good at calming people down. Used his words, not his fists. Shame he couldn't work his magic on Ashley."

Tamzin wrapped her arms around herself, tucking her hands into her armpits for warmth. "He adored Laurel, loved a nice steak - especially with peppercorn sauce. He was into trading that Elysium nonsense, and he was obsessed with the Saints."

The cold was starting to get to Cooper. The sea breeze sapped her energy and she wanted to get indoors. Though they were walking, the exercise was doing nothing to warm her. Cooper could feel a chill in her bones and a shiver ran from the top of her head down to her feet. She was about to ask Tamzin a few more questions when her phone chirped loudly, causing Tamzin to jump.

"This is Cooper."

"It's Whyte. I'm using someone else's phone. We're down by Chevington Burn. I'm waiting to hear more, but wanted to give you a heads up—"

"Spit it out."

"Someone's spotted a tent."

- CHAPTER 10 -

COOPER HELD HER BREATH waiting for news about the tent. She wiggled her icy toes and watched reflections of seagulls soaring above the calm North Sea. Tamzin, Rhett's mother, stood a few yards away, studying Cooper's face, trying to read her expression for good news. The chances of Rhett and Laurel missing their train in favour of a few weeks of wild camping were slim. Cooper thought it was more likely Whyte would call her back with the news they'd discovered two bodies. She'd heard of people dying in tents from carbon monoxide poisoning after using barbecues. After all the terrible things she'd seen in this job, all the crime scenes visited, carbon monoxide poisoning would be a relatively good outcome. Tragic, of course, but she'd imagined far worse happening to the young couple.

"It's not theirs," said Whyte when he called back. "It's blue. Just heard from the team."

Cooper mouthed, *false alarm*, to Tamzin.

The woman closed her eyes for a moment, then turned and walked in the direction her other son had gone, head bowed, hopes crushed.

Cooper put the phone back to her ear. "You sure?"

"They reported a blue tent containing fishing gear. *Property of Russell Rivers* written on it thick marker pen."

Cooper thanked Whyte for the update and ended the call. She turned her back to the wind and pulled out her notebook. She wanted to write a few notes immediately to remember later. Russell Rivers. She'd heard the name before; she was sure she had. But her mind struggled to find the memory or make the connection. The double alliteration sounded like a porn star name. Then it hit her. Russell Rivers. Ronnie Rogers.

Ronnie, or Veronica, was an accomplished blood-spatter analyst working out of Manchester. They'd used her services during a double shooting in the spring. Cooper smiled. She owed Ronnie Rogers. If Ronnie hadn't shown an interest in Atkinson, Cooper wouldn't have become jealous and made it evident to him that she wanted him back. Now she had Atkinson and his baby. Jealousy was a funny thing.

Moving away from the beach, Cooper took a sandy trail through the dunes. It was beautiful here – if you ignored the dozens of police officers scouring the area. She couldn't imagine being anywhere else. Even with all its quirks and flaws, she adored the northeast. As she reached Hauxley Lane, Cooper turned right towards a small car park. They'd set up a van with coffee facilities, maps, evidence bags and other items they'd need during the day. She found Tamzin and Ashley; they were warming their fingers around plastic cups of something steaming. She caught Denise's eye, who nodded to signal they were doing all right, all things considered.

Assured that Tamzin wasn't wandering the coast alone, Cooper retraced her steps. She wanted to clear her head. After that, her next stop was HQ.

IT TOOK LONGER THAN promised for the bank records to arrive. At least the information from Rhett and Laurel's phone service providers had come through promptly. Having secured the warrant and given the paperwork a quick scan, Keaton delegated the grunt work to Martin.

It was Friday morning and the case was moving slower than a comatose snail. Martin found a big fat nothing in the phone records, the door-to-doors had proved fruitless, and the search produced nothing of interest.

Laurel's father had arrived on Tyneside the previous day. He gave Cooper an intense grilling and threatened her with bad press if she didn't find his daughter alive – and soon. Cooper told him, "I don't give a shit about bad press. But, I do give a shit about your daughter. I'll do whatever it takes to find her or find out what happened to her. I've decided to expand the search area. Work's already begun."

Her honesty softened Bruce Deacon and he promised to stay out of Cooper's way as long as she kept him informed of any developments.

"Boss," Keaton held a receiver to her chest as she called across CID.

Cooper looked up.

"Olly Watkins from the caravan park is on the blower. His camera trap caught something. He says it might be bugger all, but he's sending the footage across."

Pressing her palms together, Cooper looked to the ceiling – in all its stained, strip-lighting glory – and thanked a god she didn't believe in.

The footage came through two minutes later. Her computer emitted a high-pitched beeping noise, and everyone crowded around like urchins at a sweet-shop window. Everyone leant forwards as a grainy, black-and-white image appeared on screen.

"That's it?" said Cooper. It was a five-second video where the hindquarters of a badger waddled into view and out again. "Very helpful."

Keaton straightened and rubbed her lower back. "Yeah, unless you're into badgers' butts, it's hardly worth getting excited over."

"Play it again," Martin said.

"Why? You into badgers' butts?"

Martin wrinkled his nose at Keaton. "Very funny. Seriously. Play it again."

Cooper hit play. Then again. And again.

"Well, young man, as handsome as that badger is..."

"It's not the badger," he said, squinting and bringing his face closer to the screen. He hit play, then quick as a flash, he hit pause. The image froze. "There. In the background."

Cooper's mouth dried up and she reached to her handbag for a bottle of water.

"I see it," said Keaton. "Someone moving through the trees."

In the distance, a dark figure crept through the treeline, moving in the shadows from one tree to the next.

"It looks like bloody Sasquatch," said Martin.

"That's no Big Foot. That a man," Keaton said. She folded her arms, her forehead creasing into three straight lines.

"Could be a woman."

"It's a man."

"How do you know?" asked Martin.

"Because women, as a rule, don't go roaming around deserted caravan parks in the middle of winter. That's creepy AF. We have a little thing called self-preservation."

"Men have a sense of self-preservation."

Keaton laughed. "Like hell you do."

"Says the adrenaline junkie."

Cooper angled her head back to peer at the bickering detectives. "Children," she warned. "That's a man. Quite a tall one. When was this taken?"

Keaton pulled up the metadata from the video file. "The twenty-eighth. Middle of the afternoon."

61

That was the day before Rhett and Laurel's bikes were seen.

"Could it be Rhett?" asked Keaton. He was five-ten, right?"

"Or a drifter?" Martin suggested. "Could've been looking for a place to stay. If he knew the caravan park was deserted..."

Keaton snorted. "The day before our two cyclists happen to disappear off the face of the planet? If he is a drifter, he's a suspect."

"Children!" Cooper's blood sugar was low; she was feeling tetchy. She played the footage once more and stared as the unknown male, almost silhouetted, vanished into the trees. Whoever he was, he scared her.

- CHAPTER 11 -

THE BANK FINALLY RELEASED Rhett and Laurel's data on Friday afternoon.

"What's the verdict?" Cooper asked Whyte.

Cooper was casually dressed in faded black jeans, a grey t-shirt and a grey blazer. Her boots were flat but polished to perfection. Whyte sat next to Saffron Boyd; he wore a smart navy suit and was hunched over the desk. His floppy dark hair hung forward as he read and re-read the bank statements.

"Last cash withdrawal from either of them was on the twenty-seventh. That was the Barclays ATM by the Life Science Centre."

"That's not far from the Discovery Museum. Do you have a time stamp?"

"Two forty-three," he told her. "They took out a hundred and fifty quid from Laurel's account."

That fit with what the guide at the museum had told them. Rhett and Laurel had left at around half-two; shortly after, they'd withdrawn some cash.

"Okay," Cooper said. "Do me a favour and get the CCTV footage from the ATM. That way, we'll have a better idea of what they were wearing and we can share the images with the media. Hopefully, someone else will come forward."

Whyte gave Cooper a thumbs up and bobbed his head towards Boyd. "Saff's been doing some digging."

Boyd ran a finger down the page. Her nails were short and painted with clear nail varnish. "I've gone over Laurel's expenses for the past year. Regular outgoings include rent, mobile, Netflix, Amazon Prime and Specsavers. I presume she pays monthly for contact lenses. She has two sources of income. Wages from an accountancy firm where she does some admin. She's part-time and her wages vary depending on how many shifts she works. I spoke to her boss. He says she's a professional young woman and a good team member, but he's also well aware that she's not interested in working admin forever and is just there until she finds a job doing something she's interested in."

"Her second income?" asked Cooper.

"Fiverr. It's an online marketplace for freelance services. She designs websites, sets up VPNs, and programs chatbots for those annoying customer service pop-ups. She makes about as much from freelancing as she does from admin. But, after her outgoings, there's not a huge deal left. She shops at Aldi and Tesco and drinks in a microbrewery near to her home. I'm afraid, I don't have much else to tell you. She hasn't used her card to pay for anything since Boxing Day."

Cooper sighed but thanked Boyd for her efforts. If Laurel's card had been used it could either mean proof of life or it could lead them to whoever harmed her. Sadly, no financial activity meant no clues.

They were no further forward.

"Update the FLO," she told Whyte, then get yourselves home. It's Friday night; go enjoy yourselves.

IT WAS COOPER'S TURN to cook dinner for Family Friday. The word cook was up for debate. For Atkinson or Julie, it meant putting love and care into a meal that took hours to prepare. Even Tina could follow a Youtube tutorial and rustle up a curry; she made a mean massaman. Cooper's interpretation of the word cook included buying ready meals or ordering a takeaway. No one would complain. It was safer that way.

Cooper called into M&S at Silverlink Retail Park. The place was heaving with people shopping after work and those starting their weekend at the cinema or Italian restaurant. She weaved her way through the store using what she dubbed her pregnancy privilege. People were far more respectful of personal space if they thought someone's waters might break at any moment.

A selection of Chinese ready meals caught Cooper's eye, and she added Peking duck, pancakes, spring rolls and spare ribs to her basket. Her cravings for sweet food had driven her to distraction all afternoon, but as she turned into the cake aisle, she spotted a familiar face.

"Hey, Neil."

As usual, Fuller didn't look well. Peaking into his trolly gave Cooper an idea why. Two six-packs of Stella, a bottle of M&S whiskey, frozen burgers and a box of Nytol.

"How're things?" she asked, knowing they weren't good.

Fuller was single, having been poetically dumped by the woman he left Cooper for. Cooper wasn't bitter, not these days. Now her main concern was keeping the struggling DI alive. Cooper had suggested he seek therapy to deal with the Summer Holt case, but his stubborn masculinity – a hangover from having a Dad who prized a stiff upper lip over all else – meant he'd refused.

"Did you hear?"

Cooper's heart fluttered, wondering if there'd been news.

"Someone created a GoFundMe for the Holts and the Hardings. It's raised a bloody fortune. Over thirty grand in only a month or so."

Cooper picked up a cake in the shape of a caterpillar, peered at it and put it back on the shelf. "That's good news. Isn't it?"

"I thought so." Neil rubbed his beard. "Then I found out what they're spending it on. They've only gone and hired a private investigator. I swear to God, Erica, he's going to make us look like fools."

"Well, he wouldn't be the only one," she muttered. "That GoFundMe isn't just good for the families, it's good for us. Every time someone shares it or the story is repeated in the press, it's another opportunity to remind the nation that Summer is still missing. It keeps her image in the county's collective consciousness. I know it's hard, Neil. I don't envy your position, but try not to be antagonistic with the PI. It doesn't matter if this investigator works for us or someone else. It's another investigator. Another set of eyes, another way of seeing things."

He sighed, his face more downtrodden than Cooper had seen it before. Being a police officer was his life. It was his identity. What would he have to live for if he lost his purpose? She appreciated his certainty, how he could wake up and know exactly what he had to do because she felt the same about policing. Only Cooper had a partner, a child, and another one on the way. Fuller had Summer Holt.

Not knowing what else to say, Cooper kissed his cheek and patted his arm. She wished she could say something wise, something to make him feel better, but she didn't have anything. Instead, she bid him goodbye and continued her shopping. Her sweet cravings hadn't disappeared in the last five minutes, so she picked out a chocolate cake and some ice cream. Deciding that Atkinson and Julie would appreciate a glass of dessert wine with their cake, she steered her trolly to the liquor aisle and picked one off the shelves. It wasn't until Cooper joined the queue at the checkout that she paid attention to the pretty bottle of plum-coloured liquid. Its label featured a pink and yellow heart and the word Elysium written in a stylised font.

Cooper paid, put the items in the boot of her BMW and headed home. She found a space at the end of the road, heaved the shopping bag onto the crook of her arm and fumbled for her car keys from her blazer pocket. She was about to unlock the front door when an uneasy feeling swept over her.

It was dark, the street lights casting long shadows down the street. Cooper turned and stared into the night. "Hello?" she called anxiously.

"Hello."

Cooper jumped, spun on the spot and thrust the heel of her palm into Atkinson's chest. He staggered back into the open doorway and rubbed his breastbone.

"Welcome home," he gasped dryly.

"You scared the shit out of me." Cooper scanned the street again, then followed Atkinson indoors.

He took the shopping from her and kissed her cheek. "What's got you so on edge?"

She shook her head, feeling silly. "Nothing. I just had a weird feeling, like I was being watched or I'd forgotten something."

"I was watching you." Atkinson unpacked the spring rolls, read the instructions on the box and turned the oven on to preheat. "I looked out the bedroom window and saw you parking up."

"Yeah, it was probably that." Cooper sat down at the kitchen table and undid the laces on her boots.

"And if you've forgotten something, it's probably your phone. I tried to call you three times."

Cooper opened her purse, rummaged for a moment, then swore under her breath. "Pregnancy brain," she muttered. She pulled her feet from her boots, crossed one foot over the opposite knee and massaged her toes.

Atkinson continued to prep dinner, explaining that Tina was in the shower and Julie was in the living room reading the latest Portia Holt bestseller. He read the instructions for the other items and cut the corner off a packet of jasmine rice before putting it in the microwave. Cooper offered to help; after all, it was her turn to cook. Atkinson gave her a *don't-be-daft* look and presented her with a cup of lemon and ginger tea.

Reaching the dessert items, Atkinson's face spread into a wide grin. "Cake? Very nice. I'll have to go for a run tomorrow to burn this off."

"You love running."

"True." He picked up the bottle of dessert wine and turned it until the label faced him. "Elysium? My favourite."

Cooper let go of her aching foot and stood up. "Elysium! That's what was bugging me. Elysium."

Atkinson looked lost.

"Rhett's mother said something about Elysium."

"That's your missing cyclist?"

"Yeah. I met his mother on Tuesday. She's a nice lady, but she's going through hell. When I asked her about Rhett, she mentioned something about Elysium. What's Elysium?"

69

Atkinson put the bottle down. "Well, aside from being a tasty alcoholic beverage, it's the idea of an afterlife in Greek mythology. It's different to Hades in that only those related to the gods or chosen by the gods could live a blessed and happy life in the Elysian Fields."

Cooper sat down and played a pit-a-pat tune on her belly. Her baby played too, his or her little feet kicking a rhythm of their own. Cooper didn't think it would have any bearing on the case if Rhett had been buying and selling wine. Unless he had debts that they didn't know about. Even then, most business folks used the courts to claim back money, not their fists. It was only the likes of the Blackburns and the Roker Boys who would kill or maim someone over unpaid debts. But why harm Laurel as well? To leave no witnesses?

Once again rummaging in her bag, Cooper pulled out her notepad and scrawled a message to herself for Monday morning.

Look into Rhett's business ventures.
Did he have a side hustle like Laurel?
Check for business accounts.
Call Hampshire local intelligence.

If Rhett Campbell had even the slightest connection to the mob, Cooper wanted to know about it.

- CHAPTER 12 -

JACK FROST CONTINUED TO tiptoe around the northeast on Saturday. During the morning the temperature barely got above freezing. Ice crystals formed into fractal ferns and flowers, painting every window and car a frosty white. At night the pavements resembled ice rinks, slowing traffic to a cautious pace. A cloudless sky of inky blue glowed silver with dazzling stars and a mid-winter moon.

In Tynemouth, Cooper and Atkinson packed a grab bag in preparation for when Cooper entered labour. The bag was a gift from Julie and Tina, an expensive weekender Cooper could use for many years to come.

First into the bag was an oversized Guns N' Roses T-shirt Cooper could wear as a nightgown. She added a couple of magazines, a book, maternity pads and a nursing bra. They packed snacks, a wash bag and a pair of slippers. Atkinson downloaded television shows and podcasts to an iPad to keep her entertained and distracted during the early stages. When the downloads were complete, he placed the tablet and charger in the bottom of the bag.

Sitting on the edge of their bed, Atkinson handed Cooper a gift bag. She smiled in appreciation and peered inside. Reaching in, she pulled out three newborn-sized sleepsuits in neutral colours. Safari-themed in shades of sand and khaki, decorated with paw and hoof prints, the tiny clothing melted Cooper's heart. She held one to her chest and looked at Atkinson with tears in her eyes. He read her mind and nuzzled close to her. They had so much love for someone they'd never met. Girl or boy, they couldn't wait to meet their baby.

THERE WASN'T THE SAME scene of domestic bliss in Willington Quay, where Keaton sat alone sipping her fourth beer and shouting at a rugby game she was watching on catch-up. Her life was a depressing mess. Christmas had been especially bleak and wretched. She'd spent the day with her brother Riley trying to skirt around the elephant in the room. Keaton's girlfriend had cheated on her and left a chasm of a hole in her heart. Riley tried his best to make Christmas dinner, but every mouthful was a reminder of April's absence. She was a caterer, a great chef and a pastry wizard. No matter what magic Riley worked with the sprouts, it would never match April's version. After eating in silence, they'd agreed to get pissed and watch the least Christmassy thing they could find on Netflix.

Keaton drained her beer and crushed the can in one hand. This wasn't how she wanted to live: lonely, seeking comfort in a can of Carling. She turned off the game and rubbed her eyes. Her skin felt greasy and she couldn't remember if she'd brushed her teeth that morning. If next Christmas resembled the one just passed, Keaton didn't think she'd survive it. She wanted to love someone and be loved in return, but she knew she'd never meet someone sitting in her fat pants on a lop-sided sofa. If she wanted to get back out there, she had to do just that – leave the damn house. That meant getting washed and dressed. Try as she might, Keaton still lacked the mental fortitude for something as basic as personal hygiene.

She turned the game back on, lay down on the sofa and told herself the pain would end soon.

It had to.

KEATON WASN'T THE ONLY member of the team thinking about Christmas. That evening, Oliver Martin walked hand in hand with Saffron Boyd through the streets of Newcastle; he felt like a kid on Christmas morning.

Boyd's dark blonde hair formed loose curls beneath a black beret-style hat. She wore a black double-breasted winter coat and flat knee-high boots over jeans. Her skin was bright and pale, her lips bee-stung and dark pink. Martin thought she looked like a doll with doe eyes and long lashes. But it wasn't just Boyd's adorable features that made him feel lucky to be seen with her. She was kind, sweet-natured and had an innocent sense of humour. In other words, he was smitten.

It had been Boyd's turn to plan their date. She'd chosen an escape room near Grey's Monument. Martin had never been to an escape room before and Boyd couldn't wait to show him what it was all about. They took a lift to a space designed to look like a subterranean cave. Martin felt like some sort of Geordie Indiana Jones. They solved the series of clues in just short of the sixty-minute cut-off time, leaving the venue feeling energised and accomplished.

"You're a genius," said Martin as they walked down Dean Street towards a tapas restaurant. At the top of the bank, a bus pulled away from its stop. "I'd never have guessed the number of pebbles in the jars corresponded to the combination lock."

"I had an advantage. I've done a few before," Boyd said modestly. You get used to recognising clues and start looking for them in the right places. Besides, we wouldn't have got out in time if you hadn't remembered where we put the skull and the diamond."

Boyd squealed as she slipped on the icy pavement, sliding off the curb and into the road. At the same time, the bus's tyres lost their traction, and fourteen tonnes of metal and diesel hurtled towards her.

Martin grabbed Boyd by both hands, preying the tread of his boots would hold firm on the slick ground. He pulled her back to her feet and onto the curb. Holding her body close to his, their hearts thundered as the bus careened down the hill. The driver regained control, turned into the skid, and brought the vehicle to a stop behind a queue of traffic. It was a miracle no one was hurt.

"Saved your life," he said, half-joking, half-serious.

Martin stared down at Boyd, her lips parted in a soft gasp. He couldn't help himself; he leaned down and kissed her. It was electric, their lips melting together, their bodies pressed close. They forgot about the cold and the people around them as they got lost in each other. Eventually, they broke apart, both breathless and grinning like idiots.

"Oh, sorry, that's my phone," Boyd said. "One second."

She pulled away, spoiling their embrace to retrieve her phone from her coat pocket. Martin wasn't prying, but he couldn't help reading her message.

Everything okay? It was from her father, his third message this evening.

Yes, she typed quickly. *Having a nice time.*

Nice? Martin thought. That wasn't a great endorsement. He'd just saved her from becoming road kill. He'd have described their night as bloody fantastic, but then his parents didn't text him every hour on the hour to check up on him. Male privilege, Martin thought. His parents didn't need to worry about him – he was a bloke.

They took a left towards the tapas place. He'd looked it up online after Boyd told him she'd book a table. It looked authentic, and Martin had his eye on the fried goat's cheese with honey.

Another buzz.

Are you getting a taxi home? her father asked.

Yes. Have one booked at ten.

That was news to Martin. He'd hoped for a couple of cocktails, some dancing cheek-to-cheek.

Text me when you get home.

Will do. Love you.

Feeling deflated, Martin let his mind wander. Boyd spoke quietly, chatting about a holiday she'd once taken to Spain. He wasn't listening. He enjoyed their dates and had agreed to take things slowly. But something about their dates seemed almost childlike, nothing more than kissing and always home by half ten. The constant parental text messages may as well be an old chaperone watching their every move for signs of impropriety.

It wasn't as if he wanted the modern approach either: sext, hook up, ghost, repeat. Still, he thought there was room for something somewhere in between. He wanted Boyd to be his girlfriend; he wanted a physical relationship. Had something happened to Boyd? Something traumatising? Martin had never been one for heart-to-hearts or serious conversations. He never knew what to say or how to start a dialogue. He'd have to overcome that fear someday. Just not today.

He sighed and took her hand in his once more. "What lagers do they serve at this place?"

- CHAPTER 13 -

CRAIG MILTON TESTED THE ground with a shovel. The blade fell heavily, hitting the hard earth with a dull thud. Frost dusted fields for as far as he could see. Winters were long and hard in these parts – for both humans and livestock. His flock of Cheviots would need to be fed hay until temperatures rose a few degrees.

Craig tightened calloused fingers around twenty-kilogram bags of sheep feed and tossed them into his trailer. He may be getting on in life, but his grip was that of a twenty-year-old rock climber. The feed was labelled sheep nuts, and though it contained no nuts, it was filled with wheat, meal, minerals and oils. Everything a growing lamb needed.

Craig climbed carefully into his tractor, his joints aching more than usual. He'd applied a layer of anti-inflammatory gel over his hips and lower back, but the analgesic effect had yet to kick in.

Putting the vehicle in gear, he headed down a bumpy track. It was early afternoon and having been up since four, he was famished and in need of some sustenance. Emma's famous cider and onion soup should be bubbling away on the hob, a loaf of seeded bread growing in the oven. He smiled, almost able to smell it.

He slowed as he passed the flock on a steep hill.

"Yan, tyan, tethera, methera, pimp," he mumbled instinctively.

Sheep rustling may seem like a problem for a bygone era, but it was on the up again and counting sheep was still an essential part of shepherding. Organised criminal gangs laundered money at livestock markets or stole stock for illegal butchery.

"Sethera, lethera, hovera, dovera, dik."

As he drove, Craig made a mental note of any general maintenance to be added to his ever-growing to-do list. Fence posts needing attention, a squeaky barn door, a stile on its last legs.

Craig brought the vehicle to a stop by a barbed wire fence marking the boundary between his and his neighbour's land. Something small and white was caught on the barbed wire. About the size of a credit card, it fluttered in the breeze. A stickler for keeping a tidy farm, Craig got out of the tractor, moaning as he did so, and plucked the white fabric from the wire.

It was an Altura clothing label. Craig examined it, turning the shiny material between his aged fingers. He didn't recognise the brand name, but another name caught his attention. In blue biro was a faded, blurred phone number and the name Laurel Deacon.

———

COOPER PUT THE PHONE down and pursed her lips. Not much had happened in the ten days since Rhett and Laurel's bank statements had come through. Conversations with Rhett's mother and Laurel's father had garnered nothing new. She'd found no evidence of Rhett being involved with the mob, and while her suspicions of him having his own business were correct, nothing appeared untoward. Rhett bought and sold random goods on eBay and Amazon, fad items that became hugely popular one minute then disappeared the next. He'd arrange a shipment from China and then handle distribution in the UK. Though he turned over a decent amount of money, his profits were low. It hardly seemed worth the effort.

Getting to her feet, Cooper approached a large map of Northumberland pinned to the wall. She took a sticker and placed it over Craig Milton's farm. His property lay near Stobswood, west of Widdrington. It didn't look far from the area they'd been searching, but it was at least ten kilometres from where their bikes had been seen.

Cooper looked around. Unable to find Keaton, she turned to Whyte. "I need you to head to this location right away. A farmer found a clothing label with Laurel's name on it."

His eyes widened. "No way?"

"Way." Cooper checked her watch; it was mid-afternoon. "We've lost daylight now. Head up there and have a chat. Get the label to the lab, I'll organise a thorough search to start at daybreak."

CRAIG PLACED THE CLOTHING label in the cab of his tractor where it couldn't fly away in the wind. He'd recognised the name from the news and dialled 999 straight away. The operator put him through to a detective chief inspector who asked him to keep it safe without handling it too much. She told him someone would come and speak to him soon. Craig knew it was ridiculous, but he was worried about the police coming to his farm.

"What if they think I had sommat to dee with it?" he murmured.

Unable to sit still, he began to pace the field on the boundary of his land. He rubbed his dodgy hip as he walked. "Divint be daft, lad."

But what if Laurel — and what was her fella's name? — Rhett? What if they were lying in a ditch somewhere on his property? Craig shoved his hands deep into his pockets and glanced around at the fields and hedgerows stretching across the horizon. He couldn't just stand about not knowing.

Craig tightened his scarf and set out on foot. Warning himself that he might find two bodies, he braced himself. Like most farmers, he was accustomed to death, one had to be when working with animals, but he'd only seen a dead human once before. That was when his dear mother passed away in his arms. He choked back the memory and pressed on. No use dredging up things like that.

Still, as Craig walked, he couldn't help himself. He was at a stage of life when one attended more funerals than Christenings. Death was inevitable. It lurked around every corner. Craig only wished it didn't lurk anywhere on his land.

"Ah, crap." Craig stopped walking.

- CHAPTER 14 -

ELLIOT WHYTE GOT OUT of the pool car at the end of a quiet country lane and opened a heavy metal gate. He drove through, then got out of the car again to close the gate behind him. Whyte took a moment to stretch his legs. He wasn't the most outdoorsy of the team. He preferred watching television or hanging out in the pub with his mates to hiking and cycling. While he enjoyed the occasional game of five-a-side, he wasn't like Tennessee had been, always on a family walk on the weekends. Still, there was something peaceful about the countryside in winter, especially Northumberland. In the darkness, the fields and farmhouses looked greyscale, frozen in time like a black and white photo from days gone by. Whyte wondered if the place had changed in over a century.

He continued along the uneven trail until he was flagged down by an elderly gentleman and the most giant dog Whyte had ever seen.

"Craig Milton?" Whyte asked, lowering the driver's window.

"Aye. That's me."

Whyte had been told Craig was in his early seventies. But the man before him wasn't frail like his father, robbed of charm, strength and intellect. He was a sturdy man with bright eyes and a grip that, when he shook Whyte's hand, almost crushed it. *Use it or lose it*, Whyte thought, telling himself to get more fresh air and exercise.

He got out of the car, keeping one eye on the ginormous grey, shaggy hound. It yawned, flashing teeth the likes he'd only seen during Shark Week. Gulping, Whyte froze like a statue as it approached and nudged its great cannonball of a head into his crotch and gave him a good sniff.

Whyte was a sneeze away from a vasectomy.

"Divint mind Cheviot."

"He's called Cheviot?" asked Whyte, his voice trembling.

"She. And, aye, 'cause she's the biggest beast in Northumberland. Soft as clarts, though. You'll have a marra for life if you tickle her under her chin."

Whyte had no intention of putting his fingers anywhere near the creature's mouth; she was over sixty kilograms of lean, wolf-killing muscle. Instead, Whyte swapped his office shoes for waterproof rubber boots and let Craig and Cheviot lead the way.

It was a good ten-minute walk to where Craig had left his tractor. Whyte zoned out for a moment while the old farmer told him about the machine's inner workings, gears and horsepower. Suspecting the man had a lonesome existence out in his fields all day, Whyte let him talk, waiting for a natural pause before drawing him back to the case. He pulled on some nitrile gloves as Craig handed him the clothing label.

"I was lugging some sheep feed doon here when I saw it stuck to the boundary fence."

Whyte placed the label in a clear evidence bag before examining it. Laurel's name, though blurred, could clearly be read in neat, rounded handwriting. Whyte turned on his torch and moved a circle of light back and forth over the fence. In the rural darkness, it barely made a difference.

"Hang on a sec," said Craig. He climbed into the tractor and turned its headlamps on, almost blinding Whyte. "Better?"

"Much." Whyte blinked several times, temporarily blinded.

"I, erm, I found sommat else."

Whyte turned his attention from the fence to Craig, blinding himself once more. The farmer reached into the cab and pulled out a carrier bag; Whyte recognised its Tesco stripes. He placed the bag on the ground in the pool of light in front of the tractor.

"It was behind one of the big horse chestnuts ower that way." He pointed to his left.

The bag and its contents were soaked and muddy. After all, they could have been out there for almost a month. Whyte reached in and pulled out a blue bra.

AT DAYBREAK, TENS OF officers searched Craig Milton's farm as well as those of his neighbours. They looked through their homes, rummaged through barns and explored outbuildings. No stone was left unturned.

Cooper stood with Whyte and Keaton near where Craig found the carrier bag. They huddled under umbrellas while dark skies iced the county in drizzle. Keaton topped up their travel mugs with tea from a thermos.

"A bra and a pair of briefs?" mused Cooper.

"Women's briefs, to be specific," said Whyte.

Cooper's ankles felt swollen against the sides of her waterproof boots. Her baby had been unusually active all night, preventing her from getting more than an hour's sleep at a time.

"They're probably Laurel's," said Keaton. "Too much of a coincidence otherwise, but we don't know it for certain. Could anyone identify them?"

Cooper shrugged. "Other than Rhett? I doubt it."

"Her father?"

Both Keaton and Cooper stared at Whyte. "Yeah. I know. Forget I said it."

Cooper would ask Denise to update the family and tell them that a clothing label from Laurel's jacket had been found. They'd keep the information about the underwear to themselves until they received DNA analysis from the lab.

Keaton rested her large frame against the side of Cooper's car and blew into her travel mug to cool the tea. Cooper rubbed her lower back.

The big woman looked at Cooper with concern in her eyes. "You in pain? Get back in the car. Have a seat."

"I'm fine," said Cooper, though she wasn't, "and I have two theories."

"SA?" suggested Whyte. "Someone sexually assaulted Laurel, maybe killed her, and then tried to dispose of her underwear or hide it?"

Cooper nodded. "That's one theory. We'll know more when we get the DNA results back."

"The other theory?" asked Keaton.

"Laundry bag. Rhett and Laurel were cycling from place to place and wouldn't always have laundry facilities. Perhaps Laurel put her dirty items in a carrier to keep them away from the rest of her luggage."

Keaton blew on her tea once more then took a sip. "So, how did it end up here? We're nowhere near where their bikes were spotted."

"Remember Billy Gilmore, the birdwatcher? He said a pair of backpacks were on the grass at Hauxley. If whoever stole their bikes also stole their bags—"

"Which would make sense."

"Then they might have come down here to sort through the bags and decide what to keep and what to get rid of."

The three detectives moved out of the way so Craig Milton could shepherd a herd of soggy sheep through a gate into a neighbouring field. They waited silently until the man and his ovine associates had passed.

Keaton was the first to speak. "So, some thieving little shit stole their bikes and bags, legged it down here and sifted through their belongings. He discarded anything he didn't fancy and cut the label out of Laurel's jacket so he could keep it or sell it on. But before he could sell the bikes, Squires, that scrawny mummy's boy from Ashington, nicked them."

Whyte rubbed his eyes with his free hand. He looked as tired as Cooper felt. "Or someone assaulted and killed Rhett and Laurel, then tried to hide the evidence."

Cooper moved away from the group and walked along a lane surrounded on both sides by tall trees. The most likely explanation was a combination of both theories. A single person could have done it all: sexual assault, murder, theft. Still, they had no bodies and no murder weapon.

Another kick. This baby was going to be a footballer, for sure. That or a cage fighter. She was about to admit defeat and take a seat in the car to rest her feet when a miserable, sopping-wet, uniformed officer appeared at the far end of the field. He moved at a decent pace, considering the undulating terrain. He held up a clear evidence bag.

"Thought you'd want to see this," he panted when he was within earshot. "We found another clothing label."

When he reached her, Cooper took the bag and held it under the umbrella. Like the one from

Laurel's jacket, this label had been cut out and discarded. No name or number this time, just a brand and size. Musto, size large.

"Rhett's?" asked Keaton. She and Whyte had walked over to join Cooper the moment they heard the officer's voice.

"Only one way to find out," she replied. "Let's speak to his family."

- CHAPTER 15 -

IT WAS STILL EARLY when Cooper arrived at the Travelodge in Cobalt Business Park. She found the Campbells, Bruce Deacon and FLO Denise Oswald in a breakfasting area that smelled of coffee and cereal. If Cooper wasn't mistaken, someone had burnt their toast.

Denise rose to her feet as soon as she saw Cooper. She greeted the detective with a handshake then guided her away from the families. "Any news?" she asked in a hushed tone.

"We found some clothing labels on farmland; one had Laurel's name and number on it. There was some underwear too. It's likely Laurel's, but I don't want to distress her father unnecessarily."

"Wait for DNA before mentioning it?"

Cooper nodded at Denise, who offered to get her some breakfast and a coffee. "Just a tea, please. Herbal if possible."

Scattered throughout the breakfasting area, people dressed in business attire sat alone, their expressions glazed. Travelling for work was tiresome and lonely; none of the diners looked keen to get to the office. Being a detective was hard work; it was a demanding and high-pressured position. Still, despite her job coming with the ghosts of those she failed to save, Cooper couldn't see herself doing anything else.

Dealing with monsters beat dealing with monotony.

At the far side of the room, Bruce sat with Tamzin and Ashley. Though they shared the same tired and glazed expressions as the commuters, their faces were forlorn and filled with dread. Their postures slumped and downbeat, their clothing acting as comfort blankets. Tamzin played with the cuffs of her knitted cardigan and cast hopeful glances around the room, willing someone to talk to her. Any conversation would be better than the dark thoughts tumbling through her mind. Ashley and Bruce either didn't see or didn't care. The former stared intently at his phone; the latter read a tabloid.

Seeing Cooper approach, Bruce stood. Laurel's father was a tall man of around six feet with a swarthy complexion and a head of thick, black hair. At five-eight, Laurel was tall for a British woman. Though she inherited her father's height, her colouring must have come from her mother.

"What is it?" he asked, his eyes wide with trepidation.

Cooper sat and placed some printouts on the table. "These clothing labels were found on farm-land in Northumberland. The farmer who found them recognised Laurel's name and called us."

Bruce Deacon pulled one of the images towards him and ran his fingers over it as if stroking his daughter's hair. "Were these found near Hauxley?"

"No. Further south. About ten kilometres away."

He looked confused but asked no further questions.

Tamsin stifled her tears, dabbing at her eyes with the frayed cuffs of her cardigan. "And you think this one came from Rhett's coat?"

"I think it might have," Cooper said. "We're testing it for DNA, but I'd hoped you or Ashley recognised the brand."

"I— I'm not sure," said Tamzin.

"It's the sort of brand he'd wear," Ashley said. "Right size, too."

Cooper watched mother and son exchange a helpless glance. "Did Rhett send you any photographs of him cycling? Maybe wearing a Musto jacket?"

Ashley slumped back. "We haven't texted in a long time, DCI Cooper." He pushed his chair back, its legs squeaking against laminate flooring, and left to fetch himself a glass of apple juice.

Tamsin reached into a voluminous handbag to retrieve her phone. "He sent a few pictures when they first set off, but it was mainly of the scenery." Her thumb slid back and forth over the screen as she searched her images. A weak smile spread across her face, and she turned the phone towards Cooper.

Rolling hills of the Cumbrian countryside were speckled white with a fine layer of snow. "Very scenic," said Cooper.

Rhett's mother flicked her thumb again and a photograph of Rhett and Laurel perched on their bikes emerged. "Oh. How about this? It's a bit blurry."

Cooper squinted at the screen; it was slightly out of focus. Rhett wore a black cycling jacket, but she couldn't make out the brand name. "Could you send it to this number, please?" Cooper handed Tamzin her card. "We might be able to enhance it."

THAT AFTERNOON, COOPER SWUNG by Nixon's office to give him an update. In predictable fashion, he told her the case wasn't progressing quickly enough. Had it been a few months ago, Cooper may have taken the man's grouchiness personally. These days it was like water off a duck's back. She was too pregnant to care what Nixon thought of her, especially as he still wouldn't cave to her requests for a new DI.

Back in CID, Whyte was yelling at someone down the phone.

"Don't ask," mouthed Boyd from behind a stack of witness statements from the drive-by shooting.

Cooper found Martin with newly replenished supplies from the vending machine. He opened a packet of Munchies and offered one to her.

"Cheers."

Martin chewed a couple of the chocolate-covered snacks, opened his notepad and flicked to a page near the back.

"I spoke with Rowan from the Discovery Museum. He couldn't remember what brand of jacket Rhett was wearing."

Martin looked chuffed with himself; Cooper suspected he was about to give her good news.

"But, the lady who runs the BnB where they stayed on Christmas Day said he was wearing a Musto jacket."

"How did you word the question?" asked Cooper. There was a big difference between asking someone to describe a jacket and asking if someone was wearing a Musto jacket. One left it open, the other planted ideas in a person's memory.

"I asked her to describe what Rhett was wearing when he and Laurel arrived at her place. She described a day-glow woollen hat, a head torch, a black Musto jacket and fluorescent yellow leggings. She thought the leggings were a touch too figure-hugging for a man. Said she could see his meat and two veg."

Grimacing, Cooper thanked Martin for his efforts.

"That's not all." Martin opened a file. "I checked the ATM footage from the day they visited the museum." He handed her a still. "You can clearly see the brand name on the left chest."

A crack of thunder shook the building. The sky had turned a murky grey while Cooper had been in Nixon's office. She stood up, her belly getting in the way, and went to the window. With her hand shielding her eyes from the office lighting, she watched with disgust as sheets of rain flooded the car park.

"Nightmare," said Martin. "I'm supposed to be getting the bus home. Wonder if my Dad'll pick me up." His cheeks flushed rubescent.

"No shame in having your parents care enough to collect you from work, Martin."

Cooper remembered the day she started at Northumbria Police. Her parents, though they cared, had already left the country. She walked home from North Shields station every day.

"Tina's netball team are playing tonight," Cooper said, looking out at an angry sky. "I'm guessing it'll be moved indoors."

Martin chuckled. "You'd better hope so, boss."

"Well, if it's not, you can expect a short-tempered DCI tomorrow morning."

Martin gulped.

- CHAPTER 16 -

LED FLOOD LIGHTS ILLUMINATED the netball court, turning night into day. Rain pitter-pattered off the tarmac, wind rattled a chainlink fence. The referee, a statuesque woman with pencilled eyebrows and hair pulled back so tightly it caused her skin to stretch, inspected the court. She declared the surface playable, causing a collective groan to rumble from both teams.

"Now, now girls. You all know netball is an outdoor sport. I remember playing in the most awful blizzards in my day. Very character building."

"Yeah, but that was the dark ages." A teen with the surliest expression Cooper had ever seen rubbed her upper arms for warmth. "They hadn't invented health and safety then."

"Or child protection," grumbled another player.

A tall girl with thighs that could give Keaton a run for money added, "Character building? Everyone

95

knows that's just what posh people use to justify torture."

The referee had clearly heard it all before. She shook her head dismissively and addressed both sides. "If either team feels they are too fragile to play outdoors, they can easily forfeit the match."

All fourteen players rolled their eyes but said nothing.

Cooper and the other parents watching from beyond the chainlink fence felt their pain. They'd all wanted the game moved indoors. A mother, far better prepared than Cooper, erected a chair and some sort of pop-up tent. Cooper, Atkinson and Julie shared a golf umbrella.

The Tynemouth Sharks huddled together for a team talk. Playing in bottle-green netball dresses with bare arms and legs, they seemed to shiver as one, teeth chattering as their coach tried to extract an ounce of enthusiasm. Tina stood back from the group as if she was an outsider, a substitute or an imposter. Whether she was uncomfortable or unwelcome, Cooper didn't know, but the second the whistle blew, her daughter transformed.

The quiet mouse was gone. A vicious predator took her place. Wearing the WD bib of wing defence, Tina stood tall, commanding the team. She yelled orders over the noise of parental cheers, rain and wind. Water dripped from the ends of her hair with every quick pivot. She was a thorn in the side of the opposition's wing attack, a shadow stalking her relentlessly.

Every time the opposition gathered momentum and tried to get the ball to their WA, Tina intercepted, scanned the court for an open player and had the ball back in their goal third in a matter of seconds.

Julie, Tina's grandmother, was impressed. "Go on, Tina! Shoot!"

Cooper hushed her. "She can't shoot. She plays defence. And she doesn't like us cheering."

"Nonsense, dear. Everyone else is cheering."

"It distracts her, Mum. Please don't cheer."

"Then why the hell are we standing here in the sopping rain if I can't cheer for my granddaughter?"

"We're still supporting her. Just not vocally." Julie never fully understood Tina and what made her unique and brilliant. "She appreciates that we're here. And you can clap all you like. Just please don't call her name."

By the time the third quarter began, the Sharks were up twenty-one to eleven. Tina caught the ball in mid-air, landed on one foot, pointed to where she wanted the goal attack to run and threw the ball with precision. The goal attack took aim and scored. Twenty-two.

Atkinson put an arm around Cooper and pulled her further under the umbrella. "The last time I saw Tina this intense, she was defending a seagull from her grandma."

WHEN THE FINAL WHISTLE blew, Julie ran over to hug Tina. She pulled away, looking embarrassed.

Cooper and Atkinson, respecting her hatred of close contact, gave her congratulatory fist bumps instead. While most of the Sharks asked their parents if they saw their great goal or fantastic footwork, Tina changed subjects with ease.

"What's for tea?" she asked, pulling joggers and a sweater over her soaking uniform.

"After a performance like that?" asked Cooper. "Anything you bloody well like."

ON THURSDAY MORNING, COOPER opened her emails; the DNA results from the clothing labels were back. Keaton, unable to control her curiosity, hovered over Cooper's computer screen. She crossed her fingers, hoping for good news.

"Bollocks," said Keaton.

"Balls," echoed Cooper.

They gathered the team for a morning briefing. Boyd and Martin sat next to each other in the front. Whyte and Keaton hovered near the back of the room. Like parents supervising a soft play, they kept an eye on their colleagues. Though CID was usually a well-oiled machine, Cooper was glad the likes of Keaton had her back.

"DNA results are back." Cooper smoothed the front of her blazer, picked up a folder and retrieved photocopies of the results to hand out. She handed the pile to Boyd, who took one and passed the rest on.

"Let's start with the bikes. Aside from Rhett and Laurel, the only DNA present was that of the thief, Squires, and a close female relative to Squires."

"His mother?" asked Martin.

"I'd assume so, but swing by and ask for a sample from her just in case."

Martin nodded. "No problem, boss. I can do it this afternoon."

"As for the clothing labels, it's more bad news. As you can see, the only DNA present belonged to Rhett, Laurel and the farmer."

"Should we take a closer look at the farmer?" asked Keaton.

Cooper paused for a moment. She'd spoken to Craig Milton twice now, once on the phone and once in person. She perceived him to be sincere and helpful.

"I don't think that's necessary. His property was thoroughly searched and he seems the honest sort. Whyte?"

Whyte lifted his chin. "I agree. I reckon he's clean." He pushed his hair back and hesitated before speaking. "But killers do like to involve themselves in investigations. If it turns out he had something to do with Rhett and Laurel's disappearance-slash-murders, we'll be done for."

He was right. Nixon would throw the book at them if they neglected to look in detail at everyone involved in the case. "Good point. Keaton, can you action that?"

Keaton confirmed that she could.

"Great," said Cooper. "I'll hand you all over to Elliot Whyte now. He had a breakthrough with the drive-by shooting case."

Whyte moved to the front of the room and set a can of Coca-Cola on the desk. "On Friday, January tenth, Tommy Jenkins, a nineteen-year-old dealer from Roker, was shot in the head. He survived but is still in a coma at Sunderland Royal Hospital. SOCOs reopened the street the following evening. Gill Side Grove was once again closed on Wednesday, January fifteenth, this time for resurfacing work."

Keaton started to chuckle. "I can see where this is going."

"The smart arses contracted to do the work let the tarmac clog up the drains. Light rain wasn't a problem, but the downpour we had on Tuesday caused the whole street to flood. Now, according to residents, the street didn't need resurfacing. It was in good nick and had been resurfaced fairly recently in 2014."

"It's not like the council to waste money," said DI Neil Fuller from the end of a row of seats.

"Quite," said Whyte. "But I think the road being resurfaced unnecessarily a few days after a drive-by seems like a bit of a coincidence."

"Did you speak to the council?" asked Cooper.

"Yes, I did. And they have no record of approving the work. I reckon the drains were clogged on purpose—"

"Because the weapon is down there?" Cooper closed her eyes and shook her head.

"Now your average gangbanger doesn't have the brains or funds to hire road resurfacers, have them pose as the council and do a suitably crap job on purpose. We're looking for someone – or some organisation – with money."

"Like the Roker Boys or the Blackburns?" asked Keaton.

"Exactly. The drains are being cleared as we speak, and we have a team ready to search for the gun."

"Good work, Whyte," said Cooper as he took his seat. He tried not to smile but Cooper could tell the compliment meant something to him. "Okay, let's move on. Fuller?"

Neil Fuller had a narrow face, a pointed nose and small eyes. His fingers were thin and his nails a touch too long. This combined with his fuzzy facial hair, gave the man a murine appearance. Despite looking like he should be following the Pied Piped, Cooper felt sorry for Fuller; he was working a truly awful case.

Fuller stood, wringing his hands. He never used to be so squirrelly.

"Five-year-old Summer Holt has been missing since June. She disappeared from her garden in Ponteland."

Fuller gave everyone a quick reminder of the case, but it was hardly necessary; everyone in the country had heard of Summer Holt. Every newspaper featured her pretty face, every port and check-in desk displayed her photo.

"Three-year-old Timothy Harding, known as Tim, went missing from Riverside Park in Durham in August. I'm working closely with Durham Police. Whilst we don't have anything to suggest the cases are connected, it makes sense to pool resources. The parents have hired a private investigator. He's ex-GMP, and based on my first impressions, he seems like a sound, if very sarcastic, bloke. We all agree we need to renew interest in both Summer and Tim."

"You could do another live interview with the parents," joked a tubby officer in uniform.

"After last time?" Fuller paled at the memory. "I don't think so."

"Don't dismiss the idea too quickly, Neil." Cooper raised her brows at him. "The interview may have been a complete disaster, but it did get Summer back into the public's consciousness. Ask Durham if they'd consider a joint press conference. Perhaps some reenactments. February twenty-first will mark six months since Tim went missing. We could use that to drum up some press."

"Unless we find them by then." Although Fuller's statement was hopeful, the hope didn't reach his eyes.

Cooper wondered if he'd had a single night of unbroken sleep since taking on the burden of a missing child. She faked a smile and tried to sound optimistic. "Here's hoping," she said.

- CHAPTER 17 -

FEBRUARY CAREENED INTO NORTH Tyneside with high winds, loose roof tiles and fallen trees. The pretty winter of frosty windows and snow-covered fields was gone. This was a winter of dull grey skies and the constant threat of rain. Wheelie bins toppled and rolled down back lanes. The wind whirled litter into corners, forming spirals of crisp packets, fag ends and flyers. Mini maelstroms of suburban flotsam.

Cooper tried to get comfortable in her BMW, but her back ached and she hadn't slept well for a few nights. Putting a pillow between her knees helped, but she still tossed and turned. Her phone rang and connected through the car's Bluetooth, interrupting Metallica's Master of Puppets.

"This better be good," she grumbled.

"Boss." It was Keaton. She sounded sleepy but excited. "I've just heard from Martin. There's been a breakthrough. I'm on my way in."

"Tell me more," said Cooper, fastening her seat-belt around her swollen midriff.

"Little old lady from Sunderland called to say she got a lift from some geezer over New Year when she was up Blyth way. He drove a black pickup like the one Squires described. She says the bikes were in the back."

"Why's she only coming forward now?"

"She was out of the country. Been in Spain enjoying some warmer weather."

Cooper couldn't blame her. It was bloody miserable in Tynemouth that morning, had been for weeks.

"Fair enough," she said. "Sounds like we're headed Wearside. You got your passport and insurance ready?"

"No need. The granny's coming to us. Says she loves a trip out and asked if we can pick her up from Haymarket."

Cooper told Keaton to send Whyte.

"Already done. He met her ten minutes ago. They should be at HQ in fifteen to twenty, depending on traffic."

Stifling a yawn, Cooper wondered what time the woman had got up. It was only eight-thirty and the Metro would have taken her about forty-five minutes. "Okay. I'm on my way. I'll be as quick as I can."

She drove through Tynemouth and joined the A193 through North Shields. Cooper hit the brakes outside the Magistrates, where an enormous tree hadn't survived last night's storm. She turned right to head up Linskill Terrace and was halfway up the street when a thunderous noise made Cooper bring her car to a standstill. Another tree – having been tortured all night by the wind – finally caved to gravity and crashed down over the BMW's bonnet. Neither Cooper nor the residents of Linskill Terrace were going anywhere soon.

Two hours later, with sore, soggy feet and a temper like a teen who'd lost their phone, Cooper finally arrived at HQ. Her car had been towed and she'd spent a small fortune getting an Uber to work during surge pricing. God only knew what the mechanic would charge her later.

Apparently, she should be happy to be alive. She'd be happy when she had her car back.

After taking five minutes to calm down and change her socks, Cooper felt her mood lift when a warm coffee was handed to her.

"I know," Keaton said, "I'm a star. Granny's name's Mildred Houghton and I reckon she's at least a hundred years young. Sharp as a tack though. Whyte's keeping her busy with a crossword. She's running rings round him."

Keaton pushed the door to CID open and held it for Cooper.

"Nine down. Inebriation."

"Nice one, Mildred."

Mildred Houghton was dressed in a canary yellow summer dress. She wore it over thick woollen tights and a long-sleeved fleece. An elegant cloche hat decorated with daffodils covered her delicate silver curls. Long beaded necklaces jangled against each other as she turned to smile at Cooper with perfectly white dentures.

"You must be the famous DCI Cooper. I love your hair, by the way." She turned to Whyte. "Do you think I should shave my head?"

"I think you're beautiful the way you are."

"Oh, you smooth-talking rogue. Are all detectives as sweet as you?"

"We try," he said with a wink.

Cooper held out her hand. "Call me Erica. DS Keaton said you saw our appeal for information regarding Rhett Campbell and Laurel Deacon's bikes. You think you met the man who stole them."

"No *think* about it, Erica. I know I met him. "She tapped a finger against the side of the cloche. "Memory like an elephant."

Cooper took a seat opposite Mildred. She smelled of lavender and honey, and her sunny demeanour worked wonders on Cooper's mood. "Tell me everything."

"See, Erica, my sister is a stubborn old fool. She never learned to drive and is scared of flying. Bless her, she's never been anywhere fun. Hardly ever leaves Blyth. Never been to Disney World. Never danced the night away in Havana with one of Castro's handsome bodyguards." She sighed wistfully at some enticing memory. "But alas, my adventure days are behind me. These days I like to get a nice Airbnb in Spain or Greece for a couple weeks each winter. Much better for the old bones, you see. And those Spanish gents know how to treat a lady."

"I bet."

"Last year, I learnt how to tango. Want to see?" She offered Whyte her hand.

"Yes, please," said Keaton.

"Not right now," said Cooper. "So, your sister lives in Blyth?"

"For her sins. I visited her over New Year to try to convince her to come to Spain with me. I told her I'd get her good and drunk so she'd sleep through the flight, but she wasn't having any of it. Anyway, Erica, we were putting the world to rights in a nice little coffee shop when I told Virginia – my sister – that we should go to Woodhorn because we had nothing better to do that day. I had my iPad with me, so we looked up how to get there using public transport, and it was going to take over an hour on the bus. That's not a problem for me, but Virginia has an irritable bowel. Trains she's okay with because they have toilets, but local buses don't."

"I see." As interesting as Mildred's sister's bowels were, Cooper hoped she'd get to something useful soon.

"Then, you'll never guess what, Erica. The gentleman at the next table offers to drive us. How lovely is that? He offered to be our tour guide as he'd been there a few times before as long as we paid for petrol."

"This man was a total stranger?"

"Yes," said Mildred. "Didn't know him from Adam."

"And you felt safe taking a lift from a stranger?"

"He had his little girl with him. He said she'd find Woodhorn dead interesting." She reached across the table and patted Cooper's hand. "Besides, I know krav maga. If he tried anything, my knee would be in his groin and the heel of my hand in his Adam's apple before he could say hadaway and shite."

Mildred punched her arms towards Whyte, her fingers curled back in some form of palm strike. "See. I might be old, but I'm fast."

"Indeed you are," said Cooper.

Whyte slid his chair away.

"And this man was driving a black pickup as described in our press release?" asked Cooper.

"Yes. On the outside, it had seen better days. There was rust around the wheel arches, and it was covered in muck. The inside was immaculate, though. Very clean."

"Don't suppose you saw what type of pickup it was?"

"It was a V-reg Nissan, Erica. And there were two bikes in the back. One was black, and one was orange. The black one was on top of the orange one, so I didn't fully see what was written on it. I saw *cannon* and assumed it was called cannonball. Then when I saw the news, I realised it was Cannondale."

Cooper could feel hope and excitement rising in her chest. She could hardly contain herself. These were the moments she lived for. The moments when a breakthrough, a new lead, or a credible witness turned up. They had a witness who had met the man who stole Rhett and Laurel's bikes.

He was their prime suspect and the one most likely to have harmed the missing pair.

"So, you and Virginia get in the pickup with this man and his daughter. When was this exactly? What happened next? What did he look like?"

"One question at a time, Erica. I'm ninety-six and I don't like to be rushed."

Cooper apologised. Keaton tried not to laugh.

"It was the thirtieth. New Year's eve's eve."

That was the day after the twitchers saw the bikes at Hauxley Nature Reserve.

"We drove to Woodhorn. Have you been? It's terrific. There's the colliery, the big park around the lake, nice little café. I bought him and his daughter hot chocolates to thank them for playing tour guide. Virginia couldn't have one; she's not good with dairy. I think he must have been from the area. He had such good local knowledge. A very nice man."

"You thought he was nice?" Cooper asked.

"Not now. Now I think he's a murdering bastard. But then, yes I did. Very nice, actually."

Cooper tried to calm Mildred. "We don't know that this man had anything to do with—"

"But you think he *could help your enquiries*. "Mildred mimicked the tone of the six o'clock news anchor. "We all know what that means. Right, what else did you want to know? Yes, what he looked like."

Mildred took a length of beaded necklace in her hands and twirled it around her index finger several times.

"He looked like a bit of a scallawag. I could see him in leathers riding a Harley or hanging out in some dive bar in the Bronx." She gave a nostalgic smile. "Ah, dive bars in the Bronx. Those were the days. Where was I? His looks. I'd say he was between thirty-five and forty-five. He was about six feet with dark skin. Not dark like a minority, dark like someone who spends time outdoors. Weathered. Tanned, even in winter. You know the sort."

Cooper didn't. She spent most of her time indoors under fluorescent lights.

"He had thick dark hair with the odd grey around the temples and a few days' worth of stubble. Oh, and he had a tattoo on the back of his left hand. I can't remember what of. No, wait, it was a barcode."

Cooper noted all of this down. It was a tremendous start. They'd confirmed the make and reg of the vehicle and got a decent description of the driver. She would ask Mildred to speak to an officer and have an E-FIT put together.

She thanked Mildred, who asked Whyte once again if he'd like a tango lesson. He declined and showed her towards the door.

"If you think of anything else you can reach me on this number." Cooper handed the flamboyant woman her card.

"I can think of something else now." She flashed Cooper a mischievous look. "You're going to kick yourself, Erica."

"Why's that?"

"His name, of course, you silly goose. Don't feel bad. I suffered terrible baby brain when I had my first. His name was Russell Rivers."

- CHAPTER 18 -

RUSSELL RIVERS. *PROPERTY OF Russell Rivers.*

Cooper hadn't been this annoyed since some low-life Cumbrians trashed her car and sprayed *Pigs* over the bonnet.

"Get him on the phone. NOW!" Cooper slammed her hand on a desk so hard she hurt her wrist.

Elliot Whyte, who never flinched, not even when dealing with serial killers, recoiled as if he was facing a rabid gorgon.

"Oh, you're in for it now," said Keaton, sitting down and eating from an invisible tub of popcorn.

"It's not my fault," pleaded Whyte. "Don't shoot the messenger."

"Now," she repeated.

Whyte dialled the number for the police station at Amble. "DCI Cooper for PC Dumble, please." He held the receiver to his ear for a few moments, passed it to Cooper, and then moved to hide behind Keaton.

Cooper remembered standing on a cold, bleak beach, speaking with a tortured woman whose son had vanished. She remembered the look of resignation on Tamzin's face when the search proved fruitless. She breathed slowly through her nose, calming herself before speaking.

"Dumble. During the search on January fourteenth, you reported a tent containing fishing gear."

"Yes, ma'am."

"And the words *Property of Russell Rivers* written on it."

"Yes, ma'am."

"Describe the tent."

Dumble hesitated. His voice laced with the anxiety of someone who knew he was in trouble but didn't know why. "It was pretty small. A two-man tent – I mean a two-person tent. It was turquoise."

Cooper was beside herself. Her heart raced, her blood pressure peaked. She felt hot, feint even.

"Turquoise?" she growled. "You didn't tell DC Whyte it was turquoise. You told DC Whyte it was blue."

"Yes, ma'am. Like bluish-green."

"Bluish-green? Greenish-blue? Listen, you absolute, useless f—"

Keaton took the handset from Cooper before she found herself on the wrong side of HR. "I'll arrange for someone to get a statement from PC Dum Dum and send someone to see if the tent's still there."

"It won't be." She ground her teeth as she spoke. "It's their tent. Rhett and Laurel's tent. We had him, and we bloody lost him."

ELLIOT WHYTE SPLASHED WATER over his face, gripped the edge of the sink and gathered his thoughts. The tent definitely looked green in the photo Hampshire Constabulary provided; they'd described it as such. Still, he should have gone to see the tent with his own eyes. The team had trusted his word; he'd trusted Dumble's word. People relied on him, none more so than Rhett, Laurel and their families.

He descended a flight of stairs, knocked on a door and entered a windowless office that Whyte suspected may have once been a broom cupboard.

"You're the Collector?"

When Cooper told him to get his arse to Local Intelligence to see someone called the Collector, he'd pictured a Dick Tracy type in a well-fitted suit and a cool hat. Cedric Bell was a bitter disappointment.

The room had a pungent smell of old cheese and cheap deodorant. A desk was littered with empty drinks cans and plastic models of various superheroes, both DC and Marvel.

"In the flesh." Cedric picked something from under his thumbnail, examined it, and popped it in his mouth. "And you might be?"

"DC Whyte. Cooper sent me."

"Ah, and how is the lovely Erica Cooper? Still beautiful as ever?"

Cedric Bell, with his shirt buttons done up incorrectly and a ketchup stain on his cuff, was certainly no Dick Tracy.

But he was a dick, thought Whyte.

He ignored Cedric's questions about Cooper and got to the point. "We have a lead on someone called Russell Rivers. He's not in the PNC or PND. The DVLA have no record of him, and neither does HMRC. Wondered if the name meant anything to you."

Cedric's chair creaked as he adjusted his weight. He leaned back and rested hands over his chest, steepling his fingers together. He seemed to enjoy making Whyte wait. No wonder Cooper didn't want to come down here.

"Russell Rivers? Yes, it rings a bell. Pardon the pun."

Whyte didn't get it.

"Bell, boy. My name's Bell."

Whyte still didn't laugh. "Do you know him or not?"

"It's a known alias of Ewan Underwood. It's his rapper name."

"Excuse me?"

Cedric stuck his finger in his ear and started digging for treasure. "He had a Jack Russell called Russell – very imaginative – and his mother's maiden name is Rivers."

"That's his pornstar name. Your rapper name is the street you grew up on prefixed with something like L'il or MC."

Cedric shrugged, then spread his arms wide and adopted a smarmy expression. "I grew up on Two Ball Lonnen in Fenham. Guess that makes me Biggie Two Balls."

Gross.

"Anyway, Ewan Underwood?"

"Hmm. Yes, he's a nasty piece of work with a record going back to his teens. You'll find him and all his misdemeanours in the database. Last I heard, he and his wife lived in Blyth."

***

THE COLLECTOR WAS RIGHT. Russell Rivers may not be on any official records, but Ewan Underwood was. That afternoon, Cooper gathered the team in CID. Despite her earlier outburst, Cooper felt like they were getting somewhere. They had a name; a solid, tangible lead.

Though everyone meant to be at the meeting had arrived, not everyone was paying attention. Officers checked their emails or had a quick scroll through their phones. Others hurriedly typed, trying to finish their latest report before Cooper got started. Coffees were poured, gossip was exchanged, chocolate bars were unwrapped.

Keaton coughed. "Last one to put their butt on a seat and turn their phone off has to do the Starbucks run for the next fortnight."

There was a rush as officers and detectives clambered over one another. Martin was last to his seat.

"But I come by bus," he said.

115

"I see your mouth moving, but I can only hear excuses."

Cooper waited for the chatter to die and for eyes to settle on her.

"I'll keep this brief as you will all need an early night. On December twenty-ninth, Rhett and Laurel's bikes were spotted here at Hauxley Nature Reserve." Cooper pointed to the map. "The following day, on New Year's Eve, the bikes were seen in the back of a pickup truck, being driven by Russell Rivers – an alias for Ewan Underwood. More on him later. Two weeks later, on January fourteenth, Rhett and Laurel's tent was spotted on the banks of Chevington Burn." Cooper pointed south of Hauxley. "However, thanks to a major F up, we only found that out this morning. The tent was labelled, *Property of Russell Rivers.*"

The team shuffled and fidgeted in their seats. They were antsy, sensing they'd get some action soon.

"So, who is Ewan Underwood? Keaton?"

DS Paula Keaton got to her feet and spoke without consulting her notes. "Ewan Underwood, forty-two of Middleton Street, Blyth. Married. Four kids. I'll skip the muggings and shoplifting and get to the nasty stuff. At twenty, he was jailed for punching a man for cutting in line at McDonald's on Northumberland Street. The man hit his head and was unconscious for six weeks. Once a free man, Underwood struggled with alcohol and drug addiction. Eight years ago, he broke into the home of a young couple, restrained the man, raped his girlfriend, then robbed them blind."

The room was silent. Boyd covered her mouth, looking sick. While some visibly felt pity for the victims, others swelled with rage against the perpetrator.

"Thanks to our wonderful justice system, he served seven years. Ten months ago, in early April, a similar attack took place in Berwick. Another couple, a man restrained, a woman..." Keaton's voice faded. She cleared her throat before continuing. "They ran tests and found Underwood's DNA. No doubt about it. When Blyth Police went to arrest him, he'd gone to ground. His family and friends either didn't know where he was or didn't want to tell us. Either way, he's on the run."

"But he's not doing a great job of it." Whyte stood. "He's wanted for a violent crime, and I hate to say it, but he's probably done the same to Rhett and Laurel, only this time he's escalated and killed them both. He nicked their bikes and slept in their tent. Next thing we know, he's playing tour guide for little Mildred Houghton. He's meant to be on the run. Why's he still in the area?"

Whyte had a point. This Underwood either didn't have the means or intellect to leave the northeast. That, or something was keeping him here.

"His kids," Cooper said. "Mildred said he had his daughter with him. His kids are why he stays local. They're his weak spot. He's been sleeping rough, camping, probably bedding down in that pickup, but I bet you a grand he's been sneaking home to see his wife and little ones whenever the coast is clear."

Heads throughout the room nodded simultaneously, those who had kids especially so.

"You said we'd need an early night?" Keaton asked.

Cooper pushed her files into her handbag and rubbed her lower back. "Yes. Get some sleep, everyone. We have a pre-dawn raid to look forward to."

- CHAPTER 19 -

MOST OF THE TEAM were home by six. Cooper collapsed on her sofa, unable to face cooking, cleaning, or even conversation. She was exhausted. And though she pretended to be annoyed, she was pleased Nixon told her to keep her *big, pregnant belly away from the raid* and leave it to Keaton and Blyth Police. At least she'd get a lie in.

AT WHYTE'S FLAT IN Jesmond, he switched on the TV and waited for his microwavable steak ragu pappardelle to finish cooking. When it beeped, he brought it to the living room and ate it straight from the container. He called his father's nursing home and waited for reception to connect him.

"Hi, Dad. It's Elliott."

Whyte's father made small talk for a few minutes, asking Whyte about work. But it was short-lived. Within minutes Brian Whyte thought he was speaking with his old school friend, James. Whyte didn't correct him, he just reclined into the sofa cushions and let the old man speak.

On television, a news reader announced Francisco Peña, a Dominican wanted for murder, had filed an appeal against the Home Secretary's decision to extradite him. Whyte half listened to the news, half enjoyed the sound of his father's happy, engaged storytelling. He was recounting a night in his twenties that may or may not have actually happened.

The news switched to a reporter in Roker. Whyte recognised Gill Side Grove, which had been torn apart so teams could access the drains.

"Sorry, Dad. I mean Brian." Whyte pulled a face. Though he didn't mind indulging his father's fantasies – it didn't do any harm to let him think he was chatting to James – he never got used to using his first name. "Sorry, Brian. I'll have to call you back."

Live on air, a scene of crime officer emerged from the drain. In his hand was a clear plastic bag.

Inside the bag was a gun.

"Thank fuck for that," smiled Whyte.

IN WILLINGTON QUAY, KEATON picked up her post as she crossed the threshold. She threw the junk in the recycling bin and leafed through the bills: overdue, reminder, action required. Without April's income, Keaton was struggling. She'd never ask her dad for help, and she didn't want to put too much pressure on Riley. Her teenage brother contributed when he could, but he only worked part-time between college lectures.

"I had an idea," Riley said when he saw his sister arrive home.

"Did it hurt?"

"That never gets old." He handed her a bottle of Corona. "They were on offer. I know we need to save money, and my phone contract's up soon. I checked with the guys in the phone shop at work, and they can do unlimited data for under twenty-five quid a month. We pay over sixty a month for broadband, so I say we just cancel broadband and hotspot the internet from my phone. I know it means you can only use the internet when I'm home, but it'll save over seven hundred a year."

Keaton placed the bills on the hallway table and patted Riley on the arm. "You always were the brains in the family, weren't you?"

"I'm the looks too."

Her brother was amazing; she was lucky to have him. Keaton smiled to appease the worried look in his eyes then disappeared to her room. There she could let her sorrows and loneliness rise to the surface and escape in quiet sobs.

B BASKERVILLE

NEIL FULLER LEFT AMBERLEY Primary School in Killingworth and turned left, crossing the road at the roundabout and heading up Citadel East. He'd heard about the Russell Rivers fiasco, and while all detectives make mistakes, he was still glad he wasn't in Elliot Whyte's boots.

Killingworth was quiet that evening. Though there were many cars, the streets were empty of pedestrians. This route home from the primary school was his new Thursday evening routine since joining the community choir a few months ago. He'd needed something outside of work to take his mind off the little girl he'd failed to find.

His first week there was awkward. He was terrified of meeting new people and barely opened his mouth. But the others were welcoming and he felt at home with his new friends. Fuller didn't even care if his singing was bad; he was just grateful to spend a few hours each week being with people who didn't know his role at Northumbria Police. Fast forward a few weeks, and he was singing his heart out during the songs and chatting away during the breaks.

He paused outside the Shire Horse. The pub looked warm and inviting, but he thought better of it. It was only Thursday and he knew if he slipped in for one, he'd end up having six. His phone rang. Not recognising the number, he let it go to voicemail as he continued walking. When it rang for a second time, he decided to answer.

"Fuller."

"Good evening. This is Malcolm Dorsey calling."

It took Fuller a moment to place the name and accent. Malcolm Dorsey was the private investigator the Holts and Hardings had hired.

"Oh. Evening, Mal. What can I do for you?"

Fuller turned right when he passed the White Swan Centre, pausing to let a bunch of youths with a pair of mean-looking mutts pass.

"I wanted to check something with you. I was under the impression there's no real link between the two cases, that the families aren't connected."

"That's correct," said Fuller, letting himself in and wiping his feet on the doormat. He didn't mind Dorsey calling but would have preferred he stuck to office hours. Choir practice had helped him detach, now his mind was back in CID.

"Hmm."

"What do you mean hmm?" Fuller asked, frowning.

"The families told me the same thing – that they don't know each other, or at least they didn't until their children went missing. But then I found out Michael Holt and Cyrus Harding both graduated from the same uni in the same year."

It was Fuller's turn to go, "Hmm." He turned on the oven and took a pie and a bag of crinkle-cut chips from the freezer before asking. "Which uni?"

"Northumbria."

"Same course?" he asked.

"No," Malcolm said. "So, it's probably a coincidence. Just wanted to give you a heads up in case it wasn't."

Fuller hung up. Malcolm was likely right about it being a coincidence. After all, how many people graduated from Northumbria each year? Thousands? Maybe even ten thousand. Still, as he put the pie and chips on a tray and bunged them in the oven, the thought troubled him.

-CHAPTER 20-

SHORTLY BEFORE FIVE A.M., Keaton met Sergeant Sharma from Blyth. He had a soft voice but a handshake like a vice. He told Keaton they'd been watching the house since the previous afternoon; if Underwood was in there, they hadn't seen him.

Keaton knew it was a long shot. The man was on the run, and though he'd been hiding in plain sight, staying local, sneaking home to see his wife and children, the chances of him spending the night there were slim. Still, they'd quiz his wife and search for evidence.

At this time, the street was still dark, illuminated only by streetlights. Police vans blocked either end of the road and the back lane, their engines and headlamps switched off. Everyone spoke in hushed tones.

"Nice area," said Keaton.

"Yeah, it's not bad." Sharma secured his body armour as he spoke. "It's pretty safe round here, not much trouble, other than the Underwoods, that is. I live nearby on Cypress Gardens." He glanced towards a team of officers just itching to get going."

"Ready?" asked Sharma.

"Born ready."

Though she sounded confident, the sudden noise of raids always startled Keaton. The near silence of the street was replaced by shouts, the banging of doors being forced open, and the clanging of boots on stairs.

To an outsider, it looked like chaos. Keaton waited back with Martin while Sharma's specialist team got to work.

"Clear," he called over the radio after a few minutes. "Underwood's not here."

"Wardrobes? Under the bed. Let's make sure he's not doing a Canoe Man," Keaton said.

Several years ago, John Darwin faked his death after canoeing in the north sea. His wife claimed over a quarter of million pounds in life insurance while John secretly lived in the house next door.

"Check for any hidden rooms."

"We're clear," repeated Sharma. "You coming in?"

Every home was different, and Keaton never knew what to expect. Some houses were so clean it seemed impossible their occupants had ever lived in them. In other houses, it was clear the owners were hoarders, unable to throw anything away. The Underwoods' house was a mixture. As Keaton stepped inside she registered a doormat covered in dead leaves, cobwebs and flyers for takeaways. The rest of the hallway was clean and well-presented. A large family photograph hung above a radiator.

Ewan Underwood stood with his arms around his wife, who carried a little girl. A small boy with a cheeky toothless grin held Underwood's leg, and two older boys stood together in matching checkered shirts.

"This way," Sharma said. He pointed to the living room. "The wife's in there with her two little ones. No sign of the older boys."

Keaton approached a tired but angry-looking woman. She wore a pink dressing gown, fluffy slippers and a scowl that would frighten a hungry bear. It had no effect on Keaton.

"Gemma Underwood? I'm DS Paula Keaton."

Gemma's hair was a fiery red, the glue from cheap extensions easily visible at her roots. She still had sleep in the corners of her eyes and long, fake lashes. Her daughter sat next to her on the sofa, bright-eyed and full of energy; her youngest son wide-eyed and afraid. Their living room was cluttered but clean. A wooden chest, filled to the brim with toys, was tucked beside the sofa, a dark jacket hung from the back of a chair, and a cup of cold tea sat on a side table.

"What's this all about?" She clenched her children's hands as if she could protect them from the world.

"I'd appreciate you answering some questions about your husband."

Gemma rolled her eyes. "If you think I'm going to bad mouth me man in front of his bairns, you've got another thing coming."

"How about DC Martin stays here and watches cartoons with your kids? We can go in the garden and bad mouth him there instead."

Gemma's face cracked and she laughed, pointing a finger at Keaton. Her nails were acrylic and painted scarlet. "That was funny." She got to her feet and switched the television on, flicking through the channels until a bright yellow cartoon character with a high-pitched voice appeared on the screen. Martin shuffled closer to the set as if she'd put the show on just for him.

They walked through the back of the home, passing through the Underwoods' kitchen, where officers looked through every cupboard and container.

"D'ya really need to ransack the place?" asked Gemma.

Once outside, Gemma sat on a wooden bench and faced Keaton. "I know what you're thinking. That I'm an idiot to stand by Ewan after all the bruises and everything else he's done."

"I don't think you're an idiot, Gemma. You're life's your own business." Keaton looked around the garden. Children's toys covered an overgrown lawn. "I don't think I could stay married to a rapist, though."

"Technically, he was never convicted of rape." Gemma's scowl returned as if the load of constantly defending her husband, and therefore her choices, was beginning to weigh heavy. "It's the bairns. Kirsty would be okay if she never saw Ewan again; she hardly knows him. But the boys... Boys need a father."

Keaton thought of her own father. He was a violent man, not like Ewan Underwood, but still, she thought Riley was doing much better without him in their lives. The Underwood children would be just fine without their low-life criminal father. Boys needed role models, and Ewan Underwood was far from one of those.

"He can be a lovely man. Proper sweet when he wants to be." She picked up a piece of Lego from under the bench and played with it for a moment before tossing it into the lawn, where it would lie in wait for an unsuspecting bare foot. "He dotes on the bairns when he's sober. Buys all sorts for them."

Steals all sorts for them, Keaton thought.

"Not that he's ever sober for long. I've tried so many times to get him to quit."

A cough caused Keaton to look up. Sharma joined them in the garden, holding the jacket from the living room. He handed it to Keaton, who examined it as she spoke.

"Black. Musto. Looks to be a size large. And let me guess, yes, the label's been cut out."

"That was a gift for our Shaun." Gemma reached out to take the jacket from her.

"This is evidence," said Keaton, holding it out of reach.

"And that's not all." Sharma presented Keaton with other items belonging to the missing pair: a Swiss army knife, a digital camera, and a prescription for codeine made out to Miss L Deacon.

"Gemma," Keaton softened her tone and sighed. "Ewan's in serious trouble. Robbery and sexual assault, taking of bicycles, stolen goods, maybe even murder. I know you want a father for your children but trust me, you're all better off without him. You'll be safer without him. Your husband is a violent man and he needs to be locked up. We can help you create a new life, but only if you help us."

Gemma stiffened, preparing herself. She was a tough woman – it took one to know one – and Keaton knew she'd never betray her man.

"Help us, Gemma. Where's Ewan?"

To Keaton's surprise, Gemma burst into hysterics. "You're shitting me, right? I thought you were here to gather evidence. That and to convince me to testify against him. You're telling me you're here to look for him? That's hilarious."

"Why is that hilarious?"

"Because he called me last night."

"Where from?"

"Prison, you fool." Gemma tried to control her giggles; Keaton tried to contain her anger. "Your lot picked him up yesterday for the thing in Berwick. He's being held on remand in Durham."

- CHAPTER 21 -

"WELL, THIS WEEK'S BEEN a colossal fuck up."

Martin swirled beer around the bottom of his pint glass.

"Not really," said Whyte. "Embarrassing? Yes. As bad as you're making out? Not quite. Besides, I heard you got paid to watch Sponge Bob yesterday. You're living the dream."

The pair were sipping pints of Deuchars in The Victory, a pretty, white pub in South Gosforth near the double roundabouts. It was a busy Saturday night. An electric fire heated the room and the clientele were in good spirits. Most of them, anyway. A seat opened up by the fireplace and Whyte made a dive for it.

"Look, we wanted to find Underwood and we found him. Just because you and Keaton didn't get to slap the cuffs on him doesn't mean it was a complete failure."

"It was a waste of time and resources. Nixon's going to hit the roof."

"That wouldn't be anything new. Besides, he was picked up after we'd all finished for the night. Yes, if we'd rerun his name at two in the morning, we might have had a head's up. But, as far as I'm concerned, it's a win. Not only do we know where Underwood is, we found items belonging to Rhett and Laurel in his house." He checked his watch. "I can squeeze in one more before I need to head off. I'm going to the bar. When I get back, change the subject."

Whyte didn't mind talking shop, but Martin was in a gloomy mood, fixating on negatives instead of positives. He needed a distraction. A young bartender with rosy cheeks and braces asked Whyte what she could get for him. Whyte didn't think she looked old enough to serve alcohol, but perhaps that was his age speaking. He was told the same thing countless times when he had his first job pouring pints, so he kept his thoughts to himself. He ordered a pint for Martin and a half for himself – he had church tomorrow.

Walking back to the table, Whyte could feel the warmth of the fire. Though he enjoyed weekends, he was eager for Monday to roll around and wondered if Cooper would let him come with her to Durham's category two prison. He wanted to see Underwood in the flesh.

He handed Martin his drink and they clinked glasses. "Right, what are we going to talk about now?"

"We're two blokes in a pub on a Saturday. We have two choices," Martin said. Sports or women?"

"Sports," said Whyte, and for fifteen minutes, they waxed lyrical about the teams of the north-east: Whyte's Sunderland AFC, Martin's Newcastle United, and the forgotten step-child of the region, Middlesbrough.

"Time for me to go," said Whyte. "You calling Saff?"

Martin shrugged. "Probably not. She doesn't come out to play after ten."

Whyte stood to put his coat on. Though no more snow was forecast, it was still bloody cold and he planned on walking back up Matthew Bank to Jesmond. "You two still taking things slowly?"

"Painfully. If we go any slower, we'll go backwards and just be mates again."

"Not getting any?"

"I wish." Martin examined his pint as if searching for an answer. "I can't take her to mine with my parents in the next room, and she's never asked me to hers. It's not like I'd pressure her into anything. But it would be nice to be alone with her. I get the feeling she doesn't trust me, doesn't feel safe with me."

Whyte sat back down. He couldn't leave Martin looking so morose.

"It's not you, buddy. She likes you. I can tell by the way she looks at you. It's kind of gross, actually. She gives you those big, doe eyes like Ariel looking at Prince Eric."

"The Little Mermaid?"

133

"I watched a lot of Disney growing up. But seriously, it's not that Saff doesn't feel safe with you; she just doesn't feel safe full stop."

"What do you mean?" Martin asked before taking a big drink.

"Ever notice how she never wears heels, only flats? And how she doesn't wear make-up or revealing clothing?"

"She doesn't need to. Saff's gorgeous."

"True," Whyte said. "But it might be more than that. Maybe she's protecting herself; women can't run away in heels. And, you know what the world's like. Something happens to a lass, and some brainless plank's bound to say, *what did she expect, dressed like that*?"

Martin put his drink down and fixed Whyte with a hard stare. "What do you know that I don't?"

Feeling torn, Whyte thought carefully about his next words. He'd already betrayed one colleague's trust; he wasn't going to do it again. Martin was a good kid, Boyd too, and her story wasn't Whyte's to tell.

"Her old DCI was a bit of a dick, her old team too." He placed a hand on Martin's shoulder. "She'll tell you when she's ready. Be patient."

- CHAPTER 22 -

COOPER COVERED HER NOSE with her sleeve, thankful her morning sickness was long gone.

The prison smelled of mildew and men. Sweaty men with stale breath and body odour kept in close quarters. There was an overriding scent of vape. A lot of vape. While smoking bans existed in all indoor areas, prisoners could vape within the confines of their cells. In Durham, the vape of choice smelled savoury but distinctly chemical in nature, like an artificial roast chicken.

Whyte held a door for Cooper. The pair were shown into a bare breeze block room with a table, a few chairs and a CCTV camera in the corner. A guard informed them that Ewan Underwood would be with them momentarily. He came five minutes later, wearing a grey prison tracksuit with his hands cuffed and his feet shackled.

"Is that really necessary?" Cooper asked.

The guard glanced at Cooper's belly. "He's been in four fights since he's been here and last night he tried to intimidate a female member of staff. I'm not taking any chances. Neither should you."

Fair enough, thought Cooper. Once upon a time, she might have been offended. *Just because I'm pregnant doesn't mean I'm not as capable as...* But after what happened in Kielder, she was happy to play it safe.

"Mr Underwood, I'm DCI Cooper, and this is Detective Sergeant Whyte. We're here to talk to you about the disappearance of Rhett Campbell and Laurel Deacon. Please, have a seat."

When Underwood didn't move, the guard shoved him onto the chair.

He was as Mildred Houghton described, tall with broad shoulders and a brawny torso that stretched against his sweatshirt. His skin had a dark, weathered look, and he'd gelled his thick, raven hair off his face. The barcode tattoo on the back of his hand warped as he clenched his fingers into fists.

"Congratulations," Cooper said.

"On what?"

"Evading Northumbria Police for ten months. That's quite an achievement."

"You've got me now, though. Haven't you?" Underwood's eye contact was intense. He didn't look away, barely even blinked.

"Yes, we do," Cooper said. "How did you manage that?"

He grunted. "I keep moving. Sometimes I slept rough or had a night on a mate's sofa, but mostly I kipped in the van. Once or twice I'd rent a room – somewhere I could pay cash and didn't need ID."

Whyte propped his elbows on the table. "What happened to Rhett and Laurel?"

"Nee idea. Never met them."

Something about Underwood made Cooper uneasy. The way he looked at her, the way he oozed confidence despite his surroundings. Knowing what she knew about his past crimes, she was glad the guard insisted on shackles.

"Rhett Campbell's coat was found in your home," continued Whyte. "Gemma told us you gave it to your eldest son. How'd it end up in your possession?"

Underwood stayed unnervingly still for a moment before answering, "Finders keepers."

"Where did you find them?" he asked.

"On the grass near Hauxley, at the nature reserve. Nee one was around. I took a chance and loaded them into me van."

"Ah, the pickup," Cooper said. "There's no pickup registered in your name. In fact, you don't have a valid driver's licence."

Underwood shrugged. "And?"

"Who's van is it?"

"Divint kna. Nicked it not long after I left home. Made it easier to move about, assuming I didn't draw too much attention. I stayed off the motorways and took it to a mate's to get false plates. Turns out they were already false plates." He smirked. "I nicked a stolen car. Thieved from a thief. It's kind of poetic."

"It's kind of shitty," Whyte said. "Who's this mate who arranged false number plates?"

Underwood's chest twitched as if he was going to laugh but thought better of it. "Like I'd tell you."

"Listen, you need to be honest with us—"

"Or what? You gonna throw me in jail?" He did laugh this time, shaking his head at the DS dismissively. "I don't dob in me mates. Snitches get stitches."

Cooper cleared her throat. "Let's take a step back. On the twenty-ninth of December, you were on the run, laying low in Northumberland. You saw two bikes and rucksacks at Hauxley and decided to steal them?"

"Maybe I didn't steal them. Maybe I thought they were abandoned. They were making the place look untidy. Perhaps it was my civil duty to pick up the litter they'd left lying around."

"Semantics." Cooper rubbed the bridge of her nose. "You saw the bikes and bags, and you took them."

"Correct."

"What about Rhett and Laurel?"

"I never met them, never saw them, divint kna what happened to them."

Cooper didn't know if she believed him. She looked to Whyte, who had contempt for Underwood written all over his face. He'd be a terrible poker player.

"Tell me what happened next," she said.

"I drove south and parked up in a quiet lane. I went through the bags. There was a tent which was in good nick. I thought it might be nice to camp out for a few nights. I'd have more room than the back seat of the van and thought if the weather was good I could make a fire and grill some food. There was a bag with a few items of washing in – I chucked that away. Their coats were quality. The lass's had her name written in the label so I cut it oot and did the same with the bloke's jacket."

"When did you give the jacket to Shaun?" asked Cooper. "And where's Laurel's jacket?"

"The next day. I went to Blyth to see the family. I arrived after dark, parked a few streets away and went in through the back lane. Gemma let me in; the kids were dead excited to see me. I gave Shaun the bloke's jacket and Gemma the lass's. She's not very outdoorsy; she probably sold it."

"Then what?" Whyte asked.

"I stayed the night. Want to know the details?" Underwood raised a wicked eyebrow at him.

"Spare me," he replied. "What about the next morning? You had a day out with Kirsty."

"Gemma tell you that?"

"No."

He put two and two together. "That little granny, Mildred. She was a character. She recognise the bikes?"

"Did you enjoy playing tour guide?" Cooper asked, ignoring his question.

"It was alreet. Got some petrol money and a hot chocolate oot of it. Kirsty had a good day."

"Then on the sixth, the bikes you stole from Rhett and Laurel were stolen from the back of your van."

"Which was stolen from someone else. Yes. See, it's poetic. There's no honour among thieves, detective."

"And don't I know it." Cooper took a slow breath and adjusted her weight so there was less pressure on her belly. "Here's what I don't understand, Mr Underwood. If you never met Rhett or Laurel – if as far as you were concerned, they were alive and well – wouldn't they have reported their bikes stolen?"

"I guess."

"Then why would you have the audacity to drive around for over a week with stolen bikes in the back of your pickup for all the world to see? Especially when one of them was so distinctive."

He grimaced, the corners of his mouth bending down towards the table. "Guess I'm just an arrogant sod."

Cooper shook her head. "No, I think you dared to do that because you knew the bikes wouldn't be reported stolen because you knew their owners were dead."

Underwood tensed. "Interesting theory."

"Did you murder Rhett and Laurel and steal their possessions?"

"I stole their stuff. I didn't kill anyone."

Underwood's cool demeanour cracked. Cooper saw anger in his eyes, as well as something else. Something dark. He made to run his fingers through his black hair, but the shackles kept his hands close to his waist. He licked his lips.

"I think you used the rope in your van to tie Rhett up, then you raped Laurel, then killed them both

140

and used the tools in your van to dispose of their bodies."

Underwood twisted his head back and forth till he found the guard standing in the corner behind him. "I'm done here. Time to go," he said as he stood up. "I've cooperated, alreet?" he said to Cooper. "I never met them."

"Where are their bodies?"

"I divint kna!" Underwood slammed his shackled hands on the table. The noise and vibration startled Cooper. She slid her chair back, protecting her stomach with her hands.

As Whyte asked Cooper if she was all right, and the guard dragged Underwood from the room, they heard his screams. "I never met them. I never met that Rhett or his whore."

- CHAPTER 23 -

"WELL, HE WAS A real Prince Charming." As Whyte left Durham with Cooper, sarcasm dripped off him like thick gravy. "I can see why his wife sticks by him. I mean, what a catch."

Once upon a time, there'd been a spark between Cooper and the DS standing beside her. Nothing happened between them. Instead, Cooper barely spoke to him for several years. Feeling mischievous, she said something she knew would piss him off.

"You know, you look a bit like him."

"Who?"

"Underwood."

Whyte looked horrified. His lips worked as he tried to find a way to defend himself without getting himself in trouble with his senior. In the end, he settled on, "Give over."

"I'm serious. Gel your hair back, put on a bit of muscle, hit yourself in the face with a shovel a few times, and you'll be his double."

Cooper smirked to show she was joking and relieve his pain. Though both men had dark hair, Whyte didn't really resemble Underwood. With his Roman nose and heavy brows, Whyte looked like a centurion ready to defend Hadrian's Wall; Underwood looked like the moody cousin who was never invited to Christmas dinner.

They drove north towards Newcastle. Whyte was at the wheel while Cooper played with the radio until she settled on Radio 2, who was doing a special on Led Zeppelin. The journey took thirty-two minutes and she had to stop herself from singing along to Whole Lotta Love.

Turning right into the Travelodge car park, Cooper immediately spotted Ashley Campbell. His thin figure shivered at the entrance while he puffed angrily on a cigarette. After Whyte found a parking space, they approached Rhett's scowling brother.

"Hello, Ashley. How are you coping?"

Ashley looked confused for a moment, then softened. "You know, DCI Cooper, you're the first person to ask me that. Mum's always asking how Bruce is doing, and Bruce always asks how Mum's doing. In fact, that's the first thing anyone ever says to me when they call: *How's your mum?* It's like I don't exist." He took another drag on his cigarette then, noticing Cooper's belly, apologised and stubbed it out in the bin. "Sorry."

"It's fine. You can smoke if you like, Ashley."

"No." He tucked his hands into his pockets. "Mum would kill me. I'd almost quit before all this started. Shall we go in? We can talk in my room. I'll message Mum and Bruce."

They huddled in Ashley Campbell's hotel room a few minutes later. It was unnaturally neat for a hotel room; his items were all stored away in drawers. The only sign someone was staying there was a couple of single-serve milk pots in the waste paper bin. Ashley sat on the end of his bed; Bruce Deacon sat on the drawers, his shoulders hunched and tense. Tamzin offered Cooper the seat next to the desk, but she turned it down; she'd already been sat on her backside too much today.

"Is Denise joining us?" Tamzin asked.

Cooper explained that the FLO was on another call but would visit them after lunch. "I want to talk to you more about Rhett and Laurel's personalities and habits. I know they were adventurous, but were they risk-takers?"

Bruce Deacon lifted his swarthy face. "Not really. I would say Laurel took calculated risks. When she visits a new place, she plans her route and researches any areas to avoid. When choosing which university to go to, she looked into which ones were safest for female students."

"Which is why," said Tamzin, "I find it so hard to believe they'd just leave their bikes on the grass like that. It makes no sense. They saved up for ages to buy those. They wouldn't leave them like that, even if no one was around."

Bruce nodded, causing his thick hair to fall forward. He brushed it back. "Exactly. Laurel said they were using two bike chains per bike when they were in towns and cities, and in the countryside, they'd lock them to trees or gates."

Whyte opened his notepad and made a note saying they should speak again with Billy Gilmore, the bird watcher.

"Did Denise speak to you about Ewan Underwood?" asked Cooper.

"Yes," Ashley said. He was staring at his shoes as his legs hung off the end of the bed. "Sort of. She said he had their tent and that you were looking for him."

"We found him." Cooper described how Rhett and Laurel's coats were found in his home and how he'd admitted to taking their bikes.

"Did he hurt my Rhett?" Tamzin said with a gasp. She covered her mouth, fighting to keep her fears at bay.

"He denies ever seeing your son. Or Laurel," Cooper replied.

"And you believe this Underwood character?" asked Bruce.

Whyte shook his head. "We'll be talking to him again. And no, I don't believe him." He took some photos taken in the Underwoods' home out of a file and handed them to Bruce. "Do you recognise any of these items?"

Bruce studied the photos. "That's her wash bag," he said, pointing to a purple bag with a floral print. "She had it the last time she visited me."

Cooper already suspected as much, especially after the team found prescription medication made out to Laurel.

"Laurel had a prescription for codeine," said Cooper. "Was she in pain?"

"She was cycling four hundred miles. I'm certain she was in pain. But no, I think it was an old prescription after some minor surgery she had last year. She probably packed it just in case."

Bruce handed the photographs to Tamzin, who pointed to an item behind Laurel's wash bag. "That's an epi-pen. Might be Rhetts."

"He had a nut allergy?" asked Cooper.

"Yes. Quite a bad one. Not so bad he couldn't be in the same room as them, but if he ate even a tiny crumb of one, he'd be in a bad way."

Cooper thought about this for a moment before turning to the parents of the missing couple. "Bruce, Tamzin, I know all parents want to think of their children as responsible and careful – I have a teenager myself, and I try to always think the best of her – but please don't rush to answer these next two questions. First, would Rhett and Laurel leave their bikes unsecured, even if they thought they'd only be a few minutes?"

Cooper was thinking of the early theory that Rhett and Laurel had nipped into the trees to have some intimate time. Get jiggy with it, as Keaton had said.

"No," said both parents together.

"At least, I highly doubt it," added Bruce.

"And Tamzin, would Rhett ever be without his epi-pen?"

"Oh no." She shook her head vehemently. "Had it on him at all times. At all times. Caused some problems getting into nightclubs, but no, DCI Cooper, he wouldn't be without it."

As Cooper plodded along the blue and magnolia corridor of the Travelodge, she thought about the case. If Rhett would never be without his epi-pen, and Laurel would never leave the bikes unsecured, then there were only two possibilities.

One. Underwood was telling the truth. Something – who knows what – happened to Rhett and Laurel, causing them to abandon their belongings. Then Underwood, being an opportunist thief, took them for himself.

Or two. Underwood was a lying piece of shit. He harmed the young couple, either by attacking them when they were unawares or luring them into a false sense of security with the charming tour guide act he used on Mildred Houghton. Then he hid their bodies and stole their possessions.

It was Cooper's job to find out which possibility was correct.

- CHAPTER 24 -

AFTER PICKING UP A meal deal from the Boots at Silverlink, Cooper and Whyte returned to CID, keen to move forward with the case. Cooper called Billy Gilmore; Whyte called Adam Squires.

Billy Gilmore was confident the bikes weren't locked to anything. "They were just lying on the grass. There was stuff they could have locked them to, like the gate or one of the trees. But like I said, they were just lying there."

"Perhaps they were locked together?" Cooper suggested. As a teen, she and Cindy would lock their bikes together using the logic that you'd need to be pretty strong to carry two bikes.

"Nah. Sorry. I didn't see any locks at all."

Cooper thanked the man and hung up. She turned to Whyte, who was doing the same thing.

"Well?"

"Squires said there weren't any locks on the bikes when he took them from Underwood's van."

"You think he's telling the truth?"

Whyte shrugged. "I guess so. It matches what Gilmore said, and although he's a scumbag, he doesn't really have a reason to lie."

"But," said Cooper, thinking aloud. "Suppose Underwood had an interaction with Rhett and Laurel. If he attacked and assaulted them in the same manner as the other couples he robbed, he could have taken the keys off them to unlock the bikes."

"Squires said the van was full of tools. Maybe he had bolt cutters."

"But that doesn't fit with Gilmore," Cooper said. "And I'm inclined to believe him. He's a decent witness."

Whyte stood up and looked out the window. "We've scoured Hauxley. There's no sign of their bodies."

"We need to find his van." Cooper wondered if Underwood had given the cyclists a lift. Maybe he used the tools in the van to attack or torture them. Most likely, he used it to transport their bodies. If they found the van and found Rhett or Laurel's DNA, they'd have the proof they needed.

IT HAD BEEN A tiring few days. Tuesday was primarily spent grilling Underwood. Cooper didn't like being in the same room as the man, but at least his defence lawyers kicked her out of the room every couple of hours to allow them to speak to him privately. They were prepping him for his trial regarding the crime in Berwick. It was a waste of time as far as Cooper was concerned. The prosecution's case was watertight, thanks to Underwood leaving his DNA on both victims and their property. Add to this the brave testimony of the female victim, and he'd be going away for a long time. Life, Cooper suspected, given his priors. Still, everyone, even scum like Underwood, was entitled to a defence team.

On Tuesday evening, Cooper and Atkinson got some fresh air by watching Tina play netball. Luckily the weather was a significant improvement on their last outing. Though it was dark and cold, at least there was no snow, rain or hail in sight. It had been a crisp evening, and the Sharks played exceptionally well. Tina was brilliant as always and came off the court talking about a rumour that some of the team would be nominated to play for the county.

On Wednesday, Cooper returned to Durham jail, this time with Keaton, and battled with Underwood's lawyers to get access to him. Knowing the husband-and-wife legal team had three children of their own, Cooper tugged at their heartstrings using terms like *missing children, worried parents, they could be out there somewhere, injured, needing help.*

It worked.

"Once again, Mr Underwood, why did you keep the bikes for a week? You could've stashed them at your home or hidden them somewhere. It was rather brazen of you to leave them in the back of an open pickup all that time. It leads me to believe that you knew the owners were dead and wouldn't report them stolen."

"Look, I'm getting real sick of being asked the same questions over and over. Maybe I kept the bikes for so long 'cause I'm a bloody idiot. You might be surprised to hear this, but I'm not exactly Einstein. I didn't do so well in school and this place..." He looked about, gesturing to the jail in general. "It isn't packed to the rafters with clever kids. The ones with books smarts all ended up with jobs like you ladies, or those ambulance chasers out there." He tipped his head towards the door.

Smart move, Cooper thought sarcastically. Insulting the people sent to help him get back home.

"I was an idiot for keeping the bikes that long, but I thought I'd get a better price for them than Gemma would. Regret it now."

"Because they were stolen from you, or because it's got you caught up in a potential murder case?" Keaton asked.

Underwood shrugged and fixed his dark eyes upon hers. "Does it matter? I fucked up. But I'm telling ya, I never met those kids. Never laid eyes on them."

Cooper and Keaton sat quietly, hoping Underwood would feel the need to fill the silence. They were right.

"I stole their bikes. Stole their bags. I admit that. I'll take those charges. As for the rest, nowt to dee with me."

Cooper leaned forward. "Where's the pickup?"

"How should I know?"

151

"Where did you leave it before you were arrested?" Keaton asked.

"Can't remember."

"You know," said Cooper, "you're mighty uncooperative for someone who says they're cooperating."

A slow, creepy smile spread over Underwood's weathered face. "Just my nature, love."

"I'm not your love."

For three hours, Cooper and Keaton tried to extract information from Underwood, tried to catch him out or make him contradict himself, but he stuck to his story like a fly on dog shit. He wouldn't give up what happened to Rhett and Laurel, nor would he give them the pickup's location.

Cooper asked Keaton to join her in the corridor. "What do you think?"

"I think I want to tie him up, use him as a punching bag, then force him to watch while I do bad things to someone he loves. See how he likes it."

She could always rely on Keaton to keep it real. "Aside from that?"

Keaton folded her hefty arms and snorted. "I think he's hiding something. Unfortunately, we don't have a shred of evidence that he actually crossed paths with Rhett and Laurel. His story could be true, and we have nothing to prove otherwise. Shit."

"Relax," said Cooper. "It's not like he's going anywhere. He can't do another runner."

The bigger woman paced momentarily, her boots squeaking on the floor. "Can I at least do him for theft?"

"Knock yourself out."

They reentered the room; Underwood looked up, his eyes as calm and frosty as ever.

"Ewan Underwood, I am arresting you under section twelve five of the theft act: the taking of pedal cycles," said Keaton. "You do not have to say anything—"

"Yeah, yeah. Not my first rodeo. I know it off by heart."

Underwood lifted his hands, they may be cuffed, but his intention was clear. He wanted to shake Cooper's hand.

"I'm a bad man, DCI Cooper, but I'm no murderer. I'll plead guilty to theft and assist you however I can, but I'm telling ya, I didn't kill those kids."

It was those words that kept Cooper awake that Wednesday night. She tossed and turned, not because of Atkinson's snoring or her baby dancing in her belly, but because – despite her best efforts – part of her believed him.

- CHAPTER 25 -

A GAGGLE OF JOURNALISTS gathered outside South East Northumberland magistrates' court. It was a small modern building in Bedlington, conveniently located next to the police station and a branch of Greggs, meaning local officers didn't have to go far when charging suspects or seeking carbohydrate-rich grub.

"Someone must've tipped them off," grumbled Keaton as she and Cooper clambered out of the BMW. "Probably his lawyers. They love a bit of publicity."

A wave of excitement preceded an approaching police van.

"It's him." A photographer pushed to the front of the crowd.

"Get out of my way," said another.

"Ewan, Ewan. Over here. Leslie Jacobs, Shields Gazette."

"Mr Underwood. Ruri McGregor, The Journal."

This continued until Underwood was led from the back of the van. He walked tall, shoulders back. He met every member of the press with the same intense eye contact he used on Cooper. One by one, the press fell silent.

Defiant, thought Cooper.

As he passed, they regained their confidence, shouting to the back of his ebony head of hair.

"Why did you take Rhett and Laurel's things?"

The man posing the question, a boy really, looked fresh out of school, with shaggy blond hair and an innocent face unblemished by the jaded pursuit of headlines. He gulped as Underwood stopped in his tracks and turned to face him. Though flanked by two police officers, Underwood cut an intimidating figure.

"Because I could."

The police officers, strapping men in uniform and high-viz, tried to guide Underwood away.

"One minute won't hurt," Underwood told them, resisting their efforts. "Let the nice men and women ask their questions. They're just trying to earn a living."

There was a sea change in the atmosphere. Suddenly Ewan Underwood was no longer a vicious rapist and burglar; he was a champion of honest, hardworking investigative journalists.

"Where are Rhett and Laurel?"

"Are they dead?"

"Did you kill them? Give us an exclusive."

"No, give me the exclusive. We pay well, Mr Underwood."

Cooper couldn't believe her eyes. "He's turned this into a press conference."

As they headed to the front door, unable to watch any longer, Keaton added, "No. He's turned this into a circus."

———————

GRIPPING A GREEN FELT-TIP pen in her tiny, chubby fingers, Summer Holt drew a small circle on a sheet of white paper. She put the lid back on the pen and placed it back in the pencil case. She crawled into her playhouse and nestled into a velvety cushion with her favourite picture book. She turned the pages admiring cartoon images of trees, fields and animals. This was the closest she got to playing outdoors. She longed to be outside, to splash in puddles in her wellies or smell flowers and pick up pretty pebbles. But it was not to be; she was stuck in the basement.

It wasn't so bad, she told herself, as long as they stayed quiet. She and Tim got new toys every month, sweeties twice a week, and they both had drawers full of new clothes.

Summer ran her palms over her yellow tutu and matching ballet slippers. Yellow was her favourite colour. When she grew up, she was going to be a famous ballerina. Or maybe an astronaut.

The basement was much nicer these days. Not as nice as home, but it wasn't the dark, damp place it used to be. When she and Tim both had coughs, the man brought them medicine that tasted of oranges. He installed a heater and a fluffy rug, hung up some posters and let them paint flowers on the brick walls. The ants and the spiderwebs were long gone, but Pumpkin still lived under Summer's bed. Every day she'd use her toy sweeping brush to sweep Pumpkin's droppings under the rug and down the gaps between the floorboards. She didn't want the man to get rid of Pumpkin, to squash her like he had the giant spider. Summer thought the man secretly liked her and Tim. He was only scary if they made too much noise.

Summer sighed as she heard Tim start to cry. Here we go. She ran from the playhouse and jumped on his bed beside him to give him a cuddle.

"Shh. It's okay."

"I hurt my finger."

"Let me see." Summer kissed his finger and told him to be more careful. "It's not bleeding."

Tim's toy tool kit was spread over his bed. He'd been playing mechanic again, pretending his bed was a car.

"We should tidy up," Summer said, looking at a clock on the wall. She couldn't tell the time – not properly – but the man had given her a few lessons, and she now knew the hours and what half past meant. It was half past three. "It'll be snack time soon."

"I hope it's ice cream," Tim said.

"Me too."

As they tidied the wooden screwdrivers and hammers into the bag, Summer thought of another time when she'd had ice cream. She'd been playing in her garden at home when a shadowy figure waved at her from the pool house. Summer thought it was her daddy, so she ran over to him. But it wasn't her daddy. It was the man. He said he'd brought ice cream for her mummy and daddy and that it was only polite to offer her one too. It was strawberry, her favourite flavour.

"Where does Bogies go?" asked Tim, holding up a green teddy bear they named Bogies.

She pointed to a toy chest. "In the box."

The strawberry ice cream was the last thing Summer remembered about being at home. It made her fall asleep, and when she woke up, she was in the basement.

As the door at the top of the stairs opened, Summer turned her eyes to the little window high up the wall. She could hear an aeroplane. By the time the man reached the bottom of the stairs, she could see it too. Summer liked planes; they reminded her of home. Ponteland was near the airport and she often watched planes landing or taking off from her bedroom window. Perhaps she wasn't far from her mummy and daddy's house. If only she could escape, maybe she could walk home.

DEAN AND KAREEM, THE *dream team*. Dean Starr let go of his partner's hand. He and Kareem had lived together for over a year. Though they had no problems living as a gay couple in Bedlington, they didn't take unnecessary risks. Dean's family and friends were cool with his sexuality, and his colleagues were an open-minded, modern bunch. Still, the police station and magistrates' court often had undesirables coming and going. When they walked past this part of town, it was best to look like two mates, not two lovers. It was unfortunate, but it was safe.

"What's going on?" Kareem asked as they got closer.

"Something high profile by the looks of it," Dean said. He could see a police van and a few uniformed officers. There were men and women in suits who just screamed plain-clothes police, a gang of chavs rubbernecking because they had nothing better to do, and a bunch of excitable journalists acting like school girls at a BTS concert.

"Come on. Let's have a gander."

Kareem beckoned Dean to follow him. His partner was like an inquisitive kitten, and everyone knew what happened to curious cats.

"I dunno," Dean said.

"Pussy." Kareem winked and then used the railings to pull himself onto a small wall. He offered his hand to Dean, but he refused and climbed up by himself.

The man they escorted into the building didn't look like he was attending court; he looked like he was holding court. He stood with the cocky posture of a rock n roll heartthrob and had the tattoos to match. His eyes were like onyx, hard and cold. Dean swallowed painfully. Something felt worryingly familiar.

"Is that who I think it is?" he asked.

Kareem looked intently at the accused. "It might well be." He jumped from the wall and sidled up to a female photographer. "'Scuse me, darling. Who is that?"

Dean couldn't get away with calling random women darling, love or sweetheart. He was too much of a big, beardy bloke. On the other hand, Kareem was non-threatening with his slim build, cheeky smile and adorable curls.

"You not watch the news?" she asked. She lowered her camera to reveal a round face, scarred from acne and chickenpox.

"Too depressing," said Kareem.

She chuckled. "Too right it is." She pointed her camera back at the man as he was led away. "That's Ewan Underwood."

"What did he do?" Dean asked, hanging back slightly.

She chuckled for a second before stopping herself. "Sorry, shouldn't laugh, it's just you'd get a quicker answer if you asked what he hadn't done. He's got a rap sheet longer than the Tyne. Assault, robbery, theft, rape, you name it. Now it looks like murder."

Dean looked at Kareem and felt a shudder run down both legs. He didn't feel so good.

"You know those two cyclists who went missing? The pair from down south?"

They shook their heads.

"Christ, you two really don't watch the news, do you? Well, they were doing the coast and castles route when they disappeared without a trace. That

Underwood fellow is the prime suspect. Only word has it, there's no real evidence. From what I hear, he admits to stealing their bikes, but there's nothing to actually tie him to the missing kids. No bodies, no blood stains, nowt."

Dean focused on the back of Underwood before he disappeared from view. His stomach didn't feel right. He could feel saliva flooding his mouth. He swallowed it back down, and despite his better judgement, he asked, "Do you have a photo? Of the cyclists?"

The woman pulled back from her camera and pressed a button. She flicked through the last few images she'd taken before switching it off and storing the expensive piece of equipment in a purpose-built bag. She removed an iPad from a satchel and brought up a news story.

"Here you go, lads. That's Rhett Campbell and Laurel Deacon. Missing since just before New Year's."

Dean barely glanced at Rhett; his eyes were drawn to the missing woman. Strawberry-blonde hair framed bright-blue eyes. She looked fresh-faced and kind. He took a deep breath, the icy air stung his throat and lungs, making him feel light-headed, as if he'd taken too big a hit from a bong.

"You all right?" Kareem asked.

Dean shook his head. "I think we should go home."

- CHAPTER 26 -

DC SAFFRON BOYD WAS having a dull Friday morning: paperwork, following leads, typing statements. It didn't bother her. Boring beat the high-adrenaline stuff. Still, she was getting better in stressful situations, especially now she'd learned to trust the team at Northumbria Police. They were nothing like her old team – not that they were ever really a team, simply obedient little minions for their volatile leader. Here, everyone seemed to genuinely care for each other. They all had their backstories and spats, but gossip was kept on the QT, and if you wanted to talk, there was always someone to listen. Similarly, if you needed to be there for someone, there was always someone to be there for.

Putting a highlighter pen back in its packet, Boyd returned to CID with a stack of paper in her arms. She dumped the files on a desk and noticed a pink envelope addressed to *Saff*. Boyd sat and examined the envelope, looking around to see if anyone was watching her. It smelled faintly of roses. She slid her thumbnail under the seal and tore the edge in a straight line.

A Valentine's card.

The occasion had completely skipped her mind. After all, the last Valentine's card to land on her desk was from her former DCI. *Don't think about that now.*

She laughed at the image as she studied the card. It wasn't soppy or sentimental. Instead, a picture of an asthma inhaler, the blue type she used to use as a child, was wrapped with the words *you take my breath away*. Boyd snorted before opening the card.

Happy Valentine's Day, Saff.
I have a surprise for you.
Meet me at Tennessee's bench.
Yours, Oliver

OLIVER MARTIN HADN'T FELT this nervous since he cycled to Amelia Ewing's house to ask her to their sixth-form leavers' dance. Her dad had stood two feet behind her the entire time, fixing Martin with the sort of stare that made hard men cry.

She'd said yes, but their brief romance was nothing more than awkward teenage fumblings whenever they could get a few moments away from her parents. He thought about his current situation. Well, they say history repeats itself.

The bench was cold, and he shuffled around for warmth. He looked up eagerly when he heard a sound, only to be disappointed; it was just a granny with two pugs and a toy poodle. All four snarled at him as they passed by. Hoping no one could see him, Martin grabbed a small mirror from his pocket and checked his reflection. He'd do. He shoved it away again as soon as he saw Boyd turn into the waggonway.

"Hi," she said.

"You came." He sounded surprised.

"Of course. Thank you for the card. It was cute."

"All the others were covered in hearts and roses and dodgy poetry. I thought, maybe..."

"Relax," she said, reassuring him. "I liked the card."

Martin padded the seat, but then something occurred to him, and his eyes widened with worry. "Shit. Sorry. Is it too isolated here? We can go to the park or Starbucks."

Boyd moved away, her expression sad. "You know, don't you?"

Martin nodded. "Sorry."

He didn't know if he was apologising for what happened to her, for knowing and not saying sooner, or for picking a quiet place to talk to her when he knew fine well she preferred to be around people – around witnesses. He felt like a prize idiot.

"Did Whyte tell you?"

He shook his head. "No."

Whyte had sparked a curiosity. Google had done the rest.

"I would have told you eventually." She bit her lip. "It's just—"

"Hey," he said, standing and taking her hand. "You don't owe me any explanation."

Martin steadied himself. He wanted to spoil her and make her feel special, but he worried his gesture was too big. Would she pull away from him?

"I— Er— I got you a present. Well, I got us a present."

Boyd moved into him and rested her head on his chest. "Do tell."

He wrapped his arms around her, cuddling her close. Was he about to make a huge mistake? "I booked a hotel."

Her body stiffened. Shit.

"No. It's not like that," he said urgently. "I booked two rooms. You have your own space, your own key. I thought we could get out of town for a bit. It's a lovely place near the border. Nice farmland walks and that. It's got a pub attached to it with open fires. We can have a few beers, eat pub grub, play chess by the fire."

"You play chess?" she looked up, her brows raised.

Martin painted mock insult over his face. "My grandad taught me. I'm not just a pretty face, you know? And, yeah, anything else is completely up to you."

He felt Boyd sink into his arms, her body relaxing. "When do we go?"

"At the end of the month, so there's no rush."

Boyd looked up with her big eyes. God, he couldn't resist those. She smiled. "It sounds perfect. I can't wait."

As the sun peeked from behind a big, grey cloud, Oliver Martin felt like a prize idiot no more. He felt like a king.

A STEADY STREAM OF traffic rumbled over the Tyne Bridge. An occasional car horn and the distant tune of an ambulance's siren punctuated the constant moan of engines as commuters fought their way home. The great, green arches needed a lick of paint, but they would always be a symbol of the north, a testament to the men who built it and the times they lived in.

Keaton walked to the mid-point of the bridge. It was dark and the water below appeared like a black snake carving its way through jewelled city lights.

For years, Keaton had mocked Valentine's. A pointless holiday for the commercialisation of love. Cliché roses, tripe sentiments in cutsie cards, a bottle of pink, fizzy wine and obligatory sex. When caring people were in love, they didn't need a day to prove it; it was in every morning kiss, every simple gesture. Yet, as Keaton stared down at the Tyne she found herself wanting nothing more than someone to present her with a pink teddy bear and a bunch of flowers. It was pathetic.

She was pathetic.

As a couple strolled past her arm-in-arm, they gave her a cautious look but carried on, saying nothing. That was when Keaton noticed the sign: *In distress? Call this number.* She sighed and took out her phone. The screen was blank of texts or missed calls, only an email offering a ten per cent discount on pizza awaited her.

A few days ago, she'd registered with a lesbian dating app but hadn't finished activating her profile. Thinking, why the fuck not, Keaton added a few photographs where she didn't look too big and too muscly. Maybe somewhere in this city of students and footy fans, there'd be someone like her: a lonely heart needing company on the fourteenth of February. It was that or the bloody Samaritans.

The algorithm did its thing, and before long, Keaton was flicking through profiles, her back resting against the green railings of the Tyne Bridge as a small vessel passed beneath. Her thumb froze over a picture of a beautiful woman with a round, friendly face and rosy cheeks.

April. Twenty-nine. Loves cooking and cuddling. Looking for m or f aged twenty-five to thirty-five who likes good food and good company.

Feeling like her stomach was about to dive into the river, Keaton's hands shook and her mouth dried. It was the worst possible match the dating site could have made. Her loneliness was like cancer, creeping through her lymphatic system, destroying her from the inside out. She began to type: *I miss you.* Then, hastily deleting the words and overcome with anger and grief, she hurled her

Google Pixel phone off the bridge and into the depths of the Tyne.

Too high to hear the splash, now she could call neither April nor the Samaritans.

- Chapter 27 -

Having been a single mum for fifteen years, Cooper was used to milestones going unnoticed. Tina didn't know Cooper's birthday until she was ten years old. Even then, it wasn't as if her father or grandparents could take her shopping for presents. Mother's Day didn't happen in the Cooper household, and Christmas was only about her daughter. Surprise gifts and meals out weren't something that happened to Cooper.

So, it was lucky for Justin Atkinson that Cooper had little to no expectations for their evening together. For when she arrived home from CID, she found her partner supine on the sofa, a cold compress on his forehead and a tumbler of amber liquid in hand.

"Happy Valentine's," she said.

The tall, greying man froze. He looked scared and embarrassed in equal measure. "Oh."

He sat, taking the wet cloth from his head and running it over his face.

"I'm so, so sorry, Erica."

She giggled in the way she did early in their relationship when he brought out her youthful sense of humour. "You look like I'm about to murder you."

"You might."

"You know I'd take a mosh pit and a lager over flowers and a table for two any day of the week."

Atkinson downed his brandy and pushed himself to his feet, the seriousness of his day weighing heavy on his shoulders. He'd been called to a house in Redcar to investigate the death of a young boy. According to Cleveland Police, the parents were wrecks, crying and sobbing, unable to contain their loss. That was until Atkinson arrived, took one look at the body and knew all was not as it seemed. The child had been starved over several years, his head strangely large for his undersized, skinny body.

"It was truly awful today. I'm not sure how much longer I can do this job."

Never once in their relationship had Atkinson considered a change in profession. He was the top dog of northeastern SOCOs and was always updating his skills at courses and conferences.

"But you love your job," Cooper said.

"Not when little kids are murdered by their own fucking parents."

Cooper could count on one hand the times Atkinson cursed. She didn't swear much, but she talked like a sailor compared to Atkinson.

He hugged Cooper, told her he loved her then repeated the sentiment to her belly. Her words from a moment ago returned to him and he laughed. "You're thirty-six weeks pregnant. I'm not letting you anywhere near a mosh pit."

"Well, it's a good job I downloaded the new Suicide Silence album." She held up her phone. "My feet are killing me. I'm going to chill in the bath and listen to some deathcore."

A raised brow.

"Yes, you can chill to deathcore," she replied. "Well, I can. While I'm in the bath, I'll order us some food. Do you fancy tacos from Lobo? Then you can either tell me about your hellish day, or we can act like it never happened. Your choice."

The front door clicked into place. Tina waltzed through the living room clutching her school bag in one hand and a heart-shaped box of chocolates in the other. Before Cooper could ask if the chocolates were from Josh and if she could have one, Tina disappeared upstairs.

"I'll run the bath for you," Atkinson said, shepherding Cooper into an armchair. "Least I can do. Then you can relax to deathcore in peace."

KEATON TURNED OFF THE A19 at Cramlington the following morning and joined the A189. They were heading north to Bedlington, a town famous for terriers that resemble fluffy lambs. They'd received a call that morning that two gentlemen

171

wished to speak to Cooper about Ewan Underwood. They had no further information besides their address – Cherry Tree Drive.

Keaton turned into a cul-de-sac and parked opposite a house with a tidy drive decorated with evergreen shrubs in planters. It took Cooper two attempts to get herself out of the car seat, the first time, her weight caused her to topple back into it. As they approached the door, it swung open and a small man with warm brown skin and glossy black curls beamed at them. He glanced at Cooper's belly then at Keaton's height.

"Blimey, you're huge." He immediately covered his mouth with his hand. "Forgive me."

Cooper looked at Keaton. "I'm going to assume he's talking about you."

"Same to you," said Keaton.

The man stepped aside. "I'm Kareem. I'm the one who called. This is my boyfriend, Dean."

Dean glowered at him.

"Oh, don't give me that look. You've been out the closet longer than you've been in it."

Dean was a well-built man with rosy cheeks and an upturned nose. He had a thick, light brown beard and reminded Cooper of a young Santa Claus.

"Forgive Dean. He didn't want to get involved."

Dean grunted. "Not my circus, not my monkeys. Nothing good comes from getting involved in other people's business."

Cooper and Keaton sat on a stylish striped sofa and were handed bottles of sparking water by Kareem. In the corner, an old shaggy dog lifted its head from its basket then went back to sleep.

"Ignore Dean. He needed to speak to you as much as I did. It was making him sick. He got all nauseous and has had a tummy ache since Thursday."

"What happened on Thursday?" asked Cooper.

"We saw Ewan Underwood at the magistrates' court."

Internally, Cooper rolled her eyes as she remembered Underwood lapping up the attention of the press.

"We recognised him," continued Dean.

"From the news?" asked Keaton. She opened her bottle of water and managed to stop it from fizzing over the rim.

"No. I can't stand newspapers. All the hate-stirring, catastrophising and polarising nonsense. Never mind the WAGS and Love Island celebs." Kareem made air quotes as he said the word *celebs*.

"Pfft." Dean shook his head. "Like you don't know every sordid detail of the last season of Love Island."

"Am I telling this story, or are you?" asked Kareem. When Dean said nothing and returned to reading a magazine with a man in a life jacket on the cover, Kareem continued. "I recognised him from real life. Dean and I bumped into him. It was New Year's Day and we'd been kayaking off Druridge Bay. We needed to blow the cobwebs away after Dean's wicked New Year's Eve party."

Dean flicked a page over, then added, "It was pretty wicked."

"We spent about ninety minutes on the water, then dragged our kayak back up the beach and carried it to the car. We were going to go to the Drift Cafe because Melanie likes it there."

"So do I," said Dean. "They make nice sandwiches."

Cooper agreed but asked, in case she needed to speak to her, "Who's Melanie?"

"The dog," said Kareem, pointing at the basket in the corner.

Perhaps not.

"She comes with us. She loves kayaking. Well, to be precise, she loves being with us on the kayak. She can't actually kayak."

"No opposable thumbs," Keaton said, flexing her thumb back and forth over her palm.

"Exactly. But here's where it gets interesting—"

"Stop dramatising," said Dean.

"Shh," said Kareem. "Melanie starts tugging on her leash. The old gal doesn't have the energy she used to, so she usually just plods along at a gentle pace, but she starts pulling like Rudolf on Christmas Eve. She pulls us out of the car pack, down the lane and into the woods just north of Druridge Bay Country Park. We thought she was after some fox poo; you know how dogs are. But guess who we see."

Cooper knew without asking; she could picture the big man with black hair and dark, chiselled features prowling through the undergrowth. "Underwood?"

"Exactly. Only, he's not alone."

174

It felt like a dozen spiders crawled over her scalp. Cooper's heart slowed as she shared a look with Keaton. The DS had a wary look in her eye and a sheen over her brow.

"Go on," Cooper said.

"He was with a woman," Kareem told her. "Now, we don't read the papers or watch the news. We would have come forward sooner if—"

"Describe them," Cooper said, her teeth biting down on her lower lip.

Kareem began to pace around his living room. "The man, Underwood, was big with shaggy black hair and dark skin for a white guy. Em, what else? He seemed outdoorsy, dirty, almost as if he'd been sleeping rough."

"And the woman?" Keaton asked, her eyes trailing Kareem as he paced.

"She was younger. They seemed like an odd couple. He was older and scruffier; she was young and dolled up to the nines. It was the missing girl – Laurel."

Cooper placed her bottle of water between her knees and sat on her hands to stop herself from fidgeting. Dolled up didn't sound like Laurel. Yes, she was an attractive young female, but from the photos she'd seen of her, she preferred a minimal approach to makeup. "How was she dolled up?"

"Loads of makeup, long painted nails, big false lashes. Like a bird from Love Island," he said, looking pointedly at Dean.

Dean folded his magazine away and turned to the detectives. "He's right. Her clothes were plain, but she wore a lot of slap. It was definitely her.

Once we saw the picture of her, there was no denying it. Those eyes are really distinctive. She was awkward, like. Didn't say a word the whole time we chatted with Underwood."

"What did you talk about?"

"The dog," he told Cooper. "Nothing incriminating. He didn't give his name or owt. I thought mebies we'd interrupted them, that they were lovers and wanted some privacy."

"Or they were having an affair and didn't want witnesses," added Kareem.

Joy and despair in equal measure. Joy, because they finally had a witness. A man matching Underwood's description was with a woman matching Laurel's description three days after he took their bikes and bags. Despair, because Cooper could only reach one conclusion: Underwood must have kidnapped Laurel and held her captive somewhere. Knowing what he'd done to women in the past made Cooper's skin crawl. She felt sick, and her stomach hurt for Laurel.

No. Not for Laurel. Her stomach just hurt.

Cooper doubled over as her uterus contracted.

- CHAPTER 28 -

KEATON HELPED COOPER INTO the car and looked at her like she was a wounded animal she couldn't get to the vet in time.

"You can chill, Paula. It's just some Braxton Hicks contractions. They're annoying but nothing to worry about."

"You sure?"

Keaton might look like the big bad wolf of CID, but those who knew her knew she was a softie on the inside.

"I'm sure. I'm not about to have this baby in the pool car."

Keaton's face relaxed as she helped Cooper with her seat belt. "Good. Because, knowing Nixon, he'd send us the cleaning bill." She started the engine, put the car in gear and left Cherry Tree Drive with Dean and Kareem waving them off from their doorstep. "Now, what the hell are Branston Pickle contractions?"

"Braxton Hicks," Cooper said. She chuckled and rubbed her belly. "My uterus is practising for labour."

"Sounds painful. You sure you're okay? We can go to the doctor or the walk-in centre."

Cooper patted Keaton on the shoulder and reassured her with a smile. "It is pretty painful – nowhere near as intense as the real thing, though. They feel different too. When I had Tina, the pain started in my lower back and moved round to the front; these are just over my belly."

As they joined the A189, the clouds rolled in, blanketing Northumberland in grey.

"Can I do anything?" Keaton asked.

"It's just stress. Carrying the hopes of the Deacons and Campbells can be a little fucking much. As much as I need a herbal tea and a walk, I need to find those two poor missing kids. Dead or alive, we need answers. The families need closure."

As she said the words, Cooper thought of Summer Holt and Timothy Harding. Not two poor missing kids. Four.

BACK IN WALLSEND AND aware that some gentle exercise would make her feel better, Cooper slowly walked laps around the incident room while Keaton brought Whyte, Boyd and Martin up to speed. She'd had two paracetamol and was ready to ease her stress by providing peace for Bruce Deacon and the Campbells. That peace may come in the unfortunate news that their children were dead, but it was better than the purgatory they were in now.

"This is good for the investigation," said Whyte. He sat on a table and scratched his chin. "Two witnesses can put Underwood with Laurel. The CPS can use that."

Martin shifted uncomfortably. "He kidnapped her?"

"It's an unfortunate possibility," Cooper said.

Martin paled. "So, where was she in the three days between Underwood taking their things and when the kayakers saw them?"

"A good question," Cooper said. "Where was she while Underwood visited his family or when he was driving Mildred and Virginia around Woodhorn and going for effing hot chocolate?"

Whyte's voice was low when he spoke. "That creeps me the F out. I don't mind admitting it. How guys, and it's always bloody guys, can do unspeakable things and then carry on as normal. Go back to work, go back to their families, hide behind a mask of normalcy."

"Every time," Keaton said. "Dennis Nilsen continued working at the Jobcentre when he had three bodies stashed in his cupboard, and don't get me started on Shipley."

Boyd raised her hand then put it down again, seemingly remembering she wasn't in primary school. "Do you think he left her at his wife's house? From what I read of your and Oliver's report, she seemed supportive of her husband despite all he's done. Could he have left her under

Gemma's supervision while he took his daughter for a day out?"

Laurel Deacon was a tall, athletic woman. Keaton described Gemma as being eight stone soaking wet. One-on-one, and things being fair, Laurel would have stood a good chance against her. But if she was tied up or injured, or if Underwood's two older sons were home, she wouldn't have faired well.

Cooper pulled her phone from her pocket and entered her passcode. "It's a theory worth investigating, and I know just the person to ask."

Atkinson answered on the third ring and blurted out, "Is the baby coming?"

After clarifying that there was still a month to go and that everyone needed to stop treating her like a bomb that was about to go off, Cooper asked about the analysis of the house on Middleton Street.

"Atkinson's going to rerun a few tests for us," she told the room, "but other than her wash bag and the camera, Laurel's DNA wasn't found anywhere in the Underwood home. There is no evidence she set foot in the property." She turned to Boyd. "You don't need to look disappointed. It was a solid idea." Then, to the room, "But now, let's focus not on where Laurel was, but where she is now. If Underwood had her tied up somewhere..."

The thought of the young cyclist being locked up like property, a toy for Underwood to return to every time he fancied it, caused bile to rise in Cooper's throat.

"...if she was tied up somewhere, she'd be dead by now. Underwood was taken into custody on the sixth. It's now the seventeenth. No one can go eleven days without water."

The group fell silent. They'd tried to keep a flicker of hope alive for their own mental health if nothing else, but sadly, facts were facts.

"Are we absolutely sure it was Laurel?" asked Martin. "I went through the file. I can't see a single picture of her in heavy make-up and with false nails."

Cooper looked at Keaton. "You were there. Good witnesses?"

"Oh, they were certain. Right height, right build. Same hair and eyes. But little Olly has a point – don't let that hair gel fool you, there's a brain under there – why was she *dolled up*, as Kareem put it?"

Oliver Martin gave Keaton a playful death stare while Boyd took some images out of a manilla folder. One by one, she laid them on a table.

"This is Ellen Grange, the woman Underwood assaulted in 2011 after restraining her boyfriend. And this is Beth Joplin, the woman in the second attack. Here are some photos from social media from before the attacks. I'm spotting a pattern. Is anyone else?"

"Holy shit." Keaton pulled the photos across the table toward her. "Underwood has a type."

Ellen Grange and Beth Joplin were both heavily made up with foundation a few shades darker than their natural skin tone, and both appeared to have lip fillers and long, sweeping, false eyelashes.

181

"It was the DNA under Beth's nail extensions that identified Underwood as her and her partner's attacker," added Boyd.

Impressed, Cooper smiled at Boyd and approached to pat her on the back, both literally and figuratively. "The sick bastard dressed Laurel to fit his fantasies."

"Gemma was the same, wasn't she?" Martin asked Keaton.

"Yes," she confirmed. "Hair extensions. You name it, she had it."

Outside, the sky darkened another shade of grey, signalling more rain.

Whyte tutted and leaned on the windowsill. "Bloody miserable out there." He looked back at Boyd. "Good connection that, Saff." Then to Cooper, "Can the CPS use it?"

"They can. I wouldn't call our case solid, but we're getting there."

Whyte looked pleased, then he lowered his heavy brows. "But why didn't she speak up or ask for help when Dean and Kareem saw her with him?"

"Good question," Keaton said. She took a deep breath, her strong chest inflating and deflating slowly. "Kareem was a scrawny bloke; he couldn't take on Underwood. His boyfriend could have, though."

"Dean seemed shy," Cooper said.

"Still, he was built like a prize bull. The three of them – Dean, Kareem and Laurel – could have kicked Underwood's arse. Easily."

"She might have been too scared," Boyd said. "I freeze up when I'm afraid."

Both Martin and Whyte paused and gave the diminutive DC a supportive glance. Cooper was missing something, but it was something that could wait for another day.

"Perhaps Underwood threatened her," Boyd continued. "If Laurel thought Rhett was alive, she'd do anything Underwood asked if it might save his life."

Boyd's thoughts were cut off by the sound of pine doors on flimsy hinges colliding with a wall. With a face like the thunder brewing outside, Nixon glowered at the lot of them.

"Sky News. Now."

- Chapter 29 -

The MP for New Forest East finished addressing the camera. Alex Lee wore a well-tailored suit and crisp white shirt, her midnight-black hair framed what would have been a pretty face had it not been marred with so much anger.

"This is a disgrace. Rhett Campbell and Laurel Deacon may still be alive if it weren't for Northumbria Police's incompetence. I want to assure the people of Hampshire that I will be raising these issues in parliament. Northumbria Police have a lot to answer for."

Cooper held her head in her hands. Whyte pulled out a seat and guided her into it.

"Turn it off," she said. "I've seen enough."

Keaton switched the news off and placed the remote on the table.

Alex Lee MP had revealed to the nation that the number one suspect in Rhett and Laurel's disappearance had been on the run for ten months and that he was in the northeast the entire time, right under the noses of Northumbria Police. The MP was furious; anger seethed out of every pore. As she spoke, a ticker tape of sound bites scrolled across the screen. *MP says Northumbria Police have blood on their hands.*

All around the incident room, phones buzzed and beeped as the news broke, and friends and family tagged them in stories. The spotlight of media attention was now on CID, on Cooper in particular. The eyes of the nation were watching her, judging her. She could imagine the way the newspapers would run their headlines. They'd call her a failure, a bumbling amateur – or worse – hormonal.

It wasn't her team who'd failed to find Underwood; his previous crimes hadn't fallen on her desk. And yet it was now Cooper who owed it to pregnant workers everywhere to make things right.

"Okay, first things first. We need an injunction to stop the press reporting on Underwood's past."

"Too late," said Martin. "He handed her a tablet displaying the latest news and skimmed from one site to the next. "They've already gone live. Everything from his childhood misdemeanours, the Maccy Dee's punch up and the assaults and robbery. This one quotes a neighbour about Underwood's alcoholism."

"Shit." Cooper chewed her lip. "There's no way they'll find an impartial jury now. Underwood won't get a fair trial."

Martin shrugged. "I doubt Tamzin Campbell or Bruce Deacon care about a fair trial."

"They should," Cooper told him. "Remember, he's not on remand for Rhett and Laurel's murder. We haven't charged him with anything more than theft. He's standing trial for rape, assault and robbery. If his defence can prove a mistrial, Underwood walks."

"Exactly." Nixon gave them all a scathing look that reminded Cooper of a parent who wasn't angry, just very disappointed. "And if this Underwood walks out of jail, you lot can walk yourselves to the nearest Jobcentre."

WHILE COOPER SAT IN the incident room, biting her nails and wondering how to handle the situation, Paula Keaton, Elliot Whyte and Oliver Martin hung around the vending machine like it was the fountain of youth. If the answer to life's problems could be found anywhere, it would be in a bag of Skittles or a can of Pepsi Max.

"Do you really think that MP will talk about us in parliament?" asked Martin.

"I'd bet good money on it," Whyte said. "Christ, the press are going to crucify us."

Keaton's thoughts weren't on the case. As she popped another brown M&M into her mouth, her mind turned to the pressure she felt to keep a roof over Riley's head.

"Hello? Earth to Keaton? Earth to Keaton."

Martin's words fell on deaf ears. She used to have a full life: family and cousins who rode the coat-tails of her sporting success, teammates who stood by her when her father disowned her, colleagues who couldn't wait to go for a pint and lap up her larger-than-life personality. Now, her brother was all she had left in the world. Her remaining family either sided with her father or were too scared of him to speak up. When she retired, hung up her boots and mouthguard, and moved back to the north, there'd been talk of reunions and meet-ups. But it was only talk. The colleagues she joined the force with moved on too. Some got married and had kids, others changed jobs to preserve their mental health, and some – like Tennessee – were dead and buried. What a boring shell of the old Keaton she was now.

"Hello?" Whyte waved his hand in front of her face. "You had a lobotomy in the last ten minutes?"

"I'm going to say it," said Martin.

"Don't say it," said Whyte.

Martin cupped his hands around his mouth and bellowed, "Saracens suck!"

Keaton snapped back to life, knocked Martin's bag of Skittles out of his hand and pointed in his face. "Saracens rule."

"Hey! My Skittles."

"You're lucky I didn't show you what it's like to be tackled by a five-ten, eighty-five-kilo woman."

Whyte laughed, "I'd have paid to see that."

Martin sank to his knees and swept his arms around, trying to corral the fruity candies towards the bin. "Are either of you going to help me?"

"No," Keaton and Whyte said in unison.

Martin gave Keaton the same look he always did when she busted his chops. It reminded her of a dopey Labrador who'd had his favourite toy taken away.

"Anyway, as I was saying," said Martin as he dropped the last of the sweets into the bin. "I tried to call you over the weekend to see if you wanted to watch the Arsenal match. It kept going to voice-mail."

Keaton tried not to show any emotion. Her personal phone was at the bottom of the Tyne, along with all the photos of April that she never backed up to the cloud. "Yeah, it's on the blink. Getting a new one next week."

"Probably for the best," said Martin. "The Toon lost four-nil."

Whyte opened a bottle of fluorescent green liquid. It fizzed and almost bubbled over. He took a swig, pulled a disgusted face and said, "Speaking of Arsenal, my Gunners-loving flatmate's moving out at the end of the month. Wondered if you'd like to take his room."

Martin grinned. "Me?"

"No, Martin. The Prince of Wales. Yes, you. You said you fancied moving out of your parents' place."

Martin was made up. He and Whyte shook on it and excitedly started disguising the cooking schedule, which from what Keaton could gather, was actually a re-heating schedule. Not that she could talk. She hadn't exactly been eating a balanced diet recently. She was pleased for Martin, but a stabbing pang of jealousy hit Keaton in the gut. She wished she'd asked first. Riley wasn't home much, and the new house didn't feel like home yet. Still, Keaton knew she'd never have asked Martin to move in. That would have meant opening up to the guys and telling them what had happened.

Show no weakness, she told herself.

Keaton slapped the hugging men on their backs and said, "Right. I'll leave you lovebirds to it. If anyone needs me, I'll be solving crimes."

- CHAPTER 30 -

BY LATE FEBRUARY, RHETT and Laurel had been officially missing for fifty-five days. No one had seen them in sixty-five days. Cooper, fresh from once more asking Superintendent Nixon to protect her and her team from negative press regarding Ewan Underwood's ten months on the run, found Keaton in the incident room.

"Bad news, boss." Keaton put the phone down and span her swivel chair around to face Cooper. "Just been on to the phone companies again. Rhett and Laurel's phones still haven't been switched on. There's nothing to trace."

Cooper had expected that. Underwood, though locked up, wasn't talking. Rhett and Laurel's bank accounts were untouched, and the searches for the pair and any evidence connected to them had been called off. The Campbells and Bruce Deacon had returned south. They were sad, grieving and let down.

LEAP YEAR DAY FELL on a Saturday. It was a brisk six degrees, and though the sun shone brightly, grey clouds on the horizon warned the northeast to prepare for more drizzle that evening. The roads were quiet and lonesome as Hayley Daniel drove north on a winding track to a spot dear to her and her late husband's hearts.

To her left, in the baby seat, one-year-old Alfie babbled along to children's songs. After the fourth rendition of Baby Shark, Hayley had enough. She switched the radio off, causing Alfie to squeal and threaten to cry.

"No," she snapped at the infant.

Alfie's lip wobbled, and though he didn't cry, his eyes showed fear.

Hayley stopped the car and put her head in her hands before scooping up her little boy. "I'm sorry, sweetie. Mummy's just tired."

She was always tired.

Hayley knew she was a good mum. Her own mother told her so, and her brother-in-law too. But Hayley didn't feel like a good mum. She felt exhausted and angry most of the time. It had been six months since her husband's murder, and though she could deal with her own loss, she couldn't stand the thought that Alfie would grow up never knowing or remembering Tennessee.

Pulling on a thick, woollen cardigan, Hayley checked her reflection in the visor mirror. She used to be a bonny wee thing with bright brown eyes and shiny hair; she was once signed to Tyne Tees Models and had a small part on Byker Grove. Between post-natal depression and having to cremate her childhood sweetheart, Hayley hardly recognised herself.

She wiped a tear from her eye.

"Time Mummy pulled herself together," she said. "How about I be strong for you, and you be strong for me?"

Alfie laughed and Hayley felt forgiven. Her son was beginning to look more and more like his dad. He was the forgiving sort too.

Secured Alfie into a baby carrier she could wear like a backpack, Hayley opened the car boot and took out an ornate wooden box. Inside was something very precious that she had to let go of – Tennessee's ashes.

***

"HERE WE ARE," HAYLEY said after she'd walked for twenty minutes. She removed her baby-carrying backpack and settled Alfie against the base of a tree. He looked around, his eyes bright and curious at his new surroundings. Hayley wiped a droplet of drool from the corner of his mouth and sat next to him, the urn in her lap.

"This is where your father proposed. We were barely out of school, and everyone thought we were crazy to get engaged so young."

A tiny firecrest landed on a branch, its sage wings and impressive dandelion-yellow crest glistening in the sunlight. The pair silently watched the bird with its black eyemask until it flew away.

"Maybe one day, Alfie – when you're much, much older – you'll bring a girl here and ask her to marry you."

Her son gurgled and lurched forward so he could crawl through the grass. A pain grew in Hayley's chest. This was much harder than she thought it would be. She stroked the cold china urn and lifted it to her lips. She kissed the lid and whispered, "Your son's here. You wouldn't believe how much he's grown. He's going to be as tall as you, maybe taller."

The urn felt heavy. It and its contents weighed around five kilos, but the weight of what she was going through made it feel like a tonne. Hayley grieved for all the memories they'd never form. Alfie would take his first steps soon. Her mind conjured images of her and Tennessee beaming with joy as their baby walked unaided. She imagined them hand-in-hand at Alfie's sports days, sitting in the sunshine, cheering on their bairn as he sprinted across the school field. She pictured Tennessee applying a plaster to a grazed knee after a game of kickabout. She thought of them sitting on the sofa as Alfie – aged six or seven – unwrapped his Christmas presents. She could see them sitting in church, their hair grey, as Alfie married the love of his life.

These things could still happen for Alfie, just not the way Hayley pictured them – with his dad there every step of the way. To distract herself from cry-ing, she watched Alfie pull himself to his feet using the tree trunk to balance.

"Are you ready? Because Mummy's not."

She opened the urn and poured the ashes by the base of the tree, waited for the wind to pick up, and watched her husband dissipate into the chilly air. Alfie clapped at the whirls of white powder, so Hayley clapped with him. "It's pretty, isn't it?"

Alfie soon lost interest and resumed crawling across the grass. He turned a rock over, revealing woodlice and millipedes that scattered for cover, as well as a dirty, discarded wallet.

Hayley opened it. Inside, there was a pound in small change and a debit card. Thinking she should hand it into a local shop or police station, she turned the card over to read the name: R Campbell.

Silently, Hayley returned the wallet and rock to exactly as they had been; she'd been married to a detective long enough to know things should be left in situ. She screwed the lid back on the urn and, with tears in her eyes, put Alfie back in his carrier. Today was supposed to be about her, Tennessee and Alfie. It was supposed to be cathartic.

It was anything but.

Hayley had to do what she'd been dreading for six months; she'd have to speak to the woman she blamed for Tennessee's death – Erica Cooper.

-CHAPTER 31-

HE COULD SMELL THE vinegar before he set foot in the shop on Saturday evening. The place may officially be called SGF Fish and Chips, but it would always be West Moor Chippy to Fuller. The chippy was an award-winning local institution worth the fifteen-minute walk from Fuller's house. Besides, eating them on the return journey would keep him warm and nourished, and everyone knew calories consumed while exercising didn't count. Inside, the shop was as busy as ever. Friendly staff fulfilled orders as fast as customers could hand over their cash. The sounds of customers making small talk, crispy batter falling into cardboard boxes, and sharp knives on blue chopping boards were an assault on the senses.

While Fuller waited for his turn, he scrolled through his phone, dipping in and out of Tiktok and Twitter.

Ding. An email entitled, *you should probably see this.*

Hi. I was freeing up space on my laptop when I found this photo. Recognise anyone?

"Yes, darlin'. What can I get you?"

Fuller jumped, looking up embarrassed, aware he looked like just another phone zombie.

"Jumbo cod, chips and curry sauce."

While the server worked on his order, he returned to the email. There was no name, the address being an anonymous series of numbers. He quickly typed a reply asking the mysterious sender to call him. If they didn't get back in touch, he'd ask the tech team to help trace the mysterious source.

"That's fifteen-sixty, love."

Bloody inflation. He remembered the days when a large fish supper came in at nine quid. Fuller fished around in his pocket and handed over a twenty-pound note. When he took his food, he could barely concentrate on the pleasant aroma of batter and spices. What he'd just seen troubled him.

The image appeared to have been taken in a swanky restaurant or posh hotel. In the background, a painting of two horses – one bay, one white – adorned a sage green wall. In the foreground, three men in tuxedoes raised glasses of port, grinning like aristocratic Cheshire Cats. Fuller didn't recognise the man in the middle; he was reasonably tall and stocky, had cropped, light brown hair and was clean-shaven. Otherwise, he was unremarkable. It was the other two men who caused Fuller's mouth to dry. As much as he tried to enjoy his dinner as he walked back home, the food was wasted on him. Each mouthful iced his insides. If the Holts and Hardings didn't know each other, why the hell were Michael Holt and Cyrus Harding in the same room, within touching distance of one another?

THE SUN HAD YET to rise when Neil Fuller approached the gates marking the end of the Holts' driveway. Birds sang the dawn chorus while parents walked their little ones to school. He lowered the car's window and pushed a button on an intercom.

There was a buzzing noise, then, "Yes?" Portia's voice was weak and tinged with sadness.

"It's me. Neil."

The gates creaked as they opened. Fuller closed the window and drove towards the house. High walls and higher privet bushes, wrought-iron gates coated in anti-climb paint, security cameras and motion-activated lights. All this security at the front of the Holts' home and yet Summer had apparently disappeared from the back garden. A garden marked by a feeble wooden fence and a gate with a simple auto-latch. It backed onto a bridle path, leading to a park at one end and farmland at the other.

"Is there news?" Portia asked as she opened the door. She wore a dressing gown and slippers.

Fuller shook his head and followed Portia to the kitchen, where a man fried eggs in a heavy pan. He was broad-shouldered, bald and built like a tank. Fuller guessed he was in his sixties and took a stab at the man's identity.

"Malcolm Dorsey?"

"In the flesh." The PI carefully removed the eggs from the pan and laid them on buttered English muffins. He washed his hands before greeting Fuller with a sturdy handshake, "Good to meet you, Neil."

Making the Holts' breakfast? Was he a PI or a PA? An insecure voice in Fuller's head wanted to make a cutting or sarcastic remark, to be antagonistic, but he remembered Cooper's advice to work with him instead of against him. Dorsey had already proven the cooperative sort by sharing information. It was only fair Fuller did the same.

"I was hoping for a quick chat with Michael," said Fuller to Portia.

"He's in his study," she told him. "Upstairs. Second door on the left."

Fuller glanced at Dorsey, who read his mind.

He handed Portia her morning meal and made to follow Fuller. "I'll take Michael his breakfast."

Michael was hunched over a traditional typewriter with round keys. He looked up when the men entered the study and removed his glasses.

"A typewriter?" mused Fuller. "Old school."

"I find it helps focus the mind," Michael said, adopting a learned air. "With no delete button, I'm forced to consider each word carefully. To be concise in the vernacular."

While the PI placed Michael's breakfast on his desk, Fuller unlocked a tablet and brought up the image he wished to talk to him about. The picture of three men in tuxedoes drinking in front of a painting of horses.

"What can you tell me about this image?"

Michael slid his glasses back on and peered at the tablet. "That's a photograph of me."

"And?"

"And what? It's me and two randoms. Where did you get this from?"

"It's not two randoms, though. Is it? This is Cyrus Harding." Fuller pressed a finger on the tablet, leaving a greasy fingerprint.

"Timothy's father?"

"You don't recognise him?" Fuller asked, handing the tablet to Dorsey so he could take a look.

"I look a lot younger there. So does Cyrus. This picture must be years old, maybe a decade old. When was it taken?"

"You're in the photo. You tell me."

Michael glared at Fuller, revealing the aggressive side he tied to keep hidden but reared its ugly head when dealing with pushy journalists.

"Who sent you this? Was it Amelie?"

Fuller said nothing.

"Nevermind. It was obviously Amelie." Michael pushed his breakfast away, apparently having lost his appetite. "My ex. She's an attention-seeking bitch. She wants me back, you know. Tried to talk me out of marrying Portia, tried to seduce me when Summer was a baby. Look." He dipped his chin and made pointed eye contact. "I don't want Portia more upset than she already is. Can we—"

His sentence was cut short by Portia shuffling into the office, cupping a mug of tea in both hands, a little egg yolk at the corner of her mouth.

"I'm a grown woman, Michael. You don't need to protect me. What's going on?"

He rolled his eyes at his wife and muttered, "Amelie."

"Oh, what now?"

"She sent Neil this." He took the tablet from Dorsey and thrust it towards Portia, almost knocking the tea from her hands.

The study was a relatively small room, filled mainly by an obnoxious writing desk that must have weighed a tonne. With four adults crammed around it, the room felt claustrophobic.

Portia pursed her lips and looked at the tablet, muttering, "Amelie? That woman is bloody insane. Why would she send Neil... Wait. That's you and Cyrus."

"I know that. The point is, she's doing what she always does. Trying to wiggle her venomous little claws into our lives again."

"When was this taken?"

Michael shrugged. "It was a wine tasting. I can't tell you exactly when. I was completely hammered. Must have been forever ago." He snatched the tablet back and cast his eyes over the picture. "It looks like the Vermont, maybe Slaley Hall."

Fuller jabbed a finger towards the mysterious man in the centre of the image. "Who is this man?"

"Who cares?"

"I do," said Fuller, Dorsey and Portia at once.

"You're kidding me. You think this man has something to do with Summer's disappearance? Why? Of all the men in the world, you're focusing on some random I met once and don't even know. I can't remember the evening, let alone who this grinning idiot is."

Dorsey's arms were folded tight across his chest. "There's no need to be defensive, Michael. Two children vanished without a trace, and this bloke is so far the only thing we have to connect the cases—"

"Because the cases aren't bloody connected."

"This man connects the cases. If you want to find your daughter—"

"If I want to find my daughter? Listen to yourself. Of course, I want to find Summer. Now watch your tone of voice. You work for me, not for him." Michael used his glasses to point at Fuller.

"Actually," Portia said quietly, tears filling her eyes. "He works for me. Not you. Nadine and I hired Malcolm.

As the Holts descended into a heated argument about who wanted to find their daughter more and how the PI best spent his time, Fuller and Dorsey made their retreat.

"What do you think?" Dorsey asked, following Fuller to his car. The sun was higher in the sky now, sending golden rays over the dewy grass.

"I can believe two people graduate from the same university in the same year and claim not to know each other. I can't remember five per cent of the people on my course, let alone people in other departments."

"And?"

Fuller got into the driver's seat but left the door open while he spoke to Dorsey. He pulled the seat-belt across his chest and clicked it in place.

"And I can believe someone being so drunk at a wine tasting that they can't remember a photo being taken. However, if Cyrus Harding also can't remember where he was or who the other man is, then I'm calling BS."

"Same."

Fuller closed the car door and started the engine. Dorsey patted the top of the car twice and added, "Keep me posted. Let's find that little girl."

- CHAPTER 32 -

COOPER AWOKE WITH A start on Monday morning; the weekend had been emotional and her sleep had suffered. It didn't help that she felt like she had a beach ball glued to her stomach.

She couldn't believe her eyes when her phone rang on Saturday afternoon and Hayley Daniel's name lit up the screen. A small, cowardly part of her didn't want to answer and thought about letting it go to voicemail. Thankfully the braver part of her psyche won out.

It had been a short, one-sided conversation.

"I need to see you. Meet me at Tennessee's bench."

She had expected Hayley to have a go at her, for them to cry, argue even, perhaps hug it out. She had been completely thrown when Hayley told her about the wallet.

"It's here," she said, pinging Cooper the exact location. "Under the tree where he proposed."

Fury radiated off her. Cooper could feel it like the heat from an oil burner.

"I'll get a team straight over."

She wished she had the words to make everything all right. But no such words existed. What could she say that would change anything or bring him back? As Hayley ran her hand over the small brass plaque on the bench that read *DI Daniel,* Cooper pulled her coat further around herself. She wanted to conceal her belly and hide it from Hayley, not that she could. Still, she wanted to. Her baby had a father, Hayley's did not.

"You should go too," Hayley told her. "If you want to. I'd just scattered Jack's ashes when Alfie found the wallet. There wasn't much wind today. If you hurry, he might still be there."

He might still be there. Those were the words that caused Cooper to wake. Her dream had been a mix of Hayley's name on the screen, their awkward encounter and the last flakes of Tennessee she'd ever see.

Sensing her discomfort, Atkinson kissed her and told her to have a relaxing shower. "I'll make breakfast."

ARRIVING AT HQ, COOPER parked close to the front of the building. It was a bright morning, but the forecast suggested it wouldn't last. Entering the building, she wiped her feet on the mat and headed for the stairs where Martin and Boyd held hands. Their weekend away must have been a success. *Good for them*, she thought. When Boyd spotted Cooper, she let go of Martin's hand and adopted a business-like expression. Martin stood formally and nodded to Cooper. "Morning, boss."

"At ease, soldiers," she laughed. "Hope you both had a nice weekend. I could do with a little break myself."

"Can't be long now," said Martin, his eyes cast downwards.

"I'm not sure maternity leave counts as a break. From what I remember, it's not very relaxing."

He flushed. "Of course. Sorry. I'm nipping to the canteen before the meeting. Can I get you anything?"

"A coffee and paper would be great. I'll see you both in the incident room in five minutes. You remember the rule?"

"Twenty push-ups if we're late," they said in unison.

Boyd's eyes widened as she checked her watch. "Four minutes. Come on." She grabbed Martin's hand again, and they legged it towards the canteen, returning to the incident room in a record-breaking three minutes and thirty seconds.

While they waited for the last-minute stragglers, Cooper sipped coffee and read the headlines. Thankfully, none of the front pages mentioned Rhett Campbell, Laurel Deacon or indeed Erica Cooper. Famous author Portia Holt - Summer Holt's mother - apologised for the delay in releasing her next book. She explained that she was too busy focusing on Summer to make the changes her editor suggested but that the book was still available for pre-order. Oh boy, thought Cooper. The online mob would crucify her for that quick bit of promotion. Fathers of missing children might be forgiven for continuing to work, bills needed to be paid after all. But mothers were expected to stay home, nervously waiting for the phone to ring. She turned a page. Dominican, Francisco Peña lost his appeal and would be extradited to the USA to face trial for murder, Carlisle Infirmary's maternity unit had been closed following further investigation, a footballer had been caught cheating on his missus, and a major clothing manufacturer was moving its factories to China to save money, costing over two hundred jobs.

Keaton peered over Cooper's shoulder. "Any good news?"

"Not a peep."

With everyone present and seated, Cooper took a moment to fill herself with caffeine before starting the meeting.

"Right. Here we are again. Is anyone getting deja vu?" She pointed to the map of Northumberland on the wall. "The bikes and bags, seen here at Hauxley. The clothing labels found near Widdrington. And now, Rhett's wallet and debit card found here at Druridge Pools."

Keaton adjusted her belt, then asked, "Has the wallet come back from the lab?"

"Affirmative. And before anyone gets excited, there's no blood and no DNA other than that of Hayley Daniel."

The room seemed to deflate as one.

"Are we assuming Underwood was camping there?" asked Whyte. "He could have taken any cash and discarded the wallet like he did some of their other possessions."

"That would make sense." Cooper sipped her drink. "We'll ask him. Not that he's being much help. But either way, the wallet won't help us charge him. We have no bodies, and no-body murders are notoriously rare and difficult to prove. In fact, there's only one in the history of Northumbria Police."

"Donald Graham," Martin said. "Hexham, 2014."

Everyone turned to look at the young DC.

"Fifty points to Martin," Cooper said, an impressed look on her face. "But other than Dean and Kareem's witness statement, we have no evidence Underwood met Rhett or Laurel. They're solid witnesses. But still, we're talking about someone who looked like Underwood with someone who looked like Laurel."

"Is it just me, or is this the most frustrating case ever?" asked Whyte. "None of these items – the bikes, the labels, the purse – offer any clues as to what happened to Rhett and Laurel or where they are now."

"Where they are now?" echoed Keaton. "I think we all know they're dead and buried. About the only thing we can prove is that there's no proof of life."

"We either need a confession, or we need something solid. We need the bodies, or the pickup truck, or both." Cooper sighed. What she wouldn't do for a few extra pairs of hands. Or an extra brain or two. "Let's organise another search."

"That'll cost a fortune," Martin said.

"Nixon'll hit the roof," Whyte said.

Cooper agreed. "Paula?"

"You want me to ask him?"

Everyone nodded as one.

Keaton rolled her eyes. "You're all cowards."

- CHAPTER 33 -

THE RAIN DROVE ALL but the hardiest residents into their homes. It gushed from the bottoms of gutters, the drains struggling to cope with the onslaught. Fat raindrops pelted the tops of cars, sounding as heavy as hailstones.

Mike Parker wasn't a hardy individual, nor was he particularly outdoorsy. Still, he didn't have a choice about being out in this weather. There was no such thing as an indoor parking enforcement officer.

Stupid title, he thought as he trudged along the suburban streets of Bedlington, checking permits as he went. What was wrong with the term traffic warden? That's what they've been called when he was a young 'un.

As he rounded the end of Victoria Court, Mike spotted a dinged-up Volvo whose permit had expired. Bingo. He entered its details into the system, printed the ticket and placed it in a plastic envelope. After fixing it to the car's windscreen, he continued to Victoria Way. That was one benefit of this weather, thought Mike. No one was around to give him grief about his job. Folk hated parking enforcement offices for giving them fines but were quick to whinge that nothing had been done about some bird from three streets over nicking their space. It was a no-win situation.

"Oi, oi. What do we have here?"

The top of the street was a dead-end. There was space for three cars to park, and the road had been widened slightly so vehicles could turn around. Taking up most of the room was a hideous RV. Not as big and grotesque as the ones the Yanks loved, but still, Mike bet the neighbours hated the sight of it. He could barely see the windscreen and had to stand on his tip-toes to check if it had a permit. It did. Whether it was in date or not, he had no idea. He'd need a step ladder to find out. So big was the camper van that it partially obscured the vehicle next to it. He wouldn't have even known the black pickup was there had he not given the RV a close-up inspection.

Black pick up.

The words rang a bell. Mike pulled out his mobile and held it close to his body to shield it from the rain. He typed a quick message to a colleague.

Alreet, Specky. What were the details of that pickup we were supposed to be keeping an eye out for?

The reply came quickly, as he knew it would.

I'd rather be a specky four-eyes than an ugly twat. Black V-reg Nissan. Why?

I've only gone and found it!

Mike peered through the vehicle's windows until his phone vibrated again.

If there's a reward, I want half.

He laughed. Specky could kiss his hairy arse.

COOPER WASTED NO TIME. As soon as she got the call, she contacted forensics. Atkinson and his team were there within the hour. She sent Whyte as her eyes and ears; if there were anything worth knowing about the scene, Whyte would tell her. Or, he'd better bloody tell her after the whole tent debacle.

True to form, he called within minutes of arriving. "I have good news, bad news and news that will definitely piss you off."

Cooper stood and walked to the window. The wind was howling outside, trees swayed, and the grass looked flat as if it were trying to duck under the gale. Whyte's words bothered her. She wanted to hear the good news and cover her ears for the rest. Things like this were like plasters; best to yank them off quickly.

"Urgh. Let's get it over with, then. Hit me."

"Right. Well, bad news first. Atkinson thinks the rain will have destroyed all evidence on the exterior of the car. He doubts they'll be able to get prints."

That was disappointing but not unexpected. Underwood's vehicle would have been there since his arrest for the Berwick rape and robbery. He'd been held on remand ever since; that was almost a month ago.

"Never mind. Next."

"The good news – and this is potentially excellent news – is that the tarpaulin covering the bed of the truck was secured perfectly. Atkinson reckons whatever's in the bed will be as Underwood left it. If any of those tools, ropes, etcetera have Rhett and Laurel's DNA, he'll find it." Cooper tried not to swear with joy. She formed her hand into a fist and punched the air. That was bloody good news. If they could tie Underwood to Rhett and Laurel themselves, rather than just their possessions, they might stand a chance at securing a murder conviction – bodies or no bodies. She told Whyte as much and asked for the news that would piss her off.

"You won't shoot the messenger?"

"I make no promises," said Cooper.

"Here's the thing, Victoria Way is a dead-end road. The end where the pickup was found is separated from Schalksmuhle Road by a few bollards."

"Why do I recognise that street name?" Cooper heard Whyte gulp. "Spit it out."

"Because that's the address of the magistrates' court. You and Keaton probably drove past it. Underwood was stood outside the court fielding questions, all the while knowing a key piece of evidence was at his two o'clock. The bastard was playing us. Having the time of his fucking life."

- CHAPTER 34 -

THE MINI-BUS DROPPED A downtrodden Tina back home not long after seven, her expression somewhere between surly and depressed.

"Hey, champ," called Cooper.

She ignored her mother's greeting and began rummaging through the kitchen cupboards.

"I take it the Sharks lost?" Cooper asked.

Tina removed a packet of salt and vinegar crisps from the cupboard. "Lost? We were crucified."

She moved to the living room and collapsed on the sofa.

"Want to talk about it?"

Tina crushed a crisp between her thumb and index finger. "No. I want to eat my feelings."

Cooper sympathised. "That, I can help you with. Give me a few before Justin gets home and insists I have something healthy."

She offered her the packet and Cooper scooped several into her mouth, savouring the salty flavour and crunchy texture.

"Why don't you go and see Josh for an hour? Take your mind off it."

Tina made a huffy noise. "Nah. He's in a mood because I kicked his butt in biology today."

It seemed everyone was in a mood: Tina because her team had lost at netball, Josh because he was dating a genius, and Cooper because she'd been outwitted by an alcoholic, violent criminal. Hopefully, Atkinson would have some news that would put a smile on her face.

He arrived home with some lamb chops, a bag of vegetables and an apologetic demeanour.

"No DNA?" asked Cooper.

"None yet, I'm afraid." He started unpacking the vegetables while Cooper turned the oven on. "But leave it with me. If it's there, we'll find it."

Cooper sank onto one of the chairs at the kitchen table. "I know. But if it's not there..." She thought of Underwood and all the misery he'd caused in his life. "He has to be put away."

"And he will be. He's already locked up. Even if you can't prove these murders, he'll undoubtedly be found guilty in the Berwick rape and robbery."

"He'll be out again in ten. And that's assuming there's no mistrial. Jesus. What if he ends up back on the streets?"

Atkinson chopped carrots into neat slices. "You can't let him get to you."

"You haven't seen him." Cooper shook her head. "His eyes. They're black and soulless. It's like locking eyes with the devil."

He put the knife down. "He scares you?"

She considered the question. He unnerved her; that was for certain. "A bit," she admitted. "I'm more worried about him setting foot outside a jail again."

Adding another carrot to the pan of vegetables, Atkinson sighed. "There's nothing that can be done right now, and worrying about it won't do you or the little one any good. The pickup's in the lab. There's a lot to go through before we're finished. All the equipment in the truck bed, the cover itself, the interior, the upholstery. Be patient."

He was right, as usual. Stressing wouldn't solve the case any quicker. Still, being patient wasn't a strong point of hers.

———

"I BLOODY KNEW IT."

When Cooper pushed the doors to CID open on Wednesday morning, she was greeted by the sight of DS Elliot Whyte punching the air in jubilation.

"It was the Roker Boys. I knew it. I've got the bastard."

Cooper sat on a swivel chair and turned to face the delighted detective. The drive-by shooting on Gill Side Road had been troubling Whyte; the victim was still in a coma. "Come on then. Spill."

Whyte sat on the edge of the desk and offered Cooper a bite of his muffin. She declined.

"We finally caught a break. Doorcam footage. This woman, Aashi Sabeer, had been in India visiting family all this time. Only got home on Monday. She had a scratch on her car, so she checked the footage from when she'd been away. She'd only gone and caught the whole thing on camera."

Now it was Cooper who punched the air. "Bloody brilliant. About time we had some good news. You managed to ID the shooter from the footage?"

"Not exactly. It's grainy, and you can't see the shooter's face."

Her spirits dampened.

"But what you can see is golden." Whyte couldn't contain his glee. "As the car rolls into frame, you can see the shooter lower the window and take the shot. He wipes down the gun and then drops it down the drain. Here's where it gets interesting. The genius takes a swig from a can of Pepsi and hoys it out the window where it lands in Aashi Sabeer's garden and rolls under a bird feeder."

Cooper burst into laughter. "He went to all the effort of cleaning the gun, hiding it down the drain and having the road resurfaced. When all the while, his spit is all over a Pepsi can. Tell me the lab managed to get DNA from it."

"They managed all right."

She clapped her hands together, hope warming her from the inside out. If DNA could survive on the Pepsi can, there was a chance it would survive on the pickup too. "This has made my day."

"And it gets better. We got a match on the spit. It's Henry Dunn, the son of Kayla Dunn, one of the heads of the Roker Boys. We didn't get any old mobster lackey. We got a mobster's son."

Whyte shoved the remaining muffin in his mouth, jumped down from the desk and took a bow, a grin of triumph spreading over the faces of the two detectives.

Keaton put down the report she was reading. "Couldn't help but eavesdrop. Does that mean lunch is on you?"

"You have a one-track mind. I've only just finished breakfast." He pulled his debit card from his wallet. "Here, order pizza for everyone. Have it delivered at half-twelve, one-ish."

Cooper almost didn't hear her phone ring as the back-slapping and congratulatory remarks rippled through CID. The number was withheld.

"DCI Erica Cooper," she answered.

A robotic, automated voice came on. "This call is from a person currently in prison in England. All calls are logged and recorded and may be listened to by a member of prison staff. If you do not wish to accept this call, please hang up now."

- CHAPTER 35 -

COOPER PRESSED THE PHONE against her ear and turned the volume up with her thumb. The caller whispered as if he were wary of being overheard. He was a prisoner; his caution was understandable.

"I saw your name in the paper," he said. "You're the one investigating the missing cyclists. The kids from down south."

"That's right. Do you have information?"

She heard his breath quiver while people walked by. He swallowed, then said, "They're dead. Underwood killed 'em."

"How do you know?" she asked.

Another pause. "'Cause the fucker told me, that's how."

Though it was what she feared, Cooper didn't want to believe him. For one, she wasn't in the habit of automatically believing criminals. She was conflicted. She felt a pang of sadness because she didn't want it to be true. She knew their chances were slim, but a small idealistic part of her hoped there'd be a happy ending for Rhett and Laurel. But there was also hope. Another witness meant a better chance of nailing Underwood, securing a life sentence and ensuring a dangerous man never walked free.

"You're calling from Durham?" she asked.

"Aye. I'm in the same wing as him."

"What's your name?"

Cooper heard his fingers tapping against the phone while he thought. "Call me Larry."

Obviously not his real name. The name of a childhood friend, his father perhaps.

"Okay, Larry. But if we're going to move forward, I'll need your real name eventually."

"He's a bad man," he said, his voice trembling. "He ain't normal. Someone ratted on him for taking two puddings at dinner. He didn't just give him a clip; he beat the shit out of him – put him in the hospital. Took three guards to pull him off. I can tell you what he told me, but that's it. I can't go on the stand. I can't go public."

"Try to relax, Larry. You've done the right thing." Cooper needed him to trust her if she was going to get as much information as she could out of him. "I want to come and see you. Today."

"Oh. I divint knaa if that's a good idea."

"There's a McDonald's on the way. What do you want? Big Mac? Fries?"

Cooper counted down from ten in her head. She knew he'd cave before she got to one.

Five, four, three...

"A Big Mac, large fries and a chocolate milk-shake."

"Okay—"

"And a chicken nugget Happy Meal."

DRIVING ALONG OLD ELVET in Durham, Cooper had to fight the urge to pull over and scoff all the junk food for herself. The smell of ground beef and melted cheese drove her crazy. She dodged a pothole so large it had developed a personality of its own and turned on to Whinney Hill.

As it turned out, Larry was actually called Gary. Not the most imaginative pseudonym Cooper had heard. If Cooper had to make up a name on the spot, she'd go with Debbie, as in Debbie Harry, or Chrissie, as in Chrissie Hynde. After getting his real name out of him, Cooper called the prison and asked for Gary to be moved to an interview room where he'd feel safe until she got there.

After arriving at HMP Durham, Cooper entered through a metal detector and a series of doors made of heavy bars painted white. A security officer checked her belongings, including the brown paper bag containing the Mcdonald's. He had a thin frame but a bit of a gut. His uniform was immaculate, and he tried to disguise his smoking with a good spray of Eternity For Men.

"Sorry, ma'am. You can't take the toy in." He held up a character from a beloved animated film. "Choking hazard."

Cooper narrowed her eyes to thin slits and gave him a sceptical stare. "I really don't think that's necessary. He's not three."

"I know. But who do you think'll get the blame if ickle Gary gets it stuck in his throat?" He lifted the toy by its plastic hand and waved it in the air. "Me! And then I'm liable. That's not a risk I'm willing to take."

"Okay. Fine. You keep it." Cooper hoisted her bag strap up her shoulder and waited to be buzzed through.

"He's in interview room two. I'll show you through. There'll be a guard by the door. He can come in if you like."

"Is he dangerous?"

"Gary? Nah. Not unless you chat him up in the showers."

"Then I think I'll be fine."

She followed a corridor of pale blue breeze blocks to meet the man they would call Witness A if his intel proved worthy.

Gary was a diminutive man. He was seated, but Cooper suspected he was five-two, five-three, given how big he made the table look. His prison uniform was baggy, hanging off his slender frame. He shared the same haircut as Cooper, but his skin was pale and sickly. He looked up briefly, then averted his gaze, keeping his eyes down in a manner that reminded her of Tina.

"Gary? Pleased to meet you. I'm DCI Cooper."

As soon as she put the paper bag on the table, Gary reached out and pulled it towards him. He tore the bag like a man who hadn't eaten in days. Given his size of him, he may not have.

Gary shovelled a handful of fries into his mouth, then shoved his sleeves up and furiously scratched at his arms. His skin was covered in angry red lines. He chewed the fries quickly, then swallowed. "They're everywhere."

"Who?"

Gary continued to scratch at his arms, barely able to get the words out. "Insects. Everywhere. They're in the walls. They're under my skin. They got a nest inside my arm. It won't stop itching." While he spoke, he dug his nails into his arm until it bled. Blood still on his fingers, he grabbed his burger and took a bite.

Delusional parasitosis, thought Cooper. Or, Morgellons, perhaps. Some thought these conditions were physical, and others thought they were psychological. Either way, it didn't prevent him from being called as a witness; it would be up to a jury to decide if he was competent and of sound mind.

"Gary, you called me because Ewan Underwood told you he killed Rhett and Laurel. What did he say exactly?"

Gary's pupils tracked back and forth as he frantically searched the paper bag. His eyes turned rheumy, then he lifted his chin to look at Cooper. In a child-like voice, he asked, "I asked for a Happy Meal. Where's my toy?"

- CHAPTER 36 -

IT TOOK A WHILE for Cooper to win Gary's trust after turning up without a Happy Meal toy. She thought it best to tell him that there was a problem with the factory and that no one got a toy that day. He might take it badly if he thought the prison staff had singled him out.

He wiped his mouth with the back of his arm, leaving blood on his jaw and mayo on his arm.

"You promise my name won't be brought up?"

"I promise. You'll be known as Witness A in all official communication and during the trial. *If* there is a trial. It all depends on what you can tell me."

Gary played with the straw from his milkshake, his hands shaking. "Okay."

"Take a deep breath," Cooper told him. "Then tell me what happened."

With laboured breaths, he whispered, his mouth full of burger, "He'll kill me if he finds out."

That was true, but Cooper couldn't tell him that. "He won't find out. And I won't let anything happen to you."

"He was playing pool. By himself because no one will play with him except for Shiela."

"Who's Shiela?"

"This massive Aussie. That's not his real name; that's just what everyone calls him." Gary scratched the back of his head and stared at his knees. "Think he's called Darius or Demitrius. Something biblical, anyway. But, yeah, most don't want to play him 'cause if they lose, they'll owe him a ciggie, and if they win, he'll blow his top and they'll get a pool cue over their head. Or worse."

Cooper didn't want to know what *or worse* meant. She had a fair idea, though.

"I'm in my cell. It's right next to the pool table. I'm playing with the radio. It's a proper old one. You've got to tune it in old school like, none of that digital bollocks. Eventually, I get a good signal for Radio One by standing on the bed, touching the aerial with one hand and the window frame with the other. The news comes on and there's a bulletin about someone finding that lass's wallet."

"You mean Laurel Deacon?"

"Aye, her." Gary held a fry up to the light and examined it as if it may be poison. After a second, he popped it in his mouth. "Well, Underwood hears and he tells me to turn it up. I almost shat myself thinking he was gonna come in the cell like."

Cooper imagined Underwood's colossal frame and his shaggy black hair filling the doorway. He'd be as intimidating as hell.

"He listens to the bulletin then starts laughing like he's possessed."

Gary scratched the back of his hand. "Bloody insects."

Speaking of possessed, thought Cooper.

"He's laughing and laughing. Then he says, 'the idiots are looking in the wrong place.' Meaning you guys, the coppers. Meaning you're the idiots."

"Thank you, I gathered that." Cooper tried not to roll her eyes. If she hadn't wanted Gary's information, she'd have pointed out he was the idiot. After all, he was in prison because he'd hit someone on the head with a fire extinguisher over an argument about Eastenders.

"So then Shiela walks up and takes Underwood's pool cue, and I think it's all about to kick off. I'm about ready to hide under my bunk. But Shiela claps Underwood on the arm and asks where they should be looking."

Cooper leant forward, desperate to know where she'd find the missing cyclists.

"Underwood winks at him, and then he says, 'they're beyond Coquet Island.' 'Course, I didn't knaa where that was at first. I had to go to the library to find out. Then I called you."

Cooped blinked. Gloom filled her as she thought of Underwood dumping Rhett and Laurel's bodies at sea. She thought of their parents, Tamzin Campbell and Bruce Deacon. If they ever found their children's bodies, they'd be unrecognisable after marine damage. There'd be no saying goodbye face to face, no sense of closure.

Cooper heard Gary say something, but she couldn't make it out. It sounded like, "Bastard."

"Pardon?"

Gary chewed his straw. "Underwood's a bastard. He shouldn't 'ave done that to those kids."

Cooper didn't reply. She was wondering if Underwood's remark counted as a confession. Not officially, no. But in the eyes of a jury? Potentially. It was one inmate's word against the other. Would a court look more favourably on Gary – fidgety and unattractive, or on Underwood – terrifying but charismatic?

"Gary, I need you to listen carefully." Cooper adopted a soft expression and tried to hold the man's attention. "I believe you, but some people may not. They might automatically dismiss your claim because you're an inmate. They might think you're just saying this because there's something in it for you."

He looked at the bag of food, now empty save for some crumbs and grains of salt.

"There won't be any further perks for helping with the case. No reduced sentence or fancy gadgets for your cell. No day release. Do you understand?"

He nodded. "I knaa." He looked to mull over what was ahead of him. Readying himself, he said, "I'll sign the statement. All I want is anonymity."

- CHAPTER 37 -

COOPER SPENT ALL WEDNESDAY afternoon and evening talking to Keaton, Whyte, Martin and Boyd about what Witness A had told her. Martin and Boyd were quick to suggest getting a team of divers to Coquet Island, but Cooper and the others knew it would be pointless. They were killed over two months ago. If Witness A was telling the truth, their bodies could be anywhere now. For all Cooper knew, they'd already washed up on some desolate, isolated Scandinavian shore. As far as she was concerned, they were still pursuing a no-body murder.

She was about to head to Morrisons when she stopped by Fuller's desk for an update. Though for some reason, she craved cheap mince and onion pies, Cooper would do the right thing and fill her trolly with fruits and vegetables. She was planning a grilled peach and pecan salad for tomorrow evening, followed by butternut squash and mixed beans the following night for Family Friday. Realising both meals were vegan, she thought she'd better add a whole chicken to her shopping list. Atkinson would worry about her protein levels, and Julie would comment on how she couldn't be vegan if her life depended on it. Then she'd try and sound very worldly by talking about the Spanish diet when everyone knew she'd had most of her meals in Lanzarote in either Benji's, the bar she and Cooper's father owned, or the Irish Pub down the road.

"How's it going?" she asked Fuller.

Fuller shrugged. "Same shit, different day. Durham Police spoke to Cyrus Harding. He says he doesn't recall the photo being taken."

"And you believe—"

She was interrupted by Fuller's phone, which rang so loudly in the quiet room that Cooper jumped.

"That's Portia's PI," he said.

"Mind if I listen in?"

"Not at all." He answered the call and turned the speakerphone on.

Dorsey sounded both exhausted and excited. "I know where the photo was taken."

"Cyrus remembered, did he?"

Dorsey snorted. "No. I've been doing some digital detective work. The painting in the background is Harry Hall's Newminster. Took me bloody hours of scouring the internet to find the right picture. Do you know how many blooming paintings of horses are out there?"

"I can imagine."

"Fookin' millions. Managed to find the auction house that sold it and sweet-talked a lovely lady into telling me who bought it. I pretended I was a buyer and said I'd give her a finder's fee if the new owner would sell it to me."

Cooper was impressed. She raised her brows at Fuller, who said, "Nicely done."

"Yeah. Made up some cock and bull about Harry Hall being my great-great uncle of something. Anyway, long story short, it's in the lounge of the Northern Counties Club. It's an exclusive—"

"I've heard of it," Fuller said. "Some of the big wigs round here are members. Do you think our mysterious third male is a member?"

"Perhaps," Dorsey said. "Do you think they'd give us their client list?"

Fuller looked to Cooper. She shook her head. "I doubt it. Those sorts of establishments always boast of discretion."

"Who's that?" asked Dorsey.

"DCI Erica Cooper," Fuller told him. "And I agree. We'd need a warrant."

There was a pause, and then Dorsey said, "Leave it with me. I'll find a way in."

Cooper leant into the phone. "By becoming a member?"

She heard Dorsey laugh. "No. You think they'll believe a big, bald bastard like me wants to join some swanky private member's club? I look like a British Joe Rogan and sound like Liam Gallagher. Besides, they probably have rules about keeping the riff-raff out. To become a member, you'll need to be nominated by two other members, some bollocks like that."

Cooper tried to picture the man. She hadn't heard of Joe Rogan, so she imagined a bigger, balder Liam Gallagher instead.

"Like I said. Leave it with me. I'll find a way in."

"Legally?" asked Cooper, but Dorsey had already hung up.

THE INCIDENT ROOM WAS unusually quiet on Friday morning. A good sign. It meant officers and detectives were out chasing leads, confirming statements and talking to the public. There was no hum of computers, and the printer was switched off. Martin checked that Boyd still wanted to hang out that evening, then went to meet Keaton in the West End to follow up on a stalking case. Boyd poured Whyte a coffee and offered Cooper the same.

"No, thank you," she said.

Boyd picked up a stack of files and moved to the corner of the room to type reports.

The week had passed quickly. Cooper and Whyte spent the previous day at Durham Prison reviewing the finer details of Witness A's statement. Times, vernacular, everything. So far, the prosecution would rely on four key pieces of evidence. One, there was no proof of life. Two, Witness A heard Underwood confess. Three, Underwood admitted to stealing the bikes. And four, Dean and Kareem said they saw Underwood with Laurel. If

Atkinson could add some DNA to the mix, they'd have the bastard.

Whyte pulled out a chair. "You look ready to burst."

"A few weeks to go. You can't get rid of me just yet," she said.

"Is Tina looking forward being a big sister?"

Cooper was about to answer when a phone began chirping.

"I'll get it," Whyte said.

While Whyte talked, Cooper closed her eyes and softly rubbed her belly, looking forward to their Family Friday meal. Her baby was especially active that morning. She felt under and around the baby bump, wondering if the baby was stretching or playing keepy-up. She thought of Tina and pondered Whyte's question. Yes, Tina seemed very excited about the baby. Aside from suggesting names, she'd spend her own money on plush toys for the nursery and books to read to her little brother or sister. Perhaps things had worked out for the best; Tina could have all the love that came with a baby without the responsibility. She'd still get to live her life.

"Coop?"

Cooper opened her eyes.

Whyte covered the receiver and smiled. The gesture softened his sharp features. "You said you wanted one more bit of evidence. We might have it."

"DNA?" she asked hopefully.

"No. Not that good. But another inmate says they heard Underwood talking about Rhett and Laurel."

Cooper slid her chair across the room and picked up a phone. She pressed a button and joined the call.

"Sir, I've added DCI Cooper to the call. She's the senior investigating officer in the Rhett Campbell and Laurel Deacon investigation. I'm going to remain on the line."

There were a few seconds of silence, then a deep male voice said, "You called me *sir*. Ah divint think anyone's called me sir in me whole life."

"Can you tell me your name?" he asked.

"Archie."

"Okay, Archie. Tell us what happened."

There was a chance Witness A, Gary, had blabbed about his conversation with Cooper. She wondered if Archie was jumping on the bandwagon, trying to get a free meal out of her. She waited, but no demands came. Archie seemed more than willing to talk.

"I was in the barber's getting my hair cut."

"The barbers?" asked Whyte.

"Aye. It's a skills training thing. I applied but didn't get in. Apparently, I can't be trusted with scissors."

Cooper and Whyte covered their mouths, trying not to laugh.

"So, Big Phil's cutting my hair. He's deaf as a post. He won't put his hearing aid in, so he's no craic and can't hear a word I'm saying. Underwood's in at the same time getting a trim and shave from Prince Harry."

"Prince Harry?" asked Cooper.

"He's ginger, and he's called Harry. Not the wittiest nickname, but it works. Now Big Phil's not chatting on to me, so I listen in on Underwood. He's three chairs away, but we're the only ones in, and I've got mad good hearing. I'm like an alert dog or something. It's like a sixth sense." He paused. "Well, it's one of the five senses, but just boosted a bit. You know what I mean?"

"I understand," Whyte said. "What did Underwood say?"

"He said he ran into the cyclists at Hauxley. He said he knew straight away he was going to nick their bikes. He reckoned he could get good money for them. But after chatting to the pair and seeing the lass up close, he decided to have some fun."

Fun. For such a joyful word, it sent shivers up Cooper's spine.

"He offered to show them a badger sett nearby, and the pair left their bikes and followed him into the woods behind the caravan park. Once alone, he said he hit the bloke over the head with a rock. Knocked him clean out, apparently."

The thought made Cooper feel queasy. Saliva flooded her mouth. She swelled it down and tried to focus as Archie continued.

"The lass ran but... Maybe she was tired from riding her bike. Either way, Underwood caught her. He said he punched her in the head, knocking her out too. He dragged her back to where the bloke was lying and tied her up. Once she came to, she made him watch while he killed her boyfriend."

"Jesus." Whyte looked as peaky as Cooper felt. "Did he say how he killed Rhett?" asked Whyte, his voice trembling slightly.

"Said – Rhett, was it? – said he was face down, and he bashed the back of his head with the same rock until his skull caved in."

Taking a deep breath, Cooper asked, "What else?"

"He held the lass captive for a few days. Assaulted her multiple times a day. I can give you details, but – you're a woman – it might not be easy to listen to."

"None of this is easy to listen to," Cooper answered honestly. "But, I've done this job a long time, and I want to hear everything Underwood said."

While Archie talked, Cooper made notes, focusing on facts rather than emotions. She felt detached from the monologue as if she were watching from a distance as he described Underwood abusing Laurel in detail. The perversion of it turned her stomach. Cooper didn't speak, but she could sense Whyte's unease and Archie's need to keep talking, to relieve himself of the words he'd heard.

"At one point, a couple almost caught him."

Dean and Kareem.

"When he got sick of her, he took both bodies out to sea in a skiff he stole from a driveway in Amble. He said he weighed them down with scrap metal. Then, afterwards, he cleaned the boat and dumped it somewhere."

"Did he say where?" asked Cooper.

Archie laughed. "He might've done. But that was when Big Phil finished my hair, and I had to leave."

Cooper spent a few moments explaining to Archie – who would now be known as Witness B – that there would be nothing in it for him if he made an official statement. No rewards or reduced sentences. She said Whyte would type up everything he'd said so far, then come to speak to him to add any further details and have him sign a statement. Archie said he understood.

When they hung up, Cooper turned to Whyte. "I think one inmate dobbing on Underwood might be nothing more than a grudge. But two?"

"Two? That's either a conspiracy, or we're finally onto a winner."

- CHAPTER 38 -

A COLD WIND ICED the back of Cooper's neck as she walked across the car park. Spring may have been on its way, but that didn't mean anything in the northeast. Spring could bring sunshine and daffodils; it could equally bring sleet and snow. Right now, it smelled slightly of snow. Despite the weather, Cooper decided to keep her Braxton Hicks contractions at bay with a herbal tea and a short stroll to Tennessee's bench.

Cooper was an atheist. She didn't believe in higher powers or an afterlife, but still, she spoke to Tennessee as if he were there. She knew it was for her own comfort, but like many placebos, it worked. She chatted about the case, about Tina and the baby, and about seeing Hayley. When she'd finished her tea, Cooper walked around the biodiversity park and climbed to the top of the sundial. She checked the time on her watch and compared it to the shadow that pointed across a gravelly circle. Whyte should be back by now.

She met him at the entrance to HQ, and together, they ventured upstairs to meet Keaton in the incident room. After bringing her up to speed, they discussed Witness A and Witness B's statements.

"So both of them report Underwood saying he dumped the bodies at sea?" Keaton asked.

"Yeah. Witness A said *beyond Coquet Island*, but Witness B just said *at sea*," explained Cooper. "However, he specified that Underwood stole the skiff from Amble and Amble's the closest town to Coquet Island."

"I'd call that a match," said Keaton.

"Ditto," said Whyte.

Keaton tightened her ponytail. "We can see if any boats have been reported stolen. That would help."

"I'll sort it," said Whyte. "The other thing I like about this is how Witness B said Underwood was almost caught by a couple. We didn't release anything about Dean and Kareem seeing Underwood and Laurel at Druridge. If the witness fabricated the story, that's one hell of a coincidence."

"I agree," said Keaton. "Could we follow this further and get more witnesses? We could talk to these Shiela and Prince Harry characters."

Cooper pursed her lips and moved them from side to side while she thought. "Potentially. But we have to be very careful. If we speak to Shiela, he'd easily work out who the witness was, same for Prince Harry. I can't risk having the witnesses hurt or worse. They've trusted us with their safety."

"Snitches get stitches," Keaton said.

"Exactly." Cooper gave her a pointed look before turning to Whyte. "Did you find anything else out at the prison?"

"Yeah. I spoke to a few guards to see if the witnesses were the sort to devise a scheme to frame Underwood. Witness A made it clear Underwood's a dangerous character. If he's charged with murder, he might be moved to a different wing or over to Frankland."

"And?"

Whyte shook his head. "They move in different circles. The pair are never seen together."

Cooper struggled to her feet and rubbed her back. "Right then. Time I update Nixon. Wish me luck."

THE DOOR TO NIXON'S office was open. Cooper knocked on the door frame, causing Nixon to look up.

"Ah, Cooper. Come in. Take a seat."

She padded into the room and tried to pull the chair facing his desk from under the table. It was heavy, and the metal legs seemed to stick to the floor.

"Here, take mine." Nixon rose to his feet and offered her his ergonomic swivel chair.

Cooper didn't have to be told twice. "You're feeling generous."

"You seem shocked."

"Generous enough to fork out for a new DI?" It was worth a shot; shy bairns got nowt.

He didn't say no, but he folded his arms and stared at her disapprovingly, which was practically the same thing.

"I hope you're here because you have news," he said, changing the subject. "Hampshire's CC won't let it drop. They want a name. Someone has to pay for what happened to those kids."

Cooper crossed her legs at the ankles and played with her bracelet, running the links through her thumb and index finger as if she were counting rosaries. *What happened to those kids.* Nixon's words repeated in her mind while she visualised what Witness B told her. She could see Rhett and Laurel trusting the charismatic Underwood, feeling the back of her head twinge as she thought of the rock smashing into Rhett's skull. Nausea began to creep up her throat as she remembered what Laurel had been through. As someone who had been held captive before, she didn't have to imagine her terror; she'd felt it for herself. Her attacker hadn't sexually assaulted her, but he had stripped her naked, and the memory felt like a clamp around her brain that she'd never get rid of.

"Cooper?"

"Sorry, sir. I was somewhere else." Cooper pulled her shoulders back. "We have witnesses. Four of them. Two are a couple from Bedlington who recognised Underwood when they saw him being taken into the magistrates' court. They think they saw him with Laurel in the woods around Druridge Bay Country Park. They were mucky as if

239

they'd been camping or sleeping rough. They described them both as having dirty hands and muddy knees. Laurel was heavily made up with false nails and eyelashes. Underwood seems to have a fetish for women who wear a lot of make-up; his wife and victims all have a similar appearance."

Nixon lowered his eyes while he listened and then nodded for her to continue.

"The other two witnesses are inmates from Durham. They both report overhearing Underwood confess to Rhett and Laurel's murders. Elliot Whyte checked with some guards, and whilst the witnesses may have grudges against Underwood, it's unlikely that they are working together. Witness A is willing to testify that Underwood said we were searching for the bodies in the wrong place and that we should be searching beyond Coquet Island."

"He dumped them at sea?"

"It seems likely, sir. Witness B overheard Underwood saying that he murdered Rhett and kept Laurel captive for several days before stealing a boat from Amble and taking them out to sea."

"Physical evidence?" asked Nixon.

"Their possessions. Underwood admits to stealing their bikes, and some of their belongings were found at a house on Middleton Street where his wife and children live. Other than that, we have nothing.

Nixon signalled for Cooper to stand; their conversation was almost over. "It's good enough for me," he said. "Charge Ewan Underwood with the murder of Rhett Campbell and Laurel Deacon."

She stood and smoothed her shirt over her stomach. "Yes, sir."

The prosecution would have a tough job securing a conviction. Murder charges without a body were incredibly rare, but they weren't impossible. There would be plenty of time before the trial to gather more evidence. Hopefully, something concrete would turn up, something guaranteed to secure a guilty verdict.

"Hopefully, that will get the chief constable off my back."

At the door, Cooper turned. "What does he have on you?"

"Excuse me?"

"Hampshire's CC. You told me you owed him a favour, but I've never known you to be the sort to worry about replaying a favour. I reckon there's more to it."

Nixon frowned. "Do you now?"

"You said he's from up here – a Geordie ex-pat. Are you the reason he moved down south?"

"Quite the detective, aren't you?" Nixon's expression was part annoyance, part admiration. He was impressed, but it killed him.

Cooper smirked. "I try."

He growled, then shook his head in resignation. "I suppose I can trust you to be discrete. I'm not proud of this. That bastard and I were up for the same promotion, and he beat me to it. As payback, I slept with his wife."

Cooper's eyes widened, and she left without saying a word. On the plus side, she was no longer visualising the horrific deaths of the two young cyclists. On the downside, she'd accidentally imagined Nixon having sex. She didn't know what was worse.

- CHAPTER 39 -

OLIVER MARTIN PAUSED ON the pavement of his new street. His belongings were piled into a pyramid of cardboard boxes; having never moved house before, he was surprised at how much stuff he'd accumulated over the years. He'd always liked Jesmond and was thrilled to be moving to the vibrant, leafy suburb filled with bars and restaurants.

Houses in Jesmond were expensive to buy and to let. He was grateful that Whyte gave him first dibs on being his new flatmate. The sun peaked from behind a cloud, warming his face. The door to the neighbouring terrace house opened and two young girls in crisp, white taekwon-do doboks ran to their car, chased by their father. Martin huffed as he picked up the first box and carried it to the front door. He rang the bell and heard Whyte's feet jogging down the stairs to welcome him.

"Hey, roomie," beamed Whyte. He slapped Matin on the back and took the box from his arms. "Here, let me give you a hand."

It took them twenty minutes to move Martin's things to his room. By the time they were done, Martin's arms were burning, sweat seeping through the grey marl t-shirt he wore.

"These are your keys," Whyte said, handing him a keyring with two Yale keys. "Follow me. I'll give you the tour."

Whyte showed him the kitchen first. It featured pale wooden cabinets and an oven that looked older than he was. A back door led to a fire escape and two parking spaces at the rear of the property. Though the kitchen was clean, it smelled different to the one at his parent's place. He was used to the scent of pine; Whyte was clearly a citrus man. The combined living and dining room was spacious, with a leather couch and wide-screen television. A dining table with six chairs stood next to a bookcase.

"I cleared you a shelf," he said.

"Thanks," said Martin, wondering what he'd put there. A family photograph or some of his comics, perhaps. "But I think you're forgetting something."

Whyte counted on his fingers while going through a mental checklist. "You've signed the contract, I showed you the gas safety certificates, showed you where the fire extinguisher is, gave you your keys..."

"Beer," Martin said. "You forgot it's beer o'clock. Moving's thirsty work. Time to show me my new local."

Less than ten minutes later, Martin was in the nearest pub, nodding in approval. The Lonsdale was situated next door to West Jesmond Metro Station. The beer was reasonable, the pool tables well-maintained, and the staff friendly. What more could he need?

The bar began to fill as the afternoon turned to early evening, the clientele ranging from eighteen-year-old students to old-timers in their eighties. Some dressed casually in jeans and jumpers, others dressed to impress in dapper suits or tiny dresses. Large screens broadcast the football, with half the room cheering Newcastle and half the room not giving a monkey's.

"That's one good thing about living round here," said Whyte. "There are so many people from out of town. I could sit here in my Sunderland shirt and no one would bat an eyelid."

Newcastle played Southampton at St. Mary's. At the seventy-ninth minute, Saint-Maximin put one past the Saint's goalie to put the Magpies in the lead.

"Get in," cheered Martin.

"Bollocks," said Whyte.

"Speaking of Southampton—"

"No." Whyte cut him off and pointed a finger in his face. "Don't even think about talking about the case. New flatmate rule. No work talk outside of work."

By the bar, a woman with an hourglass figure in a tight-fitting top and flared skirt laughed with friends. Her brown hair was pinned into Victory rolls, her plump lips painted bright red. She caught

Martin's eye, not because he was attracted to her, but because he knew her.

"Hey, that's April. Keaton's missus."

"So it is," said Whyte, looking over. "Wonder if she's around."

Martin jumped from his seat and weaved a path through the crowd. "Good to see you, April. It's been ages. How're things?"

She looked awkward, smiling nervously. "Fine, I guess."

"Paula out tonight?"

"I wouldn't know."

That seemed a strange answer. "You two have a fight? Sorry. Is that a personal question? I've had a few pints. Tell me to mind my own business."

Martin wasn't drunk, but he was definitely beyond tipsy. April looked confused. She turned her head for a moment and looked to be considering her response.

"A fight?" she asked. "Did Paula not tell you?"

"Tell me what?"

April bit her ruby lip. "We broke up. She threw me out."

Martin's jaw dropped. "What? But she adores you."

"She does. Or did. I dunno. I know I messed up, though." April shrugged and picked her drink up from the bar, walking away to rejoin her friends.

"Wait," Martin called. He caught her back up. "When was this?"

"Months ago. Not long before your colleague was killed."

Martin returned to his seat and sat silently next to Whyte, trying to process what he'd just heard. It didn't make sense. For months Keaton had been putting on a front. When they asked her about her new home, April and Riley, she acted like everything was fine. As if they were a happy little family.

"Come on," he said, standing back up. "We need a taxi."

"Where are we going?" asked Whyte.

"Willington Quay."

"HOW COULD WE NOT have noticed?" Whyte sat in the back of the taxi with his head in his hands, each speed bump forcing his palms into his eye sockets.

"She's a professional. She doesn't bring her drama to work."

Whyte raised his head. "It's not drama."

"I know that. You know that. But this is Paula Keaton. The Pitbull. You know what she's like. Offence is the best defence, never back down, never show weakness. That's not an attitude she can turn on and off."

Whyte thought back over the past few months. Had they missed something? Was she quieter than usual? Moodier? He couldn't recall. Whyte joined the team in the spring of last year, coming on board at the same time as Boyd to help with a double murder involving the head of a crime family. It had been a long process trying to get on Cooper's good side. Entirely his own doing, he admitted.

Still, it was bearable because the others had been so welcoming. Keaton especially. From the get-go, she treated him as she treated everyone else, by which he meant she teased him mercilessly.

The taxi pulled up outside Keaton's home. The sky was dark, and one of the street lights was out. Another blinked tiredly as if its bulb would die at any moment.

Martin hesitated by the door. "Are we doing the right thing? She's going to hate us for turning up like this."

Whyte rapped his knuckles on the door. "We're her friends. Would you rather she was angry with us or that she continued suffering alone?"

When the door opened, Whyte couldn't believe his eyes. He hardly recognised Keaton.

She looked thinner. Weaker. A stained, oversized t-shirt hung from her shoulders. Keaton never wore her hair down, but she did now, and it was greasy and unkempt. Puffy skin around her eyes showed she'd been crying.

Confusion and embarrassment painted her face. She quickly hid it, correcting her posture and pulling her hair back. She forced a smile. "What are you two losers doing here? Let me guess, you need some real muscle to help with the big move?"

She flexed her biceps.

Whyte and Martin glanced uncomfortably at each other. Martin had known her the longest. He was shy and clumsy with his words at times, but it was best he tried to take the lead. Whyte nodded at him.

"We know," he said.

Two words. That was all it took for Keaton's facade to falter. Tears rushed to her eyes, her body
shaking.

"You should leave," she said, sobbing. "It's not a
good time."

Martin stepped over the threshold and wrapped
his arms around her. Whyte followed and did the
same. "We're not going anywhere."

- CHAPTER 40 -

THE BATHROOM SMELLED OF coconut shampoo and deodorant. Cooper stared in the mirror while Atkinson smoothly ran hair clippers over her scalp.

"There you go," he said once he'd finished.

Atkinson bent to pick up the towel from the floor and shook the tiny hairs into the bin. Cooper admired her fresh buzzcut, running her fingers and palms over her head.

"Thank you," she said. She was about to say it looked great, but a contraction caused her to wince.

Her partner's face lit up, and he ran along the upstairs corridor, searching for their grab bag.

"False alarm," she called after him. "I'm getting bloody sick of these."

"They must be annoying."

"Annoying? Try painful."

"Are you sure you don't want to start your maternity now?" He looked at her with admiration and concern.

Cooper applied toothpaste to her toothbrush. "Not really. I'll just be sitting at home bored all day. There are still a few weeks to go. I'd rather have the time after the little one's here."

He kissed her head. "That makes sense. Well, if you need me, I'll be in Penrith helping Cumbria recover evidence from a multi-vehicle accident."

"Rather you than me," Cooper said dryly. "And if you need me, I'll be interrogating a murderer all day."

Atkinson returned the grab bag to the cupboard. Laughing, he said, "Rather you than me."

KEATON SEEMED IN GOOD spirits when Cooper picked her up from HQ. She played with the radio, switching between nineties dance and rock ballads.

Cooper slapped her hand away from the touchscreen display. "Turn November Rain off at your peril," she warned.

"But Fat Boy Slim—"

"Fat Boy nothing. I'll dump you at the side of the road if you skip the mighty Guns N' Roses."

Keaton laughed. "You're feisty today; I like it. Hope that bairn of yours inherits it. You remind me of this bad bitch who used to play for Wasps. She was a tiny thing, not very strong, but she was fast, and she could cut you down with a stare."

Cooper hadn't thought much about what traits she hoped her child would inherit. Atkinson's height, book smarts, kindness and empathy were all great attributes. Perhaps she'd pass on her logic and determination. Worst case scenario, she'd pass on her cooking skills, and Atkinson would pass on his dance moves.

They stopped at the Claypath Deli and bought two croissant croque-monsieurs from a couple with big smiles and friendly demeanours. They drank tea and ate their breakfasts on wooden seats in a small garden area out the back. Cooper described her weekend; Keaton said she met up with Martin and Whyte but didn't elaborate.

As they drove the short distance to HMP Durham, they went over the case. At the moment, the prosecution would rely on four key events: Underwood being in possession of Rhett and Laurel's bike and bags, Dean and Kareem's testimony that they saw Underwood with Laurel at Druridge, and the two anonymous witnesses whose stories both suggested Rhett and Laurel were dumped at sea. They would also introduce Underwood's previous convictions, but only those where the MO remained the same. He'd shown a habit of targeting couples, robbing them and assaulting the women.

The defence had no alibi. They'd argue the lack of physical evidence and try to discredit the witnesses. Easily done when your witnesses were convicted felons.

Cooper parked the car and stopped the engine. "You ready?" she asked Keaton.

"I'm full of carbs," she replied. "I'm ready for anything. Now let's see if we can get owt from this bastard."

TAMZIN CAMPBELL GOT OFF the bus at Havelock Road, opposite the SeaCity Museum in Southampton, and walked north around Watts Park to Bruce Deacon's office. She pushed the door and a small bell chimed. The place was empty, so she took a moment to look at his available lettings. Most were three-bedroom flats catering to students in the Highfield area. Others were family homes and holiday lets. For a few minutes, Tamzin forgot about her troubles and found herself staring at holiday villas, fantasising about a week in Puglia, a fortnight in Antigua, or a long weekend in Bruges. *Fool,* she told herself while gazing at a pale blue beach house surrounded by white sands and lush palm trees. *You can't even cope with a flight to Newcastle. As if you could go to Italy.*

"Tamzin, is everything all right?"

Bruce emerged from a back room. His dark hair was slicked back, and he wore a tailored suit that complimented his long limbs. As someone whose husband had passed – not that she missed the good-for-nothing low life – she admired Bruce for being a single dad all those years. Balancing his businesses and raising a young girl without a woman must have been hard. She admired him.

She dug in her coat pocket and pulled out a handkerchief to fiddle with. The action calmed her like a security blanket. "Yes. Well, no. It's never all right, is it? Have you heard?"

Bruce's tanned face hardened. He looked older than his years, more tired.

"No. Not that." Tamzin felt guilty. "They haven't found them. Sorry if I made you think it was over."

"I'm a fool," he said. "To keep wishing for a happy ending after all this time."

"You're not a fool." Tamzin touched his arm. "We're all wishing for the best. But I can't bring myself to believe it. I think it's time I stopped getting my hopes up. It'll only be worse... In the end."

Bruce dipped his chin. "You're right. So, what's the news?"

"Denise called."

Tamzin liked Denise Oswald, their family liaison officer. She had a calming influence and a sympathetic ear. Under different circumstances, Tamzin could picture her and Denise as friends, visiting coffee shops to discuss what books they'd read or films they'd seen.

"They're going to charge Ewan Underwood with Rhett and Laurel's murders today."

The tall man sighed. "But..."

"It's called a no-body murder, Bruce."

"That means the police are convinced they're dead?"

Tamzin gave a weak smile. "Sometimes I think we're the only ones to think otherwise. Denise reckons it'll help bring us closure. I'm not so sure.

I know it's naive, but I sit at home staring at the door, willing Rhett to walk through it. I just want my little boy back."

She wanted a hug, wanted him to wrap his arms around her. Only in a platonic way, but it would help. She was single, her son was missing and her other son wasn't one for physical contact. She missed it. Laurel was always so affectionate. She always greeted Tamzin with a hug or kiss on the cheek. She'd even call her Mama Campbell sometimes. A tear rolled down her cheek. She hadn't just lost a son; she'd lost her soon-to-be daughter-in-law. This was a cruel, cruel world.

"Maybe Denise is right." Bruce loosened his tie and looked to the floor. "It's been months. As much as I can't stomach thinking of Laurel as de—" he couldn't quite say *dead*. "As much as I hate to think of Laurel in the past tense, perhaps it is time to draw a line under this nightmare. I can't be in limbo forever. It's time to mourn and move on."

- CHAPTER 41 -

UNDERWOOD LOOKED BOTH DETECTIVES up and down as if they amused him. He looked paler than Cooper remembered; spending twenty-three hours a day indoors had that effect on people. His eyes were like coal, and crusty blood coated his nostrils. Hopefully, someone had given the scumbag a quick one-two on the nose.

"Mr Underwood, this is DS Paula Keaton. I don't think you've met."

His lip curled. "I've not had the pleasure," he said, giving her a once over.

Underwood sat on a plastic seat in front of a wooden table in a small, breeze-block interview room. He wore a surly expression and standard-issue prison uniform, indicating he'd been denied enhanced status and the right to wear his own clothing.

"I doubt this will shock you," Keaton told him, pulling out a chair for Cooper, "but you aren't my type." She sat, rested her forearms on the table and leaned towards him. "From what I hear, you like your women dolled up and non-consenting."

Something flashed in Underwood's eyes. His obsidian irises burned with something Cooper couldn't quite read. Anger, or something more thrilling. Did he see Keaton as a sparring partner, someone to have a spot of back-and-forth fun with?

"Truth be told," he said, turning his eyes to the DCI. "I sometimes have a bit of a fetish for pregnant women."

"That's enough," growled Cooper. She didn't know if he was trying to shock her or charm her, but either way, she wouldn't allow him to disarm her. "This is a murder investigation." She unfolded a map of Northumberland that included Holy Island, Coquet Island and the Farne Islands. "You killed that young couple. Where did you bury them?"

"I can't help ya," he said.

"Give over," smirked Keaton. "We have witnesses."

"Did these so-called witnesses actually witness me kill anyone?"

The two women faltered long enough for Underwood to know their answer.

"Yeah, I didn't think so. Forgive me for not trembling in me boots."

Keaton flicked a look under the table. "They're not boots. They're trainers, and crappy ones at that." She slid her chair back far enough to plant her pair of men's motorcycle boots by Bruno Marc on the table. "These are boots."

"Very nice."

"You know what else would be nice?" Keaton didn't wait for him to answer. "Being released before your little girl forgets you exist. In fact, if you want to be released at all, you'll need to demonstrate remorse. Tell us where their bodies are."

He leaned back and folded his arms. A few strands of dirty brown hair fell in his face. He blew them away. "I would if I could."

"Don't you want to see your daughter again?"

"Of course I do."

"Then tell us. Bruce Deacon will never get to see his daughter again. It's time to put him out of his misery."

His black eyes rolled dramatically. "You two are boring me. Always the same old questions." He placed his palm over his mouth and pretended to yawn.

Cooper shifted her weight in her seat. She was uncomfortable. "If they're where I think they are, they'll turn up eventually."

Cindy didn't.

The little voice in her head caught Cooper unawares. Her best friend throughout her teens had been pushed into the Tyne and was never seen again. While many bodies bloat and make their way to the surface, not all of them do. If Underwood secured the bodies in a container that was resistant to water and marine life damage, they could remain hidden until Cooper was long gone.

Cooper decided to change the subject; she'd revisit where he hid the bodies later. "Let's talk about why you kept Laurel alive for a few days."

"I didn't."

"You killed her the same time you killed Rhett?"

"Oh, here we gan. No, that's not what I said, and you know it."

Cooper tried to hide her pleasure. She liked that she could wind him up like he'd done to her. "We have not one but two witnesses who saw you in the woods just beyond the sand dunes at Druridge Bay."

"I never met Laurel."

"You talked to them about their dog."

Underwood shrugged. "I like dogs. More than most people. Definitely more than most coppers. And if I met someone with a dog, I likely talked to them about it. But, like I said, I never met the lass."

Cooper was about to press him when Underwood wagged a finger at her. "Hang on a minute. How about I ask you a question? If two people supposedly saw me with this Laurel bird, why didn't she ask for help?"

"Could be many reasons," Cooper answered. "Perhaps she thought you could overpower both her and the couple."

He took that as a compliment, flexing his upper arms and lifting his shirt to reveal rippling abdominals.

"Put it away," warned Cooper.

"Alreet, I'll give you that one. I could take on three at once; it wouldn't be the first time. Let's have another one of your theories."

"If Laurel didn't know Rhett was dead, she'd have put up with your bullshit in the hope of not endangering him further."

Underwood met Cooper's gaze and seemed to look straight into her soul, into the depths of her insecurities. "If Laurel didn't know Rhett was dead?" he said, repeating her words back to her. "To be fair, you divint knaa he's dead."

Keaton leaned across so she was in his eye line instead of Cooper. "Only because you won't tell us where their bodies are. But regardless, we can show no proof of life, and that'll be good enough for the jury."

"Come on, one more theory. This is fun."

Cooper was going to tell him to get stuffed, that she wouldn't play his game, but Keaton threw another theory his way.

"Maybe she had Stockholm syndrome?"

"Mebies you're clutching at straws?"

Cooper's uterus contracted; it hurt enough for her to moan aloud.

"Boss? You okay?" Keaton got to her feet.

"I'm fine. I'm fine," insisted Cooper. "Bloody false labour. Give me a minute."

Though the breeze block room was chilly, sweat trickled down her back. She could smell whatever was being served in the staff canteen and as much as she wanted to get out of there and away from Underwood, she had a job to finish. "This is your last opportunity to help us, Ewan, Mr Underwood. Tell us the truth now, and it could influence your sentence."

More pain radiated through her.

The suspect's lips hung apart as if the answers to Cooper's questions were about to spill out. Instead, he said, "You divint look so good. I mean, I knaa this is your job, but we can take a break." He gestured around him at the tiny claustrophobic room. "I'm not gannin' anywhere."

"I said I'm fine," Cooper snapped. "It's just Braxton Hicks contractions." Another shudder of intense pain caused her to double over and groan. She gripped the table's edge until her knuckles turned white. "No. Not false labour. Real labour. Shit."

- CHAPTER 42 -

"GUARD," CALLED UNDERWOOD. HE stepped back from the table to give Cooper space.

A confused prison officer entered and took in Cooper's pained appearance.

"What did he do to you?" he asked.

"I didn't do owt, ya daft sod. She's in labour."

All the things that could possibly go wrong clouded Cooper's mind. She thought of tearing and blood loss. She wondered if the baby was breech or if she'd need a caesarian. What if there was a problem with the anaesthetic and she died never knowing her baby? What if they were born with the cord around their neck?

What if, what if, what if.

She'd been so caught up in the excitement of having another child that she didn't stop to consider the dangers. Now the anxieties shrouded her so thickly she could barely breathe.

"Call an ambulance," Keaton instructed the guard.

"Calm the hell down," Cooper said, talking to herself as much as anyone. She leaned over the table, letting her arms take some of her weight. "We have plenty of time. Keaton, you can drive my car." She turned to Underwood. "Ewan Underwood, I am officially charging you with the murders of..."

Underwood jumped backwards, avoiding Cooper's amniotic fluid as it flooded from the in-seam of her trousers.

"...the murders of Rhett Campbell and Laurel Deacon."

Keaton looked at the liquid seeping across the floor. "I thought you said we had time?"

"I thought we did," said Cooper.

"That baby's in a hurry," Underwood said, his back against the wall. "Was the same with my third. It's called precipitous labour, and if it makes you feel better, it happens in around one in fifty births."

Cooper scowled at him. "It doesn't."

"Just trying to help. I can list the complications if you like."

Keaton held up both hands. She pointed one at Underwood. "You, keep your mouth shut. And you." She pointed at the guard. "Call an ambulance."

The guard stuttered and looked around for help.

"The number's nine-nine-nine," Underwood said, enjoying himself.

"I know the number, smart arse." The guard rubbed his hands together and made the call.

263

When he hung up, he shook his head. "Bloody government. There're none available."

Keaton was furious. "What do you mean *none*?"

Underwood laughed. "As in zero, nought, nil, nowt."

"Get him out of here before I punch him in the face." Cooper felt as if her entire torso was tightening. As if she wore a Slendertone belt on its maximum setting with no way of turning it off.

The guard did as instructed.

"Come on," she told Keaton. "Back to Plan A. We'll take my car."

Keaton helped Cooper to the main entrance, where curious eyes followed their every move. As they signed out and exited the building, they were shocked to see flashing blue lights in all directions.

"Uh oh," Keaton said.

"Oh, fucking hell," Cooper said.

The road was closed in both directions. Some tosser over both the alcohol and speed limits had hit a pedestrian. The man died instantly, and officers scoured the ground looking for evidence. The driver had taken off in the opposite direction and hit a tree at the top of the road. He was dead too.

A PC with a regretful face brought them up to speed. "The road's blocked. We can't get any vehicles out until his car's been towed. How about we walk you down this way, and then one of the panda cars can take you to the hospital?"

Cooper wondered how many of the contractions she'd dismissed earlier in the day were actually real. It didn't matter now; she was in the throws of labour whether she liked it or not. "Okay," she said breathlessly. "Let's go."

They'd only taken two steps when another contraction hit her, this one more painful and prolonged than any she'd experienced with Tina. Cooper felt a terrifying urge to push.

She grabbed ahold of Keaton. The last time she'd felt helplessness like this was when she saw Tennessee's mutilated body. "We don't have time," she cried. "The baby's coming now."

COOPER STARED AROUND THE white subway tiles covering the walls of the prison medical room. There were twenty beds in the twenty-four-hour in-patient suit. As a doctor hurried to close a curtain around her, Cooper counted the empty beds. Prison, it appeared, was the only place in the country where you could see a GP or get a hospital bed without waiting six weeks to two years.

Not now, she told herself. Now wasn't the time to internally rank about the state of things. She was about to give birth. In a prison, no less. As a Northumbria Police DCI, she'd never live it down.

Keaton and a nurse helped Cooper remove her clothes and put on a flimsy gown that covered her front but was open at the back.

"Call Justin," she said.

Keaton held up her mobile. "Done. He's on his way."

"Call my mum, too,"

B BASKERVILLE

"Okay. Justin's coming from Penrith, but I can ask Whyte to bring her down."

Cooper shook her head. "No. Not here. I need her to go to mine and be there for Tina coming home from school."

"Gotcha." Keaton took Cooper's phone, so she could retrieve the number and left the room to make the call.

The nurse stood at the end of the bed. She was pretty, with long auburn hair secured in a bun. With round, chestnut eyes and a slim waist, Cooper would put money on the inmates injuring themselves on purpose just to be in the same room as her.

"We don't have stirrups here, I'm afraid. Being a male prison, there's no need for them. Now I think of it, we don't have speculums either. But if you butterfly your knees open, I'll try to get a look at your cervix, see how dilated you are."

What else didn't they have? Cooper lowered her knees to either side. The room was cool and the breeze felt pleasant on her clammy skin. "Tell me you have pain relief."

"We have Entonox." She attached a mouthpiece to a gas canister and handed it to Cooper. "Use it sparingly. That's our last canister, and we don't know how long we're going to be here."

That wasn't what Cooper wanted to hear.

266

- CHAPTER 43 -

THE TERRACED HOUSE ON Latimer Street, Tynemouth, could only be described as organised chaos. Organised because it was spotless and sterile, thanks to Julie's obsessive cleaning. And chaos because every surface was covered in gifts and cards.

Atkinson picked up a card from the mantlepiece and read the greeting. "Who's Rebecca?" he asked.

"Becky the Techie. She's a cyber wiz, works out of Byker."

He closed the card and admired the cute picture of a baby elephant under the words: *It's a boy!*

That very boy lay in Cooper's arms. He was four days old and perfect in every way. Cooper, on the other hand, was far from over the trauma. During her rapid labour, her body hadn't had time to adapt. As a result, her pelvis had partly dislocated. Without an epidural, she passed out from the pain. When she awoke, her baby was wrapped in flocculant towels that smelled lavender. She remembered the guard bursting in and covering his eyes as he shouted that the road was clear. Her baby was taken by car to the neonatal unit while an ambulance rushed to get Cooper to surgery. It was another twenty-four hours before she'd get to hold him. She wasn't sure she'd ever be able to fully articulate the relief she'd felt at that moment.

When they'd returned home, both Cooper and Atkinson were utterly overwhelmed. They'd assumed parenting would be like riding a bike, but they were wrong. Atkinson had two sons, twin boys, studying at Edinburgh University; Cooper had a fifteen-year-old. But having a baby again after all that time had been more difficult than she'd imagined. The baby didn't take to breastfeeding like Tina had, and Cooper had to learn to express. Sometimes it felt like she couldn't even change his nappy correctly.

There was a noise as Tina arrived home. Her steps were accompanied by a thump-thump of crutches. The night after Cooper gave birth, Tina played in the season's penultimate match. She landed badly, twisting her knee and rupturing her anterior cruciate ligament. She'd miss the final game, the one that would decide if the Sharks were league champions.

Tina dumped her bag and came straight to Cooper and the baby. She smiled at him as he gripped her little finger. "May I?"

"Go ahead."

Tina scooped him up and carefully sat on the sofa, wincing as she swung her injured leg up. "I can't get over how tiny he is."

"You were that small once. Smaller, in fact."

Tina's smile softened into a pensive expression. Her eyes lost all expression. Cooper signalled to Atkinson to give them a moment.

"What is it?"

In a parallel universe, Tina would have been due to give birth this week too.

Tina wrinkled her nose. "Nothing."

Thinking netball might be a more accessible subject, Cooper said, "It must be frustrating, having to hobble around on those things."

"I don't mind the crutches. I'm just pissed – sorry – that I won't be healed in time for the next match."

ACL injuries took a notoriously long time to heal. It would be a miracle of science if Tina was fit by the end of the month.

"The coach's going to put some of us forward for the county team. I guess that doesn't include me anymore."

Poor Tina. She'd had such a rough run of things. Between an absent father, a sick mother, school bullies, and a miscarriage, it was a wonder she wasn't a complete wreck. Now her only real hobby was in jeopardy.

"There's something else," Cooper said. "I'm a detective. I can tell these things," she added with what she hoped was a wry smile. "But you know me. You don't have to talk about anything you don't want to. Are you thinking about how things might have turned out?"

Tina stared at a blank television. "Sort of. But it's okay. Really, it is." She looked to be chewing her words over. Eventually, she said, "It's Josh. He wants us to... You know."

"And you're not ready?"

"God, no. Never again."

Cooper didn't know if Tina was being serious, but she appreciated that she'd opened up. As she pushed herself to her feet, she realised she needed another painkiller. She took her baby back and kissed Tina's head through her bushy hair. "Stay strong. If he loves you, he'll wait."

KEATON RANG THE DOORBELL but didn't wait for anyone to answer. "Coming through," she declared, wrapping her hulking arms around Atkinson.

He gasped as she let go, rubbing his ribs.

The rest of the tribe followed Keaton: Whyte, Martin and Boyd.

She, Martin and Boyd made a beeline for the infant, surrounding his bassinet, cooing. Whyte approached Cooper and gave her a bag containing two ginormous rib eye steaks.

"Everyone always buys stuff for the bairn. Figured you two might need an iron boost."

Cooper burst into tears. "Oh, my God. Sorry. Ignore me. I'm just—"

"Enjoy. And don't apologise. You just gave birth in a prison. That's pretty damn..."

"Badass," Tina said.

"Exactly," Whyte said. "Now, are you going to introduce us?"

Cooper stood. She felt faint, exhausted and a little frightened. Still, she was pleased the team dropped by.

"Everyone, meet Daniel Benjamin Cooper." She reached into the small woven crib and touched Danny's foot.

Keaton slung her arm over Martin's shoulder. "Daniel? As in?"

"As in Jack Tennessee Daniel." Cooper's tears continued to stream down her face. It was Tina's idea to name him after Tennessee, and she couldn't resist.

"And Benjamin was your father's name?" asked Keaton.

"That's right."

Martin asked if he could hold Danny. Cooper saw no reason why not. "Just support his head." The young man was a natural, holding the baby just right. Danny whimpered for a moment, then made happy noises. Cooper, Boyd and Keaton all shared the same look.

"What?" asked Martin when he noticed.

"Are you feeling broody?" Keaton teased.

Martin didn't look up; he was entirely captivated by the infant. "A bit," he admitted. "But not till I'm proper old, like in my thirties."

Keaton slapped him round the back of the head. "Hand him over. My turn. I practically delivered him."

That wasn't entirely true; Cooper wasn't the only one to pass out during her labour.

271

Boyd started to chuckle, then tried to disguise it as a sneeze.

"What's so funny?" Martin asked, taking her hand.

She had that worried expression she often wore as if saying the wrong thing may get her hurt.

"It's okay," Martin told her quietly. "You're among friends. I'm sure we'll find it funny too."

She took a deep breath and looked at Cooper. "I just thought it was humorous how you're a detective chief inspector and your baby's called DB Cooper."

Cooper didn't get it. But she hoped her baby didn't share a name with a character from a Netflix show or the lead singer in a pop group.

Atkinson, still keeping his distance in case Keaton hugged him again, widened his eyes. "DB Cooper! I hadn't even thought of that."

"Will someone tell me who DB Cooper is before I hit you all with one of Tina's crutches?"

Boyd took Danny, holding him close. "DB Cooper spent forty-five years on the FBI's most wanted list. He's a cult hero. He hijacked a plane, extorted over two hundred grand and parachuted somewhere over southwest Washington. He was never caught."

"So, you're telling me that not only was my baby born in prison, but he also shares his name with one of the most wanted men in history?" Cooper rubbed her head in despair.

"Badass," said Tina.

ONCE EVERYONE HAD A turn holding Danny. Atkinson made them all cups of tea and handed out plates of Swiss roll. He fed Danny his bottle and looked at him with such a tender expression that Cooper found it hard to watch.

"Almost forgot," said Keaton.

She handed Cooper a pile of cards.

"From work."

Cooper opened the first one. It was from Nixon. He wished her well and told her to take all the time she needed. Another card was from Neil Fuller. He said he had news, but it could wait until she was back at work. Her heart leapt, but they couldn't have found Summer Holt; she'd have heard about it on the news. The final card was addressed to DCI Cooper, Northumbria Police, Middle Engine Lane, and was affixed with a second-class stamp.

Cooper ran a fingernail along the seal and removed the card. A pair of tiny wooden feet were glued to the front with New Baby written in glitter pen.

"That's pretty," said Atkinson. "Who's it from?"

Cooper opened it and instantly felt sick.

Dear DCI Cooper,

I hear congratulations are in order. With God as my Witness A, there's nothing better than being a parent.

Love and hugs,

Ewan Underwood.

Cooper covered her mouth in case she vomited. The card fell to the floor as she grabbed her phone and dialled HMP Durham.

"It's Cooper. Have Gary Burke, Witness A, moved to solitary for his own protection. NOW GOD-DAMMIT."

- CHAPTER 44 -

SPRING WAS IN FULL swing in Northumberland. It was late March, and every garden, village green and hedgerow was blanketed in golden blooms of daffodils. While the air was warm and smelled of nectar, the water remained icy cold.

Finn stood on a stepping stone and stared into the lake. It was only a foot deep in real life, but in Finn's imagination, he stood on a precipice to inky ocean depths.

Param pressed the edge of a wooden sword into his back. "Walk the plank, matey."

Finn hopped forward onto the next stone. It wobbled, but he kept his footing. Pirate Param followed.

"I said, walk the plank. Down to Davey Jones' locker with you. Yarr."

And so they continued until they reached the north shore of the lake. Finn turned, whipping his own sword from his belt with a flourish. "I am

275

Finn the Fearsome. Tell me where you buried the treasure."

The boys ran into the woods, the sound of clashing swords echoing off ancient trees. Disturbed by the commotion, birds flew from their roosts.

In the distance, Finn and Param's mothers' voices floated on the breeze.

"Don't go too far," shouted Finn's mum, "and don't get too clarty. Those trousers are brand new."

The boys fled to the shadowy depths of the wood. Beyond the tree line, a field of menacing-looking cows stared at them.

"Sharks are circling the island," declared Finn, pointing his sword toward the cows. "Tell me where the treasure is, or I'll feed you to that great white yonder."

"No, no, anything but that." Pirate Param dropped to his knees and raked his hands through the soft earth. "It's around here somewhere, I swear. Rum, gold rings, bangles and goblets. More treasure than you've ever seen."

"Swear on your parrot's life."

Param stroked an invisible parrot on his shoulder, Finn's sword directed at his throat. "I swear on Polly's life."

Dramatically, he rolled away from Finn's reach. He fell at the base of the tree and glanced up. A blue cross denoted the park manager's plan to remove the tree, but that meant nothing to the boys.

"Behold, matey. X marks the spot."

Finn held his sword in the air. "Shiver me timbers. We found the treasure. Dig, matey, dig."

Finn dropped to his knees, ruining his new trousers. They used their swords to scrape at the ground, making slow progress until Poseidon's roar filled the air.

"Finn Abbot-Morrison, what did I just say about your trousers?"

Finn's mother looked furious. One hand on her hip, one pointing an angry finger at her son. "Why do you never listen?"

The boys looked at each other, eyes wide and fearful.

"Avast. 'Tis the sea monster," yelled Finn. "Swim for your lives."

The boys ran, their arms windmilling as if swimming the front crawl.

A scream caused Finn to stop in his tracks. He turned to see his fellow pirate fall into a hole, possibly an animal burrow. Param clutched his leg, his back bucking wildly with pain. He was hurt. Properly hurt. Finn knew instantly this wasn't something they could just stick a plaster on and continue playing. Param's mouth formed a perfect oval as he gasped for air and tried to scream.

Saddened, their game faded away as Finn broke character. "Mam! Mam! Param's broken his leg."

He watched the two women begin to run in their direction and turned back to Param. His friend wasn't only in pain; he was afraid. Deathly afraid. A skeletal hand poked out of the ground, its skin and tendons all but disintegrated. Around one finger, covered in mould and fungi, a pale wooden ring, varnished to a high shine, glowed like amber in the sunlight.

Finn crawled into the hole and touched his friend's shoulder. "You did it, Pirate Param. You found the treasure."

———

"YOU STRANGLING A CAT, or what?"

Fuller was halfway through his choir homework when his neighbour banged on the wall and told him to pipe down. He held what he hoped was a perfect C until he ran out of puff, then grumbled that the grumpy bastard next door could have just taken his hearing aid out.

Taking a seat on the sofa, Fuller continued to hum the ditty. He turned on his television and flicked through the TV guide for a film. It was Saturday, and he fancied something action-packed with plenty of explosions.

He'd settled on Bruce Willis film when a thought occurred to him. As the opening credits scrolled by and the director and screenwriter's names flashed on the screen, Fuller wondered if he'd ever seen one of Michael Holt's films. He paused the movie and opened the Internet Movie Database on his phone. He searched for Michael Holt and scanned a list of his works. All pretentious nonsense by the looks of it, with none scoring above four stars. He doubted he'd be interested in any of them; by the looks of things, his last success was eight years ago.

Fuller restarted the film, watched a balding Bruce Willis punch a bad guy in the face and paused it again. He picked up his phone and called another muscular, bald guy – Malcolm Dorsey.

"No, I haven't got into the Northern Counties Club yet. I've got a plan, though."

"Not why I'm calling. Remind me what the Hardings do again?"

"Nadine's a cosmetic surgeon. Makes the best boobs north of the M25. Her words, not mine. Personally, I hate fake tits."

"And Cyrus?"

"He loves them. Nadine's a big ol' E cup. Doubt she operated on herself, though."

Fuller laughed. Dorsey was growing on him. "You know fine well what I meant."

"He's a stay-at-home dad. Course Tim's not there, is he? So, basically, he's unemployed."

"What did he used to do?"

"Can't remember. Hang on a minute while I check my notes."

While Fuller waited, he watched the rest of the fight scene. Bruce Willis kicked the guy in the gut and pulled out his gun.

"I'm back. He wrote shitty dramas for ITV but was laid off years ago. He thinks Amazon or Netflix will come knocking any day now."

"Hmm," Fuller said. "Interesting."

"I doubt it. They're probably all period dramas. Lots of tea and sympathy and not a car chase in sight."

"Not what I was getting at." Fuller tapped the remote against his knee. "Michael and Cyrus claimed not to know each other. Yet, they went to the same university, had been photographed together and worked in the same industry. Let me ask you this – If Summer and Tim were found alive, that would be the story of the year, the story of the decade, right?"

"Right."

"And if their loving fathers wrote a heart-wrenching film of their abduction – the inside scoop – that's the screenplay all the agents would want, isn't it?"

Dorsey let out a low sigh. "It would be fucking gold dust."

SCENE OF CRIME OFFICERS sealed off the northern edge of Druridge Bay Country Park. The rest of the park remained open, but instead of enjoying the trails, the public seemed intent on hanging around the police cordon like flies on shit.

The police arrived first, providing basic first aid to the injured boy and his traumatised mother while they waited for a paramedic. The forensic team came next. Hong Evanstad, a Korean-born SOCO, took one look at the hand and called the team at CID.

It might have been Saturday and Keaton's day off, but there was no way she'd miss this. Besides, it wasn't like she had anything better to do. She pulled on a pair and boots and a windbreaker and headed to the deposition site.

She found Hong carefully brushing soil away from the bones of a left thumb revealing the trapezium and scaphoid. In the adjacent field, a herd of cows stared at them, intrigued by the fuss.

"Could be a coincidence?" said Keaton. She stepped aside while protective screens were erected. If the bones turned out to be Rhett, or Laurel, or both of them, it meant their no-body murder now had a body. In theory, a conviction would be easier. Those who died of natural causes didn't, as a rule, bury themselves.

Hong raised a brow as he exposed the left radius. "Coincidence? If it looks like a dead cyclist and smells like a dead cyclist... This is Rhett Campbell. I'll eat my bunny suit if I'm wrong."

Keaton squatted down to her haunches. "How are you so sure?" She was in a bad mood. As much as her heart-to-heart with Whyte and Martin had helped, she was still angry and bitter at her situation. She knew it made no sense, but she kept blaming herself. If she'd been a better girlfriend, a better lover. If she'd worked less overtime and been home more. Until she could forgive herself, Keaton was doomed to a short-tempered life.

"The ring. It's on the left ring finger. Any old wooden ring would rot away in the wet soil, but this one is built to last as you'd expect with an engagement ring. It's been lacquered to perfection. As a result, very little water damage. Next, the average woman doesn't have hands this size, and the radius suggests a height of – hmm – close to six feet. Five-ten, five-eleven maybe."

He put down his brush. "The bones are young and strong. This is a man who worked out. This is Rhett Campbell."

Keaton stood. Beyond the police cordon, rubber-neckers held cameras and phones in the air. She'd have to disperse them soon; there'd be more police and forensic vans arriving, and they'd need clear access.

A crime scene photographer approached. Hong leaned backwards out of the way, waiting silently while he took his time to capture the image of the skeletal hand against the backdrop of burnt umber soil. The process repeated with each bone Hong uncovered.

"How long is this going to take?" Keaton asked.

"How long's a piece of string?"

"Long enough to tie round your neck."

Hong laughed. "Aren't you going to praise me on my use of an English idiom?"

"You're taking to it like a duck to water."

Hong frowned. "That's a good one. I'll try to use that in conversation tomorrow. But, in answer to your question, all night. I think we're looking at a fairly deep grave. At least as far as amateur burials go. The hand is higher than the rest of the body as if the perpetrator was in a hurry and didn't quite finish throwing him in before piling earth on top. The animals dug about a foot, maybe a foot and a half. We might have to excavate at least another foot to reveal the rest of him. Then we need to bring in ground penetrating radar to find the second corpse."

Keaton looked left and right. The wooded area north of the lake was reasonably small. It wasn't like they were dealing with Keilder Forest again. Hopefully, she'd hear something by dawn.

"Where's Margot?" she asked.

Margot Swanson was a talented forensic pathologist in her fifties. She was a massive flirt and used to scare the crap out of Tennessee.

"On a cruise. She's been informed. Her ship docks tomorrow morning on the south coast. She's going to take the first flight up to Newcastle. Her diary's cleared for Monday."

Keaton clapped the SOCO on the back and walked to a clearing where she could smell sweet-scented flowers and feel the sun on her neck. Keaton hadn't been to the morgue in a while, but that wasn't what bothered her. They'd found a body, and there was a ninety-nine per cent chance it was Rhett. She knew she could handle the following stages of the investigation alone and didn't need Cooper's help. Still, she wondered if she should call her. She shouldn't. She was on maternity leave and entitled to time off to bond with Danny and adjust to her new life.

Hunching her shoulders, Keaton made a decision. *You need to call Cooper,* she told herself. *For one reason and one reason only: she'll bloody kill you if you don't.*

- CHAPTER 45 -

IT WAS FIVE A.M. on Monday when Fuller was awoken by the vibration of his phone. He seldom put it on do not disturb mode because it was that rare for anyone to call him. Rubbing the sleep from his eyes, he saw it was Dorsey. The PI was employed by Portia Holt and Nadine Harding, who had hired him to help find their children. Unbeknownst to the two women, Dorsey watched their husbands the closest. Wondering why the PI would call at such an ungodly hour, Fuller feared the worst.

"Summer?"

"Malcolm Dorsey, but close."

"Very funny."

"I thought so," said Dorsey, chuckling. "Just calling to say I'm in."

Fuller sat up in bed. He turned on the bedside lamp and flinched at the sudden brightness.

"In where? Not the Northern Counties Club? Tell me you didn't B and E."

"Relax. I didn't break in. I got a job with the agency that does their cleaning. Had to forge a few references, but it was easy enough."

For some terrible reason, Fuller pictured Dorsey in drag, pushing a vacuum around like Freddy Mercury in the video for I Want To Break Free.

"This is definitely where that photo was taken. Unfortunately, I can't get into their database. Their cyber security's pretty good, but I managed to unlock an iPad and get into their private Facebook group. It doesn't go back far enough to find the event Michael Holt and Cyrus Harding attended, but I've found a few images of the same bloke. Higher def than the one we had from Michael's ex. I'm sending them over now."

Fuller removed the phone from his ear and waited for the familiar ping and buzz of a new email. The pictures showed the same clean-shaven stocky man. In some, he wore a blazer and tie; in others, he was more relaxed. Either way, he always accessorised with a glass of port or brandy.

"Are they tagged?" he asked Dorsey.

"'Fraid not. And I can't see any comments to identify him. Can you work some facial recognition magic?"

Fuller was out of bed now. He was too worked up to go back to sleep. Perhaps he would go for a pre-dawn run. Who was he kidding? He'd have an early breakfast and play about on Tiktok until it was time for work.

"There's a girl in tech, Becky. She's brilliant. She'll know what to do."

Fuller heard the sound of an aerosol being sprayed followed by a swooshing noise.

"Are you actually cleaning?"

"Course I am. I want to get paid, don't I?"

KEATON TRIED TO GET the working week off to a good start. She had a healthy breakfast of porridge, blueberries, flax seeds and flaked almonds. She even treated herself to a drizzle of honey. Other than visiting the deposition site, Keaton had been alone all weekend; Riley was nowhere to be seen. She tried to make the best of it with a movie night, but it wasn't the same without April's commentary or her homemade snacks.

She met Cooper outside the Freeman Hospital in Heaton.

"I did the right thing in calling you, right?"

Cooper stowed her phone in her pocket. She looked knackered. All women's bodies were different; some took a long time to regain their pre-pregnancy shape, and some never did. But Cooper must have been made of elastic. Her belly seemed to have vanished. Her hair was fuzzy, longer than Keaton had seen it in a while, and purple-tinted bags hung under her eyes.

Cooper yawned. "Damn right. Come on. I'm weirdly looking forward to this. Compared to baby poop, the morgue will smell all right."

286

THE MORGUE WAS COLD, with avocado green tiling and stainless steel cabinets and counters. Steel cupboards, some with glass doors, were filled with charts, files, textbooks and folders. Three metal gurneys dominated the centre of the room. One was bare, and the other two were covered with white sheets.

Cooper was wrong. The smell was as stomach-churning as always, a cocktail of death and bleach. She dabbed Tiger Balm under her nostrils, but it was akin to taking paracetamol for a migraine – it did nothing more than take the edge off.

"Oh, hello there." Margot Swanson sashayed out of her office. "Congratulations, Erica. I heard you named the wean after young Jack, God bless his soul. Lovely gesture. Ignore the smell, ladies. That's Mr Vinograd over here." She tipped her head towards one of the tables. "Chloe needs to get him back into cold storage before he becomes a health hazard."

A short, stout lab assistant scurried past Margot and wheeled the table away.

Margot's thick, glossy curls bounced with every movement. Her skin was tanned from her cruise and she looked to have put on a few pounds, most of which had gone to her boobs.

"Speaking of your youngster. Where is he? Has your mum got him for the day?"

"No. He's with Justin," Cooper told her.

"Aww. Is he on babysitting duty?"

Cooper flexed her jaw. The comment irked her. "No, he's not babysitting. He's being a dad and parenting his own child."

Admonished, Margot apologised. "You're right."

Atkinson wanted to be a hands-on father. He'd taken paternity leave and was doing the lion's share of the parenting. Thinking back over the last few days, Cooper reckoned he'd done sixty per cent of the feeds and seventy per cent of the nappy changes. After a tiring start, he'd eased back into parenthood. Cooper wouldn't admit it, but she was finding it harder. Her body and mind were still traumatised from the circumstances of the birth and the surgery that followed. She was healing, but slowly. And with Danny preferring to be bottle-fed by his father than breastfed by her, bonding was proving difficult.

Margot secured her curls in a bun and pulled the sheet back on the remaining table to reveal the cadaver. Cooper didn't have to count the vertebrae to tell it was a complete skeleton. She took in the skull with its gaping eye sockets and the ribcage, empty of lungs and heart.

"This skeleton belongs to a Caucasian male aged eighteen to thirty."

"You can tell his race?" asked Cooper.

"Easily." Margot took a set of callipers and measured various places on the skull. "The nasal bones, the shape of the jaw, the fusing on the lambdoid suture – they all point to a Caucasian male. The DNA profile will be ready soon, but I think it's safe to say this is Mr Campbell. Here, these are what remained of his clothes." She handed Cooper a clear evidence bag containing fragments of man-made materials.

"Looks like sportswear," said Keaton. And if anyone was going to recognise sportswear, thought Cooper, it was her.

"Can you tell us how he died?" An image of Underwood on top of Rhett came to Cooper. She saw him lift the rock, then bring it down with animal-like force.

Margot turned the skull over. "No. But I can tell you how he *didn't*."

Cooper and Keaton moved closer. The skull was perfectly intact, with no fractures or indentations and no sign of trauma.

Keaton shook her head. "You've got to be shitting me?" She turned away from the table and folded her arms.

Cooper felt around for the edge of the counter behind her; she needed it to steady herself. "This is bullshit."

Margot offered Cooper a chair. "You okay, sweetheart? Here. Sit."

Cooper refused and moved to the far corner of the morgue. "One discrepancy we could handle," she said, pinching the bridge of her nose so tightly she might make herself cry. "Both Witness A and Witness B swore Underwood talked about disposing of their bodies at sea. They promised to testify to it."

She could see the headlines, another story about how the pregnant DCI had been stupid enough to believe the ramblings of two of HMP Durham's finest. Another MP making a mockery of the team in the House of Commons. Another summoning to Nixon's office.

Cooper had been keen to get back to work, and the guilt was starting to chip away at her. What mother wanted to leave her baby at home in favour of a trip to a morgue and a gruesome double murder? She knew what her own mother would think of her when she found out she'd finished maternity early to get back on the case. But this revelation had pushed her back in the opposite direction and she wished she could make the choice over again.

"Underwood was supposed to have hit him over the head until his skull caved in. Jesus Christ. You know what this means?"

Keaton nodded but couldn't look up. "It means our case just collapsed faster than a house of cards."

- CHAPTER 46 -

OLIVER MARTIN PRACTICALLY FELL through the doors to the incident room. Rosy-cheeked and shiny brow, he was out of breath.

"I'm not late," he gasped, pointing to a large white clock on the wall.

"You were five seconds away from twenty push-ups," said Cooper.

He bent over, his hands on his knees while he caught his breath.

"I lost track of time, had to sprint back from Tennessee's bench."

Keaton laughed. "You realise it would have been easier to be late and just do the damn push-ups."

Martin straightened, interlaced his fingers and rested them behind his head. "But that's not the ethos we try to promote on this team."

"Quite right," said Cooper. "Are we all here? Good. Let's get this shit show started. Keaton?"

Keaton stood. "The DNA results are back. As suspected, the body recovered from Druridge Bay is Rhett Campbell." She paused to let it sink in. While none of the team actually thought the pair would be found alive, it was still hard to hear it out loud. "Which means both Witnesses A and B's stories about Rhett and Laurel being dumped in the North Sea are incorrect."

"Why would they lie?" asked Whyte. "Other than a Happy Meal, they weren't getting anything out of it."

Cooper had wondered the same thing. "They were testifying anonymously. So they weren't motivated by fame or notoriety."

"And we ruled out the witnesses colluding against Underwood?" Boyd asked.

"As much as we could do," Whyte said.

"I'm sure a lot of inmates dislike Underwood," she said. "Independently, they could have tried to influence the prosecution to get him transferred or moved to a more secure unit."

"Witness A was definitely scared of Underwood," said Cooper.

"But Witness B wasn't," said Whyte. "And it still doesn't explain how they both came up with similar stories. They both said they were buried at sea."

Keaton chewed the end of a pen until the stopper came off. She spat it into her hand and threw it in the bin. "Maybe they're not lying. Maybe they're telling the truth."

"But Rhett wasn't buried at sea," Martin said, looking confused.

"I know, genius. But what if they're telling the truth as far as they're concerned? They might have really witnessed Underwood saying those things.

Martin didn't look any less confused. "You mean he fed them lies on purpose? That makes no sense. He knew we had no physical evidence against him. Why would he then implicate himself like that?"

Cooper mulled the idea over. She had a few ideas and let them percolate in her brain while she rhythmically tapped her shoe against a table leg.

"A few reasons. One of which is prison Brownie points."

"Ah," said Boyd, catching on. "He's a sex offender, and sex offenders generally don't have a good time of it in prison. He might have worried he'd be a target. Implying he's not just suspected of murder, but is actually a murderer, may help keep him safe."

"Exactly," Cooper said. "And he may have been testing his fellow inmates' loyalty. Feed some misinformation and see what gets back to us."

"How is Witness A?" asked Boyd.

"Underwood beat the shit out of him, but he'll live."

"What if," started Keaton, "and I hate to say this, but what if Underwood is innocent?"

Cooper let out a long sigh. "Firstly, that man is not innocent. There's a small chance he didn't commit this double murder, but that's a long way from being innocent. He stole their bikes, he slept in their tent, he's a violent psychopath and let's not forget, he was seen with Laurel. Ewan Underwood is still our prime suspect unless anyone has any other ideas?"

"No one else's really involved themselves in the case," replied Keaton.

Whyte stretched his arms above his head and rotated left and right to loosen his spine. "My money's on Mildred Houghton," he said with a cheeky grin. "She was the one who gave us his name."

"And she knows krav maga," Keaton said, aiming karate chops at Whyte's head.

Cooper coughed and the team turned their attention back to the DCI. "If it turns out to be Mildred, I'll buy you all drinks. In the meantime, we need to know who is lying. Did Underwood really say those things in front of the witnesses? Or, are the witnesses time-wasting toe rags? We'll head over first thing tomorrow. Whyte and Martin, you grill Witness B. Keaton, you and I will take witness A."

There was a collective *ahhh* from the group. Not the reaction Cooper would have expected. When she realised they were all staring behind her, she turned to see baby Danny in Atkinson's arms.

"It's DB Cooper," said Keaton. She rose to her feet and went to hold the infant. "America's most wanted."

Great. Cooper had accidentally named her baby after a notorious hijacker. If she let on that it bothered her or insisted they call him Danny, it would only make things worse. Like kids on the playground, it was best to hope they grew out of it.

"What brings you here?" asked Cooper.

Atkinson bent to kiss her on the cheek. "Part social call, everyone needs a baby break now and again, and part work call. I've heard from Margot and Hong."

Keaton handed the baby back and gave Atkinson her full attention. "Did they find Laurel?"

"Not yet, but the team are persisting with ground-penetrating radar all around Druridge. The area's still closed to the public. They'll start again tomorrow at first light."

"And Margot?" asked Cooper.

"As you know, there was no sign of trauma to Rhett's skull. Nor were there any broken bones or obvious injuries. Under closer inspection, Margot noticed a nick to the right clavicle and another indentation to the anterior C6 vertebrae."

Cooper gulped. "Meaning?"

"She's not certain. It's just speculation. But, Rhett may have been stabbed in the neck."

- CHAPTER 47 -

THE INMATES OF HMP Durham were still eating breakfast when the team arrived at quarter to eight. Breakfast packs were delivered the night before for prisoners to eat in their cells the following morning. With almost a thousand residents, the smell of white bread and strawberry jam spread throughout the wings.

Cooper, Keaton, Whyte and Martin observed the wing from behind a gate made of heavy metal bars. The cells were still locked, but there was a general hubbub as inmates talked to each other through walls and listened to breakfast radio. From between the bars of one cell, a hand emerged gripping a mirror. The inmate's knuckles were calloused, and a tattoo covered the back of his fist. The mirror angled back and forth, and then Underwood's voice called out, "I can see you."

Cooper readied herself.

"Did you get my card?"

She clenched her fists. The card had been delivered to work rather than her home address, but the thought of that man trying to mess with her from his cell made her blood boil.

"I did. Thank you," Cooper said without a hint of warmth in her voice.

The mirror sparkled as it caught the light. "And how is that lovely son of yours? Lovely name – Daniel."

Cooper froze and glanced at her team. "How does that bastard know I had a boy? How does he know his name?"

"Maybe the nurse from the medical wing mentioned you had a boy?" suggested Keaton. "No idea about the name, though."

"The paper," said Whyte. "Your mum put an announcement in the Chronicle."

Cooper growled. She and Julie had a row over the announcement in the births, marriages and deaths section of the local paper. While Julie's intentions as a proud grandmother were good, Cooper hadn't appreciated it. Her business was her own; she wasn't a celebrity whose comings and goings were fair game to the paparazzi. Given her job and the danger it posed to herself and her family, she'd thought Julie's actions were naive and reckless. Julie thought Cooper was finding any excuse to have a go.

"Boss," Keaton scrunched up her face as if debating whether to say something. "Underwood seems to be keeping tabs on you. He could have contacts on the outside. It might be worth having someone keep an eye on your place. Until all this blows over, at least."

That probably wasn't necessary. Cooper was about to say as much when she thought of the alternative and how she'd never forgive herself.

"Can you arrange something?"

Keaton nodded and went to make a phone call.

Underwood, tired of being ignored, piped up again. "You're not very talkative. At least tell me if you're breastfeeding."

A guard approached his door and snatched the mirror from him. "That's enough, Mr Underwood."

"Oi. I'm allowed that. You can't just take things from my cell."

"Technically, it wasn't in your cell," said the guard. He walked to the end of the wing and addressed Cooper. "I'll have him moved to the yard, then we can bring the witnesses to the interview rooms."

Cooper thanked him just as Keaton returned. "Done," she said.

"Thanks. Probably overkill."

"Probably. But better safe than sorry."

***

"Good morning, Gary. Nice breakfast?"

Gary, AKA Witness A, ran his hand over his neck as he sat down. He had angry red claw marks down the right side of his face and neck from fighting invisible creepy crawlies and a black eye and missing teeth from fighting Underwood.

Gary winced as if the simple act of breathing was painful. His left forearm was in a cast, supported by a sling.

"It was alreet. I'd rather have a Happy Meal."

Cooper had no intention of getting the man a Happy Meal, but she said, "Tell me the truth, and I'll see what I can do."

His face lit up, and he slapped his neck. "Stop it," he told a fly or ant that only existed in his mind. He pulled his knees to his chest and rested his feet on the seat. "How can I help?"

Keaton opened a folder and retrieved an A4 piece of paper. "According to the statement you gave my colleague on Wednesday, the fourth of March, you were in your cell listening to the radio when the news reported that a key piece of evidence had been found."

"The wallet? Yeah. It was on the BBC."

"Then you overheard the conversation between Underwood and Shiela?"

"That's right. Do you have any food?"

"No," said Keaton. "And according to your statement, that was just before lunch. What time do you have lunch?"

"Twelve," he said, digging his nails into his bicep.

"Every day?"

"Every bloody day. Nothing changes in here."

"Okay," said Keaton. "Let me check my timeline. The wallet was found on Saturday twenty-ninth of February – leap year day. We released the information to the press on Monday. You heard the story on the news, then heard Underwood telling Shiela that the bodies of the missing couple were *beyond Coquet Island*. You had library time the day after on Tuesday, then called us on Wednesday."

"Aye. That's what happened."

Keaton propped her elbows on the table. "Last chance," she said.

He stopped scratching and looked at her. "Last chance for what?"

"To tell the truth."

Gary looked at Cooper for help. "That is the truth," he said.

Cooper was still open to the suggestion that Underwood lied in front of the witness on purpose. Whether to increase his social standing within the prison walls or to test who he could trust, Cooper didn't know. But if it was Gary who'd lied to her, she thought Keaton might be one to get the truth out of him. He couldn't look at the big woman, keeping his eyes on Cooper instead.

"See, here's the problem I have." Keaton ran the edge of her thumbnail between a canine and incisor and freed a poppyseed. While you were enjoying your Frosties this morning, I called the press room. We released the information about the wallet at one p.m., and it was mentioned on NewsBeat during the three-thirty bulletin. So how could you possibly have heard it before noon?"

Gary froze.

"Well?"

"Well, maybe I got me timings mixed up?"

Keaton slammed the table so hard the noise echoed off the breeze block walls. "Maybe you're pissing me about?"

Gary flinched. "Don't hit me."

"I don't have to hit you. All I have to do is tell the warden to move you back to the wing. Underwood's already beaten the shit out of you once—"

"Okay, okay." Gary looked close to tears. "He said it would be easy."

Cooper blinked. "Who said it would be easy?"

"I got a phone call from some geezer. He told me Underwood was guilty, but you lot were having trouble proving it. He offered me money if I called you and said I heard him talking to another inmate. He told me to say the bit about Coquet Island."

"What was his name?" asked Cooper.

"I dunno. He didn't give one." Gary sniffled and wiped his nose on the sling. "He just said he's put money in my canteen and that he'd pay me again once he was found guilty."

"Canteen?" asked Keaton.

"It's like a prison bank account," explained Cooper. "You get a set amount but can earn more by working in the jail, or friends and family can top it up. They can then spend the money in the prison shop."

"I like fig rolls," said Gary.

"Yeah? Well, you won't be having any of those for a while," said Cooper. "Come on, Paula. Time for us to visit the warden."

- CHAPTER 48 -

WHYTE AND MARTIN WAITED for Cooper and Keaton in a communal area. Whyte shook his head angrily as they approached.

"Little snake lied right to my face. Don't know if I'm madder at him for lying or myself for believing the bastard."

"Come on," Cooper said, "you've been in the police as long as I have. You know as well as I do that everybody lies. Let me guess, he received a mystery phone call offering canteen money for a false statement?"

"Spot on."

"Prisoners can't receive calls. They can only make them. Which means Witness A and Witness B both have contraband mobile phones. Speak to the warden and arrange to have them seized."

"Yes, boss," said Whyte. He scraped his fingers through his hair, closed his eyes and took a deep breath.

"Don't beat yourself up," said Keaton. "They fooled us all. We knew this was possible but still decided to charge Underwood."

"Exactly." Cooper patted his arm. "Someone's pulling the strings here, and for once, I don't think it's Underwood."

"So, who is?" Keaton played with the zipped pockets on her trousers while she thought. There was a rhythmical soothing swooshing noise as the puller ran along the metal teeth. "Until Rhett's body turned up, I was beginning to think they'd been abducted by aliens."

Cooper folded her arms. Her breasts were sore, and her lower back ached. She wondered how Danny was doing, if he was getting enough sleep, if Atkinson had fed him recently. She shook the worry from her mind. Atkinson knew what he was doing. "Regardless of Underwood's guilt or lack of, someone really wants to make sure he's charged and sentenced. But who? And don't you bloody suggest Mildred Houghton," she said, grinning at Whyte.

Martin, who'd been quiet up until that point, stretched his neck to the side until it emitted a loud popping noise. "I've been thinking of all the men connected to the case. There are the bird watchers, the man who owns the caravan park, the man from the museum and the farmer whose land the clothing labels were found on. I can't see any of them harming Rhett and Laurel or trying to set Underwood up. Unless there's a connection we haven't spotted yet. Which leaves Adam Squires, the bloke who nicked the bikes from Underwood. What if he murdered the couple?"

"Stealing the bikes from Underwood so he could clean them and remove evidence would make sense," said Cooper. "But putting them on the internet to sell doesn't. Unless he's a complete and utter idiot."

Keaton and Martin chuckled. They'd met Squires, and the looks on their faces implied they thought he was just that – a complete and utter idiot.

Martin suppressed his laughter. "Forget I said anything."

"No," said Cooper. "Brainstorming's useful." She wanted the team to feel comfortable making suggestions and developing their own theories. Independent thinkers made good detectives. "You got any other ideas in that young brain of yours?"

Martin grimaced. "Like you said, someone's trying to ensure Underwood spends the rest of his life in jail. Might be because he's guilty, might be to throw us off the scent of the real killer, or it might be because someone has a grudge against him."

His last remark hit home with Cooper. They'd once worked a murder scene where the victim was so disliked it was tough to decipher who had the biggest motive. Underwood, with his previous misdemeanours, would have many people who'd like to see him harmed.

She retrieved a packet of painkillers and a bottle of water from her bag and downed two paracetamol. "Look into the people who would have reason to either frame Underwood or cement his conviction," she told Martin. "Previous victims. Their friends and families. Heck, even his own family. Whyte, you go after the contraband mobiles. Keaton and I will go see the prison accountant. Between the money transfer and the phones, we might be able to see who's been playing us."

A SKINNY MIDDLE-AGED MAN sat behind a desk covered in paperwork. His creased shirt and loosened tie looked unprofessional, but his fingers flew over the buttons of a calculator at such speed he resembled a magician performing sleight-of-hand card tricks. Behind him, an espresso machine needed cleaning, and a whiteboard bore the message *Go away, I'm busy.*

The man's muttering was unintelligible as he performed his calculations, ignoring Keaton when she knocked on the glass panel of the door. Keaton knocked harder, and the man lifted a finger to point at the whiteboard. "Can't you read?"

Flaring her nostrils, Keaton entered the stuffy room without permission. She grabbed two chairs, dragging them noisily across the floor and setting them in front of his desk. "I can read just fine." She pulled out her ID and thrust it in his face. "Can you?"

He blinked and adjusted his glasses. "I'm sorry, I didn't realise you were police officers. I'm in the middle of an audit. I don't have much time."

Keaton huffed. "Yeah, I don't care. This is DCI Cooper."

Cooper tried to get comfortable in the plastic chair. "Archie Peters and Gary Burke. I want to know who's paid into their canteen in the past month."

The accountant paused his calculations. "Now?"

Keaton took a long, deep breath. "I'm sorry, is helping the police with a double murder investigation low down your list of priorities? Yes, now."

His nose wrinkled. "There's no need to be rude."

Cooper could feel Keaton's agitation mounting. She was like a frustrated child with no outlet for her anger.

"Ugh. Fine. Give me a minute." He carefully lifted his calculator and stored it in a drawer as if it were a prized possession, then began to type furiously on his keyboard. The walls were a dull grey, and the fluorescent lighting was harsh on his pallid skin.

A printer began whirring. He reached under the desk, retrieved two sheets of A4 and handed them to Keaton, who snatched them impatiently from his grip.

Cooper was comfortable with Keaton taking the lead. She was good at spotting patterns, and it didn't take long for her to find what she was looking for.

"Erm, boss?"

"What is it?"

"Only one account has made payments to both witnesses."

"Great. That must be who we're looking for. What's the name on the account?"

Keaton bit her lip and handed over the sheets of paper.

"Sorry, boss. The name on the account is E. Cooper."

-CHAPTER 49-

E. COOPER.

Her tongue dragged across her lips, a million thoughts whirling around her head. Underwood knowing about her baby boy was bad enough; hearing her own name was connected to this mess was too much. She tried to control her breathing and keep it in a steady rhythm. But she wanted to scream, to fly into a rage.

"Find out what you can. I'm calling my bank."

The room spun as she stood up too quickly. She was still weak from the trauma of giving birth, sleepless nights and pumping milk. Cooper gripped the back of Keaton's chair and closed her eyes until she felt stable enough to walk.

Outside the accountant's office, the corridor was chilly. A draft of icy air set Cooper's teeth chattering. She unlocked her phone and logged into her bank account. She scrolled through transaction after transaction, looking for anything amiss.

Everything looked as it should. She searched for HMP Durham. Nothing. Then, just Durham. Still nothing.

Convinced her current account was safe, Cooper called her credit card and savings account providers.

Keaton turned to look at her when she reentered the office. Her immediate panic may have ceased, but she still didn't feel right. A sense of foreboding filled her chest, adrenaline coursing through her veins.

"You can chill," Keaton said. "It's not from your account. Unless you have some offshore tax haven funds I don't know about."

"I wish."

Cooper sat. Across the desk the accountant entered data into a spreadsheet, his eyes flicking back and forth between his monitor and a brown folder filled with paper. He worked diligently, not needing to look at the keys as he typed. It was as if he didn't even register her and Keaton's presence.

"The IBAN gave it away." Keaton pointed to a string of letters and numbers next to the transactions.

"What's that?"

"International bank account number. The mysterious E. Cooper's account starts with DO, meaning it's from a bank in the Dominican Republic.

Cooper tapped the table to get the accountant's attention. "How many inmates here are citizens of the Dominican Republic?"

The man slowly raised his eyes from the monitor. Still, his fingers tip-tapped the keyboard as he entered number upon number.

"Not my domain," he said. "Try admin."

Then, much to Cooper's annoyance, he lifted a finger and pointed at the whiteboard: *Go away. I'm busy.*

"WHAT DO YOU KNOW about the Dominican Republic?" Cooper asked Keaton.

They sat at a wooden table in the Claypath Deli. Keaton ordered a Vietnamese-inspired sandwich while Cooper ate a bagel named after Kevin Bacon.

Keaton swallowed, then shrugged. "Not much. I know it's half of the island of Hispaniola, the other half being Haiti. And I know there aren't any inmates in Durham with Dominican citizenship."

She grinned across the table. It had taken over an hour for the admin team to search their database of almost a thousand prisoners.

"Hmm, what else? The official language is Spanish. April went there when she was a teenager. She said it's got a rainforest climate, and the beaches are to die for."

Cooper took a bite of her bagel and savoured the crispy bacon. "You haven't mentioned April in a while. How're things?"

"Oh," she pointed at Cooper. "That murderer. The one we're trying to deport. He's from the Dominican Republic."

Cooper remembered the story from the news. "Francisco Peña? I doubt he has anything to do with this."

Keaton pulled a face and finished the last of her sandwich. "Bloody delicious that was. And, yeah, you're probably right."

THE WEATHER WAS FAIR that evening when Cooper drove home to Tynemouth. Dog walkers were out in force, enjoying the new season. As she pulled into Latimer Street, she passed a panda car on the corner. A fresh-faced PC lowered his window as Cooper drew her BMW to a stop. The PC nodded formally. "Ma'am."

"Anything I should worry about?"

"An IC6 male, early-twenties, around five-ten wandered up and down your road a couple of times and paused outside number eight."

Cooper searched out number eight; it was almost opposite her house.

"Did you approach?"

"Yes, ma'am. He didn't speak much English. Said he was looking for the doctors."

"It's two streets that way," she said, nodding south.

"I know. I escorted him there and watched him go in. He hasn't appeared in the street since and nothing else has stood out."

That was a relief. If Underwood's friends or family wanted to mess with her, that was one thing. If they tried to intimidate or harm her family, it was another.

She thanked the PC. "Enjoy the rest of your evening."

"No can do," he said. "Strict instructions not to move my ass from this spot until midnight when Pugsley takes over."

"Pugsley?"

"PC Pughs, ma'am. Looks like an overgrown Pugsley Addams."

She smirked, able to picture the man perfectly. "Right. Well, I'll bring you some grub later. Let me know if anyone's acting suspiciously," she said, handing him a card with her number.

As she fed her key into the lock, her phone vibrated with a message from Tynemouth Academy.

Tynemouth Sharks win the league. Congratulations to our incredible netball team. You truly are top of the food chain.

Atkinson greeted her at the door. Steam covered his glasses, and a tea towel over his shoulder sported a small amount of baby sick. "You want to tell me why there's been a police presence on the street all day?"

Cooper moaned as she removed her shoes and coat. "Yes. But first, I want a kiss from my man and cuddles from my children. Where's Danny?"

"In Tina's room. Did you know she can change his nappy in under three minutes?"

Remembering Tina as a young child Cooper was surprised Tina could even stand the thought of changing his nappy. She'd been highly sensitive to smells and sounds. The idea of a screaming baby with a full nappy would have been Tina's own personal hell when she was around seven or eight.

Atkinson pulled Cooper to him and gave her what she craved: a long, tender kiss on the lips.

"You taste of bacon," he said when she reluctantly pulled away.

Upstairs, her daughter cradled little Danny in one arm and held a chemistry textbook in the other. Danny was sound asleep; Tina looked ready to nod off herself. Cooper hung by the door, observing them like the proud mother she was. She felt an overwhelming amount of love for Tina. She was clever in a way Cooper never would be. She was old beyond her years and had such a caring spirit. She shouldn't be surprised. Aside from raising a seagull chick named Steven, she'd cared for Cooper during her days of radiotherapy and chemotherapy. Tina had to grow up fast, taking over most of the cooking and cleaning while she was still only in year nine.

And it wasn't just Tina. Cooper was filled with love and gratitude for Atkinson and how he'd supported her from the moment he knew she was pregnant. He'd attended every scan and doctor's appointment, and he loved staying home with Danny while Cooper returned to work. After her experience with Tina's father, Cooper couldn't be happier that Danny would grow up with a real father in his life, one who would raise him to be a good man.

She placed a hand on her belly. Her body was amazing. It may be scarred and tattooed, covered in stretch marks and cellulite, but she wouldn't change it. Her body produced the two things she loved more than anything in the world. She might not be strong in the way Keaton was, but she had strength all right. She'd beaten cancer, and she'd created two beautiful human beings. Just watching them made her want to burst into tears.

"Hey," Tina said, putting her book down. "How long have you been standing there?"

"Long enough to need a tissue."

Cooper dipped into the bathroom, blew her nose and splashed water on her face. Tina handed Danny to her and shuffled over on the bed to make room. She shoved her crutches out of the way, and they clattered to the floor, causing Danny to wake.

"Oops."

"Don't worry about it. He'd have woken for a feed soon, anyway. I hear congratulations are in order? You won the league."

Tina's wrinkled her nose. "*I* didn't win the league. I've been sat here on my butt since three-thirty."

"You didn't go to the game?"

She shrugged. "They didn't have room on the bus for me. They're all at Wood's, having hot chocolate to celebrate."

Tina fished her phone from her pocket and opened Instagram. A group of young women crowded around a table, their arms over each other's shoulders. Accomplished smiles were obscured by the steam of piping mugs of cocoa.

"Aren't you going to join them? Come on, get your stuff. I'll give you a lift."

Tina shoved her phone away. "Nah. No one thought to message me. Guess that means I'm not invited."

"I'm sure that's not the case, T. They probably just forgot."

"They always forget." Tina turned her face away and played with the edge of her support bandage. "Besides, they'll be finishing up now. I'd get there just as they were leaving and they'd all have a good laugh at me sitting alone with my drink."

Cooper's heart broke. Tina was going to win in the long run. She'd go on to get perfect grades, her dream job, be well-paid and live a fulfilling life. She could picture the bitchy teammates marrying young, seeing their looks and figures disappear, and their careers stagnate. Their husbands would bore them, they'd lie about their age, and they'd find fulfilment in a bottle of happy pills or a se-cret stash of vodka they kept down the side of the couch. None of this helped Tina now. Cooper was popular at school; she'd never known the pain of being perpetually on the outside looking in. Now she felt it every time Tina came home from school with a look on her face that said someone had picked on her.

Being a detective was hard. Being a mother was harder.

- Chapter 50 -

Tim was still asleep when Summer selected a yellow felt-tip pen and added a lemony circle to a sheet of A4. This was a daily activity for the young girl, and the sheet of paper was now covered in small, colourful circles. To anyone else, it looked like an abstract piece of art. To Summer, it was a calendar.

When she lived at home, Summer knew a few days of the week, but it was here in the basement when she'd learned the rest. The man insisted she and Tim do their schoolwork. He called it homework, but she and Tim knew they weren't really home. The calendar started one Sunday with a red dot. Summer could tell it was Sunday because of the church bells. She could picture St. Mary's Church in Ponteland, its old stone walls and the England flag flying from a rectangular tower. Sundays were always marked red on the calendar because inside St. Mary's, the benches were cushioned with red pads. Saturdays were blue. Blue reminded her of the sky, and she could always hear more flights on Saturdays. Summer often wondered where the planes were off to. Somewhere exotic like Egypt, perhaps. She'd never been but had seen pictures in a book and was fascinated by the big buildings shaped like triangles. Summer put her pen down and wondered if she'd ever get to go somewhere so interesting. If she'd ever leave the basement at all.

Her best chance was on a Monday when the man went out for a few hours. Mondays were pink like strawberry ice cream because he always gave them ice cream on Mondays to make them sleepy.

Tim awoke, and after his usual five-minute cry, he climbed a short ladder attached to a plastic slide. He slid down it and clambered up the ladder once more. If only it was tall enough to reach the window. She could climb up, smash the window, run towards the airport, and find her way home.

Filled with frustration, Summer grabbed a different piece of paper and tore it to shreds. Tim flinched and stared at her with the same fearful, wide eyes he had whenever the man appeared. Summer didn't care; she couldn't stand it any longer. If she was going to escape, it had to be on a Monday. She'd have to stop Tim from eating his ice cream if he was going to come with her. He'd fall asleep otherwise, and there was no way Summer would be able to carry him. If he couldn't resist the strawberry treat, Summer would have to go without him.

THE FAIR WEATHER DIDN'T last long. April brought with it April showers, and as Cooper drove along Middle Engine Lane she was careful not to splash pedestrians. Where yesterday the people of the northeast had stood tall, their faces turned upwards, enjoying a dose of vitamin D, today they walked hunched over, faces hidden beneath umbrellas and caps. The streets smelled of wet dirt and cold metal.

She parked at HQ and approached the main entrance. A hand-written sign stuck to the inside of the glass told her, *Please use other door.* An arrow pointed left toward the custody entrance. She tried to push it but found another sign pointing right this time. Cooper found herself, sleep and caffeine-deprived, turning left and right between the two revolving doors. Rain soaked through her shoes and drenched her short hair. She peered through the doors and saw Keaton with a big grin on her face.

"Let me in, or I'll—"

"Transfer me to Sunderland. I know the drill." Keaton pushed a button and the doors began to spin. "Happy April Fool's. Don't shoot the messenger. I'd like to take the credit, but the signs were already up when I arrived. Took me twice as long as you to realise what was going on. Had to dry my hair under the hand driers in the ladies' bogs. I reckon it was that creep, Cedric."

Cooper scrubbed the soles of her shoes on the doormat. "Think I've got a date with the hand dryer as well. See you upstairs?"

"Yeah. Just waiting to see what Martin makes of the signs. I reckon he'll be out there all day."

"Bless him."

While Cooper crouched under the hand dryer, she thought of two things: the case and how much bacteria was being blasted around the room. She put the second concern from her mind. At least she was warm.

The witnesses had been paid from a foreign bank account. That made sense. Whoever wanted Underwood to take the blame was covering their tracks. Someone killed Rhett and Laurel and left their bikes and belongings out in the open to be nicked. When a known criminal took them, the real killer must have rubbed their hands together in glee. With the heat on Underwood, they'd obviously want to add to the prosecution's case, especially when they were looking at a no-body murder.

Cooper opened the door to CID and proceeded to the incident room.

It wasn't a no-body murder any longer, she thought. As upsetting as it was, with the discovery of Rhett's corpse, they now had proof that a murder had occurred. Now, she just needed a list of new suspects.

"What the f—?"

Cooper's desk, computer, phone and chair were all covered in tiny, yellow and pink Post-it notes. The brightly coloured stickers covered the legs of the desk, the back of her chair, the waste paper basket and even the bloody stapler. See lowered her brows and walked around the desk.

Martin walked in and stopped in his tracks. "Oh," he said, his face painted with delight. "A classic."

Behind him, Cooper could make out that another figure was approaching. She assumed it to be Martin's flatmate, Whyte, or his girlfriend, Boyd. It turned out to be a sour-faced Nixon. He shook his head in a paternal manner.

"What in the name of all that is holy..."

"It's an April Fool's, sir."

"I can see that, Cooper. I'm not blind. Get it tidied away. Bruce Deacon and Tamzin Campbell are due in at Newcastle any minute."

He turned and stormed out of the room.

"Well, don't just stand there grinning like an idiot," said Cooper, scowling at Martin. "Make yourself useful."

The pair were halfway through removing the sticky notes when reinforcements arrived in the form of Keaton, Boyd and Whyte. Between them, it only took a further ten minutes to return the desk to its previous state. The bin was bursting at the seams, pink and yellow squares spilling to the floor as if it were spewing Battenburg.

"Was the bank account really in your name?" Whyte asked. He looked concerned. "That patrol car still on your street?"

The car was still there when Cooper left for work. Pugsley hadn't spotted anything overnight that should concern Cooper or her family.

"It was E. Cooper. And the E might not stand for Erica. It might be Ernie or Ella. Hell, it might even be Elliot, for all we know. Keaton's requested more details."

"Do you think they used that name on the account to mess with you?"

Cooper rolled a pink Post-it between her fingers until it formed a slender tube. "Could be a coincidence. People use mule accounts for illegal behaviour. There might be some innocent sod wondering why money's been moved from his account to Durham Prison, of all places."

The sound of a burp bellowed across the room. All eyes turned to Keaton, but it was Boyd who had a hand over her mouth.

"Excuse me," she said, flushing pink and looking mortified.

"Nice," Keaton said, slapping the young lady on the back. She pointed a finger and Whyte, Martin and Cooper. "Don't think I didn't see you all assuming it was me." She stood and switched on the ancient television set. "Speaking of the Dominican Republic."

The screen flickered to a runway at Heathrow Airport. A flustered reporter addressed the camera while protestors, held back by wire fencing, held placards in the air behind him.

"What's their problem?" asked Martin. "You'd think the public would be happy to see someone like Peña deported."

Cooper watched an SO18 officer – part of the Met's aviation security force – drag a protester in a knitted cardigan towards a police van.

"Anti-death penalty protestors have twice succeeded in delaying the takeoff of flight AA1967 to San Antonio, Texas. On board is Francisco Peña, a man convicted of attempted murder here in the UK and wanted in the US for the murders of Sophia Grey and Emma Huxley in 2017."

The white plane with a red and blue striped tail began to taxi, slowly moving towards to end of the runway.

"If found guilty, Peña will likely be incarcerated on death row at the Polunsky Unit in West Livingstone, where he will await death by lethal injection."

Jeers and boos almost drowned out the reporter, who tried to move away from the noise.

"This morning, protestors storming the runway were swiftly met by security forces. Over twenty people have been arrested, with some accusing the police of heavy-handedness and brutality."

The plane turned, then gathered speed. A man wearing a suit jacket over a t-shirt began to cry.

"A second attempt to delay takeoff involved the use of drones. It is illegal to fly a drone within five kilometres of an airport or airfield; both drones were shot down and their operators detained."

Cooper sat down on her swivel chair and reached under it to adjust its height. She found another sticky note and crumpled it in her first.

Martin folded his arms. "My mum thinks we should bring back hanging. Then again, she also thinks we should bring back national service."

"Funny how the generation that wants to bring back national service are too young to have gone through it previously and too old to be eligible for it now," Boyd said dryly.

"That's what I said. She wasn't amused."

Cooper's mind went to a dark place. Standing at the side of a gravel track that snaked through an eerie forest, she looked down at the body of a person she loved. She wanted the person who did that to be torn limb from limb.

She heard the group discussing the death penalty. Keaton talked about statistics, about how the murder rate in states with the death penalty was consistently higher than those without. Still, Cooper refrained from the conversation, unable to tear her mind away from an image she'd never forget.

"It's not a deterrent," Boyd said.

"Aye, you might be right," Martin said. "But I'd still like to see a noose around that bastard's neck for what he did to Tennessee. Boss?"

Cooper cleared her throat and tried to be objective. "Of course, I would. I'd like to see him thrown to the wolves. But that's because what he did hurt us personally, and we can't let our personal heartache influence policy. We were certain Underwood, like Peña, was guilty of a double murder. Now, we're not so sure. I have a horrible feeling he was in the wrong place at the wrong time. Don't get me wrong, I think he's a vicious shit who should spend his life behind bars. But what if we never found Rhett's body and we went to court with the witnesses' evidence that he'd dumped the bodies at sea? What if he was found guilty, and we still had the death penalty?"

Keaton turned the television off, and the group sat in silence.

- CHAPTER 51 -

IT TOOK BRUCE DEACON two attempts to fasten his tie. He soothed the silky material with clumsy hands and thought of his daughter. Her sweet, easy-going attitude always helped calm him. Being a single father was tough, and he'd resented his wife for years. The pressures of parenthood had been too much for Laurel's mother, who'd left when Laurel was only nine months. Bruce had to juggle the school run with his many businesses. Though it took years, he taught himself to cook and clean. He learned the difference between French and Dutch braids, the difference between pads and panty liners, and the difference between One Direction and Little Mix.

In time, he forgave his ex, realising now that had Marta stayed, her mental health would have only declined further. He remembered her at her darkest moments and was thankful Laurel never had to witness her episodes, or worse, find her in

325

the tub with an empty bottle of pills or a razor blade.

And as the years progressed, Bruce grew to love being a single dad. His daughter inherited her mother's smile and infectious laugh, but from him, she'd inherited curiosity and enthusiasm. He couldn't have asked for a better daughter. Had he played the traditional role, working all day and leaving the parenting to Marta, he'd have missed so much. He might not even know his daughter at all. He certainly wouldn't be the same man he was now. Thanks to Laurel, he'd given up Friday nights at the pub for walks to the local church to drop her at Guides, he'd given up lazy Sundays in front of the television for cooking roast dinners and playing games in the woods.

A smile crept over Bruce's face at a memory of the two of them covered in mud, aiming guns made of twigs at each other. *Pow, pow! Got you, Dad.*

Bruce clutched his chest. Not to reenact the playful moment from his daughter's childhood but in response to sudden heart palpitations. Though she'd moved out of home a few years ago, he missed her so much. Sitting on the hotel bed to steady himself, Bruce tried to hold it together; he had another blasted press conference to attend.

He'd turned the television on to distract himself while he continued dressing, but it didn't help. The ticking of a clock drove him crazy, and the sounds of the city droned all around: the hum of traffic, the whirring of a helicopter circling the sky. Half ten. His taxi would be there soon. He'd meet Tamzin and Ashley at the station where they'd be

326

briefed before the conference began. Bruce felt for a piece of paper folded in his pocket. He hated these things. The bright lights, the cameras, the media willing you to provide them with clickbait, to fall apart or lash out. If he could turn back the clock to the days of playing in the mud will his baby girl, he would. But as he couldn't, Bruce simply wished for this all to be over.

COOPER COULDN'T GET THE taste of peppermint out of her mouth. As she walked through the lobby of HQ, a plate of Oreo cookies caught her eye. She took one and immediately spat it back into her hand. Some joker had replaced the sweet, creamy filling with toothpaste. She got rid of the offending cookie in the nearest bin and cleaned her hands with sanitiser, wondering who the prankster was and what she'd do when she got her hands on them. Part of her might come down on them like a tonne of bricks for their unprofessionalism, part of her might hug them. The stunt with the Post-it notes may have been annoying, but it did take her mind off things for a few minutes. Though she wouldn't admit it, she'd appreciated the distraction.

The press were assembled when Cooper arrived. First, Blair Potts showed Bruce, Tamzin and Ashley to their seats. A hush fell over the room as journalists and camera operators showed their respects to the grieving mother whose pain was so palpable. Cooper followed, faltering when Tamzin looked up at her. Rhett's mother was in mourning, dressed in loose-fitting black clothing. The dark fabric reflected the darkness the fragile woman felt within. Cooper understood grief, having felt too much of it herself recently. Tears carved a path down Tamzin's dry, sallow face like a flash flood in a desert wadi. She looked malnourished and dehydrated, she'd lost weight, and her body seemed devoid of nutrients. Bruce, too, seemed to shrink as if the stress of his missing daughter physically weighed him down, his shoulders hunched, his back rounded. He no longer looked like the tall, dashing entrepreneur with warm skin and hair the colour of cola. This was what losing a child did to a person.

A supportive hand patted Cooper on the back as she approached her chair. She turned to see Nixon giving her a rare look of encouragement. Without Tennessee or Sutherland, Cooper was the only one in her team who was also a parent. With Danny only weeks old, so inexplicably tiny and perfect, Cooper's protective instincts were at their peak. She felt a deep empathy towards Tamzin and Bruce, but mostly she felt like she was failing them.

Cooper sat, crossed her legs and assessed the room. Nixon took his place beside her; receipts for M&S and WH Smith fell from the pocket of his suit jacket. Cooper bent to pick them up and handed them back to him before bracing herself to address the cameras.

"On the fourth and sixth of March, two inmates from Durham Prison came forward with details of conversations they'd overheard Ewan Underwood having with other prisoners."

Cooper spoke clearly, leaning towards a microphone.

"The details presented in their witness statements gave us the confidence to charge Underwood with the murders of Rhett Campbell and Laurel Deacon."

Beside her, Tamzin shook with tears. Ashley took his mother's hand in his. He squeezed her frail fingers between his palms and whispered words of comfort.

"We now know," continued Cooper, "that these men were lying. Not only that, they were paid for their duplicity. As a result, we have dropped the charges against Ewan Underwood."

Tamzin's cries were audible; Bruce lowered his face to his hands. Murmuring voices rippled throughout the press room.

"Will Underwood be released?"

"What if it turns out he's guilty? What about the double jeopardy law?"

"Who paid the inmates to lie?"

The questions kept coming until Blair Potts commanded the room again.

Cooper took a deep breath and tried to answer some of the queries that had come her way.

"Underwood will not be released. Dropping the murder charge in no way influences his prior convictions. Double jeopardy does not apply here. Ewan Underwood was never tried or convicted for Rhett or Laurel's murders. Therefore the charges against him can be reinstated if new evidence comes to light. I want to take this opportunity to publicly apologise to Laurel's father, Bruce, and Rhett's family, Tamzin and Ashley. They have faced an unimaginable ordeal, and we owe it to them to work tirelessly to find the monster who took the lives of their loved ones. With that in mind, we will continue the use of ground-penetrating radar in the vicinity of Druridge Bay and the search for physical evidence around Hauxley Nature reserve. We once again call upon the public."

Cooper looked directly into a camera adorned with a BBC logo.

"On the twenty-seventh of December, Rhett and Laurel travelled east from Newcastle towards Tynemouth. Aside from a possible sighting of Laurel on New Year's Day, they were never seen again. I am asking the public to look at these images of Rhett, Laurel and their bikes. I am asking the public to consider their activities over the festive period. Did you see Rhett or Laurel? Did you meet them? We need you to come forward. If you know or suspect the guilty party, do not protect them. The person who killed Rhett Campbell is dangerous, and we as a community need to find them."

Cooper paused. Her eyes stung and her throat tightened. She was acutely aware of all the people in the room and how many would be watching live at home. Handing over to Blair, Cooper pushed her weight back in her chair but maintained her posture. Tamzin was supposed to read a statement but was too distraught to do so. Bruce hugged her and said he could speak for both of them.

"We are saddened to hear that the case against Ewan Underwood has fallen apart. But for all we wish for closure, we also wish for the truth. We are grateful to the police for their work in investigating Laurel's disappearance and Rhett's murder. Rhett was like a son to me. He was kind and had a wonderful sense of humour. He cared deeply for my daughter. I can not sleep knowing the man who killed him is still out there, but I have full confidence that the people of the northeast will help Northumbria Police bring him to justice."

He closed his eyes tightly, and when he opened them again, they were red and moist.

"I have spoken before about Laurel. I was a single father. She was my only family. Without her, I am broken. If Laurel is dead, I need to know. Please, please tell us where we can find her so I can say goodbye. If Laurel is alive, if you are keeping her somewhere, please do the right thing and let my angel go."

"I'M GOING TO SOUND like a dick," started Martin when Cooper returned to the incident room. "But I think Bruce Deacon is deluded."

Cooper pulled a box of Oreos from her handbag. Real ones. After the press conference, she'd nipped to the nearest petrol station and bought a pack.

"Oh, sweet," he said, opening the packet.

"I think it's admirable," said Boyd. She took a biscuit, chewed and swallowed. "It's nice he holds onto a little bit of hope."

Whyte shoved two biscuits in his mouth and spoke with his mouth full. "It's both. It's nice he's holding onto that hope, but I agree with Martin, it's also deluded. It's only a matter of time until we find her body."

Cooper grabbed an Oreo before they all vanished. "But why haven't we found it yet? Goodness knows the SOCOs have worked their arses off looking for her." She chewed slowly, thinking through the evidence or lack thereof. "Not only have we not found Laurel, but we've also found no..."

Cooper suddenly didn't feel so good. "We've found none of her blood, no one else's DNA. What if that's for a reason? What if she's alive?"

"You mean some sicko's had her all this time?" asked Whyte.

"Oh, I hope not," said Boyd, her pale, pretty face coated with all the worst things she could imagine. "I know we considered that she'd been kidnapped, but that was when Underwood was in play. If someone else has kept her alive for months, using her like... Death would be better. Wouldn't it?"

Cooper sat down, stood up, and then sat down again. Her mouth was dry, her brow clammy.

"No," she said, looking up to meet Whyte's eyes. "That's not what I'm getting at. We found no DNA other than hers and Rhett's. Maybe that's because no one else was there when Rhett was murdered?"

Whyte frowned. "You're serious, aren't you, boss?"

She nodded and saw everyone else wearing expressions of incredulity. "Underwood fucking said it. I was in labour, so I might not be quoting him verbatim, but he said something like, 'to be fair, you don't know they're dead.' And we bloody didn't. We know Rhett was murdered. We know Laurel was with him." Cooper opened her arms, a gesture to ask the group if she was going crazy or if they were thinking the same thing too. "There's no other evidence because no one else was involved."

"Shit," said Whyte.

"Double shit," said Martin.

"If you're right," started Boyd, looking worried. "If Laurel killed Rhett—"

Cooper did the maths. "If Laurel killed Rhett, and she's the one we're after, she's had ninety-five day head start."

- CHAPTER 52 -

WHYTE FOUND BRUCE DEACON in the lobby of New-castle Central Station. It was a typical mid-week lunchtime, relatively quiet and sombre. The place lacked the vibrancy of a weekend when stag parties and women on girls' weekends descended on the city. It was too late for the morning rush and too early to catch the city types returning home after a day of making deals.

With shoulders sagged and a laboured gait, Bruce stopped before the departures board. The Kings Cross train would depart at twelve twenty-seven from platform four.

"Mr Deacon," called Whyte, rushing to get to him before he passed through the barriers and crossed the bridge to the platforms on the far side of the station.

Bruce paled, perhaps wondering if Whyte was to be the bearer of bad news.

"I won't keep you long. I just wanted a quick chat. Would you like a coffee?"

The man checked his watch and looked over to the coffee shop. "Has something happened?" He reached into his wallet and pulled out five pounds.

Whyte held up his hand. "It's on me. And, no. There aren't any developments."

This was true. All they had was yet another theory. He didn't know if Cooper was a genius or just crazy, but he didn't want to raise the hopes of the man who stood before him. He was a shell of the assertive, headstrong man he'd been when his daughter first disappeared.

Whyte bought a flat white for Bruce and an Americano for himself.

"Thank you," said Bruce, raising the coffee in a reluctant *cheers* motion. "Got to be better than whatever they'll serve on the train. So what can I do for you?"

"Early in the investigation, Hampshire Constabulary wondered if your daughter and Rhett may have been hiding or avoiding someone. We looked into their bank accounts and phone records, but we couldn't see anything that would indicate that anyone had been harassing or bullying them."

"Yes, I remember," Bruce said. He stepped to his left to let a woman pushing a buggy get past. "Laurel was never one to be bullied. And I was adamant they wouldn't get involved in anything untoward, anything that would lead them to want to go into hiding. Of course, now you've found Rhett, that might not be the case."

Whyte didn't want to imply Laurel may be why Rhett was dead. Not yet. Not when he didn't know for sure. "Say Laurel did need to hide or stay off the radar. Where would she go?"

"She'd go to Rhett," Bruce said sadly. "Or she'd come to me."

"Laurel's mam. Is she...?"

"Dead?" Bruce removed the lid on his coffee and blew its contents. "The honest answer is I don't know. My wife was a deeply troubled woman, DC Whyte. I have no idea where Marta is or even if she's alive. I reached out when all of this happened, spoke to her old friends, tried to find out if anyone knew where she was, but it was no use."

If Laurel wanted to lay low, seeking refuge with someone who'd also fallen through the cracks of society would be a good place to start.

"Did Laurel show an interest in finding her mam?"

The next train to arrive at platform four will be the twelve twenty-seven service to London Kings Cross. Calling at Durham, Darlington, Northallerton, York, Doncaster, Newark Northgate and Peterborough.

Bruce picked up an overnight bag and carried it using a shoulder strap. "Not that I know of, detective. Occasionally she'd ask questions. For instance, Laurel loves spicy food. The hotter, the better. She asked me once if she got that from her mother." He shrugged. "That sort of thing. Maybe she had more questions but didn't want to hurt me by asking them. I thought I was enough for her, but maybe I wasn't."

The bony rattle of train wheels snaking along the tracks filled the station. There was a high-pitched noise as the driver changed gears and applied the brakes.

"I'm sure you were a great father," said Whyte, thinking of his own childhood and his father whose life now revolved around a weekly trip out. "You'd better go."

Bruce passed through the barriers, feeding his ticket in one end and retrieving it at the other. He turned to look back at Whyte. "Do you really think she could be out there somewhere?"

Whyte bowed his head. "I don't know." That was the truth. "But I'll look into Marta."

The train pulled into the station, and several commuters disembarked from Berwick or Edinburgh. Whyte watched as Bruce jogged over the bridge struggling with his bag. He made it onto the train just as the doors closed. Taking his phone from his back pocket, Whyte left the impressive station – Dobson's great monument to the railways' glory age – and walked towards the short-stay car park. He dialled a number as he got into his car.

"Hi Dad, it's me."

THE TRAIN STATION WASN'T the only place serving coffee. An artisan coffee van pulled up outside HQ. Cooper was quick off the mark and managed to get to the van before a huge queue formed.

She scanned the fair-trade menu and ordered two drinks, one plain and one a little more exotic. Carefully, she carried them upstairs towards the incident room, stopping briefly at the door to Howard Nixon's office.

"Come," came the gruff reply when Cooper knocked.

The Chief Superintendent looked up, his forehead creasing into a multitude of lines. "Ah, Cooper. Everyone okay after the press conference?"

"Yes, sir." She entered the office, pausing to throw a napkin into the waste paper bin. "A bit downbeat, but that's to be expected with a case dragging on this long."

Nixon scratched the back of his hand. "And yourself? It hasn't slipped my mind that you didn't take a day longer than the legally required maternity leave."

"I'm tired, sir, but I'm good."

"Touching gesture, naming your boy after DS Daniel."

Cooper couldn't help but think of Tennessee as a DI; after all, he had passed the exam.

"Thank you. He suits the name Danny. Want to see a photo?"

Nixon looked horrified. "No, of course not. I want updates on cases, not on family life. If you say you're fit to work, then that's that."

Cooper cleared her throat. She wanted to pinch her nose as she often did when stressed but needed both hands for the drinks. The hot liquid warmed her palms and she savoured the sensation.

"I'm concerned the reason we haven't found any evidence of Laurel Deacon's murder is because she's alive and well."

Nixon's stared at her with steely eyes. "Meaning?"

"Meaning there might be a reason hers is the only other DNA we've been able to tie to Rhett's murder."

He sat back and folded his arms over his chest. "Interesting."

"I think so too. I'm going to brainstorm some ideas with the team now."

She placed the plain coffee on Nixon's desk. "This is for you."

"Oh." the corners of his mouth turned down in shock or amusement. "What did I do to deserve that?"

"It's a thank you for brightening up an otherwise miserable day with a little hijinks."

"Don't talk in riddles, Cooper."

"If you're going to prank someone, sir, choose someone other than your best detective." Cooper edged to the door and smiled at Nixon. "When the receipts fell out your pocket at the press conference, I saw one was for twelve packets of Post-it notes from WH Smith. That's when it occurred to me your office is in the best position to watch everyone walking back and forth between the two *please use other door* signs. And there are brown crumbs around your bin. I bet if I look through it, I'll find the creamy middles to two dozen Oreos."

Nixon took a long deep breath and tried his best to look like a serious senior member of the police and not a naughty little schoolboy.

"Thank you for the coffee, Cooper. As for the rest of your accusations, I won't comment further without a lawyer present."

Cooper chuckled as she walked away. She'd keep the old man's secret. Couldn't have the rest of the team knowing he was human after all.

- Chapter 53 -

Means, motive and opportunity.

Cooper wrote the words in blue ink on a whiteboard then sat on a desk between Keaton and Boyd. The three women were flanked by Martin and Whyte.

To establish if Laurel killed Rhett, they had to consider three things. Was she capable of killing him? Would she want to kill him? And would she have the chance to kill him?

"Who wants to go first?" asked Cooper.

"Opportunity," said Martin. He gestured at the board. "They were alone in the middle of nowhere. Can't get a better opportunity than that. Easy peasy."

"Lemon squeezy." Keaton shuffled her hips back on the table and hummed for a moment. "We already alluded to the pair of them sneaking into the trees to have a bit of, what did you call it, Whyte, hide the sausage?" She grimaced. "You males are gross. Anyway, we thought they'd maybe snuck off for some loving, and that's why their bikes and bags were left in the open. But maybe Laurel lured him into the tree cover using that pretext so she could take him out."

"All speculation unless we get to talk to her," said Cooper, "but I agree. Opportunity gets a tick."

Cooper handed Martin the pen and he jumped from the table to add a checkmark next to the word *opportunity*.

"Who's next?"

Boyd lifted her hand. "I'll take means. Could Laurel, a slender woman of five foot eight, murder a strapping young man like Rhett Campbell? He was tall, strong and healthy. Normally, I'd say no. But as we know, the autopsy suggested he may have been stabbed in the neck. I know from my time in West Yorkshire that it takes no pressure at all for a sharp knife to penetrate human skin. I arrested this scrawny little kid once, only fourteen and weighed six stone soaking wet. He couldn't believe he'd actually stabbed someone. He kept saying, 'I just meant to cut him. I didn't think the knife would go all the way in.'"

Boyd shook her head as she thought back to her time at her previous force. "So, Laurel would have easily been capable of such an act. Physically, I mean."

On the whiteboard, under a photo of Rhett, bullet points from the autopsy report were annotated with red pen and yellow highlighter.

Cooper pointed at the report. "Damage was noted to the right clavicle and the anterior of the

C6 vertebrae. Meaning the knife entered from the front of the body."

Keaton got to her feet and pulled Martin from the table to join her. "You be Laurel; I'll be Rhett."

"Why do I have to be Laurel?"

"Because I'm the same height as Rhett, and you own more handbags than I do."

"They're satchels."

"Call them what you like. You're still playing Laurel. Here." Keaton thrust a pair of blunt stationary scissors into his hands. "Laurel was right-handed."

Rolling his eyes, Martin took the scissors in his right hand and made a stabbing motion towards Keaton's collarbone.

"Notice anything," she asked.

"Yeah," he said. "One, she'd have to be bloody quick to pull a knife and stab her fiancé without him grabbing it off her or dodging out of the way."

"Go on."

"And two, using my right hand, I'd be more likely to hit the left clavicle, not the right. I suppose I could do it like this." He changed his grip and stabbed in an outwards motion. "But that takes longer. Rhett would be even more likely to stop her. Unless..."

Martin tapped the scissors against his palm a few times, then asked Keaton to turn around. He stood behind her and wrapped his left arm around her waist as if giving her a hug.

"Steady."

"Hear me out," said Martin. "If he was walking ahead of her and then she came up behind him, maybe cuddled him from behind, then her right arm could come around this way." He brought his right arm around the right side of Keaton and pressed the end of the scissors against her upper torso.

"It would hit the right clavicle and the anterior of the C6 vertebrae," finished Keaton.

Martin put the scissors down and picked up the pen. He added another checkmark to the board. "Which leaves the tough one – motivation. Why would Laurel kill Rhett?"

Cooper got to her feet and took the pen from Martin. "If Tennessee were here, he'd say murder always came down to sex or money."

"And he was usually right," Martin said. "Should we start with sex?"

Keaton snorted and addressed Boyd. "I hope he used a better chat-up line than that when he asked you out."

Boyd blushed and muttered something about Martin being a perfect gentleman.

Martin winked at Boyd. Between Cooper, Keaton and Boyd, Saffron Boyd was the only feminine one of the bunch. Cooper liked jeans and torn t-shirts depicting the great rock and metal bands of the eighties and nineties. Keaton preferred lycra or rugby shirts. Boyd, shy and mouselike, was an elegant young lady. She wore a subtle floral blouse with smart navy trousers. She was barefaced and her soft golden hair was tied back with a cream-coloured ribbon.

Cooper couldn't help but smile as she watched the happy couple exchange flirtatious looks.

Keaton faked gagging noises. "You two make me sick. Kidding. I'm happy for you." She playfully punched Martin on the arm.

"Anyway. Back to sex." Cooper fiddled with the whiteboard marker while she thought of Rhett Campbell and Laurel Deacon. "Both of them were good-looking, youthful, healthy. They were recently engaged and everyone talked about how deeply in love they were."

"Just because someone says they're in love and acts like they're in love doesn't mean they are," said Keaton. "He still could have cheated on her. Maybe he was keeping up appearances by proposing to Laurel when, in reality, he liked getting his end away with random delivery drivers."

"That was an oddly specific scenario," Cooper said.

Keaton glared at the photo of Rhett that was pinned to the board. "Ignore me," she grumbled. Her features softened, and she rubbed a hand over her head, smoothing her ponytail. "I'm talking bollocks. If either of them were cheating, I found no evidence of it in their phone records or social media. I'm not saying it's impossible. I'm just saying there's nothing to suggest Laurel found out about some lover and flew into a jealous rage."

"What about the other way around?" asked Whyte. "Could Laurel have been having an affair and wanted Rhett out of the way?"

"Bit extreme," Cooper said. "She could have just dumped him. Which leaves money – the root of all evil."

Keaton let out a noise that resembled a bored cat. "I went over their bank records for the past year. Nothing stood out. No big payments in or out. No large cash withdrawals. And they weren't exactly wealthy. They had wooden engagement rings, for goodness sake. And they were camping to save money on their trip. In the northeast of England. In December, I might add."

"And it's not like Laurel's family stood to gain anything from her faking her death. She didn't have life insurance or anything to leave her father. Even if she ran off to find her mother, she's left her father in pieces." Whyte shook his head while he tried to think up another possibility. "But they both worked in tech. They did freelance work for Fiverr and so forth. What if one or both of them had money squirrelled away in some other format?"

"Such as?" asked Cooper.

"I dunno. Crypto?"

"Like BitCoin?"

Whyte shrugged. "I don't know much about it. I know you keep it in an online wallet rather than a current or savings account and that prices seem to rise and fall depending on what Elon Musk tweets."

"I don't think it's just Bitcoin," said Boyd. She flicked a speck of dust from her blouse then pulled her phone out. She unlocked it and began searching. "Yeah, you've got your Dogecoin, your Litecoin, Ethereum, Solana. Think there's one called Binance."

A feeling of familiarity fell over Cooper.

"Hang on. I'll go on Wikipedia," Boyd continued. "So, cryptocurrencies aren't reliant on central governments or banks. Coins are stored in digital ledgers... Blockchain serves as a public financial transaction database... In a proof-of-stake model, owners put up their tokens as collateral. In return, they get authority over the token in proportion to..."

Boyd looked up from her phone with peaked brows and apologetic eyes. "I'm not getting any of this."

"Me neither," said Martin and Keaton together.

"Go back a bit," said Cooper.

"Blockchain serves as a public—"

"No further back. When you listed the different currencies."

Boyd swiped her finger across the screen. "Litecoin, Ethereum—"

"That's it." Cooper picked up a bottle of water from the table. Instead of the green Volvic label, she pictured a pink and yellow heart. "Tamzin Campbell said Rhett liked to trade Elysium. I figured she meant the wine but thought nothing of it after we got their bank records, and nothing of interest showed up. I think she used the wrong word. I think she meant he'd been trading Ethereum."

As one, the group folded their arms and peered at the whiteboard.

"If Rhett had a nice stash of crypto saved up..." started Martin.

"But was playing the long game and not spending any of it..." continued Whyte.

"While insisting he and Laurel lived a very frugal existence. Not even springing for a proper engagement ring," said Boyd.

"Then you'd have motive." Keaton took the whiteboard marker and drew a checkmark next to *motive*. "To be fair, I'd murder someone if they tried to get me to sleep in a tent in the middle of effing December."

She locked eyes with Cooper and shook her hair. "It always comes down to sex or money."

- CHAPTER 54 -

WHYTE SLAMMED THE PHONE down, causing Boyd to jump. It was gone five p.m. and though sunset wouldn't occur for another hour or two, the sky was dark with grey clouds.

"Sorry," growled Whyte. "These crypto companies are doing my head in. Half of them don't have phone numbers, and the ones that do go to call centres in India."

"Tell me about it." Boyd stood and turned the lighting up at the wall. "I've managed to get through to a few only to be told they can't help me because of client confidentiality. One even implied I was impersonating a police officer before hanging up."

Martin stretched his arms above his head and yawned so dramatically Cooper could see a filling in one of his molars. "Count yourself lucky. I've been battling with online chat support, and the chatbots are absolutely shite, pardon my French.

Who's bright idea was it to replace actual human beings with robots and call it customer service? They just spout the same answer to every question."

Though they were concentrating their investigation around Etherium because of Tamzin's elysium remark, they wanted to cover all their bases. A person who invested in one type of crypto was just as likely to invest in others, and portfolio diversification was a phrase that kept cropping up. In other words, not putting all one's eggs in the same basket.

Keaton punched another piece of information into her spreadsheet and rubbed her eyes. They'd created a table of all the crypto companies they could find and marked off when they made contact with a human being who was in a position to help them. So far, there was only one tick.

Cooper looked at the team. They were tired, bored and probably hungry.

"Go home," she told them. "We're not going to get anywhere without warrants. I've submitted the paperwork. Now we just have to wait. We'll reconvene tomorrow and go from there."

Martin, Whyte and Boyd gathered their things, shut down their computers and headed for the lift. Cooper grabbed her coat and followed the others. Keaton lingered.

"You okay?" asked Cooper, wondering who'd volunteer for unpaid overtime.

Keaton shrugged.

"Don't you want to get yourself home to your family?"

Keaton didn't reply. She returned to her spreadsheet and picked up the phone, ready to try another company.

Something was up with her, but Cooper couldn't
tell what. She hadn't been the same for months and
each enquiry was met with a change of subject or
a non-committal shrug. Not liking to push people
into talking when they didn't want to – goodness
knew she did enough of that with suspects – she
decided to leave it. Keaton was a grown-up; she'd
open up when she was ready.

"I'm off now," Cooper said.

"Okay."

Keaton swivelled her seat so Cooper couldn't see
her face. If she was crying, she was doing a good
job of hiding it.

"I can tell something's wrong, Paula. You don't
have to talk to me about it, but at least promise me
you'll talk to someone."

The full-back froze, the phone pressed against
her ear, her body giving no clue to her emotional
state. The call connected.

"This is DS Paula Keaton from Northumbria Police. I'm calling in relation to..."

Cooper sighed and let the door close behind her.

WHEN COOPER RETURNED TO Tynemouth, her home
was warm and cosy. A delicious smell emanated
from the kitchen and the soft sounds of cheesy
music filled the hall. It wasn't Cooper's idea of good

music, but even a metalhead like herself had to admit teeny-bopper bands were mood-boosting.

Hanging up her coat, Cooper heard a noise she hadn't heard in fifteen years – a baby sneezing. She opened the door to the living room and spotted her infant cradled in his father's arms. It was a bittersweet image that filled her with hope for their family's future but also a tinge of sadness that Tina had never experienced the same. She pushed the thought aside. Kenny Roberts was a useless piece of dirt and had he not swanned off before Tina was born, he would have done so eventually.

Cooper took Danny from Atkinson and smiled at the sniffling bundle of joy.

"Baby sneezes are the cutest thing ever," she said.

"Not when they sneeze during a nappy change and fire baby poop all over the bathroom wall."

Wide-eyed, Cooper gasped. "Oh no."

"Oh yes." Atkinson hugged Cooper and kissed her cheek. "The tiles looked like a brown Picasso. All clean now, though."

"How long had he been sniffling?"

"Since late morning. It's just a cold, but the doctor said to keep an eye on him and to call back if he develops a rash or fever." Atkinson's face crumpled. "You look tired."

She was. As much as she wanted to get to the bottom of what Laurel Deacon had been up to, she was pleased to be home. Home was a peaceful oasis away from all the troubles of work. At least, it usually was when there wasn't a police car parked at the end of the road.

Talk about bringing work home with you.

352

"I'm fine," she lied. "Any news from our body-guards?"

"Not a peep."

That was good news. The thought of Underwood doing anything to harm or intimidate her loved ones filled Cooper with so much rage she had to hand her baby back to Atkinson. "How's the rest of the gang?" she asked, disguising her anger with small talk.

"Tina's sick of her crutches. I can't blame her. I'd be the same. I asked if she was eating at home or at Josh's house tonight but only got a snort in response. I think they've been fighting."

Cooper sat on the sofa and resisted the urge to lie down and have a nap. "They'll make up. They always do."

"And your mother's been a star. She's done three loads of washing today."

Right on cue, Julie's singing carried down the hall as she sang along to an early Girls Aloud track.

"Mum's here? It's not Friday." She felt guilty thinking it, but Cooper needed some quiet time. Julie was not the quiet sort.

"I asked her to stay for dinner."

Cooper made the sort of noise Tina would make.

"She's tackled that huge pile of ironing. I could hardly send her home without the offer of food. I think she's lonely, Erica."

As usual, he was right.

Atkinson placed Danny in a bassinet and sat next to Cooper. She slumped into his body, resting her head on his chest. She inhaled, talking in his scent and thinking how she could stay in his arms for eternity.

"You're pale. You might have caught what Danny has."

Whimpers started from the bassinet.

"I'm all right. I'm not sick. It's just this case."

Atkinson's body stiffened. "It's always the case. And when you solve it, there'll be another one."

Danny's whimpers grew louder, turning to high-pitched cries.

Now it was Cooper who stiffened. "You want me to give up work and be a stay-at-home mum?" she asked, raising her voice to be heard over the baby. "I thought we'd discussed this."

"I've never wanted that. But I think you returned to work too quickly. You need more time."

"I'm DCI," Cooper said, standing up and folding her arms. "Baby or not, I need to lead by example."

"You'll lead yourself to a hospital bed if you're not careful."

Cooper opened her mouth, ready to snap back with something she'd likely regret but closed it again when Julie padded in with a tower of folded towels.

"Hello, dear. Oh goodness, he's not happy, is he?"

An understatement. Danny was crying like a demon possessed.

"Come here, poppet," said Julie, putting the towels down to pick up her grandson. "Are your mummy and daddy ignoring you?"

Ignoring him? She could hardly ignore him; she'd heard quieter jet engines.

Atkinson must have read the fury in Cooper's expression because he jumped to his feet, softened his tone and suggested Cooper go and spend a few minutes with Tina while he and Julie finished dinner.

Cooper ground her teeth and took the stairs one at a time, listing Atkinson's attributes as she went: tall, handsome, intelligent, diplomatic. She could feel her annoyance ebbing away with each stair, but knocking on Tina's door, she was met by a curt, "What?"

"Charming."

Tina looked up from her sci-fi novel. "Sorry. I love Danny, but he's been crying non-stop since I got home. I know it's not his fault but my head hurts. Grandma's singing doesn't help, and Justin keeps looking at me like I'm about to blow my other ACL at any moment."

Closing her book, Tina rubbed her temples.

Cooper took a seat on the end of Tina's bed and looked around the room. She'd moved some of her furniture around since Cooper was last in there and reorganised her books by subject rather than author.

"If it helps," Cooper said, "I'm hiding up here for the same reasons."

Tina gave Cooper a conspiratorial smile. "It's nice having Grandma, Justin and Danny here, and I wouldn't change it..."

"But it was quieter when it was just the two of us?"

"Exactly." Tina shuffled up the bed. "At least when you play your metal music, you don't sing along."

"I can start if you like."

355

"Please don't."

Cooper chuckled and picked up one of Tina's maths books, putting it down again when she realised none of it made any sense to her. Maths was never her strong suit.

"You're smart. What do you know about crypto?"

If Tina was confused by the segue in conversation, she didn't show it. "It's becoming more mainstream. Loads of companies accept payment in BitCoin now. Amazon, Tesla, Burger King, even UberEats. The values fluctuate a fair bit, but if someone invested like a hundred quid ten years ago, they'd be a millionaire now."

"Really?"

"Really."

Cooper lived a comfortable life, but she'd worked hard for it. She was jealous that a hundred pounds a decade ago could vastly alter someone's fortunes.

"Maybe we should buy some," she said, dreaming of a holiday in the sunshine.

"You can have some of mine if you like."

Cooper sat up and peered at her daughter, trying to read if she was serious. "You don't have crypto. Fifteen-year-olds can't buy cryptocurrency. Can they?"

"No," said Tina. "But they can mine it."

Cooper sat very still for a moment, then she stood and pinched her nose. "Explain."

"Well, you know how cryptos are basically maths problems, and computers or *miners* try to solve them?"

"No, but go on."

Tina sighed as if explaining anything to her mother was too much like hard work. "The owners of the computers who solve the problem the fastest get a tiny chunk of Bitcoin. Having multiple computers working simultaneously decreases the time it takes to find the solution."

"And dare I ask where you found a whole rig of computers? We don't even have a PC. You use a laptop."

"School. Josh and I worked out how to get around the administrator passwords when the new Macs were installed. Anyway, there's like forty computers in the suite, so we set them to mine twenty-four seven for the entire summer holidays."

Cooper's mouth fell open. The smell of beef and vegetables permeated the room, and her belly rumbled accordingly. The problem with Tina's expressionless face was that Cooper still couldn't tell if she was winding her up or not. She had a feeling she wasn't. "When was this?"

"End of year eight."

"When you were thirteen?"

"Yeah. We tried again at the Christmas holidays, but they'd toughened up their security by then."

"I wonder why?" Cooper asked dryly. "And how much is your wallet worth?"

Tina tipped her head from side to side. "Well, like I said, it fluctuates—"

"Tina."

"Enough to pay for rent and tuition when I go to uni."

A shout from the bottom of the stairs told them dinner was ready.

Cooper had thought it before, and she thought it again – her daughter was a sneaky little genius. She shook her head and pointed a parental finger, "We'll talk about this later. Let's go eat."

- CHAPTER 55 -

"ALEXANDER GOLDSMITH."

Rebecca Hogg, AKA Becky the Techie, waited for the printer in her Byker office to finish spewing reams of images and comments. She collated the paper into a neat pile and handed it to Neil Fuller. Becky turned her chair backwards, her legs straddling the backrest. She had long hair dyed a shocking shade of purple and a beanie covered her brown roots.

"His social media's almost non-existent," Becky said, between slurps of bubble tea. "But I noticed a Twitter account had liked two of the photos he was in – Three Bears."

She pointed to the top sheet of paper. The username was spelled 3B€ARS.

"He doesn't give any personal details, but he's an avid Toon fan and retweets a lot of Jordan Peterson. I took the same username to Instagram, Reddit and Mastodon with no luck. But, on Facebook,

I found an Alex Three Bears with the same profile image from Twitter."

Becky paused to slurp her drink before offering Fuller a sip. He declined, thinking it looked like some super sweet Gen Z nonsense.

"Suit yourself. Anyway, Three Bears isn't active on Facebook either. It's not easy to tell who he is, where he's from or what he does. But, being a clever girl I searched his profile for the word *birthday* and wham, bam, thank you ma'am, there's a post from Carole Goldsmith in 2005 saying *Happy eighteenth birthday, Goldilocks. Love Granny.*"

"Goldilocks?" Fuller raised his brows and rubbed the back of his hand against his auburn facial hair. He didn't know why he was surprised she'd got this information; Becky was a whizz at this sort of thing. He only hoped she never found her way into his own search history.

"Appears to be a nickname. Hence the three bears reference. I went through Nana Carole's posts and found a family photo with a gushing caption about being so proud of her grandson Alex for graduating with a third."

"She's boasting about him getting a third?"

"Grandmas, eh?" laughed Becky while twirling a lilac braid around her finger. "Anyway, there you go. Alexander Goldsmith. AKA Goldilocks. Born sixteenth of June 1987. Goldilocks is a goldsmith in name and nature – his dad owns a jewellery store in Newcastle. Probably how he's allowed in the Counties Club."

Fuller filed the printout into a shoulder bag and thanked Becky. She was strangely alternative with her striped arm warmers and dramatic eyeliner. Still, as long as she had a laptop, she was a genius.

"Thanks for this. It's a big help," he said. "Don't suppose you have an address."

Becky smirked. "He currently resides at twenty-one no fixed abode street."

Fuller sighed, hopes dashed. "Never mind. I know where his dad works. I'll start there."

IN WALLSEND, IT WASN'T bubble tea being sipped; it was Diet Dr Pepper. Keaton placed the can on her desk and grumbled, "One single transaction six years ago. Looks like he got some money for his eighteenth birthday. There's a transfer of three hundred quid from Tamzin, followed by a cash deposit of close to a hundred and fifty quid two days later – money from aunts, uncles, and grandparents, I'm guessing. The following day he pays a monkey to eCoinEurope. That'll be where he bought the Etherium.

Martin helped himself to a sip of Keaton's drink. "Nice one. Urgh. It's flat."

Keaton snatched the Diet Dr Pepper back, finished it in one and crushed the can in a vice-like grip. "Did we get a warrant for them, boss?"

Cooper held up a piece of paper. "Approved this morning." She pulled a calculator from her desk drawer. "Who has the Etherium value over time chart?"

"Me." Boyd opened a manilla folder and retrieved a graph. She wore a smart grey suit and a dusky pink blouse. Something about the young DC seemed more relaxed – more confident – of late. Cooper was pleased.

"At the time of Rhett's eighteenth, one Ether was just over a pound. Now it's worth almost fifteen hundred."

Cooper stabbed at the calculator. After pressing equals, she looked up at the team. "You're telling me young Rhett Campbell has three-quarters of a million sat in some online wallet?"

Keaton threw the crushed can in the air, span a full circle in her swivel chair and caught it again. "I reckon he *had* three-quarters of a million. I bet tomorrow's lunch it's not there anymore."

"You're right." Cooper waved the warrant. "Only one way to find out."

It was the start of the next week when eCoinEurope confirmed what they already knew: Rhett's wallet had been drained of all cryptocurrency. Despite the company being as helpful as possible, finding out where the money had gone was impossible.

"Transferred over the dark web," the Brummy assistant told them. "Couldn't trace it even if I wanted to."

When Cooper hung up, her expression told the team all they needed to know.

"No luck?" asked Boyd.

"Luck? In Northumbria Police? Chance would be a fine thing." Cooper stood to stretch her legs. Danny's cold meant no one in the Cooper-Atkinson household had got much sleep over the past six days and Cooper was feeling it. She walked to the big window in the incident room and looked out over the car park. Outside, the AA were tending to one of the big wig's cars. It looked like a dead battery, not quite as dramatic as having a tree fall through the windshield.

"Sex and money," said Cooper with a sigh. "All this time, I thought we were looking for a vicious killer when what we really have is a greedy little madam."

"She's both," said Keaton.

Cooper turned and folded her arms. Though her team were all similar in their desire to get the job done, they were a varied bunch. Boyd was shy, quiet, well-dressed and professional. Keaton was larger in both frame and personality. Martin, the pretty boy, was still finding his feet, while Whyte was the loner, always slightly detached from the group. Now Whyte and Martin lived together, and Martin and Boyd were an item, Cooper hoped for more cohesion.

"Which leads me to the million-dollar question," Cooper said. "Or the three-quarters of a million pounds question, to be precise. If you killed your fiancé, nicked all his money and faked your own death, what would you do next?"

Whyte was the first to speak. "Flee the country."

Cooper unfolded her arms and pointed at Boyd. "And for twenty points, what would she need to leave the country?"

"A new identity and a passport."

"Bingo." Cooper grabbed her coat from the back of a chair and pulled it over her knitted sweater. "Start calling the airlines," she told Boyd and Martin. "Paula, let's take a drive to Durham."

Chapter 56

"You know, for Northumbria Police detectives, we seem to be spending a lot of time in Durham."

Keaton looked out the BMW's passenger window while Cooper drove. It was a plain Monday lunchtime with cloudy skies and temperatures in the low teens. Cooper kept to the speed limit as they crossed the border to County Durham at Rickleton. They followed the A1 south, turning off at the Carrville Interchange and taking the green-lined A690 until the Romanesque towers of Durham Cathedral came into view. Cooper entered the Walkergate car park and waited for the ANPR system to read her numberplate and raise the barrier. They walked for two minutes through an alleyway behind a Premier Inn and climbed the steps to the Passport Office. It was a modern brick building with a glass-fronted entrance. Inside, queues of concerned holidaymakers waited anxiously to replace passports lost down the sofa, destroyed in the washing machine or eaten by the dog.

As Cooper and Keaton pressed through the crowd to the desk, they were met with jeers about queue jumping. They quickly subsided when Cooper pulled her ID from her pocket and declared, "DCI Cooper and DS Keaton to see Sujan Singh."

They were shown through to an airy office where Sujan Singh seemed unusually pleased to see them. He was a slightly overweight man with glowing light-brown skin. He wore a navy dastar and greeted them with firm handshakes.

"Forgive me for my silly grin. I'm so excited to meet real-life detectives." His eyes darted to a small pile of novels on the corner of his desk topped with a chrome Newton's cradle.

"I'm a huge crime fiction fan."

Cooper smiled. "I can assure you, it's not as exciting as in the books."

"Speak for yourself," said Keaton. "I nearly won the Northumberland Plate."

Almost a year ago, Keaton dislocated her shoulder tackling a suspect as he fled across a racetrack.

"So, out of curiosity," started Sujan. "what is the worst case you've worked?"

"The worst stuff, I can't tell you," Cooper said. "It would give you nightmares."

If it gave her nightmares, who knew what it would do to the general public.

"But I can tell you about the time DS Keaton chased a Fox Terrier for over two miles because he ran off with a key piece of evidence."

"Key piece of evidence?" Laughed Keaton. "It was the murder weapon. Little shit. Sorry. Language. But he had a knife handle in his teeth and a six-inch blade sticking out the right side of his mouth. Almost sliced through some poor bloke's Achille's tendon when he ran past."

Sujan rested his hands on his belly as he chuckled. "That's a good story. Did you catch him?"

"The dog or the killer?"

Sujan thought for a moment. "Both."

"Yes, and yes."

"The thing you need to know about DS Keaton," said Cooper, taking the seat opposite Sujan because he was gesturing for her to do so, "is that she can out-pace ninety-nine per cent of the humans on the planet. I don't say that lightly. If there's a race, you put your money on this lady."

"Sikhs can't gamble," said Sujan, "but if we did, I would take your advice. So what can I do for Northumbria Police's finest."

Keaton, blushing slightly from Cooper's praise, pulled up another chair. "Mr Singh—"

"Sujan, please."

"Sujan, we believe a woman named Laurel Deacon has obtained a passport under a fake name."

"The young lady from the news? Missing, presumed dead?"

Keaton nodded. "Only, as you may have guessed, we don't think she's dead. I trust you can keep that information to yourself?"

He flicked his eyes to his pile of books and looked thrilled to be involved in a plot twist of his own.

"Of course. You can count on me, DS Keaton. Do you know what name the passport is under?"

"No," Cooper said with a shake of her head, though she had a suspicion.

"Do you know when she applied for it?"

"No."

"Do you know what address was used?"

"No." Cooper pulled a sheet of paper from a file. "But I have a list of all properties she's lived at and a list of properties associated with her family, her late fiancé's family, and their closest friends."

Sujan eyed the sheet of paper. It was a long list with seventy potential postal addresses to search through.

"This may take some time," he said.

"In that case, I'll get us all coffee." Keaton rose to her feet. "Boss?"

"Cappuccino, extra shot."

"Decaf for me," said Sujan. He was already searching a database, his fingers moving swiftly and softly over the keys.

Cooper was draining the dregs of her frothy coffee when Sujan's face widened into a picture of happiness.

"Six months ago, a passport was issued to sixteen Hazelwood Terrace in Southampton," he said.

"Where's that?" asked Keaton.

"A flat Laurel and her best friend at uni lived in," said Cooper. "It's sat empty for the past nine months. It's not far from where she was living with Rhett. She probably walked past it every day and knew it was empty when she applied for the passport."

"Probably hung onto her old key," said Keaton. She turned to Sujan and asked, "Do you have the photo?"

Sujan nodded and turned his monitor to face them. "She looked better as a redhead."

The woman staring back at Cooper had dark burgundy hair and brown eyes. Her skin had the warm, orange tones of fake tan. Still, she was undeniably Laurel Deacon.

"Murderous little witch," said Keaton in a low growl. "We've got you."

Cooper's eyes flicked to the name. "Erin Cooper."

"E. Cooper," echoed Keaton. "I thought whoever paid the witnesses to help frame Underwood used your name to mess with you."

Cooper nodded. "Me too. But she applied for the passport six months ago. It must be a coincidence." She looked at Sujan. "Who is Erin Cooper? How could Laurel steal her identity?"

He swung one of the shiny balls in the Newton's cradle and set it in motion. The spheres made a calming, rhythmic tip-tap noise as Sujan thought.

"Cases such as this usually involve a falsified birth certificate. I'd guess Erin Cooper was a little girl born at a similar time as Miss Deacon but died shortly after birth."

Cooper's insides churned as she thought of her sick infant. A maternal tug pulled at her heart and made her want to leave for the A1 north immediately.

"If she faked or applied for a replacement birth certificate in Erin's name, she could use it to apply for a passport," continued Sujan. "That's how Canoe Man did it."

John Darwin, otherwise known as Canoe Man, faked his death in 2002. He scoured graveyards and newspaper records until he found the name John Jones, a baby from Sunderland whose identity he would steal to obtain a birth certificate and passport while his wife claimed a quarter of a million pounds in life insurance.

Laurel Deacon, both gold-digger and grave-digger, looked to have three times that amount. Cooper breathed slowly through her nose and thought of Rhett and his aspirations for that money. It may have bought his dream home, paid off his mother's mortgage or provided him and his fiancée with a hefty pension. She stood and thanked Sujan Singh for his time, asked him to keep their conversation to himself for the time being, and then bid him farewell.

- Chapter 57 -

After getting nowhere with the mysterious third man's relatives, Fuller concluded Alexander Goldilocks Goldsmith was the black sheep of the family. A man living on the fringe of society cut off from his household and friends. His father described him as a good-for-nothing leech; his mother's language was far worse. They hadn't seen him in over a year, didn't know where he lived, and the number they had for him was out of service.

Fuller essentially had CID to himself. Most of Cooper's team were either in Durham or following leads. Whyte was manning the phone, waiting to hear from Cooper. His own group of reprobates were out on various calls. There'd been some organised shoplifting at the Metrocentre, an armed robbery at Ikea and an interesting case involving a group of kids in karate uniforms. A man had reported the young teens for assaulting him as they left their martial arts class. When officers discovered the entire event was caught on camera, it turned out the youngsters were the heroes of the story. They'd stumbled across him mugging an elderly lady and weren't going to stand for it. One–nil to the karate kids.

Sucking on a cough sweet because he'd strained his voice at last Thursday's choir practice, Fuller followed a hunch and typed Goldsmith's name into IMDB. Nothing. He tried again using Alex, Ally, Al and so on with no luck. Wondering if he was wasting his time looking for the third man, Fuller tried once more, looking for variations on Goldilocks or Three Bears. His mouth fell open, and the cough sweet dropped from his mouth to the keyboard, covering it in menthol-flavoured drool.

"You okay?" asked Whyte.

Fuller was not okay. An actor using the name Goldie Smith was listed as an extra in some mushy ITV drama written and directed by the one and only Cyrus Harding.

Grabbing the phone, his fingers slipped as he dialled one of his team and demanded they bring Michael Holt in as soon as possible. He then called Durham and asked them to round up Cyrus.

"Lying little bastards can't deny it any longer. I can prove they know each other. So why are they so keen on keeping it from us?"

COOPER AND KEATON WALKED as they talked, skirting the back of the adjacent coffee house until they reached railings lining the river. Cooper placed her hands on the rail while Keaton leaned against it and crossed her arms. Looking left, Cooper could just make out the castle and cathedral beyond Milburngate Bridge.

"I think we both know that passport's been used," said Cooper with a sigh. "Laurel, Erin, or whatever she's calling herself could be a million miles away by now."

The smell of the river, exhaust fumes and coffee was a heady mixture that didn't help Cooper's low mood. She needed water and another painkiller.

"She sent bribe money from the Dominican Republic. That's where I'd start looking," Keaton said.

Cooper nodded and watched a branch being carried by the water towards the sea.

"Call HQ. Find out how Martin's getting on with the airlines. We need to know where she's gone. Focus on the Dominican Republic, but if she flew out of Newcastle, she probably went via Amsterdam or Paris."

Keaton flashed a cheeky grin. "When I said that's where I'd start looking, I meant literally. Do you think Nixon would spring for two business-class flights?"

Cooper's mood lightened, but only fractionally. "I wish. As much as I'd like to watch you chase her across a white sand beach while I sip on a pina colada, I don't think we have jurisdiction."

"Pity," said Keaton.

"Pity," said Cooper.

Keaton, looking crestfallen that they'd not be on the next flight out of Newcastle, followed instructions and called HQ. She passed the message onto Whyte and updated him about what they'd discovered at the passport office.

"Hang on," she told him. "I'll get us somewhere more private and put you on speaker."

They retraced their steps behind the Premier Inn to Walkergate car park. Cooper's BMW was cold; as Cooper engaged the electrics and connected Keaton's phone to the Bluetooth system, Keaton turned the heating on and flicked a button to warm her seat.

"We good?" asked Whyte.

"We're good," Cooper told him. "Go ahead."

At the far end of the car park, a woman laden with shopping bags returned to her car.

"I've been looking into Laurel's mother. She had some problems when Laurel was little, disappeared off the face of the planet—"

"You think Laurel's with her mum?" interrupted Cooper, wondering if the Deacons had not one but two women capable of faking their own deaths.

"Erm, no. I did, but now I don't. Remember Dean and Kareem? They saw someone who looked like Laurel with someone who looked like Underwood. As we ruled Underwood out, I'd pretty much forgotten about the sighting, assuming it was Underwood with a sex worker. But Keaton says Laurel's passport photo showed her with fake tan and false lashes. That sounds like the woman Dean and Kareem described. What if they really did see Laurel, only instead of Underwood, she was with someone who helped her change her appearance and get her to the airport?"

The woman in the car park opened her car boot and started loading her bags into it.

"An accomplice? Like who?" asked Cooper.

A man in grey sweatpants jogged across the car park, passing in front of the BMW. He sped up as he reached the woman with her shopping, then sprinted from view.

"Did you see that?" Keaton undid her seat belt. "He just snatched that woman's handbag."

Keaton opened the car's door and, without hesitating, took off on foot. Cooper turned the key in the ignition and accelerated towards the woman who was crying with shock.

"Are you hurt?" Cooper asked, lowering the window.

"No. But my phone's in my bag. Can you call the police for me?"

Cooper smiled. "I'm on it."

- CHAPTER 58 -

COOPER HIT THE GAS and took off towards the exit. As she reached the barrier, it refused to raise.

"Bollocks," she cursed.

A car rolled up behind the BMW and beeped impatiently. Cooper jumped from her car, ran to the payment machine and tapped her card against the reader. It was the first time she'd run since giving birth, not that she'd run much in the months preceding Danny's arrival. Feeling every step and every heartbeat, the pain in Cooper's pelvis almost caused her knees to buckle. She fell back into her car, the barrier raised, and Cooper floored it, scanning left and right for any sign of the thief.

"What's going on?" asked Whyte.

"Just Keaton being Keaton."

She stopped at the junction. Cooper could see Keaton disappearing from sight where the road bent towards Milburngate Bridge. She was about to move in pursuit when she saw the one-way sign.

"Shit."

"Everything okay?"

Cooper ignored Whyte, made a quick decision and turned the wrong way down the one-way road. She'd lost one team member because they'd split up; she was damn sure not going to lose another one. Keaton was capable, but so many muggers were armed these days. Cooper couldn't take the chance. She'd give Keaton a bollocking for going after him alone, but right now, her anger was suppressed with fear for her friend.

Pedestrians gesticulated and yelled at Cooper, pointing to the one-way and no-entry signs. Though the road was largely clear, a grey VW was heading straight for her, its driver oblivious as he tapped at a satnav.

Cooper slammed the horn and mounted the pavement, swerving between lampposts like a slalom skier. The BMW bumped back down the curb, and Cooper said a silent prayer as she turned into the blind corner under the bridge. An Audi with impeccable brakes stopped in time as Cooper once more mounted the curb and brought her car to a stop in front of triumphant Keaton and a dejected mugger.

Keaton shoved the man into the back seat and read him his rights. Leaping into the front seat, she held the woman's handbag in her lap and beamed at Cooper. "Reckon the victim's still there?"

Cooper gave her the same we'll-talk-about-this-later stare she'd given her daughter only a few days ago.

"I'd think so. We'll circle round and tell her to meet us at the police station on New Elvet, then we'll leave this reprobate in their custody and get ourselves back home.

"Hello?"

Cooper had forgotten about Whyte, and his voice came as a shock.

"Can someone please tell me if you're all okay?"

"I'm better than okay," said Keaton. "I feel effing great after that."

"Speak for yourself. I need a Valium and a bath of ibuprofen gel."

Cooper turned her car around and retraced her route along Freeman's Place, the correct way this time. She briefly talked with the victim, explaining who they were and where she should go to make a statement. After filling in a form or two, Cooper left the mugger with a grumpy-looking desk sergeant and returned to her car.

"Whyte, you still there?"

"Where else would I be?" he said with a snarky tone. "Right, now you're finished testing your advanced driving skills and saving the good people of Durham, can I have your attention?"

Cooper and Keaton tried not to giggle. As much as she hated to admit it, and as much as she was in pain, Cooper might have ever so slightly enjoyed their good old-fashioned police chase. Not that she'd tell Keaton that.

"You were saying?"

"Say it was Laurel in the woods near where Rhett's body was buried. Say she was with someone

378

who looked like Underwood. Now describe Underwood to me."

Keaton adjusted her seat so she could recline. "Tall, about six feet, bit of a unit. He's got black hair, not short but not too long. Slight tan."

"Exactly," Whyte said. "Who else does that sound like?"

"You're shitting me." Cooper pictured Ewan Underwood. She imagined his posture softening, his shoulders rounding. She saw his dark hair neater and swept back off his face. Underwood's face merged into that of someone else. "Bruce fucking Deacon."

"Mr   I-just-want-to-grieve-and-move-on." Keaton thumped the dashboard. "Him and his press conference crocodile tears. He has holiday rentals abroad."

"Already checked," Whyte said. "There's a villa in Antigua, one in the BVIs and one, have a guess."

"In the bloody Dominican Republic." Cooper gritted her teeth and turned the BMW toward the A1(M). "Keep on with the airlines. Let's make sure we're not jumping ahead of ourselves. I want to know what flight she got on and what she looks like. If she is in the Caribbean, we'll call their local authorities and see what they can do."

"Erm, boss." Keaton pointed to a road sign as it whizzed past her left shoulder. "You missed the Newcastle-Gateshead turn-off."

"We're not going north," Cooper told her, a renewed feeling of purpose building in her stomach.

When Michael and Portia Holt arrived at the station with their PI, an officer told Fuller that while Dorsey had followed just for the heck of it, Portia accompanied her husband due to white-hot rage. Not caring that a police officer was in earshot, she claimed she'd murder him there and then if he had anything to do with her daughter's disappearance. Michael took her threats with his usual abrasive dismissal and proceeded to call his lawyer.

Fuller brought Dorsey up to speed and then sent him off to Starbucks with copies of the information Becky the Techie had given him. Dorsey had proven himself a decent digital detective when he identified the painting as Harry Hall's Newminster. Perhaps he could spot something in Goldsmith's old social media posts.

When Fuller entered the family room, he found Portia pacing back and forth, her daughter's velveteen mouse clutched tightly to her chest. She stopped when she saw him and raced to him, grasping his lapel with her free hand.

"It can't be true. It can't be."

Fuller gently tried to remove Portia's fingers from his coat, but she tightened her grip.

"I'm not saying Michael's to blame. I don't know that yet. But I do know he's been lying to us. Both he and Cyrus acted like they were strangers to each other."

"We didn't know them before all this happened," Portia cried, cutting him off.

"I'm sorry, but that's not true. It might be for you and Nadine Harding, but not your husbands."

Portia sniffed, released Fuller and sank into a chair, her head in her hands.

"Are you sure?"

"He and Cyrus went to uni together. They've been at events together. They were photographed together. And while they both say they don't know Alexander Goldsmith, I know he played small roles in Cyrus's productions."

She rocked back and forth, her breathing erratic. "He wouldn't do that. He wouldn't harm our little girl."

Fuller patted her arm and handed her a tissue. He hoped Summer hadn't been harmed at all, but he didn't want to give Portia false hope. She was on the verge of collapse.

"But why?"

Fuller's theory was a wild one, but it was plausible. The Madeline McCann documentary topped the Netflix chart; The BBC broke their viewing record with The Moorside. Once Michael's lawyer arrived, Fuller would know for sure. Michael Holt wasn't leaving until Fuller had answers.

With no response from Fuller, Portia seemed the gather herself. She removed her hands from her face, revealing streaming, bloodshot eyes. Steadying her breathing, she pulled her phone from her handbag.

"I need a lawyer."

"Michael's already called one."

Her face hardened. "Not for him. For me. I need a divorce. I need a restraining order. I need..."

While Portia listed all the things she wanted her solicitor to handle, he thought what she really needed was a doctor and a prescription for a potent opioid. When the call connected, Fuller left her to it and returned to CID to prepare for his interview with Michael.

Elliot Whyte approached his desk and offered him a bottle of mineral water. "Hydrate. You're probably in for a long night."

"Thanks. Speaking of long nights, how's Erica?"

Whyte gave him the basics. They'd apprehended a mugger and were on their way south to arrest Bruce Deacon. He paused mid-sentence, dragging one of the printouts Beckie had given Fuller across the desk.

"One of Goldsmith's last social media posts," Fuller told him. "Under the name Alex Three Bears. Seems like a charming bloke."

The picture showed a candid, voyeuristic shot of two girls in their mid-teens sunbathing on a field wearing only swimwear. Behind them was some sort of sculpture. Two black posts pierced the ground, something dark and round hanging above them. The comment read, *My neighbours are proper sluts.*

Whyte returned the sheet to him and uttered three words that made Fuller's heart leap. "That's Shotton Colliery."

Fuller froze and met the man's eyes. "You recognise these girls?"

He shook his head. "No. The statue. It's a big pair of boxing gloves. I drive past it every weekend when I take my Dad out."

Fuller practically slid off his chair. "If this guy still lives there..." He could hardly get his words out. "The location. Show me."

Whyte unlocked a tablet and opened Google Maps. His fingers danced over the screen as he zoomed in. "Here. Not far from the airfield."

- CHAPTER 59 -

AS THEY TRAVELLED SOUTH, past open fields of grazing cattle, the sky darkened, the gentle tip-tap of April showers playing a staccato tune on Cooper's windshield. Whyte called, excitedly telling them about a development in the Summer Holt case. Could they really be experiencing a breakthrough in both cases? Cooper wouldn't believe it until she saw it. With Whyte still on the line, she asked him to call Hampshire Constabulary.

"I want eyes on Bruce Deacon. Have someone tail him. Make sure they don't arrest him yet, though. We've got another five hours of driving ahead of us and I don't want the clock ticking on his detention before I get there."

Whyte snorted. "I'll tell them, boss, but I doubt they'll listen to me."

"If they give you any shit, have them call me."

There was silence. Cooper wondered if Whyte was processing the rare occasion she had his back.

"Whyte?"

"I'm here. Okay, I'll crack on. Safe travels."

The rain intensified. The A1 was alive with the sound of roaring engines and swishing wiper blades. Occasionally the high-pitched squeak of tires struggling to cope on the wet asphalt could be heard over the tick-tock of Cooper's indicators as she weaved between lanes of traffic. Still, through the lulling drone of the motorway's mechanical music, a different sound caught Cooper's ears: sobbing.

Switching back to the left lane, Cooper glanced sideways; Keaton was wiping her eyes.

"Paula? What's wrong?"

"Nothing." The big lady in the passenger seat started to laugh. "Nothing at all. In fact, I haven't felt this alive in months."

They passed a layby where a skinny lady in a short skirt struggled to get the top back up on her red convertible Audi.

"Did Whyte tell you what happened?"

"Whyte? No. Why? What's he done?"

"He hasn't done anything except be a good mate. I asked him and Martin not to say owt. I know you don't like him, but—"

"I like him."

Keaton laughed.

"Fine," said Cooper. "I tolerate him. But he's growing on me. He's a team player. So, what did you ask him not to talk about?"

Keaton checked her reflection in the vanity mirror. She was a little red in the cheeks, but as she rarely wore makeup, she didn't have thick smears of mascara running down her face.

"April and I split up."

"What? Why didn't you say anything? Oh, Paula, that's terrible."

"It was just before Tennessee died. I walked in one day, and she was with a man. I mean *with* a man. Right there in the kitchen. Apparently, she had a kink for getting off with strangers. I mean, if that's how people get their kicks, then fair enough, I'm not kink-shaming, but..." Her voice trailed away.

"But it's only fair if all parties know and consent?"

"Exactly. I felt like a right idiot. I had no idea. I didn't even know she liked blokes. If she'd been honest from the start, I don't know, we could have worked something out or not bothered wasting our time in the first place. I felt like a fool and a worthless one at that. If April didn't want me and only me, I couldn't imagine anyone else doing so either. I resigned myself to being sad and lonely forever, and I hated seeing myself that way, so tried to keep it hidden when I was out of the house. I didn't want to bring the team down."

Cooper felt pain for Keaton and guilt towards herself. She'd known something was up but didn't push. She'd been caught up in her business: Tina's miscarriage, her pregnancy, the new baby, the case. Atkinson was right – there was always a case.

Cooper slowed the car, much to the annoyance of a man in the VW Golf behind her. He beeped and shook his fist, moving to the overtaking lane.

"What are you doing?" asked Keaton.

"I'm going to pull onto the hard shoulder. You need a hug."

"Don't be daft. I don't need a hug. I need to chase another low life through the streets of Durham. That was mint. They should prescribe it on the NHS. Never mind popping pills and bloody cognitive behaviour bollocks. People need adrenaline."

"Speaking of pills," said Cooper. "I'll take two." She pointed to her handbag in the footwell by Keaton's feet. "I haven't even had my six weeks check, and I'm sprinting back and forth to the ticket machine because the damn barriers wouldn't open."

"Shit. You okay?"

"I might have had a little wee if I'm honest. But yeah, I'm fine. See, this is the problem, Paula. You always take care of everyone else. You checked up on Tennessee when Hayley was in trouble. You checked up on Hayley when we lost Tennessee. You we're always watching out for me as I got closer to my due date. You took in Riley. And April was like a stray cat when you met her. You need to look after yourself, and I don't just mean eating well and getting plenty of exercise. You need to rest and process what you've been through. You lost April and Tennessee within days of each other."

An articulated lorry overtook, covering the windscreen in a sheet of water. Automatically, the wiper blades sped up.

"She's out there dating: I saw her profile on an app." Keaton sighed and stared out the passenger window. "She probably signed up the day I chucked her out; she's not good at being alone. Not that I am either. I keep thinking of getting out there and meeting someone new, but I can't bring myself to."

"It's not a race; you're grieving. Give it time. Better for it to happen organically than on one of those apps anyway."

"Aye, you're probably right."

A hush fell upon the car as the rain eased, and Cooper moved into the right-hand lane to let traffic join from the slip road near Catterick. She wondered how Atkinson would take the news that she wouldn't be home tonight. Danny was poorly and she missed her little lad terribly having never been away from him for more than a working day. Tina would be fine, she was practically self-sufficient. As would Atkinson, who loved being a father, but her thoughts returned to Danny. Would he notice she wasn't there? Would he miss her?

"Well, that was the most girlie conversation I've had in a while," Keaton said, breaking the silence. "I don't really do heart to hearts."

Cooper looked over and was pleased to see a smile on the DS's face. "Same here. Want to put some music on to lighten the mood?"

Keaton took her phone from her trouser pocket and scrolled through Spotify. "How about some psychobilly?"

"What the hell is psychobilly?"

"Part rockabilly, part punk."

Cooper laughed. "Sounds mental. Is it a suitable soundtrack for two female detectives pushing the speed limit in a race against time to arrest the duplicitous father of a murderer on someone else's turf?"

"Oh, it's perfect," said Keaton.

Keaton pressed play. Cooper pressed the accelerator.

- CHAPTER 60 -

SUMMER LAY ON HER bed pretending to sleep. She daren't move. They heard the front door click closed some time ago but agreed to wait for the big hand to point to the number three before moving. She opened one eye. It was time.

"Tim. Are you awake?"

He'd eaten some of his ice cream before she could remind him not to, and they'd thrown the rest down their toilet before climbing into bed.

He stirred but fell back asleep.

Feeling guilty about leaving him, Summer vowed she'd find a way to tell the grown-ups where he was so he could be with his mammy and daddy again. She remembered a story about a brother and sister who left a trail of bread crumbs to find their way home, but she didn't have any bread. She'd have to think of something else.

Summer moved around the room, gathering everything she needed. She pushed her felt-tip pens into her pocket and removed all the cushions from the playhouse. Next, she pulled all the books from her bookshelf. It was free-standing with only two shelves and was made from pale, yellowy wood. Once the books were piled on the floor, she dragged the bookcase to her play house. Inside Tim's toy chest, she found his tool kit. The plastic ones were flimsy and bent easily in her hands, but his wooden tools were just right. She picked out the screwdriver and hammer and put them to one side. Carefully, she toppled the slide over so it lay on its side. It took a few attempts to unscrew the ladder from the slide, but once the screws began to move, she could use her hands to spin them around until they popped out.

"Tim?"

He didn't wake.

It was now or never.

Summer arranged her duvet and cushions beside the bookcase in case she fell, placed the hammer on the top shelf and climbed up. She grabbed the short ladder with four rungs and clumsily manoeuvred it onto the roof of the playhouse. She'd never climbed so high before, and the idea of falling made her nervous and slightly dizzy. Her mammy didn't like heights either, but regardless, Summer climbed further, dragging herself onto the roof. Splinters caught in her dress and grazed her knees. All her hopes were pinned on the ladder. Her plan would fail if it didn't reach the window. She'd have to climb down and tidy everything before the man got home.

Gripping it in her tiny hands, Summer slowly leant the ladder towards the window. It didn't quite reach, but Summer thought she might still be able to get to the window from the top rung. Her hands shook as she climbed. She really didn't like heights and was reminded of a time last year when her daddy took her to the funfair. As much as she wanted to ride the Ferris wheel and the big, big slide, she'd been too scared. An older girl from school held her hand and said she'd go with her, but Summer cried and cried before running out of the queue and back to her daddy. The memory made her sad, but she couldn't think about it now. Instead, she focused on reaching the window.

With both feet on the top rung, she teetered unsteadily, but the solid weight of the wooden hammer in her pocket made her feel brave. She gripped the windowsill with one hand and reached into her pocket with the other. She tapped the pane, testing its strength. It made a dull thud but didn't shatter. She could hear her mummy and daddy's voice in her head, telling her off after she knocked a plant over and broke its pot. *Good girls don't break things.*

Summer took a deep breath and hit the glass as hard as she could.

It didn't break.

FOUR PSYCHOBILLY ALBUMS LATER, Cooper turned off the M1 for the Northampton Services, where there was a McDonald's, a Roadchef and a Costa. After emptying their bladders, Cooper and Keaton bought large coffees and filled the car with diesel. Cooper was fastening her seatbelt when another call came through from Whyte.

"Laurel Deacon used her Erin Cooper passport to board a flight to Punta Cana International in the Dominican Republic via Schiphol, Amsterdam."

That wasn't a massive shock to Cooper; it was what they'd expected.

"When?"

"Second of January."

Keaton rolled her eyes. "The date they were supposed to be on the train home from Edinburgh. While poor Tamzin's been beside herself, Laurel's been sunning herself in the tropics. Bet the little witch doesn't need fake tan now."

"I'm waiting on security footage so we can confirm her appearance," Whyte said.

Cooper thanked him for the update. "Anything else?"

"Hampshire have eyes on Bruce Deacon. He's at home."

"Good. Tell them to just keep an eye on him. We're not too far away now."

Cooper felt a deep hatred for Laurel Deacon. For months she'd been worried about the girl, searching for her, preying the likes of Underwood hadn't abused or killed her. Laurel had deceived them all. She was probably walking through shallow turquoise waters that lapped white sand. Cooper could picture her sipping a cocktail and lavishing her life as a fugitive.

She hoped she was eaten by a tiger shark.

- CHAPTER 61 -

LAUREL DEACON HAD NOT been eaten by a tiger shark. She was, however, sipping a cocktail and making the most of her beachfront property. She stepped out of the ensuite bathroom in a white bikini that showed off her tan. Though her skin had deepened in colour in the tropical sun of Hispanola, she was naturally a strawberry blonde. Most of her glow was thanks to dark tanning foam by Bondi Sands.

Catching her reflection in the glass doors framing the beach, Laurel was briefly surprised. She still needed to get used to her new look, especially her dark hair and the high-maintenance touches she'd added as part of her persona. She hated acrylic nails at the best of times, finding them unhygienic and clumsy. Still, the bright pink and yellow polish was particularly offensive. But that was the point. Laurel Deacon wouldn't look like that, but Erin did. She perfectly fit the character she'd created of a rich, superficial, vain, wannabe WAG. Opening the sliding doors and breathing in the sea air, Laurel listened to the gentle sounds of the Caribbean Sea. She might not be used to her new look and name, but she would eventually.

It wasn't as if she could turn back now.

This was her life, and a fine one it was.

The ice in Laurel's Cuba Libra tinkled against the tumbler as she stepped out into the Dominican sunshine. The tiled floor of the terrace was cool underfoot. As she reached the warm sand, it gave way beneath her toes. Behind her, and as far as the eye could see, lush greenery stretched along the coast. Rocks speckled the sand, and palm trees reached for the sky.

She placed her drink on a table made from an old log and sat on her sun lounger. In the distance, her friends, Carla and Felisa, jogged barefoot along the water's edge. Laurel needed help remembering what Carla Martinez did for a living; she was a forgettable woman in her early forties with poor English and terrible taste in clothes. Felisa Alemán, on the other hand, was as insecure as she was dim, which was precisely why Laurel liked her so much. Insecure people were easy to manipulate. A few compliments here and an offer of friendship there, and Felisa, who worked at the local bank, was eating out of Laurel's hand.

Felisa waved enthusiastically as the two women stopped by Laurel's sun lounger.

"Hi Erin," beamed Felisa. "I love your bikini. So beautiful."

Laurel raised her drink in thanks and offered the two ladies a drink.

"No. Gracias," said Carla.

"I would like that," said Felisa, "but we must finish our run. Will I see you tomorrow?"

"Wouldn't miss it," said Laurel, though she had no desire to go shopping with the banker. Still, best to keep up appearances.

Rhett's money – *her* money – was held in various ways. Some of it was in a new crypto wallet spread between multiple currencies. Some was in the bank, which was where Felisa came in handy. She didn't look too closely at her ID or ask too many questions when she turned up the branch to open numerous accounts. Nor did she bat an eyelid when she wanted to transfer money back to the UK or withdraw large amounts in cash.

Cold hard cash. Money was all well and good in the bank, but bank accounts were no use if the economy failed or war broke out. Laurel preferred something more tangible; checking your balance online didn't give the same rush as holding a hundred thousand pounds in your hands, thumbing the edges and smelling the notes. Since arriving on the island, Laurel had fitted the villa with a variety of safes. Some were obvious, like the one with the combination lock in her wardrobe. Others were hidden behind fake plug sockets and air conditioning vents. A fire extinguisher with a false bottom contained over ten grand, as did a clock with a removable back.

Briefly distracted by a steely grey iguana, Laurel thought of how different this place was from

England, especially those cold days in Cumbria and Northumberland. She'd never know how she'd let Rhett talk her into cycling the coast-to-coast in the dead of winter. Sure, kissing in the snow in Alston was romantic, but it hardly compared. BnBs, freezing tents, and boring old Northumbria. Or, a luxury villa, white sands and exotic animals? Laurel had made her choice. That needy clown would have done anything for her. Anything except cash in his crypto.

Laurel rolled her eyes and felt one of her coloured contact lenses stick against her lid. She blinked a few times to set it right. Rhett might have looked like an athlete, but he was a mouse. Mice scurry the ground, noticing only the small details right in front of their noses. Laurel was an eagle circling above; she saw the bigger picture. Any idiot could see a crash was coming. One more badly timed tweet from Elon Musk and his fortune – *her* fortune – would be gone.

Laurel wasn't prepared to let that happen.

The iguana climbed upon a jagged rock and made himself comfortable, perfectly blending into his surroundings, just as Laurel – or Erin – would blend into her new surroundings. She considered her futures: rich but living like a pauper with dull ol' Rhett, or this? This was paradise. Rhett didn't stand a chance. The money and all that came with it – security, power, luxury – it was all hers now.

Finders keepers.

- CHAPTER 62 -

DURHAM POLICE DESCENDED ON Shotton Colliery like biblical locusts. They roamed from house to house. Some knocked on doors asking if anyone knew Alexander Goldsmith or if they'd seen children in the area resembling Summer or Tim. Others looked for the exact location the photograph had been taken from. Fuller, unable to stay away, watched as officers diverted traffic. It didn't take long for word to get out that the police had been asking residents about the missing children, and reporters and journalists started to arrive, searching for the headline of the year.

Feeling lonely and desperate, Fuller patted the statue of the boxing gloves, feeling the cool metal against the palm of his hand. The angel on his shoulder told him Summer was nearby; he could feel it. The devil on his other shoulder disagreed. He was a nagging voice telling him he had it all wrong, that Summer's case was an opportune stranger abduction, that she was already dead. He pushed the thought away. It would consume him if he didn't. Opening an umbrella, Fuller turned away, wandering the neighbouring streets of the Ashbrooke Estate, Jubilee Place and Station Road. He didn't know if it was his despair or an act of divine intervention, but he found himself standing outside Saint Saviours Church. He made the sign of the cross and recited the only prayer he knew.

THIS DOESN'T LOOK LIKE Ponteland, thought Summer, looking around at a row of abandoned shops opposite square semi-detached homes. Maybe it's Darras Hall.

Overhead a plane flew in concentric circles. It was small and boxy, like a toy, not like the big jumbos that flew out of Newcastle. Summer gasped as the plane circled again and two skydivers jumped from the cabin. Not liking heights, she turned away. Two men in dark clothing ran along the street. Fearing one of them might be the man, she tucked herself behind a low stone wall to stay hidden. In the distance, she could hear shouting and a police siren.

Summer waited for them to pass, then dropped a felt-tip pen on the grassy ground before moving on. Her damp dress clung to her body, her rain-soaked hair lay limp against her cheeks. Blood seeped from a cut in her knee, snaking down her leg and staining her socks pink.

She was in a churchyard. Summer looked up at the building and knew it wasn't St. Mary's. St. Mary's had a tall, rectangular tower, but this church didn't have any tower at all. She stared at it for a few seconds, wondering where they kept their bell. The building was old and made of stone with stained glass windows arranged in threes. Trees in their finest spring greenery overhung a brick pavement, shielding it from the misty rain. A noise drew her attention, and she saw another man.

Summer ducked behind a gravestone. It was too late; he'd already seen her. She peeked her head around the granite memorial. It wasn't the man from the basement; this one was shorter and had orange-brown hair. He stopped in his tracks, his face tired and frightened, his mouth open in shock. Slowly, he staggered forwards as if walking was difficult.

"S— Summer?" he stammered.

She nodded shyly, her knees sinking into the muddy ground.

He looked at her as if she weren't real, like he was hallucinating. "Summer? It's really you?"

She nodded again at the nice man, then stood up and stepped away from the headstone. His eyes brimmed with tears, but he didn't look sad. He moved towards her tentatively. "It's okay, Summer. You're safe now. My name's Neil, I'm a policeman, and I've been looking for you for a very long time. I'm going to take you to your mammy."

"Mammy?"

Summer's heart felt whole for the first time in months. As she ran towards him, he fell to his knees, his arms outstretched as tears flowed over his cheeks. Summer leapt into his chest and hugged him tightly.

"But first," she said. "We need to follow the bread-crumbs." She pointed to a green felt-tip pen in the grass, then a red one by the entrance to Saint Saviours. "We have to save Tim and Pumpkin."

- Chapter 63 -

Peter Ward, Chief Constable for Hampshire Constabulary, may be Geordie by blood, but he was
an adopted Sotonian. He hadn't managed to shake
his accent, but at least his colleagues had given up
referencing Byker Grove and Fog On The Tyne.

Ward picked up his office phone and dialled the
number scrawled on a spiral notepad.

"DCI Cooper speaking."

He'd never met the woman but knew she worked
closely with that bastard, Nixon. Just the sound of
her voice annoyed him. Professional, perky, and
distinctly northern.

Ward introduced himself. "Just a quick courtesy
call." Not that Nixon had shown him much courtesy when he bedded Gina. "Wanted to let you
know we've arrested Bruce Deacon."

Cooper swallowed down her annoyance and dropped her phone voice. "What? Why? We're still over an hour away."

"He left his house carrying two suitcases, and his passport was sticking out the pocket of his jeans."

"Fair enough." It didn't take a genius to work out where he was off to. "Okay, let him call his lawyer and stick him in a cell till I get there."

"Excuse me?" CC Peter Ward did not sound amused. "I've been in this job a lot longer than you have, young lady. I know the procedure, thank you very much. This is our case and we won't be dictated to by Northumbria Police. You're a long way from Kansas, Dorothy."

Cooper stopped at a red light and glanced at Keaton. The DS smirked and mouthed, *let him have it.*

"Apologies for stepping on your toes, sir, but with all due respect," Cooper said in a tone suggesting the opposite, "but I don't let Superintendant Nixon speak to me like that and I won't tolerate it from you either. Not unless you want me to head straight to HR. This stopped being your case when it landed on my desk, so I suggest you drop the possessive act." She was silent for a beat before adding, "Sir."

Whether it was post-natal hormones, the long drive, the thought of not going home that evening, or the bloody case, when Ward didn't reply, Cooper found herself unable to stop herself from poking the bear.

"Howard Nixon sends his regards, by the way. I believe you two used to work closely together."

Nixon had done no such thing, but her comment was enough to keep the CC shtum for a moment. She considered adding *he asked after your lovely wife* but thought that would be going too far.

Ward grunted but stopped short of an apology.

"Be here by six, or we'll begin questioning without you."

SOUTHAMPTON CENTRAL POLICE STATION was a giant white cuboid, its top floors stained grey from rain. At least six storeys high, it dominated the immediate landscape. By the time Cooper killed the engine, it was ten to six, the sky was gunmetal grey, and raindrops speckled the car park. As one shift ended, another was just beginning. The car park brimmed with greetings and small talk as officers returned to their vehicles. Those arriving gave Cooper and Keaton the once over before heading for the great rectangular building on Southern Road.

Keaton bent over to stretch her hamstrings and lower back.

"That's the longest I've sat still in a while."

"Same," replied Cooper.

Word had reached them that Summer Holt and Timothy Harding had been found alive. They didn't have all the details yet, but Durham and Northumbria Police had arrested three adult males. When Cooper heard the news, she was filled with such relief Keaton had to briefly grab the steering wheel.

Cooper pulled her phone from the hands-free magnet fastened to one of the air vents and chucked it in her handbag. Atkinson wasn't thrilled she'd be away all night, but he'd supported her decision. Danny was still full of cold and had a slight fever. The out-of-hours GP was aware and would pop over if his temperature continued to rise. Tina had hobbled to Josh's house after school and wasn't due home until after eight. Atkinson had asked her not to tell Julie that Cooper was away. He felt guilty asking Tina to lie but a night in with a crying baby was still more peaceful than a night with Julie. She was sure to call in and fuss over the pair while dropping thinly veiled digs about Cooper's absence.

Almost as soon as Cooper fastened the zip on her handbag, her phone chirped. She pulled it free, hoping it wasn't news about Danny. It was Martin. Cooper read his messages then handed the phone to Keaton so she could gander at them.

"Interesting," Keaton said, shrugging her shoulders in little circles to loosen them off after the long drive.

"That's what I thought."

A detective in a long, grey coat with tired eyes but impressive posture beckoned the two women.

"Detectives Cooper and Keaton? I'm DI McLaughlin." He nodded formally to Cooper and shook her hand. "Follow me. Deacon's in interview suite four. He's had a Yorkie chocolate bar and a bottle of Lucozade."

"Christ," said Keaton. "He expecting to run a marathon or something?"

"Think he knows he's in for the duration," McLaughlin said with a wry smile. "Love your accent, by the way. Would you—"

"No, I won't say *gannin' doon the toon* or *whey aye, man.*"

"I was going to ask if you would like a cup of tea, but thanks for the Geordie lesson."

"A tea would be great," Cooper said. "Has Deacon said anything?"

"Only that going on holiday isn't a crime. That he wanted a break after his daughter's disappearance, and that shouldn't be too much to ask."

Cooper shook her head in dismay. "He's maintaining his story? I thought he'd fold quicker than a cheap card table."

- CHAPTER 64 -

THE BROKEN BRUCE DEACON who shuffled around
with slumped shoulders and a downturned mouth
was gone. The persona Cooper spoke to early in
the investigation has returned. Back then, he'd
played the part of an overbearing man demanding
the police drop everything to find his daughter.
He'd pointed fingers in faces, curled his lip in a
snarl and stood too close for comfort. Now, sitting
in an uncomfortable chair on the wrong side of an
interview room, Bruce was unable to stand over
Cooper and stare down at her in his intimidating
manner. He could still give her that same hard
stare from his onyx eyes.

Beside him, a woman in a sharp suit with
an ambitious air about her practically salivated.
The father of the missing beauty, Laurel Deacon,
had been arrested. Every up-and-coming criminal
lawyer would be wetting themselves to take on
such a high-profile case.

Cooper wondered what the press would think when they heard Laurel was alive and on the run. They'd be orgasmic.

"You know, Mr Deacon – Bruce – if you'd just come clean when you were in Newcastle, you would have saved me a hell of a long drive, and I'd be in a hell of a better mood."

"I have nothing to come clean about, and I resent the implication that I do."

Cooper turned to the lawyer. "If this man has been honest with you, you wouldn't be advising him to stick to this ridiculous charade." She stood, somewhat relishing taking the weight off her back-side after so long in the driver's seat. "I'll give you another ten minutes." She turned to Deacon, "Tell your lawyer the truth. She can't help you other-wise."

Turning the camera off, Cooer and Keaton re-moved themselves to pace the corridor. Keaton paused at one end to do some squats and lunges; Cooper watched the clock ticking slowly towards six-fifteen.

"Right," she said, reentering the room and taking a seat. "Bruce, are you sure you have nothing you need to come clean about? Nothing you'd like to get off your chest?"

"Such as?"

"Oh, for crying... Such as why you were fleeing the country?"

"I have already explained to the arresting officer that I was *not* fleeing the country." His dark face reddened slightly, a vein bulging at his temple. "I've been through an awful ordeal. My daughter has been missing since December, and I've been at my wit's end with worry. It was actually my doctor who recommended I get away for a little break and some convalescence. He's concerned about my blood pressure. His name's Dr Malik Abdi at St. Mary's Surgery on Johnson Street. You can consult him if you like. Unless you think he's in on this laughable conspiracy you've concocted?"

"What conspiracy?" asked Cooper. "All I asked was why you were fleeing the country?"

Cooper found it hard to maintain eye contact. Firstly, because the vein in his temple continued to pulse to the same rhythm as the clock hanging from the wall behind him. It was distracting. And secondly, because Bruce Deacon was so imposing. There truly was an aura of Underwood about him.

"And though I maintain I was not fleeing, I have still answered your question, DCI Cooper."

"Okay, let's take a breath. You love your daughter?"

"Of course I do. What sort of silly question is that? I raised her by myself. It's not easy being a single father. People make judgements, you see. They think I can't give her what a mother can. You'd think in this day and age—"

"You sound like a good dad," Keaton said, leaning forward. "My dad didn't give a shit about me. Still doesn't. He didn't care if I got in trouble at school or stayed out late. He didn't care if I walked home from town in the dead of night."

"Dads should protect their daughters," said Bruce, nodding.

"I agree," said Keaton. "Which is why I'm curious you let her cycle through Northumberland in the middle of winter."

"Let her?" Bruce's brows raised a touch. "She's a grown woman: twenty-two. She had Rhett with her. He's a great man, a good head on his shoulders. I can't keep her wrapped in cotton wool forever. At some point, they have to make their own decisions. You have a daughter," he said to Cooper. "I'm sure you understand."

Cooper did understand. As much as Cooper wanted to keep Tina safe from the world, it was Cooper who had caused her the most pain. A single-mum and ambitious detective, she'd skipped meal times and school runs and exposed her to dead-beat boyfriends who would rather Cooper didn't have a child in tow. She'd allowed Kenny back into her life, a controlling man whose only interest in being Tina's father was to get closer to Cooper. And although it wasn't Cooper's fault, her biggest regret was the breast cancer that almost broke her spirit. No young teen should have to take on the responsibility of caring for a sick parent – it wasn't the way of the world. Parents looked after their children, not the other way around.

"We're here to talk about your family, not mine," Cooper said frostily. "You don't look much like Laurel?"

"A lot of people say that." Bruce raked his fingers through black hair. "She got her colouring from Marta, but she got other traits from me. Her height and the shape of her eyes. We both have hooded lids. Still, it didn't stop nosy bastards from asking

411

if she was adopted. People didn't think she was mine."

"You do have a striking appearance," said Keaton.

Cooper nodded. "Some might say you have a strong resemblance to Ewan Underwood."

"That oaf!" Bruce looked offended. Cooper was happy to have insulted him.

The lawyer raised her pen. "The man arrested for Rhett and Laurel's murder?"

Cooper brought up an image of Underwood on her iPad. "The same. Here's Underwood all dressed up for the magistrates' court. I'd say he could be mistaken for your client. Or rather, your client could be mistaken for him."

The lawyer shrugged. "Debatable."

Cooper swiped her finger over the screen to reveal another image. "Laurel looks a lot more like you in this picture."

The image showed Lauren as Erin, captured as she walked through security at Schipol Airport. Her brown hair was pulled through the back of a baseball cap, and her fake tan had marked the collar of her white t-shirt.

"What am I looking at?" asked Bruce.

"Your daughter. You say you're a good dad. A good dad would recognise his daughter anywhere, don't you think?"

Keaton pushed the iPad closer to him. "This was taken on the second of January at Schipol Airport, where Laurel boarded a flight to the Dominican Republic."

"Which just so happens to be the same place you were headed," Cooper said.

"And the same place the bribe money came from for the two so-called witnesses," added Keaton.

Bruce gulped but otherwise maintained his composure. "Nonsense."

Keaton laughed. "I tell you Laurel is alive and well, and your reaction as a grieving father is to tell me it's nonsense?"

"He was never a grieving father," said Cooper. "If he were, he would have reported Laurel missing."

"I did," barked Bruce. "I did report her missing. I was here all night giving statements."

"It was Tamzin who reported Rhett and Laurel missing," said Cooper, pulling the iPad back towards her. "You only gave a statement after the police contacted you."

Keaton tutted. "Loosing your good dad points now, Bruce."

Bruce faltered. "I was in communication with Tamzin. I knew she was going to contact you. I couldn't do it myself because I, erm..."

Keaton held up Bruce's original statement that he'd made for Hampshire Constabulary. "Because you were away on business?"

"Yes. That's right."

"Where?"

"Erm." He faltered again, his eyes scanning the table for answers.

"You can't remember where you were when your daughter became a missing person?" Cooper painted an incredulous look on her face. "That's another minus point."

"Wales," he blurted out. "I was at one of my properties in Wales."

413

Keaton made the noise of a buzzer from a TV quiz. "Wrong answer. You were in Newcastle."

Cooper couldn't help but smile. "While DS Keaton and I were driving all the way down here, Elliot White – you remember DC Whyte, don't you? Friendly guy, bought you a coffee, felt bad for you losing your daughter? – He and DCs Martin and Boyd have been busy little bees. DC Martin sent me these ANPR images just moments before I arrived."

She opened an email attachment and turned the iPad so Bruce and his lawyer could see.

"On New Year's Eve, you travelled north on the A1," Cooper said.

"Big mistake," Keaton said. "Using main roads. Your lawyer's going to have words with you about that."

"We clocked you going through the Tyne Tunnel at eight minutes past five in the afternoon," Cooper added.

"And you paid your toll via the website within the hour," said Keaton. "We told you the bees had been busy."

"Then you went to Boots at Silverlink." Cooper tilted her head and narrowed her eyes. "Right round the bloody corner from Northumbria Police HQ."

"Un-fucking-believable," Keaton said with a chuckle.

The lawyer coughed. "Be mindful of your language, detectives." Though she was warning Cooper and Keaton, it was Bruce she glared at.

"Now, our bees haven't managed to get the exact details of your transaction yet, but we do have some CCTV footage." Cooper swiped left. "I don't know about you, but this looks like two boxes of Garnier Nutrisse hair dye; I recognise the green stripe across the bottom of the boxes. What does a man with a great head of hair like yours need with hair dye, Bruce? And don't tell me you're going grey. I've met you several times, and not once has there been a millimetre of grey in that mop of jet black."

Instinctively, Bruce touched his hair, then quickly interlaced his fingers and placed them in his lap.

"I think I'd like a break," he said.

"You're not entitled to one yet," Cooper said.

"Then I think I'd like to speak privately with my lawyer."

"I think your lawyer would like to know exactly what evidence we have against you. After all, she knows she can't trust what you tell her."

The lawyer gave Bruce the same look Julie gave a sixteen-year-old Cooper when she caught her sneaking in at four in the morning: not angry, just very disappointed.

"Here's what I think happened," said Cooper. "Laurel killed Rhett."

"Laurel would NEVER—"

"Let me finish. Laurel killed Rhett in North Shore Woods at Druridge Bay. With Rhett's body still warm, she used his dead finger to unlock his phone and begin emptying his crypto wallet. She partially buried his body, then took their bikes and belongings up the road to Hauxley where she spent

415

the night in the abandoned caravan park. The next morning Ewan Underwood steals the bikes and bags. If that was deliberate on Laurel's part, then fair play, tracking down stolen bikes and trying to connect Underwood to the murders took up a lovely chuck of our time."

Cooper paused to drink some water and see if Bruce would interrupt again. He didn't.

"Laurel's a clever girl," Cooper continued. "I guess she gets her brains as well as her looks from her mother because you then came to the rescue using the main roads. You turn up with fake tan, hair dye, and what DS Keaton would describe as *girlie shit*. The next morning you help Laurel change her appearance. She dyes her hair, tans her skin and applies false lashes and nails. You also bought her some coloured contacts. I don't wear contacts, but I know people who do. They're hard to get used to; you can only wear them for short periods at first. Which is why she wasn't wearing them when you moved Rhett's body to a deeper grave."

"Bonus dad points," Keaton said. "My dad would never help me bury a body."

"But you were seen," Cooper said.

"Minus point," Keaton said.

"Two kayakers spotted you in the woods. Two kayakers and a dog, to be precise. I'm betting Melanie, the dog, could smell Rhett's body. The two gentlemen knew it was Laurel because of her beautiful blue eyes. Unfortunately, they – and we – assumed the dark man who was with her was Underwood."

Keaton shook her head. "With Rhett buried in a better grave, his crypto safe and sound in a new wallet, and Laurel cleaned up and looking markedly different to how everyone knew her, Laurel headed for Newcastle International, and you headed back south ready to play a distressed father. We have you on the A1 southbound shortly after ten a.m. on the second of January."

The lawyer propped her elbow on the table and rested her chin in her hands. As ambitious as she seemed taking on a big profile case, she was no doubt now wondering how she could best defend him.

"When you came to Newcastle and gave me a hard time, you travelled by train, correct?"

"Correct."

"When you came for the press conference, you travelled by train, correct?"

"Correct."

"Do you garden?" Cooper asked.

Bruce Deacon looked like he didn't know if he was coming or going. His facade had undoubtedly slipped. Though he retained a confident posture and a menacing stare, something was off. His fingers twitched in his lap; his leg trembled beneath the table. The vein throbbed faster.

"No," he answered, his voice steady.

"Me neither. Can't stand it. I hate getting dirt under my nails. But soil's a funny thing. It's different all over the UK. In fact, the soil around Druridge and Hauxley is rather unique."

Cooper stood; she was sick of sitting. She held the iPad to her chest and smiled as she spoke. "It's called soilscape twenty-four and is found in less the half a per cent of England," she said, echoing Atkinson's words and marvelling how he'd even known that without having to look it up. "It's found on restored mining sites. I don't pretend to know all the science, but it's something to do with acid seepage from opencast runoff."

"What's your point?" Deacon snarled.

"The point is, we went over Underwood's truck with a fine-toothed comb and couldn't find any evidence of Rhett or your daughter. But I bet when we go over your car, we'll find soilscape twenty-four. Then you're going to have some fun and games explaining why your car was at the murder and burial site."

Bruce stammered and spluttered, the vein taking on the rhythm of a nineties dance track. "Are you going to let her talk to me like that?" he snarled at the lawyer.

The lawyer sighed and briefly closed her eyes. "My advice to you, Mr Deacon, is to say nothing more."

"Well, you're a fat lot of good. Knew I should have gone with someone older. Someone with more experience. As if you're not even going to tell them they can't search my car. I don't consent to that."

"You won't have a choice, Mr Deacon," said the lawyer, her voice deepening.

"Why the bloody hell not?"

"Because you're under arrest, that's why."

IT WAS FORTUNATE THAT Bruce had a Yorkie and a bottle of Lucozade, for he was indeed, in for a long night. It was three a.m. when Boots got back to Whyte with the full list of items Bruce had purchased on his trip to Newcastle. Unless he was considering a career change and wanted to begin a drag act, Cooper wondered how he'd explain the pink press-on nails by Kiss and pre-glued fluttery light lashes by Eylure. At shortly after four a.m. the lab called. They'd worked through the night as a favour for Cooper because Atkinson was a *solid geeza* who'd got them out of a few scapes. Cooper placed the call on speaker phone, listened to all the lab assistant could tell her, then hung up.

"Ready?" she asked Keaton.

"I'm ready to go to bed, but yeah, let's do this."

They had an officer wake Bruce Deacon and return him to the interview suite, where he sat alone after his lawyer withdrew herself from the case.

He rubbed his eyes, looked at Cooper contemptuously and grumbled, "Well, go on, get on with it, woman."

"You did a good job of cleaning your car, Bruce. Good, but not great. Soilscape twenty-four, unique to restored quarries and mines and found in only point four per cent of England, just so happened to be on the profiled suspension arms of your Mercedes."

Bruce wrapped his arms around his head and folded until his head rested on the table. "It was all Laurel's idea."

"Oh, bad dad," Keaton said. "I'm disappointed in you, Bruce. Shouldn't you be protecting your little girl at all costs?"

"I was protecting her! I did everything she asked of me. It was all Laurel. I didn't know. I promise I didn't know. She called me, told me what had happened, what she'd done. I couldn't believe it. Not my Laurel? Not Rhett?"

"Bruce Deacon, I am—"

Bruce interrupted Cooper with his pathetic pleas. "I was just trying to help. I was protecting her. I panicked and messed up. I took the wrong route and missed the chemists I was supposed to go to. Laurel was furious. She told me I had to buy her time, or she wouldn't tell me where to meet her once things died down."

"You're as bad as each other," said Cooper.

"I'm innocent. I didn't hurt anyone."

Rage surged through Cooper's body. She kicked a chair, causing it to hit a wall with enough noise to make even Keaton jump. "You are NOT innocent. Rhett was innocent. Rhett didn't hurt anyone. What was his crime, Bruce?"

"Nothing. Nothing." He peaked at Cooper through his fingers. "But he wouldn't cash in the crypto. She knew a crash was coming; she works in cyber security. Laurel knows all about that online business. But Rhett wouldn't budge, kept saying it was for their future."

"How awful of him," said Keaton dryly.

"And he was cheap. The wooden ring, the low-cost holidays... I'm not making excuses. It just wound Laurel up; she didn't want to see it wasted. And she was right, wasn't she? It crashed yesterday."

"It dipped," Keaton said. "Hardly a crash."

Laurel Deacon was an avaricious, murderous witch who deserved to rot in jail. Bruce Deacon was a sheep in wolf's clothing. He acted tough, but in the end, he'd given in to Laurel's greed as much as his own.

Cooper picked up the chair and returned it to the desk. She rested her hands on the table and towered over Bruce as he had once done to her. "Bruce Deacon, I am charging you with conspiracy to murder and perverting the course of justice."

Bruce tore at his hair. "But I didn't kill anyone," he begged.

"Neither did Maxine Carr," said Keaton, "and we know how people feel about her."

- CHAPTER 65 -

TYNEMOUTH SHED HER WINTER coat on the morning of Good Friday, with clear skies and an unbearably bright sun. The grass took on a healthy, vivid green, the trees were alive with blossom and insects, and the air smelled of pollen.

Though the sun shone brightly, summer was still far from the northeast. Cooper put on a pair of sunglasses, appreciating the relief they brought her eyes. There was a nip in the air, and while some seaside visitors regretted their attire, hugging themselves for warmth, the team from CID dressed in thick coats and sturdy boots.

Steering Danny's buggy to the left, they entered Tynemouth Park, an area set back from the beach with a miniature golf course, a play area and a boating lake. Short, well-tended grass and flowerbeds in full bloom surrounded the lake, which was dotted with model boats with white sails. Keaton took charge of the buggy while Cooper warmed her hands against a cardboard cup filled with strong coffee. Danny giggled as a mute swan glided toward them, hoping for some crumbs or seeds.

"Any word from Hampshire?" asked Martin. He and Boyd walked hand-in-hand behind Cooper, Whyte and Keaton.

Keaton flashed him a warning stare. "Work talk, for Christ's sake? It's a bank holiday."

Whyte laughed. "Nothing like marking the crucifixion of our lord and saviour by taking his name in vain."

"You do it all the time," said Keaton.

"I know. But it's Good Friday. Doesn't feel right."

"I didn't have you pegged as a God botherer."

"I'm not, but—"

Martin let go of Boyd's hand to put his arm over her shoulders. "But he does go to church every Sunday."

The group stopped to stare at Whyte, wondering if Martin was serious.

"What? You look like you've never seen a Catholic before. I take my dad every Sunday. It's our, I don't know, our father and son time."

Cooper looked at Whyte in a new light, then looked at her own son, who was feeling much better than he had earlier in the week. Danny, wrapped up in his favourite blanket, appeared mesmerised by the sun dancing on the lake's surface like a million fireflies. She and Atkinson had no plans to Christen or Baptise Danny. Still, she hoped with Atkinson as a father and stories about Tennessee, the man he was named after, that he'd grow up with a solid moral compass and respect for those he held dear.

"Back to your question," said Cooper, pausing to put her coffee cup in a recycling bin. "Yes. Deacon's not doing well on remand."

"Poor thing," Keaton said, her voice laced with sarcasm.

Cooper agreed. She had no sympathy for the man. While his doppelgänger, Underwood, would be fine and dandy at her Majesty's pleasure, Deacon was unlikely to thrive in jail. His new neighbours would see through his height and demeanour; they'd take one look at him and know he'd never been in a real fight before. Well, she thought, he may have been by now. The ironic thing being that despite all this, Deacon was still safer in jail than out of it. As Cooper predicted, the press and public were after Deacon in equal measure. He was a weak man who should know better, manipulated and pathetic. Unlike Underwood, who'd relished the media attention outside the magistrates' in Bedlington, Deacon had to be dragged in, a towel covering his head. His daughter, on the other hand, had captured the imagination of Brits from Lands End to John o' Groats. She was sexualised in the media and portrayed as a black widow. A sexually charged femme fatale who stole Rhett's heart, his money and his life. It was only a matter of time before Channel Five made a three-part series about her. Which was more than could be said for young Summer Holt, thought Cooper. Michael Holt and Cyrus Harding were so sure of their hair-brained scheme that they'd arrogantly started work on the first draft of their screenplay. Of course, other than as evidence for the prosecution, it would never see the light of day now. When a film or documentary eventually came out, which it undoubtedly would, it would be Michael and Cyrus who'd be the subjects of the show, not their children.

"I can't believe the Dominicans won't deport Laurel," Whyte said, his breath condensing before his face. "I know we don't have an extradition treaty with the Dominican Republic, but still, they could play ball if they wanted to."

They formed into single file to allow two joggers to pass as they circled the boating lake. Keaton brought the buggy to a stop while everyone caught up. The park was alive with the sound of birdsong, water lapping the lake's edge and the quiet chatter of locals on the chilly spring morning. In the distance, the soft rumble of traffic and car radios carried on the breeze.

Boyd's dark blonde hair wafted over her face as the wind picked up. "I'm not surprised they're telling the UK government to get stuffed. We extradited one of their own to the US. Peña's awaiting his execution at some Texan hell hole."

"Poor thing," said Keaton, echoing herself with even more sarcasm than before.

"So, Laurel Deacon gets away with murder?" Martin shook his head. "If I had it my way, we'd be on the next flight—"

"Yeah, Keaton already tried that on Nixon," said Cooper, bending to pick Danny out of his buggy because he'd started to whimper. "I can't repeat what he told her in front of this one." She smiled at her baby, feeling more relaxed than she had in a long time.

Keaton pinched Danny's left earlobe between her thumb and index finger and adopted a baby tone to her voice, "Let's not pollute your precious wee ears with what that nasty pasty told me."

"You don't seem bothered," said Whyte.

"We can't win them all," Cooper told him with a shrug. They left the park and headed right along Grand Parade. To their left, the sea was choppy as the tide went out. Crowds enjoyed the beach, taking advantage of the bank holiday despite the low temperature.

"Remember that, or this job will drive you all insane," added Cooper while Keaton pushed the empty buggy.

"We're already insane," she laughed, holding a hand towards Martin, who gave her a fist bump.

"Aye. You don't have to be mad to work in CID," he said.

"But it helps," they all said as one.

Cooper led the team away from the shore and up Percy Park Road, a street with grand three-storey homes on one side and a broad field on the other where dads played football with their sons and daughters. The air was tinged with the smell of vinegar as families hurried past, clutching fish and chips from Marshall's. It was Good Friday, after all.

"Besides, we might not have Laurel in custody, but we still solved the case." Cooper turned left onto Latimer Street. "Which means," she said, looking at each of the team in turn, a wry smile on her lips, "I get a new DI."

Martin frowned, "But Nixon said you had to find Rhett and Laurel."

"No. He said we had to solve the case. We did that. We know who killed Rhett Campbell. Bruce Deacon is going to jail for a long time, and if Laurel Deacon sets foot on British soil, the CPS will slap her with a life sentence faster than she can say, 'I'd like to speak to my lawyer.' We solved the case; I want a DI."

"She doesn't even have to come home to Britain," Boyd said, nuzzling up to Martin for both physical and emotional warmth. "I checked, and we have extradition treaties with the US, Mexico, Cuba and a host of Caribbean islands. Even Haiti. She can't leave that half of the island without being arrested and sent back here. She's basically in a jail the size of Estonia."

The front door opened and Atkinson welcomed the team into their home with arms as wide as his smile. Dressed smartly in jeans and a white shirt, his apron was speckled with a cream-coloured sauce.

"A tropical prison with a shit tonne of money to her name," said Whyte. "Not exactly HMP Bronze-field."

Cooper ignored Whyte and Boyd and stepped forward to kiss her man. Atkinson loved being on paternity leave with Danny, watching him change daily and seeing the curiosity in his brilliant blue eyes. So while Cooper took Danny for a stroll with the team, he'd indulged in one of his favourite hobbies: cooking.

He was a keeper, Cooper thought as they all followed her into the terrace house and wiped their feet on the doormat. Inside, Julie and Tina were helping to set the table. Julie hummed an Ed Sheeran track while she placed wine glasses and tumblers on coasters. Tina, who was moving comfortably without her crutches now, lined the cutlery up with a precision Atkinson would approve of.

They settled around the table, filling glasses and fantasising about a business trip to Hispañola. Keaton asked Julie about the bar and if they'd had any interest yet, and Tina, finding a friend in the other quiet soul of the group, talked to Boyd about school and GCSEs. Still, the chatter abruptly stopped when Atkinson entered the dining room with one of the biggest fish Cooper had seen. There was a collective gasp as he placed the turbot in the centre of the table.

"Whole roast turbot, with garlic and lemon new potatoes," he beamed. "Buttered samphire, salsa verde and a French sauvignon blanc."

Atkinson opened the wine and poured everyone who wasn't driving a glass, including Cooper, who had expressed milk earlier, and Tina, who was allowed a small measure.

"Oh, I almost forgot," said Atkinson, diving back into the kitchen. He returned with a cheese toasty and placed it next to Tina's plate. "Just in case you don't like the texture of the turbot."

The remarkable man sitting opposite Cooper might not be Tina's father, but that small gesture of understanding and compassion made him more of a dad to her than Kenny had ever been. As Tina's face flushed with gratitude, her co-workers tucked in, and Danny's tiny fingers curled around Julie's index finger, Cooper was reminded of a saying:

Everyone has two families: the one they're born into and the one they choose.

And on that Good Friday in Tynemouth, Cooper was blessed with both.

- CHAPTER 66 -

LATER THAT NIGHT, WHILE Erica Cooper slept soundly in her home near Long Sands Beach, another woman who went by the name Cooper strolled along a beach four thousand miles away. This beach was still warm after sunset, and the delicate, powdery sand felt soft beneath her tanned toes.

Erin Cooper, aka Laurel Deacon, was saddened as she thought of her father. She'd never see her dad again, never go home.

This is home, she told herself.

And home was paradise. With that thought, her despondency washed away like the tide. Remorse wasn't a word Laurel would tolerate. It would dampen her spirit, and not one to believe in karma, she embraced the salty oceanic air with thoughts of a job well done. Laurel Deacon had gotten away with murder. She might be trapped here, but as long as she kept her head down and stayed on the right side of the local authorities, life would be sweet. She'd never worry about money, count pennies or dread bills ever again.

It was surprising how little she missed Rhett. It helped that he'd hate it here. Too hot, too humid. Who needed a luxury beachfront villa in the topics when they could be freezing their bits off pushing a bike up a snowy hill in the arse end of Cumbria? Laurel laughed and stopped to look at her ring finger. It was bare now, free of that hideous wooden engagement band. Gemstones adorned all her other fingers, for Laurel now wore a sizeable portion of her wealth in diamonds and emeralds. She admired them in the moonlight, marvelling at how they twinkled like stars.

Above an inky sea, the full moon illuminated a path beneath it, casting the rippling water into a sharp contrast of watery peaks and troughs. In the distance, a stormy squall brewed. Lightning flashes filled the sky with white, thunder following like an echo. Such a dramatic sky, but all she felt was peace. Laurel pulled her shawl over her shoulders and smiled as she walked barefoot and free. She loved her evening strolls along this section of beach, where she could leave the coloured contacts at home and embrace the anonymity of darkness.

The ruffles of her long skirt danced in the breeze while the dried palm fronds rustled behind her. Stepping around the many sea shells scattered in the sand, Laurel turned around to head back to the villa before the storm reached the shore. She could feel the drop in pressure and electricity in the air. She didn't mind the storms; they were the price one paid to live in paradise. Besides, she had a warm shower and a chilled bottle of wine waiting for her.

———————————

UNBEKNOWNST TO LAUREL, THAT wasn't all awaiting her at the villa.

In the shadows of angular kitchen fittings, clad in black and armed with a Beretta 92FS, Carla Martinez whispered to a colleague, "She's coming back. Are you ready?"

"Si." He moved to a recess behind an American-style fridge-freezer so he'd be completely hidden from view to anyone entering the kitchen from the rear of the property. "You're sure it's her? The woman wanted in the UK?"

"Hundred per cent," answered Carla. Her friend Felisa Alémén, who worked at the bank, was the first to become suspicious of the new English girl with no family or friends, no job or backstory. They'd spent the next few weeks getting to know her, gaining her trust and watching her movements. "Erin is Laurel Deacon. She killed her man for his Etherium fortune."

"Now we do the same?"

"Si."

Only Carla wasn't doing this for her own gain. She patted the pockets of her trousers, now bulging with the money they'd found in the fake plug sockets on their first sweep of the house. She knew as soon as she put the gun to Laurel's head and the machete to her neck, she'd tell them where to

432

find the rest. She'd hand over her jewellery and the code to the safe. Then Carla would bag it all while Sergio took care of Laurel. She'd seen the butcher slaughter and carve up a whole pig in under three hours before, and Laurel weighed less than a third of the average domestic sow. By dawn, Laurel would be disposed of, and the poorest residents of San Cristóbal would wake up to surprise gifts through their letter boxes. It would buy medicine for the sick, food for the starving and school supplies for the young.

The door handle turned; Carla steadied herself.

Laurel wasn't the only one with two names. Carla Martinez combined the initial syllables of her first and last names – Car and Ma – to form her nickname, *Karma*.

Laurel stepped barefoot into her beautiful new villa and closed the door behind her for the last time. Believing it would keep her safe, she locked the door. She turned as a familiar face stepped out of the shadows and raised her weapon.

Laurel Deacon might not believe in karma, but Carla Martinez did.

And Karma was a bitch.

DCI Cooper will return

- MESSAGE FROM THE AUTHOR -

Whilst Finders Keepers is a work of fiction, some elements of the plot were inspired by real events, notably the murder of Sven Höglin and Heidi Paakkonen, a Swedish couple who disappeared in New Zealand in 1989. David Tamihere was charged with their murders. At the time of the trial, no bodies had been discovered. When one was, it contradicted the evidence presented by the prosecution. Tamihere served twenty years and has always maintained his innocence.

The kidnapping of Shannon Matthews in 2008 partly inspired the Summer Holt storyline. Shannon's mother, Karen, planned to earn £50,000 from newspaper rewards. Shannon was discovered in the base of a divan bed in a flat rented by Karen's boyfriend's uncle. Analysis of Shannon's hair showed she'd regularly been drugged with temazepam.

In obtaining a passport under a new identity, Laurel used the same method as 'Canoe Man' John Darwin. As mentioned in chapter fifty-six, he stole the identity of John Jones, a baby from Sunderland who died aged thirty-four days.

While Cooper and Whyte walked through the Discovery Museum, they learned the story of North Shields hero, Tommy Brown. Brown joined the navy aged fifteen. In 1942, he was one of three volunteers to board a sinking submarine to retrieve documents. Brown was the only one of the three to survive, and the records he carried from the U-boat helped the Bletchley Park codebreakers crack the Enigma code. It was only after his heroic deeds that authorities realised Brown was underage. He died three years later, saving his sister from a house fire. Brown was buried with military honours at Preston Cemetery in North Shields. If you'd like to learn more, I highly recommend visiting Newcastle's Discovery Museum.

- About the Author -

BETSY WAS BORN AND raised in Newcastle upon Tyne, living first in Gosforth, then Jesmond. In 2013, she moved to North Shields and enjoys spending time walking her Welsh terrier along nearby beaches and learning about local history.

At school, Betsy struggled with spelling and grammar. However, she doesn't believe in giving up on something because it's difficult. She finds writing novels can be compared to martial arts. They are both thrilling, exhausting, and rewarding.

It's no secret Betsy considers herself part ninja. She also works as a taekwon-do coach and is a self-confessed UFC geek. Her ideal Saturday begins with an intense workout, followed by a long bath, a spot of writing, steak and red wine, and then retiring to the sofa to watch the latest title fight. She came up with the idea for her debut novel, The Only Weapon In The Room, the morning after Rousey Vs Holm.

Betsy's writing process involves drinking ridiculous quantities of tea and hot chocolate, bouncing ideas off her friends and family and getting distracted by Twitter and TikTok.

- Be Sociable -

Facebook: B Baskerville - Author

Twitter: B_ _Baskerville

TikTok: B_Baskerville

Instagram: B_Baskerville_Author

Newsletter: You can subscribe to the B Baskerville newsletter using the form on BetsyBaskerville.com. You'll mainly hear from B when she has something to share, such as a pre-order going live, a new book release or sale etc.

- ALSO BY B BASKERVILLE -

The DCI Cooper Series:
Cut The Deck
Rock, Paper, Scissors
Roll The Dice
Northern Roulette
Hide & Seek
Finders Keepers

Stand Alones:
The Only Weapon In The Room
Dead In The Water